TWO OLD DEARS

Best Wishes

Edward Clark Haworth

9/4/17

TWO OLD DEARS

EDWARD EVANS

WORTHSIDE

About Edward Evans

Edward Evans lives in the Yorkshire village of Haworth with Lilian, his wife of forty-six years. They have three children; all have flown the nest and have families of their own. Haworth was the home of the famous Bronte sisters, and this connection together with their frequent visits to France is what provides his inspiration to write. All his books have a distinct Anglo-French flavour and it is from the sale of these that he raises money for various charities.

He has a wealth of experience which has been gained not only from his work in the nationalised industries and through his private companies, but also as a juvenile magistrate where he became involved in Youth Justice. It was during this time that he witnessed the injustice meted out to those from poorer social and economic backgrounds. He has written about this in *Babes in Gaol* (manuscript form only) where his passion to improve the system is apparent as is his vehement support for the underdog.

His second home in France is where Edward, assisted by Lilian, finds the time to write and where the couple relax and immerse themselves in the culture of Le Var and Provence.

About his books

11 PY

When wealthy businessman Robert Conway flies to New York to fulfil the dream of a lifetime – to buy a beautiful vintage Rolls-Royce – he little knows that he is bidding for more than he bargained for. Dream turns to nightmare as he discovers that the Rolls-Royce – the II PY of the title – is the confiscated property of a convicted drugs dealer, John Maitland, who will stop at nothing to get it back. As Conway and his family fall victim to a series of increasingly terrifying crimes, they gradually realize that there might be more to II PY than meets the eye.

'I have never read a book from cover to cover in my life but I started reading this at 5 p.m. on the Thursday and finished it at 11p.m. on the Friday. I couldn't put it down. It had my imagination running wild and has sparked an interest in books I never knew I had. I can't wait to read another of his books.' **James Reed**

LIKE *a* FISH OUT *of* WATER

When newspaper reporter Clive White is asked to interview a well-heeled eighty-something lady about her life history, he is expecting the usual run-of-the-mill tale of marriage and children with perhaps a bit of charity work on the side. The indomitable and spirited Alexandra Fraser, however, turns out to be a completely different kettle of fish, and she slowly reveals a dramatic and diverse life, encompassing sporting achievement on the cricket field and courageous service in the WAAF as well as a passionate wartime romance. But there's something even more remarkable about her story – for Alexandra was brought up as Alexander ... as a boy.

'I loved this book. I read it in one go and was hooked by the gripping storyline. It's full of interesting reflection, nasty bullies, revenge, love, real charity and a life truly well lived. Edward Evans has crafted a thrilling read which could so easily have slid into parody and exploitation but manages to keep its dignified head above the fray and emerges with something serious to say about the human condition. Like its main character, this book made me feel empowered, stronger and infinitely kind. Surprisingly delightful!' **Eric Page, freelance journalist**

The PIANO

The indefatigable newsman Clive White – who will already be familiar to readers of the II PY and A Fish out of Water – has gone to cover an unusual protest at a large London hospital. Unusual because for once it's not about waiting times or mixed-sex wards but a beautiful old piano that stands in the entrance hall. Originally, the gift of no less than 30s idol Noël Coward, the piano is now to go to auction to raise funds for the cash-strapped hospital.

One by the one the protesters reveal what the piano means to them, and heartfelt tales fall from their lips like old-time melodies from its ebony and ivory keys.

'The enjoyable feature of Ted Evans's novels is the way he pitches into his big picaresque historical adventures, projecting them way beyond his own biography. His personal experiences serve his stories, not the other way round.' **Jim Greenhalf Telegraph & Argus**

COME *on* GRANDDAD *hold my hand*

COME on GRANDDAD provides a vivid and informative portrait of someone with Alzheimer's. It is a disease much feared, yet, as we see here, with the understanding and love of those surrounding the sufferer, much can be done to ease their condition.

'I couldn't put this book down. It's a definitely eye opening and will make you look at people who suffer with Alzheimer's in a whole new light. It has clearly been written with love and care, capturing emotions and feelings in such a beautiful way. At some points I had tears rolling down my face, at others I was laughing out loud! Each character is well thought out and expressed in a way that brings them to life. I can see myself reading this book again and again and will be recommending it to friends.' **Miss C. L. Fothergill**

For the RIGHT REASONS

Like Edward Evans' previous book, II PY, For the Right Reasons is fast-paced and action-packed. Set mainly in East Berlin just a couple of years before the fall of the Berlin Wall, the novel tells the story of down-to-earth Yorkshire businessman Robert Conway who accidentally becomes involved in an assassination attempt on the East German President's life. His heroic efforts to rescue the President win him special freedoms in the East and during his travels he stumbles across secret plans for a terrifying act of sabotage against the West.

'A really good read. The author obviously knows his subject well. Exciting and extremely interesting. I am looking forward to reading Mr. Evans' next book.' **Margaret Waterhouse**

MOONCAR

The deadliest and most feared weapon in the British arsenal – the Rolls-Royce Armoured Car spreads fear into the hearts and minds of the Irish people. This symbol of British might was deemed invincible but now it was in the hands of the Republicans who would use it to devastating effect!

This is a tale of victory, tragedy and pathos, not least the expression of a man's undying love for one woman.

Also by Edward Evans

I enjoy writing and to use an Agatha Christie expression, it keeps the little grey cells alive. By meeting and chatting to people from all walks of life, I am able to glean a wealth of ideas for my novels. However, the greatest pleasure I get from my writing is to donate £1 from each book sold.

So far, we have raised over £16,000 for the following charities:

II PY
– The Bradford Day Shelter

LIKE *a* FISH OUT *of* WATER
– RAF Benevolent Fund

***The* PIANO**
– Specialist Autism Services (formally known as Sacar)

***Le* PIANO**
(French translation) – Specialist Autism Services

COME *on* GRANDDAD *hold my hand*
– Alzheimer's Charity, 'Friends Together'

***For the* RIGHT REASONS**
– Help for Heroes

MOONCAR
– Alzheimer's charity, 'Friends Together'

***

TWO OLD DEARS
– funds will be donated to disadvantaged children

First published in Great Britain in 2015 by
Worthside Holdings Ltd
Worthside House
2 Belle Isle Road
Haworth
West Yorkshire BD22 8QQ

Printed in Britain by Grosvenor Group
Typesetting and page layout by McColm Design

A catalogue record for this book is available
From the British Library

ISBN 978-0-9928642-8-6

Contents

Dedication

I am dedicating this book to our good friend Dennis Luyt, who died at the young age of ninety-one as a result of an accident. I say young because that is what he was; despite his age, he was young at heart. He had a wonderful memory and could recount cricket matches and scores going back thirty or forty years; the same with tennis and football. He was also completely up to date with current affairs and could converse on almost every subject. We enjoyed both his and his wife Tineke's company in many of the pubs and restaurants around Amsterdam, Leiden and Sassenheim in Holland. He will be sadly missed by us all. Tineke, I am pleased to say, is an avid reader of my novels, as was Dennis, and has been our friend for over sixty years.

This book is also dedicated to Margaret Hargreaves, another very good friend of twenty-five years and whom we lost this year. She too is sadly missed. It is unbelievable that she could die so young when she was so full of life. She really did live life to the full both in England and in France.

She leaves behind her husband Ken who I can count on as one of my best friends, and her daughter Lauren who is blest with Margaret's love of life, and who is now living in Australia.

Acknowledgements

I would like to thank Maureen Harris for her help with this book. It is seldom I have met a woman (or should I say, person – we can't be sexist, can we?) with such a fantastic sense of humour and from my point of view, the entertainment world has lost out on such talent.

Not for the first time, I would like to thank Lilian, my wife, for the hours she has spent not only reading and re-reading the script, but also adding her ideas to the plot and the dialogue, which in this book have been considerable. Her patience has been inexhaustible, especially when I felt the story was not right or I had run out of thoughts. I'm a very lucky person to have such a wife.

I wish she would allow her name to be put forward as a co-author.

It may surprise you to know that the two ladies mentioned above are the two old dears I have written about, but of course, I have had to change the story a little to protect their identity.

Our friend Jill Buchanan is someone I can never thank enough! She too put in many hours of work on the book before I dared present the manuscript to my editor and face her vicious pen and honesty (which is what every writer needs as we all feel our books are as good as the best). Jill is tireless in her efforts to help me.

Finally, thanks to my editor Christina Harkness whose

help with all my work is special. Every writer needs a good editor because when we are writing, we are too close to the work to see or realise we have made a mistake, and often when we re-read the work, we still do not see the errors or inconsistencies. My editor does and I believe I have one of the best.

Introduction

Dear reader

Allow me to introduce myself: I'm Clive White, an investigative reporter for the *Mail*. I've worked for the paper for years, too many I'm sure most of my colleagues would say, but what the hell! I enjoy my job and whatever the young ones think, I still sniff out a good story now and then, and my editor George Stevenson, with whom I have an excellent working relationship, seems satisfied, so no doubt I will be here for a few more years yet ...

One of the strangest and yet most amusing stories I have ever investigated was the case of the two sisters, Edith and Maud Trenchard. Two dear old ladies who had been arrested for suspected armed robbery. Over the years, there had been a series of unsolved robberies and burglaries, both in the UK and on the continent and, I believe in the USA where the perpetrators were disguised as old ladies, but perhaps this was too much of a coincidence. They looked so vulnerable, so incapable, so ... old. How on earth could they in any way be accused of carrying out any crime, let alone where a sawn-off shot gun was used in a modern bank with all the latest surveillance equipment and security systems in place.

There was no question about it – the sisters were well off

1

and not without money. In fact, they lived in some style, residing in a rambling old mansion situated in hundreds of acres of beautiful countryside in a village called Little Riddington, near London.

Certainly the house was big and old, and when I went to visit, I found it very well maintained and truly magnificent. Set in a late1920's time warp, you can imagine the décor. The entrance hall faced a massive staircase which split into two galleries with many doors leading off, to who knows where. Enormous settees and chaises longue graced the rooms, subtly interspaced with Diva mirrors and displays of Ostrich and Bird of Paradise. Paintings hung on the pastel decorated walls, which offered an airy lightness to every room.

Each room offered a touch of opulent splendour and there were more paintings – magnificent works of art attributed to the likes of Monet, Manet, Titian, Van Gogh, and Joshua Reynolds to name but a few; all of which were admired for what they were and not what they were worth. Some rooms featured numerous pictures and models of racing yachts, dedicated to various races, in which they had participated, including the America's Cup.

Numerous rooms had an individual theme created by their father in the 1920s; a music room which held a Bechstein piano and many other instruments from guitars to violins, and to my astonishment, they were still used as both ladies were accomplished musicians. These ladies must have been popular in their day as they were featured in photographs with the great band leaders such as Roy Fox, Jack Payne, Henry Hall and musicians like Fats Waller, Sidney Bechet and even Satchmo Louis Armstrong. I really couldn't take it all in.

A huge corridor of indoor plants led the way to an amazing conservatory, also fully furnished in the style of the 1920s. This really took my breath away; but here we had the real thing, almost a forest of beautiful tropical plants, inter- dispersed with statues that befitted the era.

Edith, who was a cool 91 years of age, appeared to be the strongest and most capable of the two – forthright and decisive, whilst Maud, a very young 89-year-old, came over as a simple, pleasant little character who wouldn't say 'boo to a goose'. She was the kind of person, always doing as she was told and was often scolded in front of people by Edith. She appeared to accept this as her lot. 'Yes, Edith. No, Edith.' You know the type.

Bif, the chauffeur/gardener, I eventually found out was Edith's son and Alice, the cook was her daughter; but in reality they all mucked in together. They simply gave the pretence that they were employees. It was a strange situation, and then of course, there was Maud's son, Stanley, who was the General Manager. He had an authoritative air about him and looked after the estate in effect, employing whoever and whatever was needed to keep the place going; he was also what would be considered a financial whiz kid, adding to the family fortune. But where were the fathers, the husbands? No one ever talked about them and there were no signs anywhere of a man ever being there. It was a mystery I was determined to solve.

I was tipped off by the local Chief Inspector Baldwin that the police had arrested a couple of elderly women suspected of armed robbery. Well, I ask you, who could resist that?

Chapter 1
In Custody

I arrived at the police station to be greeted by the Chief Inspector who took me straight into his office, closing the door behind him. He sat down behind his sumptuous desk, inviting me to sit opposite, before bursting into uncontrollable laughter.

'Clive,' he began, still trying not to laugh. 'You are not going to believe this! Bacon, one of my constables, has arrested two old dears for armed robbery. They're in the interview room now and I just can't believe it. I'm sure they are in their bloody nineties. The one doesn't know whether she is on this earth or fullers, and the other one pretends to be intelligent but hasn't a clue where she is. Come and have a look at them.'

We walked into an area adjacent to the interview room to look at them through the two-way mirror, and I too couldn't believe my eyes. They looked so angelic, totally unconcerned about what was happening, chatting about this and that and whether they would be home in time for tea. One of them, I later found out, was called Maud; she never stopped knitting and was without a care in the world.

'I've asked them if they want a solicitor,' Baldwin continued, 'but Edith the taller one, replied, "Oh no, we already have our own. He's been with the family for fifty years you know. Ah! Is that what you are trying to do, young man, take the work away from him? Well, it won't work. We like Mr Higginbotham and anyway, we don't know you, do we? That's right, isn't it, Maud?" To which, Maud replied: "Yes, Edith."'

Baldwin continued: 'I then asked for their solicitor's address and what firm he worked for and she replied, "Ooh, he doesn't work for a firm. He's Mr Higginbotham." And when I asked whether she had his phone number, she told me she didn't have it with her but it was on the fridge door in the kitchen!'

Now we are getting somewhere, I thought to myself, and despatched PC Littlewood to get the number.

We returned to Baldwin's office, leaving the two old ladies in their own little world, chatting about nothing and waited for the officer to return with the solicitor's phone number. It wasn't too long before we were disturbed by Constable Littlewood, a grey-haired old stager, who really should have been put out to grass years before.

'Sorry guv, but I couldn't find my way round, or anybody at home,' Littlewood said in an apologetic tone.

'Are you sure? There must be someone at home. These two couldn't look after our cat, let alone themselves.'

'You should see the place, guv! It's massive. I almost got lost.'

'Did you hear that, Clive? He tells me he almost got lost and couldn't find anyone at home,' Inspector Baldwin continued, getting angrier by the minute. 'He's a bloody policeman and he almost got lost.' He paused for effect. 'For God's sake. Can't you be trusted to do a simple job like that?'

'I'm sorry guv.'

'Oh, get out.'

A red-faced Littlewood departed, leaving Baldwin shaking his head in frustration and quite frankly, not knowing what to do with the old dears. He opened the office door and yelled, 'Bacon!'

'Guv,' Bacon called back.

'Come in here a minute.'

Seconds later, Constable Bacon walked through the door. He was a roly poly sort of man, a little rough round the edges, which gave the impression he was a jovial fellow and a bit soft, but far from it. He was a stickler for doing everything by the book. To him, everything was either black or white with no shades of grey.

'Have you seen them? Have you taken a hard look at them?' Baldwin asked, the moment Bacon walked in.

'Yes, guv.'

'Well, what do you think? Are they capable of pulling off a robbery in a bank?'

'Guv, I hear what you say, but they were positively identified by Sharon Spencer, the bank clerk who was held up at gunpoint. She's convinced even thought they were disguised as two old ladies.'

'They *are* two old ladies, for God's sake!'

'How were they caught?' I asked the officer.

'They were shopping in Marks and Spencer's and Sharon bumped into them. She apologised and one of them replied, "That's all right, dear." Sharon said she recognised the woman's voice as well as the pearls she was wearing, which had a distinctive blue clasp in the middle. She quietly went outside looking for a policeman and found me. She convinced me, so I arrested them, and here they are.'

'You do realise that if you are wrong, a) you'll look a right prat, and b) I won't want you working here with all the publicity this will bring.'

'What had they got on them when they arrived?' I asked.

'The taller one was still wearing the pearls and the other had all the usual things plus £600. That alone made me suspicious and–'

'What about the other?' Baldwin interrupted.

'All she had, guv, was a bag of knitting.'

'Did you ask her where she got the pearls?'

'No, guv.'

'Have you checked where the notes came from?'

Bacon just shook his head.

'What the friggin' heck have you *done*? You arrest two old women who don't look capable of walking into the bank unaided, let alone robbing it at gun point!'

'I didn't lock 'em up.'

'Why not? You've done everything else in accordance with the book.'

'I didn't think they would run away.'

'What? Two armed and dangerous robbers, and you didn't think they would run away. How did they get to town?'

'I didn't ask.'

'Christ! You're as bad as Littlewood. Give me what you've got. I'll go and talk to them.'

As Baldwin held his hand out, Bacon stuttered, 'I haven't got anything.'

'What? You've arrested them and you haven't got anything? Are you friggin' mad?'

'Nothing they say makes any sense.'

'Then why friggin' arrest them? Go on, join bloody Littlewood and get some of the reports up to date.'

Baldwin went into the interview room and I went into the adjacent room to watch the next round. The two old biddies were still chatting as though nothing had happened.

'Good afternoon, ladies. I'm Chief Inspector Baldwin and I've come to have a chat with you.'

'Good afternoon, young man and what are we doing here?' Edith replied. Maud carried on knitting.

'I wish I knew. Our Constable Bacon believes you have robbed a bank and he's brought you here to ask you a few questions,' Baldwin replied. 'Well, did you?'

'Did we what?'

'Rob the bank.'

'Young man, when I want some money, Stanley makes sure I have some.'

'Who's Stanley?'

'He's our manager.'

Baldwin turned to the mirror, rolled his eyes and shrugged as if to say, 'What the hell can we do with these two?'

'Now, how did you get to town?'

'We didn't. Bif took us to Marks and Spencer's.'

'I see, and how did Bif take you to Marks and Spencer's?'

'In the car, of course.'

'And where is Bif now?'

'We don't know, do we, Maud? Do we, Maud?' Edith repeated, almost shouting to get Maud's attention.

'No dear,' Maud replied. 'But he will be back at four o'clock.'

'Did you come in a taxi?' Baldwin asked.

'Are you stupid, young man? It's Bif, our chauffeur and he is to meet us at four o'clock.'

Baldwin looked at his watch. It was already after four-thirty. 'Look, I'm going to see whether I can get your solicitor's phone number. I want to see if you have someone to look after you.'

'Young man, we are perfectly capable of looking after ourselves and we have all the help we need, thank you.'

'Come on, let me check your address. I just need to be sure. Is it 17 Watling Street, Little Riddington?'

'Yes, that's it. Now, young man, Maud will need to go home soon.'

'Oh, by the way, where did you get those lovely pearls?' Baldwin asked casually.

'Oh these,' Edith replied, touching her neck. 'Maud

bought them for me from Marks and Spencer's a few minutes ago. She liked the colour of the centre clasp.'

Baldwin again turned to the mirror and sighed. Shortly afterwards, he came out, whereupon I immediately volunteered to go and get the address and phone number of their solicitor. I must be honest, I was feeling very concerned for their welfare. They were vulnerable and would have been easily bullied by someone other than Baldwin. He was very experienced and had a heart, but he was not always around.

I set off, arriving at Watling Street only to find the numbers ended at 15. I continued for about half a mile before turning back to the village to ask where Number 17 was. Naturally, the best place to enquire was the Little Riddington Village Post Office.

'Yes, it's just over a mile down the road. You'll see it. There are two stone gate posts and one has 17 on it. Good luck,' the post mistress said, her lips pursed in a knowing manner.

'Thanks.'

I turned the car round and made my way back along the road from whence I came until I arrived at the gate posts, where sure enough 'Number 17' was etched on one. I turned into the entrance and drove down the road. Three-quarters of a mile later, I pulled up at the front door. Littlewood was right. It was an enormous place, and I couldn't believe my eyes. There, also parked in the drive was a 1932 Duisenberg Phaeton, which I knew was worth a small fortune, particularly in this condition. I walked towards the main door but was intercepted by a man who looked in his late fifties, early sixties, wearing a chauffeur's uniform from the 1920s.

'Can I help you?' he asked politely.

'Yes, I'm looking for anyone who may be able to help. My name is Clive White. I'm from the *Mail* and–'

He stopped me in mid sentence. 'Go away. We don't talk to the newspapers. Go away.'

'I'm sorry. I am–'   I tried to explain the circumstances, but was immediately shouted down.

'Go away! Go away.' The raised voice attracted attention, and we were quickly joined by another man whom I deduced to be Stanley.

On a whim, I said, 'Good afternoon. You must be Stanley?'

It took them both by surprise and immediately placated the situation.

'Yes, I'm Stanley.'

'Look, I am from the press, but ...' I emphasised, 'I am not on press business. I was at the police station investigating a crime when two ladies were brought in. One of them was called Maud.'

'Oh God! Are they lost again? I wondered where they had got to. They know where to go, and someone would always ring for me to pick them up.'

'No, not at all. They are suspected of being involved in an armed robbery at the National West Bank a few months ago.'

Stanley laughed, but when I look back, it seemed a forced laugh, which made me a little uncomfortable, even suspicious. The other man just looked on nervously.

'I'm Clive, incidentally,' I said, holding my hand out. 'And you must be ... er ... Bif?' At last he smiled and his nervousness disappeared as he took my hand and confirmed my thoughts.

'They *are* in trouble, but I don't think there is anything to worry about. The police would like to interview them with their solicitor and they don't know his number. They told me it was on the fridge.'

'That's Mr Higginbotham. Don't worry I've got his number,' Stanley said, leaving me in Bif's tender care. Naturally, we talked about the Duisenberg.

'They have had it since new in 1932.'

'I thought it was new,' I said, smiling. Those few words really endeared me to him as he began to open up a little more.

'I love my cars,' he said, directing me to follow him. However, we were stopped short as Stanley came out and shouted at Bif:

'Mr White has better things to do than waste time talking about cars to you. Go on, get on with your work. I'll see to him.'

You know, a reporter is always suspicious of situations like that and no one more than me. Had he got something to hide or was it that he was unsure of strangers, anyway? He gave me the number and I returned to my car, having a last look at the Duisenberg and giving the thumbs up to Bif. I left the house, armed with Higginbotham's phone number, leaving a very worried-looking Stanley behind. I retraced my steps back to the road, only this time, I made a mental note of all I saw.

The moment I was able to, I phoned Higginbotham, introduced myself and appraised him of the situation, letting him know I was somewhat worried and asked if he could get to the police station as soon as possible because the two sisters were becoming very confused. I told him I would meet him there.

He sounded like some Dickensian clerk, very precise in everything he said and very correct in the way he spoke to me; in fact he sounded as though he was from that age and also caught in a time warp. I was genuinely looking forward to meeting the man.

'How have they been?' I asked Baldwin the moment I arrived.

'No change.'

'I've contacted their solicitor and he will be with you shortly.'

Shortly, was however immediately, as Rachael Temor, a police civil worker brought Mr Higginbotham through to the Chief Inspector's office. I could not believe my eyes; his clothes were also from a bygone era. He wore an old-fashioned dark three-piece suit, with the inevitable gold hunter watch and chain across his waistcoat pocket, winged shirt collar and old school tie. His ubiquitous black patent leather shoes were so highly polished, you could almost see your reflection in them. His swept-back hair added the finishing touch.

'James Higginbotham,' he said, announcing himself to the inspector with his hand outstretched.

'Chief Inspector Baldwin,' the inspector replied.

'Now what's all this about?' Higginbotham asked.

Baldwin outlined the case against the sisters to which Higginbotham added:

'You know this is absolute rubbish. Do you know how old they are?'

'Not yet.'

'Well, they are in their nineties and I would suggest you do not arrest anyone until you have some evidence that would at least have half a chance of standing up. I am surprised that a very senior officer like you would allow this situation to continue for this length of time. Shocks like this could easily give them a heart attack or a stroke. Have you thought of that?'

Baldwin was now looking well and truly deflated at this onslaught.

'Well, have you?' Higginbotham said, continuing the attack. 'Now I would like to see my clients and take them home. Oh, by the way, a little gift for you.'

He handed Baldwin a box which he duly opened. It was another necklace, identical to the one Edith was wearing. 'Is this a piece of your hard evidence? I've just bought it at Marks and Spencer's.'

'How the hell did he know about that?' Baldwin whispered to me as Higginbotham was taken to meet the ladies.

He spent half an hour with the sisters and then requested to see Baldwin again.

'They won't be able to answer any questions at this moment as they haven't a clue what you have been talking about. They wouldn't know where they were at any given time and the only chance we have is if Edith has entered it into her diary. So what do you want to do? Keep them in overnight whilst you make further enquiries?'

'Go on, take them home,' Baldwin replied, almost at the end of his patience.

I walked back along the corridor with Higginbotham to meet the ladies formally and hopefully get some excuse to visit, but I needn't have worried as he did it for me.

'This is Edith and Maud Trenchard, and this is Mr White from the *Mail* who very kindly called me because he thought you were in trouble.'

'Oh how kind. Thank you, Mr White. It is very nice of you to put yourself out for us.'

'It was no trouble really. I simply went to your home and met Stanley and Bif who showed me the wonderful car he has. They gave me Mr Higginbotham's phone number and he sorted things out.'

'Oh, Bif loves his cars, Mr White. You must come and take tea with us. Mustn't he, Maud?' Edith said, to Higginbotham's horror.

Maud nodded and smiled in agreement.

'I would love to, especially if I could see Bif's car collection.'

'Well, let's say Thursday afternoon, four o'clock and you will come too, won't you, Mr Higginbotham?'

'Of course. I always enjoy tea at Number 17.'

'See you on Thursday then,' I said. 'Goodbye for now.'

14

I returned to Baldwin's office to find him still deflated from Higginbotham's onslaught. 'What are you going to do?' I asked.

'What can I do? There is no evidence apart from the voice and that would be difficult in any person let alone a ninety-year-old woman. I doubt whether the notes will lead to anything. I couldn't get a warrant to search the pla–'

'You wouldn't want to,' I said, interrupting him. 'As Littlewood said, the place is massive. Their land runs for miles. The one car I saw in the drive was worth over a million. Anyway, I have been invited to *take* tea on Thursday,' I said, mimicking Edith's manner. 'So I'll let you know if I find anything.'

'Until you do, or Bacon brings fresh evidence, things will be left at that. Just another unsolved crime,' Baldwin said as I left his office.

Chapter 2
The First Recorded Crimes

For all of Higginbotham's demeanour, he was undoubtedly a very sharp solicitor. It was obvious he worked for some very exclusive clients as neither Baldwin nor I had ever heard of him. However, I think he was just that bit too clever for his own good. The point he made about the necklace puzzled me; in fact it made me want to look into matters further, so Thursday's invitation was the obvious place to start.

I remember I was really looking forward to meeting the sisters again. I could smell a good story and it was a beautiful afternoon as I drove through the gateposts up the drive and parked next to what I presumed was Higginbotham's Rolls-Royce. I made my way to the main door and searched for the bell, but as on the previous occasion I was intercepted by Stanley.

'Good afternoon, Mr White. Thank you for coming and thank you for what you did for the ladies the other day. They are in the conservatory. I'll take you there.'

Once again, I was aware that I was not going to be allowed into the house, or at least through the front door. This only whet my appetite even more.

We arrived at the conservatory where Higginbotham was waiting for me. He opened the door and I entered into what I described earlier as an amazing place. It was an oasis of tranquillity, where Edith was seated like some twenties' diva, on a wonderful Lloyd Loom chaise longue, as if waiting for the servants to begin the afternoon's entertainment. Maud sat on a matching high-rounded armchair, hardly glancing up from her knitting.

The introductions and formalities over, Mr Higginbotham began:

'Edith ... Maud ... I want to take Mr White into the office. I would like to have a chat with him before tea if that is all right with you?'

'Of course it is,' Edith replied in a matter-of-fact manner. 'Don't be too long. It will be served at four o'clock.'

Higginbotham waved his hand impatiently, acknowledging what was said. I followed him through the house to the office, once again passing the most wonderful art deco objets d'art, which matched the surroundings until he opened the door to the office. The first thing I saw on entering was a Monet over the fireplace and then several other old masters including 'The Card Players'. For the life of me, I cannot remember who it was by, but I do remember it had been missing for some fifty years plus.

Higginbotham sat down behind the desk, which in itself was a masterpiece.

'Please sit down, Mr White.'

'Wow, what a place! I've never seen anything like it in my life.'

'No, and I doubt you will ever again. But it's all a game, you know.'

'What do you mean?' I asked.

'Exactly what I said – it's all a game. Before we start, I want some legal assurances, which will give you one of the biggest stories you have ever had. You will not be able to print, publish, or talk about the sisters until after both are dead and buried, which won't be long in view of their ages. And nothing must point to the other members of the family. Do I make myself understood?'

I was intrigued to the point of sheer amazement at the way the conversation had started. 'I must talk matters over with my editor.'

'No, forget it, Mr White, this is for you and no one else. You are forbidden in every aspect to discuss what you will hear. Still interested?'

'Um ... yes, of course. What reporter wouldn't be? But why the legal battering?'

He didn't answer and suddenly said, 'Right! We will leave matters at that. This is the first of two agreements, which I prepared in advance for this sort of eventuality, which must be signed before any discussions take place. The second we cannot discuss until the first is signed.'

He handed me an inch-thick file, which was the first agreement and insisted I read it and signed it, proposing we met the following Thursday, same place, same time. He gave me his phone number and told me to confirm our meeting and that was that. Nothing further was said.

We returned to the conservatory to join Edith and Maud for a lovely cup of tea!

'Lipton's, of course,' Edith said.

'Daddy was a friend of Thomas Lipton,' Maud suddenly remarked, looking up from her knitting. 'They loved sailing together. He built a boat to challenge for the America's Cup, you know. Edith and I went on it when we were little girls.'

'He was a very ordinary man and loved everybody, making them feel comfortable wherever he went. We loved meeting him. He was such a nice man,' Edith added.

We spent the rest of the afternoon talking trivia and as I got up to leave, Edith remarked:

'We'll see you next Thursday, Mr White? And you too Mr Higginbotham.'

'Of course,' I replied. 'Would I ever miss the opportunity?'

As we walked back to our respective cars, I tried to engage Higginbotham in conversation, but he would have none of it.

'Read and sign the agreement, Mr White, and then we will move to stage two.'

It was a very intriguing proposition and one I couldn't refuse, but I was to be tied hand and foot by the most comprehensive legal arrangement I had ever heard of, let alone be involved with.

I spent some time during the week going through the agreement clause by clause, making sure I understood what I was getting into before confirming the appointment with Higginbotham for Thursday. There were no names on the agreement, just blank spaces where the names would go and it was obvious he was being doubly careful.

I returned the following Thursday to the same routine once again, meeting Higginbotham who ushered me into the office where I duly signed the agreement. The moment that was signed, he dropped the first bombshell.

'Mr White, my clients now want to retire, which is something I have been trying to get them to do for the last ten years. Especially now as they are not getting any younger and becoming a little too careless and forgetful.'

I was open-mouthed in expectation, but still none the wiser.

'Over the years, they have been responsible for over twenty million pounds' worth of robberies and thefts, not only in this country but all over the world. They have never spent any of the proceeds or sold any of the material things. Now, Mr White, I want you to sign this new agreement which simply enforces the points made earlier that you will not disclose the names of those perpetrating the crime. You will not disclose where the crimes were committed and the nature of the crimes.

'Edith and Maud will tell you all about their escapades.

On their deaths or with their permission, I want you to give the proceeds back to those that suffered the loss, making up a story as to how you found them, or whatever. You will be paid handsomely for your efforts because the sisters are extremely wealthy in their own right. You will effectively uncover the whereabouts of the stolen goods and return them to their rightful owners, whether it be the insurance company or the owners themselves. Some of the owners did not report the crime for obvious reasons, so you will be careful when you return them. You will be able to publish the return of the goods in your paper with a brief description of how the robbery took place, but I will have final editorial rights over the story. Agreed?'

'Agreed,' I replied, not knowing whether I had been done over by an expert legal mind, or a very clever con man. I hoped it was the former.

'Furthermore, Mr White, I will warn you that both Edith and Maud are very modern in their outlook and manner. Some of the things you will hear will undoubtedly surprise you and may even shock a hardened reporter like yourself. However, whatever the situation you find yourself in, I will make something absolutely clear.' He paused to let his words sink in. 'It is my job to protect the sisters and I will do it to the best of my ability, which I have done for over fifty years as did my father before me. Do you understand?'

I agreed and signed the subsequent agreement, returning to the sisters for afternoon tea.

This time things were somewhat different.

'Ah, Mr White, come and sit down. I understand you like scones?' Edith enquired.

'Well, yes,' I replied, a little surprised.

'Oh don't worry, Mr Higginbotham has looked you up. In fact, we know all about you now and I believe you are a man to be trusted. I suppose it was the way you cared enough to get us some help when we were arrested and also the way you wrote about Alexandra Fraser that clinched it. We met her several times over the years. Fascinating story, don't you think?

'Yes I do. I wrote an article titled, 'Like a Fish Out of Water', relating to the life of Alexandra Fraser, which was serialised in the *Mail* over several weeks.'

'Well, I can promise you a good story out of this,' Edith added.

I sat down in the chair, which had been placed in such a way that I could only see the two ladies and not Higginbotham although I knew he was somewhere behind me; I could feel his presence. It was as though I was being interrogated instead of the other way round.

'It all began many years ago,' Edith said. 'In fact, when we were in our teens. Maud got into trouble when she was caught shoplifting. This was very serious in those days, but then she was caught again which made things dire. It was only our father's influence and a doctor's report which confirmed she was a kleptomaniac that she was let off, together with the proviso that she handed all the goods back. It was and still is true: she *is* a kleptomaniac. Mind you, at that time she had to stay under the control of the doctor for many weeks. I think it was part of the deal struck with the magistrates to stop her going to prison.

'It didn't end there as she could not stop; someone had to walk behind her to make sure she did not actually steal the goods, or at least she paid for what goods she had taken. This went on for years and it soon became my job, as big sister, to look after her which, Mr White, you will appreciate for a young woman even in those days was a hell of a burden. But as time went on, it became the norm.

'Father was a very respected business man as well as a philanthropist and was always being invited to functions, dances and dinners, and as Mother had disappeared from our lives when we were very young, he was often on his own. So as soon as we were old enough, he took us in turn as his partner and often the two of us were invited with him.

'Don't ask, Mr White, for neither I nor Maud can tell you anything about our mother. It has never been talked about. We had hoped when Father died, he would have left some clue as to her whereabouts. But No!

'We were not bad looking women and that, together with the rumoured fortune we had, we were always in demand at Father's functions. In fact, as we grew older we were invited in our own right and this gave us a great opportunity to visit many of the large houses in Britain and abroad, particularly those on the Cote D'Azur in France, which at the time, was the playground of the rich and famous. This was to prove a useful asset later on.

'Our father died in the late 1920s and we were left to run the place. As you can see, it is rather large. We loved the house as it was and decided not to change anything, hence we are still pre-war in our décor. We were left a fortune by Father so there were no financial worries and since Stanley came along – he is Maud's son as you have probably gathered – he has more than quadrupled the size and value of the estate. I believe we are richer than the Queen!

'Quite frankly, Mr White, we were bored. The estate was well managed by our father's appointees and in any event it was not considered a job for a woman in those days, so basically we had nothing to do.

'It was during this period that I was following Maud through Harrods and didn't see her steal the gloves. However, the store detective did and she was taken, as usual, to his office. I duly followed.

'"Come on Maud," the store detective said politely like some well-known friend, "where did you put the gloves?" It was the usual scenario. Harrods were well aware of the situation and I simply paid for the goods or put them back. We were, incidentally, very good customers of Harrods so there was never any real problem. Maud took the gloves out of her inside pocket and sheepishly gave them back.

'We said good bye to the detective and walked a little way up Kensington High Street to our car, when Maud pulled out another pair of gloves from another pocket, then another, and another and another. It was obvious to me that she got a huge buzz from beating the system. She had actually stolen five pairs of gloves and got away with it and was tingling with excitement.

'It was this moment that changed our lives forever.

'I made some pretence at telling her off, but when your sister has an enormous grin on her face at her achievement, what effect would it have had? She took me to her room and opened her ottoman chest which was full of her ill-gotten gains.

'"You've done all this? She nodded her head. Stolen all this?" I added, almost shouting. "Mmm ... yes," she squealed, nodding her head again with excitement.

'"Why have you kept it all? What if people find out?" I asked. "I'll give it back, like Father said, then I won't get into trouble," she said.

'When I asked her how on earth she could remember who to give it back to for God's sake, she simply said: "I write it in my little book."

'Well, Mr White ... that was it. She had a record of all her hits and there were well over 200 in that little book of hers. She was a registered kleptomaniac and I was just bored. The perfect duo to start a new life together!'

I joined in Maud's excitement as we sat on the bed and simply laughed.

'You clever little girl,' I said to her, as she began to relate her experiences, all the time almost quivering with suspense, especially when she described how she had nearly been caught.

'I'd like to help on the next one.'

'Ooh yes, that will be fun,' Maud said excitedly.

'Next time, let me plan it,' I said to Maud, 'and we will see just what we can get away with, eh?'

'You know, Mr White, when it came to Harrods, it didn't really need much planning.

'We knew that Mr Richardson, the store detective at Harrods went to lunch at one o'clock and we would strike then. It worked like clockwork – we finished up with 20 pairs of socks, two handbags and gloves to match and 11 scarves. It was just too easy and of no real excitement, although Maudie was still her usual self.

'We carried out a few more little raids on Harrods and Selfridges. I remember stealing our first mink coat. I persuaded Maud to take a couple of dresses off the peg and I took a couple, both of us going into the changing room. Maud put two of them on whilst I supervised. The moment she had them on, I waltzed out of the room and went to choose the coat. I took two together, as though it was one and gave one to Maud to try on. It fitted. I then took the remaining dress back together with the second coat. Whilst all this was happening, Maud calmly walked out, wearing the two dresses and the mink coat. To show willing, I paid for the one dress I had taken. £80 worth of goods for nothing and just for the cheek of it, we went back into Harrods and stole four bottles of Mercier champagne to celebrate our success.

'This is where you might think us a bit strange, Mr White, because we made a note of the price and put this money on one side so that we could pay for them if we got caught. It was the same with the coat and the dress which we decided would be useful at some stage.

'Shop lifting in those days was easier; there was no CCTV, but to us it was no real challenge.'

***

Little did I know how Maud's kleptomania and Edith's short-lived boredom were to become time-honoured partners in the daring escapades these two ladies embarked upon.

Edith was about to lay bare the facts, in more ways than one …

Chapter 3
An Unexpected Result

I suppose our first job of any consequence took place when we were invited to the Earl of Boothtown's son Henry's 21st birthday party at Boothtown Hall. In fact, he was their only child and very precious to them.

The Earl had been a politician and had lost his seat a few years earlier. He was moved up to the House of Lords when a grateful Labour Prime Minister wanted to strengthen the numbers of left-wing politicians in the Lords. However, he had managed to accumulate significant funds in the process. He bought Boothtown Hall, spending a great deal of his wealth renovating it in an attempt to satisfy his wife's extravagance as a social climber.

Our father knew George Merriweather, now the first Earl of Boothtown and often invited him and his wife to our social functions. Sometimes, they would bring their children to play with us, so we got to know them well enough. Then of course, after Father died, it was just Maud and I, but we were still invited.

I remember this day ... We pulled up in our limousine, which looked brand new, alighted like two princesses, and were escorted in. We didn't have champagne very often, but this day was special and as we entered, we were served with a lovely cold glass which made both of us very merry.

We met many of our future 'victims' and, of course, the Countess as she insisted on being called. Every time she introduced us, she just had to emphasise our wealth by stressing who our father was and where we lived.

It was a lovely evening. Maudie and I were very much in demand and we were having a thoroughly good time, except I was being pursued by Henry, the future Earl, who was a bit of a randy devil. He had always fancied me as a little girl and I was sure he still had a crush on me, which was encouraged by his mother. Only after our money in reality, Mr White. However, I could see Maudie becoming anxious and felt it was about time we did the deed.

It was all to be so simple. While everyone was dancing and having a good time, I was to slip upstairs, steal the jewellery from the Countess's bedroom, whilst Maudie was to keep a look out. She was to knock on the door if anyone was around.

I left the dance floor on the excuse that I needed the loo and made my way upstairs, eventually into the Countess's bedroom. I was about to start rummaging when I heard the door handle slowly turn. I immediately turned and walked towards the door. It was none other than Henry.

'What are you doing in here?' he asked.

'Waiting for you. I knew you were following me,' I replied, thinking on my feet, but not very well.

'Come on, come to my bedroom. It's just along the corridor,' he replied.

'No,' I replied, sighing. 'Come here. I want you now,' I said, slipping my dress off my shoulders. As I said, he was a randy devil. He was on top of me in a flash, and all over me like a rash. We fell onto the bed and in one movement, he had his trousers down and was beginning to strip me off; within seconds this rampant bull was inside me, banging away.

I couldn't believe what I was hearing! I had a ninety-year-old woman in front of me, talking in this vein, as though she was a young woman of the present day. She dressed in the twenties but lived in the present. She thought in the present; she acted in the present. Extraordinary!

By now, Maudie was becoming concerned about me and decided to investigate, gently opening the door and peering in. The shock on her face as she saw us was something I will never forget.

'Nor will I,' Maud added loudly.

Thankfully, Henry was pre-occupied and couldn't see me signal to Maud to go away. I rolled him over and started to push hard down on him. He closed his eyes enjoying every movement. I covered his face with part of the sheet and began to kiss him through it. I couldn't think what else to do. I didn't want him to see Maudie. Anyway, he seemed to enjoy it more and more as the sheet became wetter and wetter from our warm saliva. I had him desperate for more as I now sat on his thighs, pushing just enough to keep him there.

But then disaster! We could hear his mother outside, asking anyone within earshot if they had seen Henry.

'Oh, where is that boy?' she kept repeating, her stammer evident.

'Christ! It's my mother,' Henry whispered loudly, trying to get up. I held him down, signalling to Maud to get into the wardrobe.

'Please let me get up, Edie,' he begged. 'Please ...' Which I did when I saw Maudie was safe. The rampant bull was now just a little lamb, as we grabbed all our clothes, straightened the bed and escaped into the anteroom.

The last thing we heard was someone exclaiming: 'Oh, don't worry, he'll be off with one of the girls, knowing your big lad.' I started laughing but he covered my mouth to stop me, and was now beginning to regain his composure. We heard his mother come into the room and rummage in the drawer of her dressing table. She muttered something to herself and made to leave. But already Henry was beginning to show me again what a big boy he was, as he began to fondle me with one hand, still covering my mouth with the other. I don't know why, but I remember thinking he would make a good pianist.

We thought we heard the Countess leave but we could still hear some movement. I knew it would be Maudie making her escape so I began to fondle him again. This time it was a mistake as he was in control. I was trapped against the wall and there was no sophisticated foreplay, just a straight bonk against the wall – something I had to put up with for the sake of the job.

'Be careful,' I begged, as he began rutting like some hog hired for the purpose.

Then came such words of wisdom – the result of his great education, and his subsequent Master's Degree in Medicine.

'Oh, don't ya worry, Edie … er. You can't get pregnant … er …when you do it standing up. Aaaarh!' He had climaxed.

'Too bloody late in any case,' I muttered as I untangled myself from his grip.

We got dressed in total silence, not even looking at each other. It was as though I had performed a specific function and was dismissed.

I rejoined the party, finding Maudie here having a wonderful time, and wearing a silly grin all over her face as I went to talk to her.

'Who's been a naughty girl then?' she said in a shrill, singing sort of voice, her eyebrows raised.

'I wouldn't have been if you had warned me in time.'
We continued having a whale of a time until I heard Henry talking to a group of his friends. 'She fucks like a rattlesnake,' I heard him say.

I was so incensed that I approached the group and added: 'I had to. His penis is so small, he couldn't satisfy any woman.' I then walked away, crooking my little finger. The whole bunch just stared open-mouthed with little Henry becoming more scarlet by the second.

At last I was able to have a word with Maudie: 'Well, did you?'

'Yesssss,' she said excitedly in that squeaky voice which became her trademark after every job we did.

'Where …?' That was enough of the question to get a response.

'In the car.'

We left the party around midnight before the balloon went up and the news broke that the Countess's jewels had been stolen. I knew no one would suspect the two little rich girls of anything. But it was a thrill to get home and find that Maudie had stolen seven pieces including her best necklace, which she had acquired whilst her son was having his wicked way with me.

There were all sorts of rumours about the robbery. Naturally, the staff bore the brunt of the investigation from the police. I heard later that Henry had vouched for me, to the delight of his mother. The conclusion was that it was a professional job by a cat burglar.

Well, this cat burglar had made a right mess of it. I realised after eight weeks, and four weeks of morning sickness that I was pregnant, which was going to curtail my activities and mess up Maud's life as well. It was a terrible disgrace in those days to become pregnant out of wedlock, so I knew we would have to go to our villa in France.

We had a glorious villa in Nice and still have, not far from the Promenade des Anglais. That created another problem as half the English wealthy folk spent the winter in Nice and I dreaded bumping into them. I was not going to let poor little Henry know the child was his as I no longer respected him for what he had said about me. We therefore decided to do one, possibly two more jobs before we went to France, especially as I didn't show.

Chapter 4
Fabergé Eggs

At that time during the summer, we would be invited to at least one party a week if not more, so we could be selective. I wouldn't say we were good time girls but at least we enjoyed the social life and as a result, we received many invitations.

On this one occasion, we accepted an invitation to Jack Short's party, which was to be a formal dinner dance. He was a wealthy industrialist who had made a fortune in steel, which was rapidly growing in importance by the day as trouble was brewing in Germany. He was, however, one of those distasteful men – the not so nice tranche of the nouveau riche. He had to brag about all the things he had, how much he had paid for them and, in particular, the four Fabergé eggs which he had displayed in a glass cabinet in the ballroom, so that the world would see and admire. This is what motivated us to make the effort and go.

It was here that Maudie had a brainwave. She had read about Richard Drew, an American who had invented a one-sided sticky tape. It was her simple question that made me realise the opportunities this might generate.

'What if we covered the glass with this sticky tape and then smashed it. Would the pieces still stick to the paper?'

'I would think so. We must try it,' I replied excitedly, feeling the way Maud felt when she had done something wrong.

Well, we bought some of this new sticky tape from

Harrods, of course. We had to order it as it was a new thing. They always claimed they could get anything for their customers so it was a challenge for them. Our maintenance man ordered it; we didn't want to draw attention to ourselves. When it arrived we practised with it in the back garden and it worked a treat! None of the glass fell to the floor, but most important of all, when the glass smashed, it made no noise.

That was it ... Jack Short's Fabergé eggs were the next target!

We knew they would have already arranged an escort for us as most of our friends and family did. It was thoughtful of them, but we often dreaded who might be chosen for us. Not once did we like the choice of escort we were given. It seemed par for the course ... every time.

The day came and we got dressed up for the evening in all our finery. We set off in our new Le Mans Bentley just to show off, arriving ten minutes late – the fashion in those days.

We were greeted by Jack who immediately introduced us to our escorts. Mine was Bellamy Winterton, a son of another industrialist, James Winterton of the automobile industry and Maud's was David 'Clingy' Cross who was like a leach and wouldn't leave her alone. Mind you, at this moment they were more interested in the bloody car than us. It did cause a bit of a stir in the rest of the male fraternity and a little animosity from the women as they thought it was not the thing for ladies to do.

Anyway, I was no lady then as I had breached another code. We had bought it on a whim because Maud had said we could make a quick getaway in it, not realising that there were only about four in the country and everywhere it went, it attracted very much attention. But it was fun to go out in and Peter, who was our chauffeur at the time, would let her rip on the straights, always sitting Maudie next to him, with me on the outside of our specially fitted bench seat so we could both sit in the front. However, this time I drove, leaving Peter at home.

Jack had to do everything in style and, of course, it was 'dwinkie poos' on the terrace before dinner. However, I must have attracted the wrong sort of escort at that time as James too was all over me, unless news had got around about me and dear old Henry, and they all wanted to try it. The gong rang out twice; the first time to usher us to the dining room, and the second time, just in case we hadn't heard the first one.

'You're very cynical, Edith,' Maud exclaimed.

Well, I really hated all this pretence. I think it was one of the main reasons I turned to crime.

James seemed to think that touching my bottom was included in the aperitif and that the first course offered a quick grope of my leg and knee, so I decided to stop him. The claret had just been served with the main course and I saw my opportunity. He lifted his glass to have a drink and at the same time his left hand gently ran down my leg.

I think all lechers were ambidextrous in those days. He reached my knee, bending very slightly forward. The moment had arrived.

'Ooooh,' I screeched as I stood up, knocking his claret all down him. 'You naughty boy,' I added, smiling and giving him a big kiss on the cheek as if to say you're forgiven. That did it. He turned the colour of his wine and remained so for many minutes.

He left the room to get cleaned up, but it didn't work and he looked a sight in a borrowed shirt. I could see many of the men smirking. In fact, Jack was struggling not to laugh. The ladies of course, were giving me nasty looks. Maudie caught my eye and just winked.

Dinner over, and I was reluctantly escorted to the dance hall where we were allocated our tables by place cards.

Poor old James had to sit next to me and was expected to have the first dance.

'Why did you do that and embarrass me in front of everybody,' he whispered curtly.

'Darling, you embarrassed yourself. Don't do it again!'

'You won't get another invitation to any party if I have anything to do with it.'

I thumped him across the face and shouted: 'Don't be so rude!' The band immediately stopped playing and a deathly silence came over the room. 'He wants to take me to bed and get in my knickers,' I exclaimed loudly as I flounced off the dance floor, shedding crocodile tears. This brought an element of sympathy and allowed me to stay on, but he left immediately. At least I had got rid of him and it gave me chance to look at the glass display cabinet with the four Fabergé eggs in it. Not my cup of tea, but I suppose they were wonderful pieces or whatever.

We knew the glass case would be locked and it was obvious that the only way in would be through a broken pane. At least I now knew the best way to do it. So when another lecher went to get us a drink, we discussed how we were going to achieve it.

It was after midnight when the first of the guests began to leave. The band had finished for the evening and many of the men had gone into the games room to have a smoke, leaving their women in the lounge to discuss knitting or my behaviour.

This was our appointed moment. Maud went into the ballroom and as the lights were still on, she closed the door behind her, leaving me outside to keep guard. It was nerve-racking waiting in a corridor where you could be seen from both ends, except if you pressed yourself firmly into the depth of the doorway. I was never the slimmest of people so you can imagine what it was like when I heard voices.

I waited several minutes for Maud before I realised something must be wrong and had the nerve to open the door to find out what. Her hands were covered in sticky paper from fingers to thumbs, and there she was, shaking them like some petulant child having a paddy as she tried to flick the stuff from her fingers.

'What the hell do you think you are doing?' I asked.

'I couldn't tear it to shape and every time I tried, a bit stuck on my hands,' she began somewhat apologetically. 'I tried doing it with my teeth but it only made matters worse,' she continued, almost in tears. In the early days the paper was very sticky and not like the Sellotape of today; it was more like strips of fly paper.

—If you remember that stuff, Mr White?

I was now very concerned and, to Maud's chagrin, I wanted to call the whole thing off.

'Come on, let's get out of here before we are missed,' I whispered, 'but we'll come back later.' That at least perked Maud up especially when I left the French windows to the terrace unlocked.

'Where's the powder room?' I asked the young waiter who was now collecting the guests' coats.

'Just along there, Miss,' he replied.

It was almost where we had come from and a splendid place to hide should there be trouble. We found ourselves casing the joint; in fact, wherever we went we were looking for opportunities. There was a ground floor window in the toilet so at least there was another escape route and I decided I would leave that on the latch as well to provide another exit, just in case.

Jack was outside in the front porch, saying good night to all his guests so we made a big thing of telling him how much we enjoyed ourselves and what a wonderful cook he must have, which he corrected with the word 'chef'.

Oh, I hate industrialists. They always have to show off.

3 5

'Sorry about young James. I hope it didn't spoil your evening,' Jack said.

'Oh, not at all. He's such a boy, and boys *will* be boys.'

'That's the spirit,' he said as we left to get into the car. 'Fine young woman that,' I heard him say to his wife.

I know it was stupid, but I just had to be a little tease for my own peace of mind. I walked over to Jack, put my hands on his arms, pulled him close to me, kissed him full on the lips and whispered loudly so his wife could hear, 'Ooh, I love powerful men!' No doubt he had a row with his wife that night.

We got into the car, goggled up, and with a huge roar of the engine, I drove back home where we immediately changed to go out again. We lived about two miles away from Jack Short's, and for obvious reasons, we couldn't use the car so it was bicycles or nothing. There was never anyone about at that time of night so we were fine.

We decided to wear trousers and dark clothes, Hepburn style, as they were dark and all the fashion, then cycle over and take it from there. There was not a soul about and we thought it would be easy, but when we left the bicycles outside the main gate, we never considered the fact that we would have at least four hundred yards to run to the house with our kit – sticky paper, a hammer, a pair of scissors, a screwdriver and a torch. It was almost pitch black, particularly when a cloud covered the moon. Furthermore, we didn't consider for one moment the journey back, not only with the tools but also with the swag, possibly being chased by household staff or even Jack himself, armed with his shotgun.

We arrived at the ballroom terrace, the right one thanks to a temporary break in the clouds. To my astonishment, they had left the door unlocked. We opened it and slowly walked in, shining the beam on the cabinet.

This time we had scissors, and cut the paper to size, stuck

it on the glass and hit it with the hammer. It hardly made a sound even when we had to gently knock the glass around the edges. This was the easy part. Maudie took the eggs out, but where to put them – we had forgotten a bag. Our only saviour was the Kathryn Hepburn trousers. They had very fashionable large pockets and that had to suffice.

It was time to go when Maud had a brainwave. She felt we must break one of the outside panes to make it look other than an inside job. I cut the paper, covered the outside glass pane and she hit it. Disaster number two! Although the pane and the paper fell out, making no noise, the vibration made another pane fall out, shattering on the floor. The noise immediately woke the family dog which started barking, and as we hot footed it across the lawns to the gate, we could see the lights go on upstairs.

Bloody Jack let his dog out, which came charging at us, catching up by the stride. I wasn't as swift as Maudie with the great lump inside me; in fact I had to stop for a second. I turned to see the dog was now within a few yards of me and thank God I had the hammer which I began waving frantically. I was in sheer panic when it leapt at me. I fell backwards onto the grass but the downward stroke of the hammer hit it full on the nose as I went down. The dog withdrew, screaming in pain.

Maudie came running back to help, just in time for Jack to fire a blast from his shotgun; fortunately too far away to do any damage. Frightening enough though. We could both see the other doors opening as members of his staff came out to join the chase, but we were now within a few feet of our bicycles and behind the wall. Seconds later, and we were away, still clutching the tools of our trade and pedalling like mad.

We were home in ten minutes or so, creeping very slowly into the house so as not to wake our staff. We both went into Maudie's room to look at the swag and despite the fall, thankfully there was no damage to the eggs.

The whole episode certainly gave us a buzz and I remember, we hugged each other and danced around, playing with the eggs as though they were toys.

The Liverpool & Preston Insurance Company sent an investigator round to question all the guests to see if they had seen anything. So did the police, but it was another unsolved crime. The press made a meal of the fact that another well-off household had been robbed.

Maudie began to take matters seriously, reading about all the latest technology used in criminal detection and decided that we must now wear gloves at all times; she had read about burglars being caught by the fingerprints they left behind. She also thought we needed to plan more thoroughly. For example, we hadn't thought about carrying the goods home. What tools would we need and where would we put them, and most of all, what would be our means of escape? We had to have more than one escape route should we find ourselves trapped.

Maud was certainly taking things very seriously and we were becoming more professional by the minute.

However, we were still very naïve with regard to crime and punishment. We still believed that if we got caught and handed the goods back, we would not be punished, just as Father had done for Maud, but until then we had to prevent the goods from being found.

—Mr White, you will be the only person outside the family to know a family secret. We have a priest's hole, which despite the Yanks having the house during the war, no one has ever found, and the goods are all in there from day one, including Maud's notebook with all the details. We would like you to return these to their rightful owners.

Edith handed me a little case containing four Fabergé eggs, plus a rather beautiful diamond necklace worth a considerable amount of money these days.

'I will give you details of where these should go. You can make up a story of how they were discovered, can't you?' Mr Higginbotham said. He obviously felt we had come to the end of our first visit. 'I'll phone you when we have another day available.'

'That will be good,' I replied.

Armed with the eggs and the necklace, I then said my goodbyes to all concerned. I was almost in a daze at what I was discovering, but I managed to phone the insurance company and Jack Short's family with the details and left them to argue out the claim. It was a sensational start to the stories that were to follow.

The Mail *headline read:* 'Tip-off Leads to the Solving of a Fifty-year-old Robbery'.

Chapter 5
Fancy Dress With the Fascists

We soon forgot the little episode at the Winterton's and life was back to normal, especially as our invitations continued and, in spite of the fact that Maud had dropped out of most things which included our previous activities, it seemed excitement was no longer in vogue. She simply wanted to be with Peter, our chauffeur and handyman, and that was good enough for me.

However, she couldn't resist the thought of having a crack at Mortimer de Clancy's place when we received an invitation to a fund-raising party for the British Union of Fascists (BUF). It was well known that de Clancy was a right- wing supporter, and we were all, including Peter, very anti the Nazis; it wasn't difficult for me to persuade her to have a crack at the place.

Anyway, it was because they needed funds that we became involved with Sir Mortimer de Clancy. He was from one of the oldest and richest families in the country. His ancestors could be traced back to William the Conqueror and further than that in France. His wealth gave him access to all the major political figures, not least the aristocracy. Suffice to say, his influence was enormous.

De Clancy decided to hold a fancy dress party at his Belleford home, one of the major stately homes of England, situated in forty thousand acres. He invited all the wealth of England in the hope of converting a large number to his point of view and, of course, any tangible gifts, such as jewellery, paintings or other objets d'art were welcome, all of which would be sold at an auction on the night. Well, it was too much to refuse.

There was massive unemployment at the time, and in spite of being victorious in the last war, there was talk of another on everyone's lips. There was great anxiety by now because the Nazis had almost taken over the political scene in Germany. The problem for us all was that this talk and fear of the consequences was spreading all over Europe.

We had read that the Jewish people were the first to be singled out for punishment with all their rights and privileges being removed, followed by anyone who could be considered not normal. Then we read that Italy, led by their dictator Mussolini, was the next to be controlled by the Fascists and despite all the talk of appeasement and compromise, some of us were beginning to prepare for the worst.

Britain itself was in the depths of the Fascist era with the BUF being led by Sir Oswald Mosley. It was now believed to have over 50,000 members and growing quickly. They needed funds.

—Mr White, I remember even your paper, the *Mail* supported them with a headline: 'Hurrah for the Blackshirts!' I'm sure it was something like that.

The party was to be held on the 5th November, Guy Fawkes Night, and not only was there to be a buffet dance, but also a massive bonfire party, followed by the auction. Together with the dance and buffet, there were other forms of entertainment in other parts of the house, including a more private discussion with senior members of the BUF. It was too much to resist, especially as we had never been there before. I recall that Father didn't like the man and always referred to him as a charlatan.

It was fun going to the theatrical costumier to get our fancy dress. I went as a whore from Victor Hugo's, Les

Misérables as I thought it was appropriate for what I had already achieved. Maud dressed up as a very glamorous titled lady from the 1800s.

The drive to the main door was at least a mile from the road and was lined with young members of the BUF, and at the entrance we were greeted by almost a private army of Mosley's Blackshirts – the pick of the membership with the insignia emblazoned on their sleeves and caps. They were, without doubt, there to evict any undesirables and to stop any unanticipated trouble.

We had taken delivery of our Duisenberg a couple of years or so earlier, and had never had the opportunity to use it, so this night was its launch, We stopped in a line of cars waiting to pull up to the main door, when I decided to get out. Peter, good as gold, got out of the car to open the door, but this caused pandemonium with the bully boys who came running over, demanding we return to the car. They manhandled Peter to the front of the car and tried to jostle Maudie and me back in.

This was too much for me and I would have none of it, slapping the Blackshirt across the mouth and marching past, stopping only to kiss the next one on the head, and leave a very smudgy pair of lips in the middle of his forehead. They were both totally bemused and were saved from my further abuse by Sir Mortimer himself who came to apologise for their behaviour. I did the same with him as I did with the bullies but this time kissed him full on the lips, especially as I knew he was taken by this whorish look alike.

Maudie did look lovely and was quickly taken off by several admirers. I was sure I would have been except that the men were worried to be seen with me. That was until the drink took hold.

We were all, several hundred of us, ushered into the main hall to be served champagne or whatever we liked, plus the most delicious canapés you could imagine. He was certainly pushing the boat out.

'He certainly was!' Maud added.

When nearly all the guests had arrived, Mortimer opened the formal proceedings. He thanked everyone for their attendance and explained where the different types of entertainment were being held. He then had the gall to make this further announcement:

'I think our menfolk will be interested to know that there is a presentation by Sir Oswald Mosley in the Blue Room.'

—Mr White, I'm sure I would have made a bloody good suffragette because there was no way I could put up with that sort of talk.

I moved forward so that I could be heard. 'Why have you invited me then?' I yelled, before adding, 'Just for the entertainment?'

He hadn't a clue who I was, despite my kissing him on the lips when we arrived. He was rescued by his aide who clearly had to whisper my name.

'I'm sorry, Miss Trenchard. Clearly that was very remiss of me. Of course, everyone is welcome to hear what Sir Oswald has to say. After all, you do have the vote now.'

Well, that last remark went down like a lead balloon in many quarters. Patronising bastard, I thought, listening to the rumblings of discontent from the womenfolk.

He was saved by an enormous bang from outside, which seemed to shake the very foundations of the house. We all turned to look out and see a huge display of fireworks which had commenced and a massive bonfire which suddenly burst into flames. The display was really fantastic as the fireworks had been imported specially from China.

'It was one way to try and change the government. Fortunately, we now have a more civilised way,' he shouted into the microphone, hoping to get a laugh, but the noise and hubbub drowned his words.

We had only been there for half an hour or so when we saw the donations pouring into the boxes, each guarded by three huge BUF thugs. The big white five pound notes, the blue one pound, and the orange ten shilling notes were falling into the boxes like confetti. One box was filled immediately and instantly taken away to be counted and locked in the safe. The envelopes followed, each with the names of the donors written on them, and each filled with jewellery to be auctioned later on.

Maud caught my eye as she slipped away from her chaperone, signalling me to go to the powder room. I immediately knew what it was about as she had that look in her eye. We managed to get away, entering this massive but beautiful room. He had really thrown money into this palace; words are not enough to describe the opulence of the place. Even this little powder room, which was small in comparison to the rest of the house, was quite magnificent.

—Mr White, our house is not small, but Belleford made it seem tiny!

Maud was so excited; she began to chatter the moment we entered. I had to shut her up simply to check whether anyone was in the toilet. We were on our own, thankfully. The bonfire and fireworks had captured most of the guests' attention, especially as the warm punch captured their hearts and minds, all of them becoming a little more susceptible by the minute.

'Let's do it!' Maud said excitedly.

'It will have to be quick as they'll move this lot soon enough,' I replied. 'First thing, let's find out where they are keeping it and go from there.'

So began one of our most daring robberies and what turned out to be the easiest.

We raced back downstairs just in time to follow another box being taken, as we found out, to the Estate Office, and in spite of the consternation caused by us entering the room, Maudie here was more than a match for them.

'You dropped this,' she said in her little girl lost voice, fluttering her eyelashes at half the Blackshirt army. She often did this, so much so, I never knew whether it was pretend or real. It worked as she handed the note to the man in charge and exclaimed, 'Oooh!' looking at his biceps, as if to indicate how big and strong he was.

'Thank you, Ma'am,' he said, raising her status to that of the aristocracy. Can you find your way back?'

'Well, I would like a big strong man like you to help us,' she said, again fluttering her eyelashes.

'Give it a rest for God's sake,' I whispered. But it was too late; we had to have this Sergeant Blackshirt as our bodyguard back to the main hall.

'There you are, Ma'am,' he said, turning to leave, but not before Sarah Bernhardt here had whispered, 'Thank you,' again in that little lost voice.

'Did you see it?' she whispered excitedly.

'What?'

'The safe – it's a Joseph Loch – the same as ours. You know the one Father bought to keep his papers in. It's dead easy to get into.'

'How would you know?' I asked, totally astonished at what I was hearing for the first time.

'I used to practise listening to the way the tumblers slotted into place. They made a specific sort of noise. I once did it in five minutes.'

I just stood there open-mouthed, unable to utter a word … in total shock.

'What did Father say?'

'Nothing, but I think he knew because he caught me playing with it a few times. Anyway, I could get into it in about ten minutes. I never read Father's papers or took anything from him.'

'I don't believe this and anyway, where did you get the

ten shilling note from?'

She opened her Dorothy bag which was only small but was crammed full of notes.

'Where did you get that?' I asked, exasperatingly.

'Sorry,' she mouthed, shrugging her shoulders, one hand held despairingly in the air.

'What else have you got?'

'Nothing now.'

'What do you mean "Nothing now"?'

'Well, I found these lovely emeralds and I had nowhere to hide them, so I put them into Tony Glazzard's pocket. It should cause a bit of a laugh if he gets caught. Anyway, he was too touchy.'

'Talk of the devil,' I remarked as Tony joined us.

'I hope it was something nice,' he replied.

'Yes, Maudie was just saying she had lost you.'

'Well now, you've found me. Come on, let's dance.'

The alcohol was flowing and this whore was becoming more popular by the minute, which was a damn nuisance because now I was intent on casing the joint, looking for weaknesses in the system. But with my unwanted admirers, it was not easy, especially as mine host Mortimer was one of them, much to the obvious annoyance of Helen his wife who looked at me daggers each time we passed her on the floor.

Maud had it easy; all she had was Mr Wandering Hands to deal with, which she kept restoring to their proper place. I had a man who simply wanted to take me to bed. I think it was the early pregnancy that did it as it makes one look voluptuous. Anyway, I danced Mortimer out onto the terrace, followed by Helen, desperate to stop me having my wicked way with him. Mr Hands came onto the terrace with Maudie who followed me as she was worried what might happen.

Thankfully, I saw them and whispered to Mortimer,

'Later ... your wife's coming.'

—Mr White, he was hooked and now thought there was a real chance of getting what he wanted!

'Go and sit over there,' Mortimer whispered, and made his way back to the dance hall just in time to meet his wife coming out.

'She needed to sit down in the fresh air,' Mortimer said, taking hold of his wife and joining the dance.

I couldn't believe it. I now had an excuse to walk in the fresh air and with Maud realising the same, she quickly got rid of Tony, at least for a few minutes.

'You go and get some drinks,' Maud said. 'I'll just look after Edith for a minute or two.' He went off like a little boy to do mummy's bidding.

'Quickly, come on, Maudie. Let's have a look round there. It's roughly where the Estate Office should be.'

We walked at least a hundred yards to almost the back of the building before we found what we were looking for, and of course, it was just like so many. It was situated in a huge courtyard, attached to the stables, where there was a garage with their six cars, including his two Mercedes limousines, which the bloody traitor had to have. Then there was the machinery store, the food store, where they hung the meat after killing – venison, beef, hares and pheasants – all that sort of thing. The tractor shed housed a couple of new Ferguson tractors; there was what you would consider normal security around as it was just an outside working office. The BUF Blackshirts were giving the appearance of guarding the place with their show of strength, but they too were also very casual about the whole affair.

When I thought about it later, I realised that no one would expect the tenth richest man in the country to be robbed. I decided that I wanted to take the money and the jewels, not only for the thrill of it, as Maudie would say, but also because I did not believe that Mosley's lot should have all this money to support his own ideals. I thought that all Sir Mortimer was doing was hedging his bets in order to keep his fortune intact, just in case the Germans conquered us as well ... similar thoughts held by many of the other rich folk around at the time.

I could see very quickly the weaknesses in the Estate Office's security but as I said before, we had to check all possibilities especially the escape route should things go wrong. We therefore wanted to case the joint properly from every angle. We retraced our steps back into the dance hall where poor old Mr Hands was anxiously waiting for Maudie to reappear and I followed, leaving her to fend off his attentions, only to find I was still in demand. We had a great time for the next hour or so when once again, I signalled to Maudie to take a natural break, and once again. we trooped upstairs. Only this time we decided to take a look in the upstairs rooms.

Sir Mortimer did not sleep with his wife, we discovered as we entered this extremely opulent bedroom. His wife's room was adjoining with the key on his side. Hers too was fit for a film star. We took advantage of the time to check his wardrobe and the drawers, and save for few sovereigns, there was very little worth taking, but then as I opened the door to leave, I came face to face with another Blackshirt guard.

'What are you doing in there?' he demanded.

'Shush, you'll embarrass him,' I replied loud enough for Maudie to hear.

He stepped back as he saw Maud escaping, dress ruffled and almost off the shoulder. She turned back to look in the bedroom. 'You naughty man, you shouldn't treat a girl this way,' she said in a loud whisper.

'Sorry Miss,' the Blackshirt said, trying hard not to laugh, and leaving the two of us to return to the dance floor.

'He's a very naughty man, but good fun,' I added, putting my forefinger across my lips as if to say mums the word. We could not stop laughing as we trundled down the stairs, so much so that Sir Mortimer wondered what was so funny and walked toward us.

'And what have you two ladies been up to?'

That did it, we burst out laughing again. 'You naughty boy,' I said, taking hold of his arm, leading him back onto the floor and flirting with him outrageously. We just hoped Blackshirt hadn't seen.

There was no way we could go back upstairs to continue casing the joint; it would have been too difficult and too great a risk. However, it had begun to rain heavily and as the bonfire became less attractive, the numbers in the house swelled, so much so there were elements of confusion as some of the guests were trying to find their way round the place. The rain then turned to a thunderstorm, and as you will probably know, the electricity supply in those days was often affected by these conditions. Sure enough, some half an hour later, the lights went out and there were screams of delight, not least indignation in certain corners. That said, within seconds there were dozens of candles brought in and all the torchlight candles were brought in from outside and relit.

The first thing I noticed was that the rest of the money that had been gifted was being taken away and so too were the enveloped gifts for the auction. Many of the Blackshirts stood round the dance hall with candle torches but the whole scene was becoming farcical.

This was our opportunity – never mind the escape route. We quickly got rid of Mr Hands and made our way through the house to the Estate Office again. There was no one there; it was unbelievable. The safe was, of course, locked but as Maudie said, it was very easy to open. I quickly ran to the car, getting absolutely drenched only to find Peter fast asleep, oblivious to everything.

'Wake up! Come on,' I shouted. 'Bring the car.'

It started with an almighty backfire and a pall of smoke, as if I wanted to draw attention to what I was about to do, but it was raining that heavy, no one appeared to notice. I stood on the running board like some Al Capone gangster and directed Peter to the Estate Office. I could not believe it. There was only one person there ... Maud. She was standing outside the door with four boxes and a pile of papers which she was holding onto like grim death.

'It's all here!' she exclaimed, handing me the papers. 'I told you it was simple, but these will interest someone.'

'Close your mouth, Peter,' I said, seeing the shocked open-mouthed look on his face. 'Maud will explain later.'

We quickly loaded everything into the car.

'Is that everything?' I asked Maud.

'Yes,' she replied, adding, 'and you had better take these,' handing me a couple of handfuls of sovereigns.

'Where on earth did you get these? Don't tell me ... Sir Mortimer's bedroom,' I whispered out of Peter's earshot.

'Look after these. Pop them in the drawing room will you please, Peter?'

'Now let's get out of here. Take the car away, unload this lot in the garage and come back in about an hour.'

He duly left, and in all that time there was not a soul to be seen. Every member of the BUF and the staff of Sir Mortimer's household were now on candle duty in the hall, or up the stairs and outside the powder rooms.

We made our way back to the dance hall with the candles. Maud went the way she came and I simply got soaked, running back to the hall via the terrace. I was immediately given a candle torch without a second look at my demeanour and waltzed in. It really was bedlam in the hall. People were dancing with candle torches, being careful about bumping into one another, and whilst it really was good fun, there were many little accidents, dropped candles – burnt fingers, spilled drinks and broken glasses. Of course, who should I bump into? None other than Sir Mortimer.

'Well, young Miss Trenchard, you look wet through.'

'I certainly am and it's all your fault.'

'My fault?'

'Yes. Yours. A couple of your guests who shall be nameless have been wanting to ...' I said, whispering the rest, 'take my knickers down, and have chased me everywhere. 'Would you like to do the same, Sir Mortimer?' I whispered again.

'I certainly would, Miss Trenchard, but I hope they didn't succeed.'

'Oh, Sir Mortimer! Of course they didn't. What sort of a girl do you think I am?' I replied, half laughing, half smiling.

'Come on, let me get these wet clothes off you,' he said, gently taking hold of my arm and leading me to the foot of the stairs. He let go of my arm and whispered, 'See you at the top in two minutes.'

I ran up the stairs, but who should I bump into but the big brute of a Blackshirt guard who had seen me coming out of Sir Mortimer's bedroom earlier. He looked at me quizzically.

'He can't leave me alone,' I said quietly, 'but shush,' I murmured, once again putting my forefinger to my lips, only just in time to see Mortimer coming up the stairs.

I turned and winked at him as Mortimer guided me to his bedroom. What an alibi I had made for myself. He led me into the room where I had to pretend I hadn't seen it before, ensuring that the guard wasn't in hearing distance. I swooned at everything I saw, which was difficult in the dark, even though Mortimer had a candle torch.

'I bet you bring all the girls here,' I said purposefully,

expecting him to say something to the contrary, when bless my soul he replied:

'Of course I do, they all love this bed!'

'What on earth does your wife think?'

'She likes living here and it's a price she has to pay. Come here,' he snapped, patting his hand on the bed; I dutifully obeyed.

I actually felt disgust for him and sorrow for his dear wife, but I needed to cement my alibi so I had to get to it. He was a randy individual and didn't even wait for me to slip my pants off as he began his performing arts free-style programme. I grunted in the right places, gripped him tight when I thought he would slip off the vaulting horse, yelled when I thought he was near his climax and shouted, 'Come on! Come on, don't stop,' when I knew he had finished, just to make him feel that little bit inadequate. Then I rubbed my knickers in his face and that did it – he wanted more of me.

'When can I see you again?' he said excitedly.

'As soon as you like,' I replied, pretending and sounding as though I was enthusiastic, but knowing full well I would not want to go near him again.

'Friday?'

'That will be marvellous. Give me a ring and I'll meet you anytime, anywhere. Ooh, you are a big boy, aren't you?' I said, stroking him. Then in one movement, I slipped his grasp to go to his bathroom when I realised I shouldn't know where it was. 'Where's the powder room?'

'Use my wife's. It's in there, second on the right.'

—Well, Mr White, the next few minutes were sheer Marx Brothers. I walked into the wife's bedroom, searching for the second door on the right with only the smallest glimmer of the light from his candle in the next room when I heard the bed clothes rustle. Although my eyes were somewhat accustomed to the darkness by now, I couldn't see anyone from that distance, so I decided to go over to the bed.

'Ooh, you are naughty boy,' I whispered, pretending to be shocked and turning to Lady Helen de Clancy, I leaned over and whispered, 'Shush, I won't tell if you won't!'

I'm sure I could sense that she saw the funny side of the matter, but our chance meeting was soon broken when Sir Mortimer suddenly shouted:

'Miss Trenchard, are you ready?' It was very businesslike, of course. I went as a whore and now I realised I had behaved like a whore, but by golly, I knew I had been well paid.

'I'll only be a moment,' I shouted back.

It took me a couple of minutes before I was respectable enough to leave the boudoir. I felt my way back, passing the bed and whispered, 'See you soon.'

To which Sir Mortimer shouted, 'Are you talking to someone?'

'Of course not,' I said sharply. 'I've just stubbed my toe in the dark.'

'Oh dear, hurry up now,' he said, with all the sympathy of a Praying Mantis. 'My wife will be wondering where the hell I am.'

'Yes, she will. I would, if you were married to me,' I said, trying hard not to laugh.

'Well, this will be our little secret, won't it?' Mortimer added.

'Of course. I would hate my reputation to be sullied if people knew I had had an affair with a distinguished man like you.'

He didn't know how to take that and thought it was a compliment.

'Yes, yes of course,' he replied, coughing a little.

I was sure I heard a stifled laugh from the other bedroom.

'You go first, my dear,' the patronising bastard said as he opened the door and almost pushed me out, following some two minutes later down the stairs.

Now where was Maud? I had to find her quickly to at least let her know how the land lay, but we still had no electricity and everyone still had to dance by candlelight. Well, she soon found me, looking worn out from the attention of Mr Hands. The only way to keep control of the situation was for her to stay on the dance floor and tire him out, succeeding only to tire herself out.

'God! I am pleased to see you, Edie. He's wearing me out, aren't you, dear?' she said, turning to Mr Hands. We soon found a table to sit at. 'Would you be a dear and see if you could get someone to bring a few drinks for us?' she asked. 'I'd like an orange with no gin this time. He's a naughty boy, Edie.' He just smiled.

'Could I have the same? ... I'm so hot.'

'Edie, your clothes are soaking. What have you been doing? You'll catch your death of cold.'

'I was fixing us up with the perfect alibi with none other than Sir Mortimer himself. Maud, you're not going to believe it but they are all at it, not just me. He had me in the one bedroom and his wife had one of the thugs in hers.'

'In bed?' she said, almost shouting.

'Yes, shush, keep your voice down.'

'How do you know that?'

'I spoke to them. Told them not to tell anyone and I wouldn't.'

'Edith, you're such a trollope, What would Father say?'

'Well, thankfully he's not with us and I was making sure we had an alibi. One of us had to do it. Anyway, what would Father have to say about his lovely baby daughter – the safe cracker?'

'Edith, you're terrible.'

The music stopped. There was a huge drum roll followed by the Master of Ceremonies advising us that Sir Mortimer wanted to make an announcement. Similar notification was made in all the other rooms, ordering all of us to go into the dance hall. The place was packed as everyone, including their candles, crowded into the room.

Another drum roll and Sir Mortimer began to speak:

'My lords, ladies and gentlemen. I am sorry about the electricity, but even I cannot stop lightning hitting the power lines. I hope it hasn't ruined the evening for you. I have certainly enjoyed myself.'

So has your wife, you typical bighead, I thought to myself as I saw her through the corner of my eye, coming down the stairs.

'Now we cannot hold the auction as intended, for obvious reasons ... we cannot see what we are bidding for ... so I intend to hold it the same time next week. I would therefore like to invite you all to another soirée for nibbles and drinks from 6 o'clock, with the auction starting at 7 o'clock prompt. All the lots are locked in the safe, but if anyone would like theirs back, we will only be too pleased to get it for you.'

'They will have a job,' Maud whispered in my ear.

'Why's that?' I asked.

'When I closed the safe I may have blocked the mechanism. I hope so.'

'So do I. It will give us a better chance to get away with it. You clever little girl,' I said, giving her a sisterly hug.

Fortunately, no one wanted their lots back and in fairness, I didn't expect it, but it did give us time. I was a little worried about the emeralds Maudie had stolen, putting them into the Mr Hands' jacket, but when I asked her, she was so matter of fact:

'Oh those! I took them back ages ago when I knew it wouldn't be necessary to drop him in it. He was a lucky boy.'

'Come here, you lovely...' I said, hugging Maudie again. The dancing continued long into the night but after midnight, some people began to drift off and as Peter was outside waiting, we were amongst them. We now said our goodbyes to mine host, who had to give my arm a little squeeze and remind me of my promise to see him the following Friday.

'What about Thursday,' I remarked. I wanted to bid for some of the items. 'We need to help the cause, don't we?' I continued, kicking Maudie at the same time as she was just about to say something and I couldn't chance that.

'Sorry dear, my foot slipped.'

'Yes, of course,' the pompous ass replied. 'See you on Thursday and Friday then.'

'Lovely.'

Peter opened the back door of the car for us and within seconds, we were in and away, but not before I gave a last wave to Lady Helen who had just arrived at the door. She returned the wave with a smile.

We arrived home shortly after midnight, not a bit tired, simply both excited and wanting to see the results of our ill-gotten gains. I remember we drove straight into the garage with the headlights shining directly onto the parcels which immediately made Maud shake with anticipation. We dived out of the car and scrambled to the boxes.

'Peter, would you help me take them into the drawing room? I don't think I can manage them on my own.'

'Yes, of course, I'll bring them, leave them to me,' he replied.

You only had to look at him to see he was madly in love with Maud, so I left them to it and went straight to the drawing room, Ten minutes later, they arrived with the parcels, but now Peter had twigged we were naughty young women, so we had to put him in the picture. You have never seen a man so shocked. Maud told him everything and when we started to empty the boxes, tipping them out onto the floor and counting the swag, he just couldn't move. He had never seen so much money in his life and neither had we, in actual cash. There was £9,123 in five pound notes, one pound and ten shilling notes, which would be worth nearly half a million pounds in today's value.

Having said that, I am sure one would expect at least that amount, especially with several hundred of the richest people in the country there. Someone even put a cheque in for £500. Miserable devil! Anyway, we decided that several charities would benefit from the money, including Dr Barnado's, the Soldiers, Sailors & Airman's Fund and several others. There was no way we would give this back as we considered these people were working against *their* ... no ... *our* country, just to protect their own wealth.

We couldn't decide what to do with the jewellery as this could be traced, so it went into our vault. But the biggest prize of all were the bundles of papers, which Maud had very sensibly included in the heist. It was sheer gold for MI5. Some gave the details of all the financial backers of the BUF, and their hidden bank accounts. There were confidential letters between members of the government, who were covert members of the BUF and the German Nazi Party. Even secret trade agreements with some British firms and the Nazis and, should the Germans invade, detailed plans of what cooperation they would have. Sir Mortimer was without doubt a traitor along with his leader. But it was the government officials that worried me – they were two-timing the country.

I gave Maud the job of taking the papers in person to Captain Vernon Kell, Head of MI5, but quite frankly, when she returned she was disgusted with the response. For a start, she couldn't get to see him and the man she did see, wasn't interested. In fact, he didn't believe the papers were genuine and–

'Come on, Edie, tell Mr White what I did with them,'

Maud interrupted in her little lost voice.

—She went to the House of Commons and gave them personally to Winston Churchill. You will remember when he became Prime Minister, he gave MI5 a real shake-up.

Chapter 6
The Investigation

Our sources told us Sir Mortimer had to return to London, leaving Belleford on the Saturday morning and not returning until the Monday evening, following which, for the first time, since the dance, he decided to look in the safe. Maudie was right. She had messed up the mechanism and it couldn't be opened. The local locksmith was called but he couldn't get the safe open either, so it was now up to the manufacturers to perform a miracle.

It was now Wednesday afternoon when Sir Mortimer was called from his study to witness the safe being opened. It was the policy of the company to open a safe in front of the customer to ensure there was no hanky-panky.

I'll never forget how it was described to us when the man pulled open the safe door. Sir Mortimer fell backwards in complete shock. He wanted to yell at everyone but nothing would come out of his mouth. He was now bent forward just looking into the empty safe – speechless and unable to move.

Eventually, he came to his senses and started shouting at everyone present. 'Who's been in the safe and where are my bloody papers?' which he kept repeating time and time again. Everyone was surprised that he didn't mention the money. The realisation that he was in trouble suddenly overtook the shock of the situation.

'Get hold of Mosley quickly,' he shouted to his secretary. He then began to make his own enquiries and again not once did he talk of the money or the lots. Even the arrangements for the soirée to hold the auction were put to one side. That was until the guests began turning up in their dozens and they had to get organised.

In the meantime, all his staff were interviewed and, of course, all knew nothing of the robbery. Rumours spread that some members of the BUF were responsible and, in spite of everything, he was reluctant to inform the police.

Apparently, Mosley arrived a couple of hours afterwards, accompanied by his entourage of bodyguards. They began to rough up all the staff in the house, and as I heard later, their suppliers – the butcher, the baker etc. All of them were pointing the finger at the BUF, which was not the right approach. However, it was at least another couple of hours before Mosley and Sir Mortimer came out of the study to face the guests. The meeting had been a tempestuous one, both parties accusing the other of dishonesty and incompetence, and both equally worried about the loss of the papers. Despite a guard being on or near the study door, to prevent eavesdropping, it seemed the entire staff had overheard the conversation.

Maud didn't want us to attend the soirée but Peter pointed out that it would look suspicious if we didn't. We found ourselves pulling up outside the entrance in the Duisenberg limousine to be greeted by the head butler and directed to the main hall to be served drinks and invited to sit down.

Everyone could sense there was something wrong. We, of course, knew what, and I was enjoying myself, desperate to see how this traitor was going to get out of this mess.

Eventually, Mosley came in to muffled applause, dressed, of course, in his black uniform and followed by Sir Mortimer. Lady Helen was conspicuous by her absence.

The butler then announced:

'My lords, ladies and gentlemen, may I have your

attention please.' The room fell silent. 'Sir Mortimer de Clancy.'

'My lords, ladies and gentlemen … friends,' de Clancy began, 'I am somewhat embarrassed to have to tell you that we have been robbed by what appears to be a highly professional gang.'

Some in the room responded with loud gasps but Maudie and I simply looked at each other, desperately trying not to laugh. He continued:

'They have taken the entire contents of our safe, which was one of the strongest and finest on the market. All the money you kindly donated together with the jewellery and other items you gave to be auctioned tonight have also been stolen. I will, of course, donate £10,000 to the fund to compensate for the loss of this money.' This brought rapturous applause and murmurs of appreciation from the audience.

'But as for the jewellery, we will need all of you who contributed to give us a description of that jewellery so that it can be identified as and when it comes onto the market. And it will. We want to catch these villains and see that they receive their just desserts.'

Mosley nodded his head in agreement of the sentiment and was invited to comment.

'When we are the government of this country,' he said, 'we will ensure that this sort of crime will be severely punished so that it will be a deterrent to anyone who thinks they will get away with it. We will not allow the police to pussyfoot around. We will crack down heavily on crime.' He too received applause which gave them an easier time than I had hoped for.

They had pulled it off. They had got away with it by lying about the robbery and in a way, by blaming the police for their own incompetence.

We said our goodbyes to Sir Mortimer and just to rub salt

into the wound, I put my arm round his neck and kissed his cheek.

'Will I see you tomorrow, darling?' I whispered.

'What?'

'You promised.'

'What?' He thought for a moment, and then almost shouting said, 'Oh, go away!'

With that, the Duisenberg pulled up. Peter got out, opened the door for us and we were away.

We learnt later that Mortimer and Mosley debated long and hard whether to inform the police, but they were afraid of public opinion and the ensuing questions if they didn't. Why would they not inform the police? What have they got to hide? So, for appearances' sake, they had to do something. Of course, they lied about the contents of the safe, but that was up to them. We knew the truth would come out and it did.

Eventually, the police were informed and it was several weeks later when they came round to interview us.

'They sent a very nice young officer to question us ... and who Edith here decided to embarrass. The poor lad,' Maud interjected.

This young man, Constable David Pugh came in, and I invited him to sit down next to me on the chaise longue. I could tell he was uncomfortable, especially when he began to stutter when I put my hand on his knee.

'Now, young man, are you a detective?'

'Yes, Ma'am. Of sorts. I'm a trainee.'

'Oooh, Maud, he's a detective! How lovely,' I said.

'Well Ma'am, I n-n-need t-t-to know if you saw anything at the d-d-dance the other d-d-d-day,' he stuttered.

'No,' I replied.

He turned to Maud, who shook her head. We then had a period of silence, each of us looking at the other.

'Now, do you want to know where I was?'

'Y-y-yes,' the constable replied, nodding his head at the same time.

'Well, come closer,' I whispered and paused for effect. ' ... Now I was in bed with Sir Mortimer de Clancy, having sexual intercourse. I'm sure he will confirm it. If not, I know someone else who will.'

The poor lad just simply coughed and spluttered. He really couldn't cope anymore.

'Look, young man ... Maud was with a Tony Glazzard all night and he wouldn't leave her alone. He's got wandering hands. He is the son of Jacob Glazzard, the industrialist. Have you got wandering hands, Detective?'

'No Ma'am.'

'Ooh, I think detectives are so powerful, don't you, Maud?'

Maud nodded.

'Would you like to take me out, detective?'

'No Ma'am, I mean yes Ma'am. No ... I mean.'

'Don't worry, she's only teasing.'

'Well, thank you, Ma'am. With that, he made some excuse and hurried out of the house. Alibi confirmed. One to us!

After the questioning by the police we began to worry what was happening with the donations we had anonymously made to the charities, also what had happened to the letters Maud had given to Churchill. We need not have concerned ourselves. The latter was resolved in Parliament when Churchill stood up to address the House on the need to improve security. He also condemned various people mentioned in a letter he held in his hand, who were consorting with the enemy. Sir Mortimer was one of those on the list and although Churchill didn't reveal any names, it soon became known who they were and they were eventually blacklisted and sent to Coventry. No one wanted to know them. What was even better was that they were interned for the duration of the war and never had any influence again. Mortimer lost almost all his money and the beautiful Belleford was severely bombed, never to be the same.

***

It was time for me to leave for our villa in France. I was now beginning to show, and the last thing I wanted was for the gossips to get going. I gave Maudie the choice of coming with me or staying; I'm pleased to say she chose to accompany me.

We packed our belongings and closed the house for several months. Peter Longdon, our chauffeur drove us to London, having arranged a driver for our other car, which was loaded with enough luggage for at least a year. We caught the *Golden Arrow* to Calais and Peter continued on to Nice whilst we and our immediate luggage went by train.

This was amazing! The train actually went on the boat at Dover, which from memory, I think was the SS *Canterbury*, and rolled off at Calais. We disembarked at Calais and caught the *Blue Train* which took us direct to Nice. Father would have gone mad at the expense, especially as we booked three sleepers to take Lizzie, my trusted companion and confidante, and ourselves. I was on my own, getting very nervous about my situation and simply felt I needed my close friends and staff around me.

It was our first Christmas in France and I was a little disappointed as we were missing all the social life. Even here I couldn't join in because of the disgrace it would cause. The festive season was soon over however, and Bif was born on the 14th February. He was a lovely little lad, as good as gold, causing no problems for Jeanette, our French nanny. He actually grew up trilingual and could have been French, particularly as Maud had been fluent since early childhood with not a trace of accent, but I'll come to that.

—I know you will think I am cruel, Mr White, but I left him in France with Jeanette and the housekeeper, paying them very good money to look after him, but it was more to protect him. I couldn't bear to think of the stigma and the ostracism he would suffer in our circle of contacts.

I remember travelling back with Maud. I felt lost, but strangely, Maud seemed happier and soon I was to find out why. She had fallen in love with Peter, our chauffeur. In fact, he was a jack of all trades as well as being our driver. She confessed she had been seeing him secretly for some time and was glad to be going back. It made me feel wonderful that she had given up that time for me.

Chapter 7
Joining the Ranks

It was because of this BUF business and the treachery of some of the wealthy, influential people that I decided to do my bit for King and country. The Admiralty was recruiting women into the Wrens and I decided to join up. I did my training and I know it was probably because I was well known and well off that I shot up through the ranks. However, I'm sure that having a good education, going to university and being fluent in French also helped…but so be it.

Maudie stayed at home to look after the house and me, and cement her love for Peter, which I fully approved of as he was a lovely man. She acted as the mother effectively.

'You were not a bad cook, were you, Maudie?'

We could all feel that a war was brewing, and some of us knew that we were at least making some effort to defend ourselves, just in case. The war in Spain seemed to be a dry run on what was likely to happen should war break out, and when Hitler began annexing various countries – Austria, the Sudetenland, Czechoslovakia etc., we knew it would be a matter of when, not if.

Furthermore, Mr Higginbotham senior, was a genius. He could see long before it happened that should the war begin, it would not be too long before the Americans became involved. He also realised that they would require the right property for their headquarters and with this in mind, he did a secret deal with the Americans, leasing the entire estate to them as the HQ for the US Air Force.

We kept the individual houses where the staff lived, and a cottage for Maud and I. The clever thing he did was to ensure that the agreement took place with immediate effect, but payment would only be made as and when they began to occupy it. This assured everything was in place and this was the genius of the scheme. Not only did it prevent the estate being simply commandeered by the government for peanuts, which we knew was already happening with residences like ours, but we also had a rental income *and* a reparations clause in the arrangement.

—Mr White, I know you will think I am a terrible person, having not talked about my son during this time, but I can assure you both Maud and I went to France on every possible occasion to spend time with him. But times were very different, especially in our social circle. It would have been terrible for him and I didn't want that – the name calling and the insinuations. At least he knew who his mother was, albeit he didn't know her very well.

The Admiralty knew we were now on a war footing. We knew that it was only a matter of days before war broke out, and I managed to get a few days off. I set off for France with Maudie and Peter to pick up Bif and bring him home. It was the very day war was declared because the Germans had invaded Poland. All leave was suddenly cancelled and I was called back to the Admiralty.

However, it was a Phoney War for several months, and then the British Expeditionary Force was sent out and we all thought the war would be over soon. I had once again made arrangements to pick up Bif, when to my utter consternation, Holland and Belgium were overrun in days and there were suddenly no boats across the Channel. I was absolutely devastated. Not only was it impossible for me to go over to France, but I could not even get in touch with our nanny or the housekeeper. From that moment on, we had no contact until the war ended.

My job had almost become a nine to five one unless there was a flap on, with the result I was able to live at home, but when Peter was called up, Maud joined up too. She also joined the Navy, and because of her special language skills, she assisted the SOE (Special Operations Executive) in training those who were to be shipped into France.

She was a very brave young woman, and like many of her kind has never spoken of it. She did learn a few techniques which we used later on, but we'll come to that. With Maudie working, my easy life disappeared. I had to look after myself. Well, not altogether. I kept as many people working as I could and, of course, had the Land Army helping on the home farm.

The US Air Force took over the estate mid-1940. I can't remember exactly when, but within a few weeks, the road into the estate was built, which lasts until today and we had the beginnings of an aerodrome. You have never seen so much concrete. I must admit we got a fair bit of trouble from the tenant farmers who saw their livelihoods disappearing, but when we explained they would have a ready market for their produce, it tended to soften the blow. Also that there was a war on and we all had to make sacrifices.

In 1940, I had the biggest surprise of my life. Our cottage, miles from anywhere, discouraged visitors, but who should I see one day when I opened the front door? None other than Henry Merryweather in his naval officer's uniform!

'Hello Henry! What a lovely surprise. How nice to see you.'

'Well, I didn't expect to see this,' he said, gesturing with his hands out.

'And I didn't expect to see this,' I replied, looking at him in uniform.

'There is a war on, you know,' he said sarcastically.

'I know there is and that is why the Americans are using

the house as their headquarters. And if we are going to have sarcasm, then I'll see you around sometime.'

'No. No, Edie, I'm sorry. I didn't mean to sound rude. I was just surprised at your circumstances. Where's Maud?'

'She works in London.'

'What does she do then?'

'I can't tell you that, can I?'

'May I come in?'

'Of course. I'm sorry.'

I invited him into our living room, where he sat, looking at the décor. I'm sure he was feeling sorry for me bearing in mind our previous surroundings.

Suddenly he said, 'Edie, I am sorry for what I said at the party. I have never forgiven myself or ever will. You didn't deserve that. I have wanted you all my life and I was so excited and drunk that I made a fool of myself. May I take you out tonight?'

What the hell. There was a war on and I wasn't doing anything. Anyway, I hadn't been out on a date for weeks, so I agreed.

He took me to Boothtown Hall, and of course, I had to meet his mother; she hadn't changed a bit. She still insisted on being called the Countess.

'Hello Mrs Merryweather, how nice to see you,' I said.

'Countess ... please,' she replied with a petulant sigh. Through the mirror I could see Henry take a deep breath and roll his eyes to heaven.

'Well, this is a surprise. How are you, Edith? We haven't seen you for such a long time. How's Maud?'

'She fine. She's working in London.'

'I think it's something hush-hush, Mother,' Henry interjected.

'And what are you doing, young lady?'

'I work in London as well.'

'I suppose that's hush-hush too?'

'I'm afraid so.'

'The Americans have taken over their home, Mother. For the duration, I gather?'

'Yes. Mr Higginbotham has done a deal with the Yanks to our mutual benefit, and anyway we couldn't get the staff. All the spare land is farmland, so now we live in a little cottage on the estate.'

'Oh, poor dear.'

'Where is your father?' I asked Henry, more to change the subject than anything else.

'He's a major in the Home Guard and responsible for the defence of this little patch. He loves it and won't stop talking about it.'

The Countess was, of course, furious with Henry for belittling his father. 'It's a very responsible job,' she added loudly.

'I'm taking Edie out tonight and as it's raining, we're going into the smoke,' he announced, squeezing my hand. There were few air raids when the weather was bad.

He took me to the cinema and then to the fish and chip shop where we ate fish and chips wrapped in newspaper whilst walking along the street. All the way home, he kept apologising for his behaviour that dreadful evening. I took him back to our place and with Maud still on duty, we were alone.

'Edie, I love you and I am sorry.'

'If you apologise again, you can get out. Now! Consider yourself forgiven. Come and sit here next to me.' He came and sat down. I put my arm around him and kissed him. There was no rutting hog this time, just a gentle response.

I took him up to my bedroom and we made love. This time it was tender and real. I just wished he hadn't said those things.

He told me how much he loved me, that he wanted to marry me and be with me forever. Then I dropped the bombshell. I showed him a picture of Bif.

'A fine young lad … and he's yours.'

There was a deathly silence. Tears began to trickle down his cheeks as he took it in. 'Why didn't you tell me?' He paused, waiting for an answer, but I said nothing. 'It was that night, wasn't it?' I nodded. 'Why didn't you tell me?'

'Would you tell a rude, filthy, ignorant pig that he was your child's father?'

'No, I suppose I wouldn't. Can I see him?'

'His name is Bif and no, you can't. He was caught at our villa in the south of France when the Germans overran the place. We couldn't get down there in time to get him out. So every night I pray for him.'

'Oh God … I am so sorry,' he said, taking me in his arms and hugging me, the tears now cascading down his face. We lay down and he held me in his arms for the entire night, not wanting to let go of me for a second. But morning came round far too soon and I had to go to work.

We said our goodbyes and made another date a couple of days hence. I begged him not to tell his family about Bif until times were better. In fact, I made him promise on pain of death. I was pleased Maudie and I had shouldered this burden together for several years, but now, having told him, I felt some relief.

I would have loved to have told him that we robbed his mother of her necklace. I would, however, have said it was a punishment for him being so nasty to me.

I was happy that we had restored our friendship and that he wanted to marry me. It seemed to give me a new purpose in life and, prior to that dreadful evening, I had always been fond of him. Anyway, he telephoned me that evening and asked if he could meet me in town as he had booked a show, with dinner first.

This is like old times, I thought as I emerged from the Admiralty building at 5.15 p.m., passing the sandbags piled high outside the entrance. I felt embarrassed that I was in my uniform as I was in the Wrens and a First Officer, which was equivalent to the rank of Lieutenant Commander and senior to him. Although he was a proud man, he didn't seem to mind.

We saw each other during the weeks he was on leave. He wrote to me all the time, always keen to know about Bif. Even his mother accepted that one day we would be married and he did pop the question and I did say yes, but then he was transferred to Gibraltar and everything was put on hold until his first leave. That never came. He was killed on convoy duty; his ship was sunk with the loss of most of the crew. I can't tell you how distraught I was, even more so when I found myself pregnant again. Neither of my children had ever seen their father.

'It was a similar happening with me,' Maude interjected, 'except I had been courting my Peter for several years. He was just an ordinary bloke who loved me to bits. He had worked on our estate for years. He never wanted any of my wealth. He would never let me pay for anything and loved me for who I am. I didn't care about marriage, I just wanted to be with him forever. We were soulmates as they say today. We talked about having several children and if the first one was a boy, we would call him Stanley.

'I knew he was being shipped out overseas as he had a week's leave before embarkation and they were the most wonderful days of my life. But in my heart I knew this blissful situation couldn't last. On Sunday, the 24th July we made our way to Waterloo Station, carrying his huge kit bag. We walked slowly to platform 14 and the Portsmouth train, which was there waiting. Why couldn't it have been delayed? Why did it have to take him? He was all I had.'

Maud stopped, unable to continue, still feeling the pain of all those earlier moments. Her tears just kept coming as she sat deep in thought, clutching her signet ring as though her life depended on it.

'Did he give you that?' I asked, trying to ease her pain. She took her ring off, lifted the stone and there was a picture of her sweetheart, standing proud in his uniform; no one grand but a private that did his bit and gave his all.

'We'll leave it for now Maud,' I suggested.

'Oh no, Mr White, I must continue. Edie would never forgive me.'

'Don't be silly. This is not what Mr White wants to hear anyway.'

'Please don't say that, Edith. They are both very moving human stories and the war seems significant in your life.'

Maud continued her story but the emotion was still in her voice as she struggled to get the words out.

'The platform was packed with hundreds of soldiers waiting to board the train, many of them with their wives and sweethearts. All of them seemed so dreadfully sad. Peter boarded the carriage with me still gripping his hand, trying desperately not to let go. The door was slammed shut by the guard as he walked along the platform, closing the carriage doors on his way down to the guard's van at the back. Peter slid the window down and put his hand out to hold mine. I smothered his hand with kisses until that damned whistle blew and the guard waved his green flag.

'I looked despairingly into his eyes as the train began to move and me with it, gripping his hand even tighter. I couldn't let go until it was impossible to hold on any longer. Our hands were wrenched apart as the train quickened and I found myself running alongside. Faster and faster it was now pulling away, and I was left waving desperately. He shouted, "I love you, I love you," and then the train turned the corner and all I could see was his arm waving furiously. Finally, he was gone.

'I was numb, unable to do anything. I remember returning to our cottage where Edith took over and helped me through the trauma.

'He was shipped to Egypt where he fell. He is buried there along with hundreds more and all I wanted was to bring him home to me. They sent all his belongings to me as he had made me his next of kin. There were three letters he had written to me and not posted, which simply told me how much he loved me and how much he missed me. There were a few little keepsakes which I have kept close to me since then.

'Of course, everyone knew that I had a baby and that I hadn't been married, but in the middle of the war, no one really cared. It was a case with everyone that you lived for the moment, and quite honestly, everyone knew how much I cared for Peter and how terrible I felt when I lost him.

'We were still fortunate to be well off and could afford to have a nurse as well as a nanny. Therefore, I only had eight weeks off in total to have the baby. I was lucky really because once women had children they were virtually on the scrap heap. But my particular skills were needed.'

'What were your skills, Maud?' I asked.

'I would rather not talk about my wartime exploits, Mr White. It's another time and another story.'

'I'm sorry.'

'No need, it's not important.'

To me, as a reporter, it was important. I had begun to sniff out another story, but it would have to wait.

'I did tell Peter's parents,' Maud continued, 'that they had a grandson. Stanley. They were thrilled. I kept in regular touch with them until they died many years later.

'Stanley was a clever lad from the word go and I always made sure he knew I was his mother and what a wonderful father he had. We are well off and now doubly so because of Stanley, and it was because of this I was able to give him a very good education, which he has used wisely, not like the two of us. That said, we have had more excitement in our lives than many would have in a hundred years.'

Chapter 8
The Search

It was the same thing with me although I wasn't in the same class as Maud as far as work was concerned. Nonetheless, when my daughter Alice was born, I told them it was the future Earl of Boothtown's daughter and that we were to be married as soon as he came home on leave. But there we are!

We were having enough of war and every day I thought of Bif. We had no knowledge of his and the others' whereabouts and no idea of whether they were alive or dead. They certainly had no money and we heard rumours from various sources that people were starving in Nice which worried us even more. But now the Allies had recaptured southern France and I knew it wouldn't be long before I could go and search for him.

I left the Navy immediately after VE Day and took the first train available to Nice to begin searching for Bif. You would not believe what the Germans had done to the place. I took a taxi to our house. I didn't want to believe what I was hearing or what I saw. The Promenade had been out of bounds to the residents and huge concrete gun emplacements were still there, although the townsfolk were tearing things down bit by bit. The beautiful hotels were turned into German headquarters, housing the Gestapo and even torture chambers. Some were holding camps for Jews awaiting deportation to the Auschwitz extermination camp.

I eventually found the way to our house, only to discover it was occupied by a family who were in the process of leaving, but taking with them some of the things from the garden – statues etc. The taxi parked across the gate and I got out.

I started screaming at them in French at the top of my voice:

'What are you doing and where is my son? I picked up the first thing I could find which was a piece of an iron bar left by the Nazis as they had taken all the rest of the metal for their own purposes. The taxi driver followed me as I approached them menacingly.

'Where are the people who lived in the house before you? There was a little boy – my little boy. What did you do with them?' I screamed, not really making sense. They hadn't got a clue but at least they knew the previous occupant and where he lived.

They were in no mood to fight and wanted to leave quickly but I prevented that. It would appear they were Nazi sympathisers and had been allocated the house. Now they knew what would happen if they were caught. So it was my intention they did get caught. They were looting in the hope of getting away with something they could sell, but ran away with nothing.

In the meantime, the taxi driver had run off to find someone from the local militia, leaving the taxi still blocking their escape. They were caught and frogmarched off to whatever fate awaited them. As far as I was concerned, they deserved it.

I couldn't believe I had got the house back so quickly and that it had missed the worst of the war. The gardens suffered though and there were many ornaments missing. The building itself and the interior was a different kettle of fish. All the paintings had gone and anything else of value, which you would expect, but some of the walls were without plaster. In fact, some of the walls were missing and those that were left had the copper wire ripped from them. What was worse was the contraband that I discovered; it was amazing.

We managed to prove our title to the property very quickly, thanks to our family lawyers and began to get things back into shape. It was the villainy we encountered that really made me angry, and I was determined to do something about it.

The previous occupant had been a very busy black marketeer. What was worse however, was the garage pit where Father used to tinker with his cars. It had been secretly covered and was filled with illegal drugs, medicines, penicillin, and morphine, desperately needed to help the populous. It was a capital offence to be dealing in such goods; many had been supplied by the retreating German army or by the Americans. Even this had not been sufficient for the little shit; some of them were counterfeit and not fit for purpose, and would undoubtedly kill the patient should they be administered.

I went to the address the collaborators gave me, followed by another address and another until finally, I got lucky. I had been talking to another suspiciously rich man who was deliberately evading any questions about any wartime activity when an elderly woman who was either the man's mother or worked for him, made some comment about two English women and a little boy.

'Shut up, woman,' the man bawled at her in French. 'We know nothing here. We know nothing. Go away,' he said to me in a very threatening manner.

'Don't threaten me,' I replied, following him into the house. 'Go and get the police,' I shouted to the taxi driver. 'He knows about my son.'

I continued following the man, pressing him all the time for information, no matter how little. He was becoming angrier by the second until he snapped, and laid into me. He hit me across the face with such force, I fell over, bleeding profusely from the mouth. He walked over to me to deliver another blow when the woman shouted:

'Arrêtes, Georges!' she yelled, pulling on his arm as she did so, but a well-timed blow to her face sent her reeling across the floor.

I struggled to get up and went over to help the woman. She seemed dazed and not aware of herself, so I shouted to the man to get a doctor. He wasn't bothered and simply shrugged; he wanted me out of the place. I checked the woman again, and this time she whispered to me that I should meet her at four o'clock outside the gate. Georges grabbed me by the shoulder and, almost dragging me to the door, threw me out. There was no sign of the taxi driver anywhere.

I walked back along the street, nursing my wounds. One of my eyes was very swollen. The inevitable black one to come, I thought. At that moment, I saw the taxi driver waving furiously. He came running over, and seeing my injuries, put his arm round my shoulder and led me back to the taxi which he had hidden out of sight.

'He's a bad man, Miss,' he said in French. 'Mafia. Very dangerous. We must get away from here quick.' He drove like a bat out of hell away from the place.

In my short time inside the house I had recognised some of our belongings. When you see paintings that you know are yours, but can't prove it, and they are currently being shown off by some crooked man who made his fortune at someone else's expense during the war, it really makes you want to avenge the situation. There was quite a bit of gossip about this man and the more I heard about him, the more determined I was to get my own back.

At that moment, my first duty was to find Bif. That was all that mattered. I left my house and took a taxi into Nice to visit the Red Cross and other useful organisations, in the hope they would have heard something.

I returned to meet the woman at four o'clock as arranged. True to her word she was there, but in absolute fear that her husband, as I discovered, would find out that she had been talking to me. She told me that because the people were English, they were to be deported to Germany but they managed to escape to Italy just before. She believed they had got over the border into Ventimiglia, in Italy and away.

I had to return to England as my time was up. In those days you could not be sure if you would be arrested and locked up on a whim let alone for criminal acts, so I left all my details with the Red Cross and arranged for posters to be put around in Ventimiglia in the hope it would stir some help, including a £1,000 reward for knowledge leading to their whereabouts but it did no good.

Whilst there, I employed a full-time gardener handyman, giving him the key to the house in case the nanny and the housekeeper found their way back. The next thing I did was to employ an architect to get the house back to normal again in the hope they could or would return and have somewhere to stay. I then returned home to England to arrange my next trip.

***

This time I wanted Maud to come with me. She had left the SOE and begun an everyday life as a mother, but was missing some of the excitement she had become accustomed to. Although we were still living in the cottage, life had returned to almost normal. Our nanny started work again, looking after Alice and Stanley and all but three of our estate workers had returned to work after being demobbed. The Americans were still in the house and displayed no signs of leaving, especially as the war in the Pacific was still ongoing; there were also underlying problems with the Russians in the east. We could put up with that because it was impossible to spend what we received in rent for the place.

We travelled to Nice in our uniforms as we felt we would be more easily accepted, which was the case. There was a great affinity towards soldiers in uniform all over Europe and I know it's a terrible thing to say, but we had no shortage of money even though there were currency regulations permitting no more than £25 to be taken out of the country on any one trip.

The wealthy always have an advantage; they can invest all over the world and this we did before the war. Thanks to Father and his sailing hobby, he had US dollars in the bank and there were no restrictions. US dollars were as valuable as gold at the time and everybody wanted them.

We arrived at our house to find that work was well under way and immediately set off, again in uniform for Italy and the last known place where we had since heard Bif might be. There was a massive queue at Menton to cross the border, but two female officers in their thirties attracted the border guards' attention, and within minutes we were on the way to Ventimiglia.

It was an impoverished little village at the time. The houses were run down and in need of repair. The road surface was non-existent and I will always remember the old market hall with its produce looking almost as bad as the town itself. There was no money around, and it was years after the war before the village began to improve and become a little fashionable.

We walked to the Via Maneira, a main through way which passed between the river and the railway line, the latter being very dilapidated. The river was filthy; it stank of oil and the banks were just dumping grounds for every conceivable type of rubbish you could imagine. In fact, the area was a complete slum. But it was the border crossing from France to Italy and therefore retained some significance.

We went to the address we had been given which was on the top floor of one of the slums. We climbed up the stairs to be greeted by a somewhat impoverished Italian woman who had been sitting on the balcony.

'Madame Trenchard,' she whispered, a look of intense shock on her face.

'Jeanette!' we replied in unison.

'Oui.'

'I'm sorry, I could not get you out. They stopped all the travelling. I am truly sorry to have left you. Where's Bif?'

The conversation was solely conducted in French; it came more naturally to her than English. 'He's out playing with his friends. You won't recognise him. I'm sorry, but we were going to be deported and had no money. We just had to run away. My husband–'

'You're married?'

'Yes, I had just to survive. His name is Francesco and he has been very kind and has protected us. Bif looks on him as his father and me as his mother. Francesco has got a temporary job now, so we have a little money, but only enough to live on.'

'Where is Bif?' I asked again, becoming very agitated.

She yelled out of the window at the top of her voice in Italian, telling Bif to come home. To all intents and purposes, she was typically Italian.

A couple of minutes later, the door burst open and Bif entered. 'Si Maman,' he said. It was a great shock for both Maud and I to see before us a scruffy, streetwise, young Italian lad, who couldn't speak English but could speak French and Italian.

He didn't know me, didn't even recognise anything about me. Can you imagine anything more heartbreaking?

'This is your mother, Bif,' Jeanette said in Italian. The

poor lad looked shocked.

I walked towards him but he stepped back, unable to take in the words.

'Jeanette, why didn't you go back to Nice?' I asked.

'We had no money, and we were told if we went back we would be deported or shot, particularly if they found out Bif was English.'

'Who by?'

'The Milice.' (French equivalent of the Gestapo.)

'Do you want to go back?'

'I can't now, we have a daughter, Yvette, but Bif must. He and Yvette are very close.'

'Where's Florence?' She was our housekeeper.

'She was arrested and we never saw her again.'

We waited for Francesco to come home, to thank him for what he had done for us, before attempting to leave with Bif. But it wasn't to be that lovely moment I had dreamed of. Just as we were about to leave, Bif ran out of the house. He was not going to be separated from his new family and friends. There was nothing we could do there and then, except encourage Francesco and Jeanette to bring him to Nice in the hope he would start to remember his past.

—Mr White, you cannot imagine what the ravages of war had done to these people and particularly my son, and you cannot imagine what it was like to leave him behind, having at last found him. I would have forced the issue should it have been necessary, but Maud suggested we try another way first.

I gave Jeanette and Francesco 100 dollars and asked them to bring him to Nice, suggesting that they stay for a few days. I would make up the loss of Francesco's wages which were pitiful in any event.

They kept their word and the four of them arrived at the house the following weekend. Bif did recognise the house and went into the various rooms, knowing what they were originally. He also walked round the grounds which we were trying to recreate to its former beauty. It was a difficult time for all of us, especially as Bif spoke very little English, but even that was slowly returning.

Finally, I offered them a job with a salary which was substantial in its day and one which Francesco realised would be difficult to find elsewhere. They accepted. I gave them a further 100 dollars to get some decent clothes and, believe it or not, they remained with us all their lives. They only had one child of their own, Yvette, due to the war and she became very special to us and to Bif. They too always looked on Bif as someone special and, of course, he spent several weeks a year in Nice, where his relationship with Yvette blossomed. I wouldn't say we had solved the problem, but we had come a long way towards a resolution, which gave us time to look at other matters.

I had told Maud about the Mafia man, how he had behaved towards me and his wife, and how I had seen two of our paintings on the wall in his house. I told her what I had discovered in the garage – the drugs and the other things I mentioned earlier.

***

We were to have our first foray after the war. We were going to retrieve the paintings and what else we could get and, we were also going to hide the drugs on his property and then report him. There was still a sort of martial law; anybody found to be black marketing drugs, not just narcotics, but penicillin and the like, could be shot.

For the first time since the war, I saw that look on Maud's face. I could see she was missing the excitement.

—I would add, Mr White, that the war made us both very fit, not only physically fit with the exercise and the diet, but also mentally alert because of the jobs we had done.

I took Maud to the house where the pictures were and left her to it. She wanted a few hours to sort out the problem. Over the following week, she spent many hours blending into the background, working out how we were going to do the job. In fact, since the war, the change in Maud was amazing. She thought out her every move, the timings, the tools, the support needed. After all, this was the sort of work she had been doing in the SOE.

Eventually, she came up with a plan. Whether or not the man and or his family were Mafia, they went to church every Sunday without fail. It was the only time he was seen in public with his wife and his children, who were all in their twenties and thirties. It was a routine of theirs. They left the house at 10.35 a.m. on the dot, arriving at the church at 10.55 a.m. and left the church at 12.05 p.m., arriving home between 12.34 and 12.45 p.m.

We had an hour, absolute maximum. Therefore, we needed to be at the house the moment the man left. Maud had been in the gardens several times and had ascertained that all the downstairs windows and doors were either shuttered or barred; the doors were extremely thick with locks to match. However, they never bothered to lock or even shut the windows and doors on the first floor level, probably because it was always too hot. That was our way in. Once inside, the French windows could be opened onto the garden terrace and we could load and unload from there. It meant we would have to drive on his lawn but what the hell.

If the plans were to work, we needed an extra man, and for the first time, we took a chance on explaining to Francesco what had happened and how the man had made a fortune out of the war by sending people away and taking their property. We knew we had to paint a compelling picture of this man's misdeeds to influence both Francesco's and Jeanette's way of the thinking. We did just that and it worked. Both of them had suffered greatly as a result of the actions taken by men like him and it was enough. They were totally on our side.

We planned the raid for the following Sunday, borrowing a large Citroen pre-war van and changing the number plates. We loaded all the drugs and as many offending items you could think of that would cause them grief and set off. Francesco drove the van whilst Maud and I got ready.

Maud waited not far away with both us and the house in view. The moment she saw them leave, she beckoned us on. Her first job was to check the door, knocking to see if anyone stayed behind and when satisfied no one was in, she shinnied up the wall like a cat. Within three minutes, she was inside, opening the French windows. The van was already parked nearby with the first boxes out and on the balcony and ready to be taken inside. I raced into the lounge area where I saw our pictures and retrieved them quickly, placing them in the van. Maud began searching the house and found the cellar which should have been used for wine but was full of everything that shouldn't be. Time was getting short as we ran down into the cellar, piling the drugs and medicines behind various boxes already there.

'Look at this,' Maud whispered.

I couldn't believe what we had discovered – a box full of US dollars. We couldn't tell whether they were forgeries or not, but either way, it was illegal. Worst of all was a crate of 20 US army rifles. This made me determined to shop him. Fifteen minutes had gone and we were nearly ready to leave when we saw other objets d'art which had been stolen from the Nice Art Gallery. I remembered them very well as we often visited there. Should we take them or leave them to the police? We decided to take them with a view to handing them back to their rightful owners.

We were away in thirty-eight minutes. Even the lawn wasn't damaged as the ground was like concrete due to the hot weather and lack of rain.

I left them to go back to the villa, whilst I went to the American Military Police and reported what I pretended I had overheard. I could not let them know we had been in the house. I explained I was an officer in the Royal Navy and that I knew these men to be very dangerous.

Well, I do know the Yanks raided the place, accompanied by the Gendarmerie and found 250,000 forged US dollars, plus the illegal medical supplies. The entire family were arrested and we never saw or heard of them again. Our paintings are still on the wall in the villa.

Once again, it was necessary to return to England as our time was running out, but this time we were taking Bif with us. We knew it was extremely difficult to get past the border controls as we had no papers for him, but did at least have his birth certificate, with the father not identified. However, this was remedied later on.

It was a painful time for all of us, particularly for Bif as he had to adjust to the culture, meet Alice, his real sister, relearn the language properly and make new friends which was difficult as we were in the heart of the country, miles from anywhere, and where there was little chance of meeting young people.

At the time there was little chance of getting him into a local school because there wasn't one, so it was private tuition. Eventually, we managed to get them both into a nearby school, but Bif was embarrassed that he was from rich stock, so he simply said he was the chauffeur's son and from that moment, we let him pretend, in the hope it would help him adjust. I made sure we kept in touch with his grandparents who absolutely adored both the children. Naturally, the Countess was delighted that there was an heir to receive the title. Granddad wasn't bothered; he just enjoyed having Bif around him. Man stuff, you know, but he loved both the children.

The Americans left the house in 1947 and kept to the letter of the contract, making good where necessary.

—No, Mr White, they never found the priest's hole and yes, the stolen goods were still in it, together with Maudie's notebook!

We were now back in our own house with some of the original staff returning. The nurses were replaced by nannies except that Bif was now at school learning English, as he was already versed in Italian and French. Maud too returned and took the east wing as hers and Stanley's home, and I took the west wing. The Yanks had done us proud – the house looked wonderful!

We decided to restore the front garden layout with its beautiful lawns as it set off the house, but we kept most of the other land as agricultural, run by the management team. We bought several US army vehicles from the Yanks because there was a waiting list for any vehicle, whether it be in the form of a car or lorry ... So began the next stage of our lives.

Chapter 9
Privy to Information

I think it was the thrill of moving back into the house, and Maud seeing her ill-gotten gains in the priest's hole that made us want for the excitement again. I know it was a dreadful, horrible war but she missed the excitement of her job and longed for some action. We had both lost the fathers of our children and whatever happened now, they would be financially secure, so resuming our previous lifestyle would not have created any difficulties.

The problem for us now was finding out who had jewellery or goods worth stealing! We still had many friends, but of course you wouldn't rob your friends, would you? Once we had found out *who* our new sources were, we then had to find out *where* and finally, *how* they secured their precious artefacts.

This is where Maud here, had one of her brainwaves.
She phoned several lock and safe companies, requesting that a salesman call and give her advice on how to secure valuable items. As I've already mentioned, she has a wonderful way of putting that little girl lost act on and it really works well.

I'll never forget the first man who came to advise us. He was full of his own self-importance and worked for one of the biggest safe companies. It was obvious he thought he would be doing us a favour.

'James Hunter Smith, pronounced Smythe,' he announced, using this supercilious tone as he introduced himself.

I couldn't resist it: 'Edith Smith, pronounced Smith,' I said in a cockney accent, holding out my hand to shake his. 'I'm the cleaner,' I continued, whereupon he quickly withdrew his hand.

Maud chipped in: 'Hello, I'm Maud Trenchard and this is Bif, the honourable Bif, son of the Earl of Boothtown,' she added as Bif came in to see what was happening.

'Oh, Mother, don't let Aunt Maud call me that. Hello,' Bif said, addressing the man, and leaving as quickly as he came in, somewhat embarrassed.

Well, that did it. James Hunter Smith, pronounced Smythe, was in utter confusion so I added further to his mounting apoplexy.

'He was a randy bugger, his father. You daren't stand still for a minute and I did. So now I've got one over the brush – a titled one at that,' I said, continuing with the cockney accent. 'Well I must be off, I have work to do.'

I left Maud to it. Mind you, I could see them in the mirror and could hear everything from outside the room.

I had to smile when I heard Maud sigh heavily and say, 'Ah, since the war, you can't get decent staff, can you?'

'No,' he replied, not really knowing how to respond.

Then Maud's offensive began and I'll never forget the little woman lost demeanour. She seemed so terrified, so helpless and needed his help.

'Now, you sit down here next to me.' She began tapping her hand on the cushion of the settee. Like a confused child, he did as he was told.

'That's my job,' I muttered. 'I'm the whore of the household. I'm better at this than you. Leave him alone.'

'Well, Mr Smith,' Maud began so sweetly. 'We are in a little trouble.'

'That's why I am here … to help,' he replied.

'We spend a lot of time at our property in France and this makes our house very vulnerable. We are really worried about being burgled here and have decided that some more of our things must be locked away.'

'I'm sure we can be of assistance,' Smith interjected in a haughty manner.

'We have a big safe at the moment, but you can appreciate we are more fortunate than most and would like a new one or strongroom to safeguard our valuables. I've heard that some of the new safes are fireproof and as the insurance company insists the paintings are secure whilst we are away, we need to buy another. It's a similar situation with our house in France so I would like you to look at that as well. We must keep it secret you know; we don't want anyone else to know what we are doing. You will guarantee no one else will know, won't you, Mr Smith?' Maud added, looking into his eyes like a desperately insecure soul.

'Of course we will!' Then came the stock reply: 'Security is the watchword of our company.'

'Thank you,' Maud continued. 'We have been putting everything in the bank vault, but it's such a fag to have to load the van each time and then collect everything from the bank on our return. Sometimes, we're away three or four times a year. You understand what I mean, don't you?'

'Of course I do,' came the reply.

'Before the war, it was difficult for burglars to get here, you know. We are so far out in the sticks and they didn't have cars, but now even *they* have got cars and could get to us easily. We are terrified of losing some of our things, especially those which Father gave us, and we do need your help,' she said, moving a little closer to him.

That silly little voice made me want to get the violin out and start playing. But it was working.

'Don't you worry now. I'll fix you up,' he said, regaining his confidence and opening his obviously new, light tan American leather bag containing all his documents and pictures. These bags were all the fashion for a time.

He took out his leaflets and began his sales pitch whilst Maud moved even closer.

'Oh, they are big! Are they secure though?' she asked, peering at the leaflets.

'Of course they are. We are the biggest ...' Maud closed her ears to the rest of his patter.

'Do any of our friends have them?' she asked innocently.

'Well, I don't know your friends but we have some very important people on our books.'

'Like who? We know lots of important people.'

He opened his customer file with a flourish, which of course had to be in neat alphabetical order and said proudly, 'Well, Lord A for example, who's leader of the Conservatives in the House of L–'

'Oh! You mean George,' Maud interrupted. 'I've known George for years. He's not important. He's only in politics for goodness sake. Come here, let me look,' she said, taking the book from him. By now she was almost sitting on his lap.

He was powerless as she ran through the names.

'That's Sir Bertie ... That's Sir Reginald and Sir Freddie, and oh, I know them very well. I was at their party last month, but I didn't see a safe though.'

'You wouldn't. It's hidden behind the wine racks in the cellar.'

'What a good idea. Was that your idea?' she asked rhetorically. 'Well, you are a bright young man. Have you done anything else like that?'

He was caught...hook line and sinker. I could almost feel Maud's excitement, as he gave her a complete record of where all the safes were and how they had installed them. Not only that, he described the sort of things that they put in them. Most indiscreet in front of a woman he didn't know, notably one who had been trained by the Navy in counter espionage and who also had a photographic memory.

I then decided to take in the tea because I didn't want to make it too obvious what Maud was doing.

'I've brought you a nice cup a tea,' I said, continuing with my cockney accent. 'Is that your nice new car outside?' I asked.

'Yes. It's the latest Morris Minor Traveller,' he said proudly before trying to hustle me out so that he could finish his sales pitch and get Maud to put pen to paper.

I left them to it as she took him to see the existing safe and its location.

'Fine safes they were,' he said on seeing it.

'Were they really?' Miss Innocent asked.

'Oh yes, but a bit small. You need something much bigger.'

'Do we?'

'Oh yes, much bigger, but I'll work out some ideas and give you an approximate cost for everything.'

He was obviously a beginner at the job if he thought our safe was one of the best. I would have loved to have told him what we thought of it.

He spent the next hour or so looking for the best places to position a safe. Maud followed him, chattering complete nonsense, almost to herself, which I'm sure made him feel he was going to make a killing out of her.

'Well, I must be off now. I think I have seen enough. I'll bring my ideas for you to see next week,' he said, putting his papers away.

'Will it be as exciting as George's, hidden behind the wine rack?'

'Please forget I told you that, Miss Trenchard, but yes, it will be.'

'Oh I will, I will,' Maud said excitedly. She was certainly excited; she was now armed with information about a number of addresses worth a visit.

A few minutes later he was gone, leaving us jumping up

and down with glee. Our elated mood continued when we had received four further visits from the other manufacturers' representatives, who were all subjected to the very best of little Miss Maud's extraction techniques.

We now had a complete dossier of many of the richest folk both here in Britain and in the south of France.

Chapter 10
A Kingdom for a Pony

We now had over forty potential customers to have a go at, but decided to take on those we didn't like, even if it was purely because of their name.

Our first candidate was the retired Chief of Police from Southampton, namely Vaughan Jones, now living in Gerrards Cross. He was a social climber of the worst kind, joining any organisation where he could meet and mix with the aristocracy and the really well off.

It was obvious to anyone with any common sense that he could not be living in the style he was on the salary or the pension of even the Chief of Police, so his money must be coming from other sources. He certainly threw it about, spending cash on many major items such as fancy sports cars. He arranged numerous dinner parties and social functions; then as a cover for his lifestyle, he would organise many charity events where everyone would think he was wonderful. We decided to turn up to one of these events and take a look at the place.

Bif, who was fanatical about cars, had now passed his driving test and as our chauffeur had retired, he said he would like to take over. He had a torrid time at school and didn't want any further education or responsibility for that matter, so he became our chauffeur. He had pretended for years that he was the chauffeur's son, so I suppose it was just one step up the ladder. Anyway, we had begun to take him into our confidence and let him know what we were going to do, so he chose the cars.

We rolled up in the Duisenberg, which by now was old-fashioned but which still caught the eye, always turning heads. We wore our favourite outfits from the 1930s which added to the attraction, making us very noticeable and causing people to think, if nothing else, that we were a little eccentric.

However, we were shocked to see how tight the security was – a bit odd for a retired policeman. There were two men on the gate, looking like bouncers at a night club. I couldn't understand why they checked us in when it was a charity event, but then within a short distance of his house, there were another two security men.

The house itself was a large detached property in about three acres of garden where there were several outbuildings, including a garage for two cars. Bif managed to park the car amongst many others, where another bouncer was standing around. We made our way towards the house, behaving like two actresses exiting the stage, leaving Bif to stay with the car.

—We didn't always behave like that, Mr White. We could be quite normal!

We were immediately met by David Baker, Jones's charity organiser and another man. In fact, it turned out that Baker was the husband of Jones's daughter and somehow mixed up in the business. They both had very annoying strong Welsh accents, almost singing the words. Baker signalled to Jones who deigned to come and meet us.

'How nice to see you,' Jones remarked. 'And what brings you here?'

'We saw the advertisement that you were holding a charity event in aid of Cancer Research so we decided to come and support it,' I replied.

'That's very good of you. So where do you hail from?' he enquired like a policeman starting his investigation.

'Little Riddington. Number 17 Watling Street,' Maud answered, giving him our full address as if she was being interrogated.

'I don't know it,' he replied in a supercilious way, which really put my back up because he then proceeded to walk away as though we were dismissed.

'This one's had it,' Maud whispered. 'Whatever happens, I want to look at what's in that safe. Pompous, ignorant ass.' We found out later it was the number – 17 Watling Street that did it. It gave the impression that it was a small terraced house and not what it really was. This however suited our purpose and from that day onwards, we decided to keep it and use it. It served our purpose even more so, as most of Jones's guests were all social climbers – the nouveau riche, as one would say. We chatted to a number of them, God knows why; we had nothing in common.

Almost everyone we met began talking about what they had acquired and what their property was worth, their new car and how much they had paid for it. One actually boasted that he had just bought an Atkinson Grimshaw painting, worth £500.

'Yes, I like Atkinson Grimshaw too,' I said, joining the conversation. 'He was Father's favourite and we have six of his works. One day they might be worth something but at the moment they just give us pleasure,' I added, putting him in his place. I'm sure they thought we were boasting but it was actually a very unpleasant experience.

I remember in one group of the impressionists – I called them that, as they simply tried to create an impression – there was a man, holding his little squaw, telling us how much land he had round the house and what it was worth and that he had just bought a three-acre paddock so Felicity could have a pony. 'Suppose I'll have to join the hunt now,' he said, laughing in a superfluous way, encouraging his audience to join in. 'Just had it valued,' he added.

'What?' Maud interrupted. 'The horse?' This caused some titters amongst the group.

'Don't be silly. The house, of course. Came in at just under the half million,' he said, sticking his chest out like some bloody Diva on the cat walk.

'Where do you live then?' Maudie asked.

'Just down the road from Jonesy here,' he replied.

'That little house just down the road? And that's worth half a million?' I asked somewhat disparagingly.

'No, silly. That's just the gate house.'

'Wow!' we both exclaimed sarcastically in unison.

'And where do you live, young lady?' he asked in a demeaning manner; I was at least as old as him.

Maud chipped in: 'Number 17 Watling Street, Little Riddington.'

'And what's your little pad worth then?' He looked around at his audience for support.

'Well, I don't really know. Do you mean the house on its own, or with the outbuildings? I suppose the house would be the same as yours. We have fifty-seven rooms and I don't know how big the paddock is, but we have at least thirty-five–'

'Thirty-five acres?' one of the group enquired, sounding surprised.

'No darling! Thirty-five thousand acres and yes, we do have a pony or two, but we don't join the hunt, as we don't like hunting, do we Maud? But they are all friends of ours. Maud here is an excellent horsewoman. Then of course, there are the farms. Oh ... and I forgot Fracklinton.'

'Fracklinton! Oh, that's a beautiful village. Have you a property there too?' another asked.

'No, darling. The family bought the village some three hundred years ago and believe it or not, we have been offered a million pounds just for the race-course there, but we decided against it. So I suppose our little pad's worth about thirty million or so.

'The Americans had it for their headquarters during the war, you know, and have spent a small fortune doing it up and of course, at the moment we have a large airstrip which must have a value because all the big planes can land and take off. McMillan had to land there a month ago as there was an emergency at Northolt. It's seldom used, but they are still leasing it as an emergency reserve because of the troubles with Russia.

'You must come and see us one day,' I concluded, leaving them all open-mouthed and I hope a little more humble.

'Edie, I want to take everything from that pompous idiot as well as his little friend,' Maudie whispered.

That did it! We had the same instinct and decided to do a sortie around the house with Maudie's inbuilt photographic memory making notes of the ways in and the ways out. It was a pretty formidable place at ground level, but like most places, there is always a weak link somewhere. Jones's was the wonderful looking balcony, which was obviously where the bedroom was as it had lovely double doors opening onto it.

It had a stone balustrade round it; we decided that was the way in. As for the position of the safe, thanks to one of the salesmen, we already knew it was in Jones's office behind a large Eastern-looking screen. We had no idea at this stage what the layout of the interior was, and stood deciding what to do next, when we were disturbed.
'What are you doing?' a familiar voice shouted.

It was David Baker, Jones's organiser. 'We are just admiring the house and the way it has been positioned so to get the sun all day,' Maudie said, to my utter astonishment. Once again as she told me later, her military training came into play. When you know where the sun goes, you know where or when to break in.

'It's lovely. Our house in France is a little like this, you know.'

'That's nice,' he said and then got straight down to business. 'I understand you own Fracklinton and the racecourse?'

'Good Lord, how do you know that?' I asked, playing a little stupid, at the same time thinking this was more Maud's domain.

'We know all about you,' he replied, tapping his forefinger on his nose.

'Gosh, not all I hope!' I said, trying to generate a bit of sex appeal and flirt a bit. God only knows why because he was an ugly bugger and even Maud tried to put a stop to it by casually kicking my foot. Well, it worked and he responded.

'Would you like to see around the place?'

'That would be nice. I was admiring the balcony. It looks … erm … lovely.'

'Come on, I'll show you.' I put my arm through his and waltzed him in through the back door, with Maud dutifully following.

At least I hadn't lost my sex appeal, I thought to myself. I could feel his interest mounting. I squeezed his arm and gave him a knowing look, which he returned as we entered one of the bedrooms.

'Which is your room?' I asked.

'Oh, I don't live here. I live in the town.'

'With your wife?'

'No, I'm not married.'

'Oh really?' I said, pretending to be a little excited. I waved my hand behind my back, signalling to Maud to disappear, whilst I tried it on. I didn't have to try very hard.

'Where's …?'

'She's gone outside,' I replied. With that, he pushed me through the bedroom door which banged shut and he started to maul me all over.

He had just about undone his trousers when PC Plod

Jones yelled, 'David!' at the top of his voice.

'Christ! It's my father-in-law!' he whispered loudly, hurriedly doing up his trousers.

'Coming,' he shouted back. 'Come on, we had better go down. I'll do the explaining.'

We walked out of the bedroom and onto the landing, making our way down the stairs. I deliberately exaggerated tidying myself up. 'It's not my fault really,' I whimpered.

It was now obvious to Jones that he assumed we had been up to something, made worse when David said: 'I've just been showing her the view from the balcony.'

'Yeah, of course you have. Get in the office and you, Miss ... Out!'

I looked at him; in fact, I just stared, ensuring that he knew how I felt and also knew that there was no way I would be intimidated.

The two men walked into the office, Jones slamming the door behind him.

I bet he's jealous he saw me first, I thought to myself, laughing, only to hear Jones shouting at my new friend. I went to the door and listened.

'I've told you this before. If I catch you with another woman, I'll cut it off. And what were you doing with that tart in my bedroom?'

That did it for me. I opened the door, walked straight over to him and my fist met his left eye full on. He momentarily staggered back, absolutely shocked.

'Don't you ever refer to me as a tart again. Do you understand?'

Both of them stood open-mouthed, unable to take it in as I flounced to the door and then announced: 'We love each other, and you won't stop me seeing him.' I could see David looking for that proverbial hole to jump in.

David's eyes opened wider and wider as it began to dawn on him what was happening. I opened the door and whispered: 'Don't worry, darling. He won't dare do anything.' With that, I slammed the door behind me.

Maudie came down the stairs at the same time and we walked out of the house together.

'It's a beautiful place. Must have cost a small fortune,' I said to the bouncer on the door as we left the house and joined the others on the lawn. Maud wasted no time scolding me for causing trouble for the poor man.

'Poor man? They're crooks! Have you seen enough?'

'Yes. Everything. It's the easiest place in the world. I'm surprised ... I thought a policeman would do better.

Twenty minutes or so later, the two men came out of the house and walked towards us. I gave him a cheeky little wave just enough to let Jonesy see it, which caused him to turn round to see what David's reaction would be. I could see his embarrassment, so I smiled. We carried on looking around, playing at the tombola and partaking in other charitable games. We were talking about all the possible loopholes about a break-in and also chatting about what Maudie had seen, when low and behold David sidled up to me and said angrily:

'Why did you do that to me?'

'You told me you weren't married. Now go away or I'll really start on you.'

Once again he looked shocked; obviously not used to being treated like that, especially by a woman.

We had seen what we needed to see and so it was time to depart but not before Maud had generously given Jones a cheque for £100. It would be worth at least £2,000 in today's money. To my horror, just as we were leaving, Jones decided to thank us publicly over the tannoy.

This Welsh accent suddenly announced our names and talked about our generosity and how delighted the charity would be. It was the last thing we wanted, especially when he made the grand gesture of trying to get us onto the stand, which of course, we refused to do.

From that moment, I realised he wanted to make friends; he obviously had something in mind. I was soon to find out as he headed towards us.

'I understand you own Fracklinton Race Course! He paused for us to answer. It was a long pause ... more of an embarrassed silence whilst he waited for us to answer.

'Well, do you?'

'What?' I asked.

'Own Fracklinton Race Course?'

'Yes.'

I could see his frustration was really boiling over.

'Why didn't you answer?'

'You didn't ask. You made a statement. You told us we owned Fracklington.'

'I'm interested in discussing a business proposition with you.'

'Oh good,' we said in unison and walked away, back to the car, but not before we overheard him say to one of his sidekicks:

'I'll get those two one day.'

'Perhaps not before we get you,' Maudie sniggered.

We got back in the car and drove down the road to where we thought the other little shit lived. There was the small gate house, which was more for show than practical use. The gates were left open and there was no one about – not even Felicity and her pony. For Maud, it was a quick nosey round and back to the car.

'There's no security whatsoever. The doors have old locks and frames. You could almost push them in. We could do it on the same day,' Maudie said, her voice animated. 'It would only take me about twenty minutes.'

We spent the next two months planning every move, checking when the houses would be empty, soon discovering that the two men were obviously good friends as they went almost everywhere together. That helped the planning. The women always seemed to go out when the men did, but poor Robert's wife had another little friend she went to see.

—It's amazing what you find out about people when you watch them often enough, Mr White.

Mrs Jones was a good girl. She always went to see her mother.

Maud was responsible for getting all our equipment together and in doing so, spent several days knitting three black balaclavas, one for each of us, including Bif who was coming with us.

—She likes knitting you know, Mr White.

We decided to attack Jones's house first. We would throw a grappling iron over the balustrade and enter the bedroom via the balcony. Maudie would go up first, open the bedroom windows, slip down the stairs and let me in.

Bif was now twenty years old and fanatical about cars. He had long since passed his driving test and was ready to help us. He chose one of our American jeeps which we had acquired some years earlier from the Americans. There were hundreds of them around the country and Bif felt it would be ideal for this job as they were wonderful cross-country vehicles and were able to get away quickly, even loaded with the equipment we would be carrying, and of course, ourselves.

The day was set when we knew everyone would be out and we would have the maximum chance of success. It all seemed straightforward. We drove up the drive to Jones's house; there was no one about, so we quickly got out the equipment.

I threw the grappling hook over the balustrade whilst Maudie took hold of the rope, giving it a tug to see if it would take her weight. All seemed secure, so she quickly started to climb up. And then ... catastrophe! She only managed about three feet off the ground before the balustrade fell off, bringing the whole of it crashing down. Thank goodness the house was secluded because the noise was deafening. Bits of stone went everywhere, just missing me and Bif, but nearly killing Maudie. It was only by luck that she fell *under* the balcony.

She was determined to start again. Only this time, she was full of anger and threw the grappling iron straight through the bedroom window, smashing it to pieces, but at least it caught on the frame. She was up like a monkey and, within a couple of minutes, she opened the front door to let me in.

By now, we had lost ten minutes and we were now running a little behind time. Bif waited outside whilst Maud opened the safe and I went in to see what else I could find. Within moments, I was disturbed by Maud shouting: 'Edie! Come here quick. Look at this lot.'

There was well over £10,000 in cash, together with accounts books and diaries. This was enough for us.

—Yes, Mr White, we had taken some sacks to put things in, and yes, they did have SWAG written on them.

It took another ten minutes to empty the safe and load the car before we were away. I wanted to call it a day, but Maud was determined to do the other place, which turned out to be so easy as the door opened with the slightest of effort.

—We only took his Atkinson Grimshaw picture, Mr White. I will give you his details unless it was insured. There was nothing else worth taking.

'And I knew it would make him miserable,' Maud added.

We always left the scene travelling in the opposite direction one would expect, always away from Number 17 and on this occasion we were lucky; we passed Jones a few miles away, on his way back home, followed shortly afterwards by the other little shit. We never did know his name. Fortunately, the cover of the jeep was up, so at least we couldn't be seen, having taken the balaclavas off.

Nothing happened immediately. But it certainly happened later on. Jones would, without doubt, have been messing himself the moment he arrived home to see his papers had gone, and I couldn't believe what I was reading when we got back.

He had kept a complete record of all the criminals he was blackmailing, and where he had hidden the evidence to prevent them being convicted. This included the monies each of them paid even for the simplest of things like letting people off driving offences for a fee.

He had raised about £350 for the charity from his latest function, so we thought it would be a nice gesture to give all the money we found to Cancer Research as a donation from Mr Jones. But the treasure we found in the safe was priceless. It gave us great pleasure to send it anonymously to Enoch Powell an MP for Wolverhampton, who we knew to be honest, plus photographs of everything to the Metropolitan Commissioner.

Having done that, the shit hit the fan. It not only led to the arrest and imprisonment of Jones, but also many other criminals and those in the community you would least have expected. We had some fun out of it ourselves, as he even had tabs on his own son-in-law and it gave me great pleasure in sending photographs of him in bed with another woman and another to George Mackintosh, the local politician who was also caught in a similar position, only this time it was a man. I'm sure you will remember it was illegal at that time.

Chapter 11
Bitter Sweet Medicine

We carried out several house burglaries over the next few months, which in some way had become routine. It created a great deal of publicity in the press about the rich getting robbed; it didn't however generate much sympathy from the public, but it did require a great deal of effort from the police as they perceived it was the establishment being ripped off. There were even a few copycat burglaries, which took some of the pressure off us, but it was when they tried it on our place that we were really let off the hook.

I suppose it was during the mid 1960s, about eight years after Suez. Maudie had been called up to do a specific job in Egypt, and in France.

'Whoops! I shouldn't have told him that should I, Maudie?'

'No, Edie,' Maud replied, looking somewhat disconcerted.

Maud's military service experience was intriguing me as much as the story I had been listening to, but somehow she would clam up the moment things were mentioned. I was determined to see if I could get to the bottom of this before I finished.

We decided to take a break from the Home Counties and from our hobby because too much attention was being given to the robberies. We were described as a gang of ruthless men that would stop at nothing! We often had to look at each other to confirm we were still girls, well, maybe slightly older than that. We had been given various nicknames such as the 'Millionaire Robbers' because we only seemed to rob the rich, which seemed very close to home. If only they had known! 'Will of the Wisps' was another name given as no one had ever seen us. The *Mail*, clever little devils they were, associated us with the robberies which happened before the war. Thankfully, that was never taken up, so we were let off the hook.

We therefore thought a few months in Nice would do the trick as we hadn't been involved there since just after the war.

'And of course, the weather was always better there,' Maud chipped in.

Everything was packed and we were due to leave the following morning. It must have been about eleven o'clock at night when Stanley came running along to our wing.

'Aunt Edith, I think we have burglars! They've driven up in a big van and parked near the house.'

I quickly got dressed and raced along to the east wing, where Maud was already dressed and watching their every move. We joined her for the entertainment just to see how good they were. They were behaving like idiots, having done very little research on the place.

Of course, you may well remember the window tax in Georgian times. Father didn't like the stone used to block in the windows, so he changed many of them. For example, he made a feature of two of the downstairs windows by putting a portico and a door in front. It looked better but served no purpose; the stone was merely covered up. Well, these two silly buggers were trying to open one of the false doors!

I raced downstairs and slipped the lock, leaving the next door along off the catch. Sure enough, they eventually worked their way to that door and came in, at the same time trying to stop laughing at their own stupidity.

Maud sent Stanley and Bif outside to get rid of their van, after which they returned to join me. They were each armed with a loaded shot gun, which only contained blanks, I am sorry to say. We knew our unwelcome guests would go down the corridor and would open and check every room, eventually entering the music room where there were many cups and other silver trophies awarded for music and other things.

This room was special to us; it was somewhere where you could get away from it all. On entering, it looked as though there was a window on the opposite wall as it had two beautiful crimson velvet curtains which were permanently drawn. It was another of Father's tricks and artistry. It was also soundproofed, as Father couldn't stand our incessant hitting of the wrong notes. There was only one way in and one way out. The walls were three feet thick and the solid oak door was four inches thick. I went into the room, sat at the piano, and waited.

Maud was only about three feet away from them and when they opened the door and entered, having just the light from their torch, I began playing the piano. The chords of Beethoven's Fifth Symphony rang out, shattering the silence.

'What the bloody hell's that!' one of them exclaimed.

'Beethoven's Fifth,' I replied.

'Mr White,' Maud chipped in. 'Take away her rough edges and Edith would have made a wonderful concert pianist. She won many competitions, you know.'

'And I can still play today,' I added.

The man's little torch was pointed at me and already beginning to dim.

'Who the fuck are you?' the other asked.

'I'm the sister of the person pointing a shotgun at your head, and it will go off if you decide to make a false move.' Maud moved into the room, leaving the door open which allowed just enough light for us all to see one another. She signalled with the gun for the two men to move to the corner of the room. This immediately encouraged one of them to show how brave he was.

'You're not going to use that thing, are you?' he said. 'It would be a foolish, murder in fact, and you don't look the type.' He continued moving closer to her.

'I don't need to. You're not big enough,' Maud said defiantly.

He sneered and immediately made a bolt for the gun. What happened next I have never seen in my life and never seen since. Once more, I had no idea what Maudie was capable of. Within a split second, she had bashed the idiot under the chin with the butt of the gun, knocking him to the floor, banged the butt into his back and rested her foot on his testicles.

'Maud, what did the new eunuch say?' I asked.

'I asked him if he had anything to say,' Maud replied. 'Very little really because he was totally out of it. I told the other one to get in the corner and take his friend with him, which he dutifully did by dragging the other little bandit with him.'

Stanley and Bif had found the driver and sadly for him he was now bound, gagged and dragged into the room. I suggested we untie him so that he could at least impart the news that they no longer had a van.

'What are you going to do?' the man asked.

'We need time to think about it. We don't like people who try to rob us so I suppose we have a few options to consider. We will let you know … in an hour or two,' I replied.

Maud answered for him. 'This room is a built-in prison and you are in it. There is no possible way to escape as this is the only way out, so good night. Oh, and by the way, if any of the things in this room are damaged in any way, you will never get out,' she said, laughing. 'It's also sound-proofed, so don't waste your time using your vocal chords.'

'Oi!' one of them shouted. 'Leave it aaart.'

'You're finished,' I replied. 'As I said, there's no escape, and many have died in this room over the years. Good night.'

Maud clicked the door shut and turned the large key in the three-hundred year-old lock. The noise would have been enough to scare anyone especially in the total darkness, except for their little torch. Batteries didn't last long in those days.

We did at least have a good night's sleep, but unfortunately, our guests didn't. There was a light switch, but it was on the outside of the room, so at least we could see them properly when we returned to the room in the morning. You could hear their relief when the light went on, but for a few minutes, they couldn't see properly because of the contrast from pitch black to bright light.

Maud went in first and was immediately greeted with, 'You can't keep us here, regardless what we've done.'

'We can. No one knows you are here. You will end you days here.'

'Well, that's where you're wrong. We always let our friends know where we are.'

'But you didn't arrive. Where's your van? We didn't get to bed until late last night. Who will they believe? A dirty bunch of burglars or us?'

None of them said a word in reply.

'Now we want to know who you have burgled recently, and until you tell us, you stay here. Not here exactly but in our dungeon underground. It's where they used to bury our ancestors. The bodies are still there and it is a bit dusty. It is also soundproofed like this room, so it's the end for you.' I went into the room followed by the two lads together with their blank loaded shot guns and grabbed one of the men. The other two started to have a go but Maud despatched them.

The lads grabbed hold of the first man and frogmarched him across the lawns and the paddock to the crypt, which was a lovely churchlike building specially built for the bodies of all members of the family over the last three hundred years or so. It was isolated and surrounded by trees and couldn't be seen from the house or anywhere for that matter until you got close up.

Stanley told me the man began to panic when he smelt the musty damp atmosphere, which rushed at you the moment they opened the door. The daylight lit up the entrance and highlighted the stone steps going down to the depths of the crypt. It does have a ghoulish feel about it, not a place to be left alone in, even for the bravest of souls. The boys left him with a hurricane lamp but not before they told him about the rats and advising them to use the lamp wisely as there was only two hours' worth of oil in it.

But the coup de grâce came when Stanley shouted:

'Don't open the coffins! Two of them died of the Black Death and we don't know which one. The modern ones will have the rats in, so please be careful.'

The heavy door was closed, leaving him standing petrified at the top of the steps, no doubt wondering what to expect.

The boys came back to the house and selected anther one to be taken to the crypt. He suffered the same routine, only this time they were told that it wouldn't matter if they died now as no one would visit the crypt and when they were dead, they would simply be deposited in one of the vaults.

They began shouting at the top of their voices in the hope that someone passing would hear, but it was no use; no one ever went near the crypt. Stanley said it was an odd feeling to hear them shouting and then suddenly, a deathly silence as he closed the door.

The third man, if you'll excuse the pun, seemed the weakest of the three, and was to be our target.

This is when Maud put the fear of God into him:

'Now we have buried the other two in Father's tomb,' Maud began, 'and their lives and yours depend on you giving me the truth. I want your name and address, your phone number, and the school you went to. I also want the name of your wife or whoever you live with, where you got married and where you have worked. Here's a pen and paper. You have thirty minutes to give me all the details. If you give the wrong details, you will be left in here on your own.'

He began sweating profusely. 'Can I have a drink?' he asked.

'No. You're a dying man. You don't need it. Half an hour!' Maud replied.

We all left him to it, switched the light out and waited. No doubt, he started shouting about it being dark but we couldn't hear. We returned about an hour later.

'How can I write when you turned the light out?'

'Sorry, didn't think,' Maud said.

'Can I have a drink, please?'

'No. The details first and furthermore, we need the names and addresses of your two friends. I've told you that when the oxygen runs out in the crypt, they will be buried in the vault, and we will have to notify their next of kin, not knowing, of course, how on earth they got there. Ten minutes is all you've got now. We will check your information and if anything's incorrect, you are finished. But if all is okay, at least you are saved.'

We waited outside, and the moment the ten minutes were up, we turned off the light and opened the door.
'I've got them! I've got them,' he screamed.

I went in, collected the details and sent Stanley and Bif to check them out.

We had missed our train and delayed our holiday, which made me very angry, but we were both determined to deal with these idiots before leaving.

Stanley and Bif returned about four hours later with as much information as they could get which enabled us to question the man further. There were one or two anomalies but in the main, he had been terrified into telling the truth, particularly about the last three jobs they had done.

'What did you do with the stuff from that last job?' Maud asked.

'It's more than my life's werf.'

'Fine. Keep shouting when we pass the door. Bye for now.'

'Wait a minute,' he said nervously. 'Don't tell the others.'

'No, we won't,' Maud replied. 'They won't be dead just yet, but I'm going to check out your story and if you are lying, we'll tell your little friends and let them deal with you. Then we'll decide what to do with them.'

He gave us the complete rundown – when, where, a mental list of almost everything that had been taken and who had bought it. We did check it out and it tallied with Alan and David Wright being the main suspects, and who were antique dealers in Vauxhall Bridge Road, Pimlico. When we investigated further, we discovered they were among the biggest fences in London, Alan Wright being renowned as a crumpet chaser. It seemed we could be onto a winner here!

Maud suggested that I deal with this Alan fellow, as I had more experience in that field than she had; he was to be my responsibility.

Before anything else, we had to deal with these three light-fingered gentry. There was no way we could inform the police; it would be hypocritical, but we wanted to make sure they never came back, so Stanley and Bif took this snivelling little idiot, whose name was Peter Hill, to the crypt to give him a taste of what the others were suffering. The lads brought back the brave one for a little tête-à-tête with us.

'John Davis,' I remarked, making him aware we knew who he was.

'Oh piss off! You'll get nothing out of me.'

'That's what your little friend said, but we don't want anything from you. We already know all about you – where you live, your girlfriend's name, even what you have for breakfast. We are just deciding what to do with you. But if you do want to make friends with us, you will need to confirm all the jobs you have done and where you have taken the stuff. Mind you, we are not really bothered.'

He shrugged. 'Please yourself,' he replied.

'Well, that's it then. We're going to put you back in the crypt and you won't be found until our next burial, which may be fifty years or more. We'll leave you plenty of water and bread, but you won't be able to shave, wash, or call out for help. You'll smell a bit, of course. Take him back down.'

He started getting a little stroppy so Maud simply pressed one of his nerves and he fell asleep. He woke up in the crypt, and it added more to their terror when Bif told the other two that we thought he was dead. We imagined it would do them good to have at least twenty-four hours underground. This would also give us time to plan the action we needed to take.

***

I remember walking into Alan Wright's shop on Vauxhall Bridge Road about lunch time on a cold November day, to be greeted by Sheila, a big bosomed, super intelligent, dying to be blonde, secretary.

'Allo! They're not 'ere.'

'Who aren't, darlin'?' I asked in my fluent cockney accent.

'Al and Dave, they raart on a job.'

'Robbin' a bank?' I asked.

'Wha ? ... Oh ... funny. They're aart werkin.'

'When will they be back?'

114

'Any time I suppose. Baart ten minutes.'

'Okay, I'll 'ave a look round,' I said, as she disappeared into the office. I was amazed how well I had conversed, as it had been several years since I had been in that part of the world and used such language.

Half an hour later, Sheila came out again, this time to tell me they were on the way back.

'But they didn't say when cos the pips ran aaart.'

'I'll wait,' I said, very impressed with my fluency.

You would expect me or someone like me who had been brought up in the way we had been to know something about antiques, and sure enough it paid off. I recognised several items on show in the shop from the robbery Peter Hill had described.

Sheila came dashing out the office, as only she could, in four-inch stilettos and a skirt that would not allow more than an eight-inch gait.

'Oooh look, they're 'ere naa,' she remarked as a large Luton van pulled up outside. 'Watch yer name?' she asked. 'Trenchard ... Mrs Trenchard.'

You could tell immediately which one was Alan, as David was a fat slob of a man whose breakfast that day had obviously missed the edge of his mouth and slid down his pullover. In fact, from the state of his top garment, it would appear to be a regular occurrence.

'Morning Miss,' David said, his mouth yet more full of food.

'I'll deal wiv the lady, David,' Alan intervened, whereupon David immediately disappeared into the office. 'This is Mrs Trenchard, Alan.'

'Right, thank you, Sheila.' She too disappeared and I was left in the hands of this suave, debonair, Grecian 2000 crumpet chaser.

'Now then. What can I do for you ... er ...?

'Trenchard ... Mrs Trenchard.'

'Yeah, I know that! It's yer Christian name I want.'

'It's Edith.'

'Lavelly, Nice name. Me muvers name's Edith.'

Well, that was a put off for a start. My plan was to seduce him, find out everything I could and he starts comparing me to his mother.

'I hope I'm not like your mother.'

'No, I didn't mean that. It's just yer name.'

'I hope so,' I said, gently running my hand down my side after I had casually bumped into a table.

'Are you all right?' he asked, concern showing on his face.

'Yes, I think so. I hope I haven't bruised myself. I do bruise easily.' I had him, so much so he got a bit cheeky, just to test the water.

'I will have to rub it for you, won't I?'

'Oooh yes, cheeky. Are you always this naughty with your customers?'

'Only when there's a day in the week,' he replied, laughing heartily.

I began to wonder what I was doing in this man's company, but for some reason I was peculiarly attracted to him. It must have been the certain charisma he displayed.
'Saucy! I've only came to have a look at some of your stuff, particularly that Queen Anne table circa 1710, and those William or Victorian dining chairs. How much do you want for them?'

'Well, my little luverly, what you going to give me?'

'What do you want?'

'You to come and have a drink with me tonight and I'll sort somefing out.'

'Lovely! What time and where?'

'I know this nice little pub. It's a bit out of the way ... in the Strand.'

'I know it. It's the Wig and Pen. I'll meet you outside

Temple Station at seven-thirty. You can take me in. It's not ladylike to sit in a pub on your own. But ... what about the table?'

'We can talk about that tomorrow. I told yer I'll sort somefing out,' he replied.

I could almost feel him undressing me as he said it. 'Half past seven then. Don't be late. I won't wait,' I said. 'See you.'

I walked out of the shop knowing full well his eyes followed my every move. I don't think he could believe his luck that he had pulled so easily.

I went home to change and to discuss with Maudie what I had seen, but although I had ten minutes on my own, I could only see the items in the shop and could not get near the office or see any possible rear exits.

I told Maudie I had a date with Alan the lecher as there was a chance I could find out more, and when I asked what should I wear, Maud said:

'Vamp him! You know you like it,' only to add, 'Be careful. You know what happened before.'

I snapped at her in schoolgirl fashion.

'That's not nice' I replied. Anyway, I'm on the pill. I managed to get some of those soon to be released in the UK. I can't get pregnant, so there!'

Judging by the way Alan behaved, he was obviously the boss of the establishment, and it was obvious to me that Sheila was his choice. Whilst I couldn't claim to be as busty as Sheila, I did have a half decent figure with a good pair of legs so I decided to use these attributes to the full.

When I came downstairs, Maud remarked that I looked like some high- class prostitute on her way to do the business. I was wearing a tight red jumper, a short black leather skirt , black sheer stockings and four-inch red stilettos to match the jumper and, of course, a wide black curbing belt which was a must in those days.

She didn't mean what she said though.

'I did,' Maud interjected.

I bumped into Bif and Alice on the way out, only to be admonished for looking like someone on the way to Soho. Trying to explain to my son and daughter why I was dressed the way I was took some doing. I looked like some sleazy Mata Hari on a mission. I told them how important it was that I got information, and dressing like this was the best way for me to achieve this. They accepted the situation, so at least I felt a little more comfortable.

Bif took me in the Rolls and left me at a decent walk from the station. Thankfully, I did that as he was already waiting, but I couldn't help but notice my chaperone driving round to see if his mother was safe before leaving the two of us to walk arm in arm to the pub.

My word, I had made a hit. He had gone a bit heavy though on the Grecian 2000. But apart from that, he had made a reasonable effort.

'You look a cracker, darlin',' were his opening words.

I felt like saying, 'Do yer fink so?' in a silly, cockney, high pitched voice, but it came out as, 'Oh, really. Thank you very much.'

I certainly attracted the wrong sort of attention as we walked to the pub, but mine host was pleased to show off his bit of high-class totty.

In those days, the pub was a lovely old-fashioned place – the 'spit and sawdust' type. We sat down at a table in the corner and made ourselves comfortable.

'Chavin?' he asked. That meant: 'What would you like to drink?'

'Half of Truman's bitter, please.'

'You'll have to come again. I thought you would be at least a Campari and lemonade girl.'

Oh God, where did he get that idea from, I wondered. We all knew that tasted like medicine. 'No thanks, just a half of Truman's, please.'

The one thing I forgot was that the pub was near the City, and I knew many who worked in or nearby and who visited the Wig and Pen. Sure enough, within a few minutes one of them saw me.

'Hello Edith, what brings you here?' a man's voice said, a look of total shock on his face.

'Close your mouth, David. I'm just here with a friend, hoping to do a bit of business.' I signalled with a slight nod of the head for him to go.

He took the hint; hopefully my date didn't see, but that wasn't the end of it. One or two others also recognised me and said hello.

'You're popular.'

'Just clients.'

'What do you do then?'

'I like to think I'm in the entertainment business.'

We chatted mainly about the antique business and I know he was impressed with my knowledge, which tended to take his mind off my popularity. That was until after my third half, which he would not allow me to buy.

'I don't invite a girl out for a drink and let her pay. Goodness me! What sort of a bloke do ya fink I am?'

'Look after my bag, will you? There's two grand in it,' I whispered. 'I'm just off to the loo.' But I was a little unsettled as I had the distinct impression that the respectable-looking man on the seat next to us was listening. However, I thought no more of it.

I was just round the corner out of sight of my date, when another friend came and asked what it was all about.

'What the hell's the matter, Edith? Are you in trouble?'

'No, I'm trying to glean some information from him as he is a major fence and they have tried to burgle Number 17.'

'There a few lads here who can sort him for you.'

'You're wonderful! Thanks, but no thanks. You can do

something for me though. I think he believes I am a good time girl with a few clients, if you take my meaning?'

'I'm not surprised,' he replied, clearing his throat with embarrassment and glancing at my cleavage. 'But I must say, Edith, I do fancy you myself!'

'Wait yer turn! Anyway, you couldn't afford it,' I said in the cockney accent. 'Now go over to him and give him the impression that I *am* a good time girl and have many influential friends.'

'That part's true at least,' he said.

'You know what to say. And thanks for your offer.' He kissed me on the cheek and left. Alan saw him and he obviously had to explain the circumstances, which seemed to have worked; Alan was more attentive than ever when I returned.

'Edie, he's told me what you do.'

'I prefer Edith, please. I know I should have told you but I don't know you well enough. I would have eventually. Promise,' I said, putting on the little vulnerable woman act. Not as good as Maudie here, but good enough because it worked.

We chatted about this and that and soon I knew all about him, All he knew about me was that I was a high-class prostitute working out of Kensington Palace.

We left the pub about ten o'clock and walked around chatting for a little while, He then suggested fish and chips, and after two and a half pints of Truman's, it was a welcome suggestion. It had been some years since I had that. In fact, it was when I was in the Navy on a date with Henry.

We finished the fish and chips and he hailed a taxi.

'Where are we going?' I asked.

'Just a little surprise, nothing sordid. I live above the shop. I thought you would like a coffee or something.'

'Now ... Alan, *you* are being saucy, so I'll have a sexy cup of coffee.'

I saw the driver giving me one of those knowing looks. We eventually arrived at Vauxhall Bridge Road where I tried to pay for the taxi, but again had the proverbial reply:

'I pay for everything when I ask a lady out on a date.'

I looked at the cabbie, raised my eyebrows, shrugged my shoulders and smiled. He collected his money, winked at me and drove off.

The entrance to Alan's apartment, as he liked to call it, was by means of the side door adjacent to the shop, followed by a flight of stairs immediately facing you. At the top of the stairs there was a small landing area and his front door. Simple so far. He invited me in and immediately tried to spoil things by attempting to kiss me.

'Alan, don't be impatient and spoil things. A gentleman wouldn't behave like that. You invited me for a coffee. Come on, I'll make it for us.'

It really was a well-appointed flat, including the kitchen. A lot of money had been put into it. While we waited for the kettle to boil, he showed me round. He opened the bedroom door with a right arm flourish and directed me in. I thought I'd entered the American Embassy! Above the bed rose its national emblem – a massive eagle.

Well? he said.

'Gawdy,' I replied. 'How can you make love with that watching you?'

He became so deflated and disappointed that I felt I had to do something to cheer him up.

'Come here,' I ordered. I put my arms around his neck and kissed him. That cheered him up.

We were sitting on the settee drinking the coffee when he suddenly said:

'You know, Edie ...'

'Edith,' I interrupted.

'Sorry. You know, Edith, there's somefink about you! You've got class. I enjoyed it tonight and not because you had half a bitter.'

'Alan, shut up. You are spoiling things. I was quite happy when you said the class bit.'

'That's wora I mean. You're the first woman who hadn't taken me for a ride.'

'How do you get to the shop down there? You don't have to go out the front every time, do you?' I asked, trying to change the subject for business reasons.

'Oh no! It's just through that door there. It goes into the office.'

'Come on, let's have a look,' I said, leading the way down the stairs with him following like a little lap dog. I opened the office door and there it was … a big safe, a door to the rear alley, and a door to the front shop. I had seen it all, but now I had my date champing at the bit. I opened the shop door and walked in. There was a dim reflection from the outside street light, but in reality it was dark. After a few minutes, my eyes became accustomed to the light and I could see a dark, secluded corner. I took him by the hand and led him to this lovely Victorian chaise longue placed in the corner.

'Come here. I want you,' I said, patting the cushion and inviting him to sit down. He was quivering with excitement as I undid his trousers and pulled him on top of me. I was thinking we had much to thank the Victorians for!

'Edie, you're disgusting,' Maud snapped.

'I'm only trying to explain to Mr White what I had to do to get the information.'

Twenty minutes later, we were walking back through the office to the flat but already it had me thinking that I would like to see him again.

He took me straight into the bedroom where I immediately covered up the peering eagle and lay on the bed. He stood looking at me, and I could tell he was falling for me.

'Edith, you are special. When can I see you again?'
I patted the bed and said, 'Let's see what you're made of.'
He turned the lights down with a dimmer switch and began to strip off.

Once more, he began to quiver with excitement and sure enough he was an expert and in control of this situation. For a person with his reputation as a crumpet chaser, I would have thought he would have been a little more aggressive with his lovemaking but he was gentle and caring.

'Stay the night,' he whispered.

I couldn't refuse. I was absolutely knackered, and slipping under the sheets, fell asleep in seconds, only to be woken in the night with him starting on me again.

'I'm sorry, I can't leave you alone.'

He was amazing, but I had to call it a day after the third occasion.

I discovered he was a satyriasis, a male nymphomaniac. I didn't know at the time but it suited me.

I awoke next morning, got dressed in my whore's outfit which seemed appropriate after my night's work, put on my bright red four-inch heels and found I couldn't stand up in them. I wasn't used to all this exercise.

'Can I see you again?' he asked.

'If you like,' I said, trying to be casual.

'When?'

I shrugged, wanting to appear indifferent.

'Tomorrow?'

'Okay.' It was strange but I really wanted to see him again and I really wanted to kiss him.

'Call me a taxi, will you?' I asked.

He did just that and we stood in total silence, waiting for the damn thing to arrive.

'Oh! For God's sake, kiss me. That's if you want to!'

'I want to but you seem to be out of my class.'

'Oh, come here, you stupid lummox.' He came over and I kissed him there and then. Neither of us wanted the taxi to arrive but it soon did.

'Same time, same place tomorrow,' he called out as I got in.

'Don't be late. I won't wait,' I replied.

Chapter 12
The Game of Love

I didn't want to leave a trail as to my identity so I alighted from the taxi on Lillie Road in Fulham, walked around a bit, getting several offers on the way, telephoned Bif as to where I was and waited. I was then told to move on by our friendly local constable.

'Officer, I am waiting for my son to pick me up in the car.'

'A likely story. Move on or I'll run you in.'

'Look officer, I've been to a fancy dress party.'

'So have I. Move on.'

I moved away very slowly in the hope that Bif would arrive quickly, turning round every minute or so to see where the policeman was, only to find him still there, watching me and gesturing with the back of his hand to move on.

—I could have made a living at this, Mr White.

'You nearly did,' Maud chipped in.

I had two cars stop, with the drivers starting to chat me up. When they saw the copper, they moved on quickly.

Bif finally arrived in the Rolls-Royce and pulled up at the pavement where I was supposed to be. He saw the policeman approaching and me tottering towards him and decided to wait.

'Move on, sir,' the copper ordered.

'I'm waiting for that lady,' Bif replied, pointing in my direction.

'That's no lady, young man. Be careful.'

'That's *my* mother,' Bif said angrily, 'and if you have to book me, do so, but I am waiting.'

I arrived just in time. 'You see officer, you should never judge a book by its cover.'

'You shouldn't be dressed like that, madam.'

'Why not, for God's sake? You should not judge anyone by their attire. I want your number. My name is Trenchard. My sister is also Trenchard and she is on the watch committee, and you should not treat people like this without knowing the full facts, particularly where women are concerned. You will be hearing from me.'

'I am sorry, madam.'

'You're lucky you said that. Next time, I expect to see you at the fancy dress party. Come as you are.' We returned smiles.

We arrived home around ten o'clock and I quickly changed out of my gear, reverting to my genteel attire.

The men had been sent home terrified of telling their stories, especially as they found their van outside the house of Peter Hill, the minor grass. We left a note inside the van saying how each grassed on the others and explained who bought the stuff from them and who had bought it from them before. They were well set up and we were sure they would avoid discussing the matter with anyone. We didn't tell them we had photographs of them.

I gave Maudie the full details of Alan's office, all the exits and in particular, details of the safe and from my description, she recognised the model and even which type of lock it had. However, when she asked how near we could get with a van, I could only give details of the front of shop and that was far too conspicuous.

'I remember they parked their van at the rear and it's a fairly large van. I saw it arrive in the afternoon.'

'Do they leave it there at night?' she asked.

'Not sure, I think so, but it was very dark. Alan has asked

me out tomorrow, Wednesday. I wasn't going to go, but I will, just for you.'

'Liar.'

She was right, of course. I really did want to see him again and tomorrow soon came. 'What shall I wear this time?' I asked her.

'Oh God, Edie, you know what to bloody well wear – same as last time.'

I was excited and once again I dressed somewhat whorish.

No, that's not true. Alan seemed to like the style, so for him it was to be very naughty. This time it was a white, skinny-ribbed sweater, brown leather mini skirt, with a figure-curving black leather belt and the four-inch black stilettos. I still looked the part.

It was the same routine: Bif dropped me off and I walked to Temple Station. Alan wasn't there, and once again I was accosted twice before he arrived in his black Zephyr.

'Sorry, I'm late,' he said, rushing round to open the door for me.

'Nice car,' I remarked.

'Yes, I'm taking you somewhere special, but first I want to show you something.'

'Not that again, I hope,' I said, laughing.'

We arrived at the shop. He opened the car door, grabbed my hand and virtually dragged me up the stairs behind him. He led me straight into the bedroom, once again opening the door with a flourish. I walked in and immediately noticed the absence of the eagle.

'Come here, you lovely man. Give me a hug,' I said, squeezing him tight and kissing him.

'Come on, we've got to go. I've got a table booked at the Willow Tree in Hounslow.'

'Ooh ... very posh.'

Half an hour later and a few frolics on the way, we

arrived outside the restaurant. The doorman opened the car door for me and nearly fell over in amazement. Alan gave him the key and a pound to park it up and, as proud as punch, he took hold of my arm and walked me in.

We walked up to the Maître D'. 'Have you booked a table, sir,' he asked, trying desperately hard not to look at me.

'Yes. Alan Wright.'

'I'm sorry sir, we do not have a booking under that name.'

'I booked! Let me have a look,' Alan said angrily.

'Sir, I'm telling you, there is no booking. Now please leave or I'll call the police.'

'Could I have a word in private?' I asked the Maître D'.

'Yes, madam, come with me.' We entered his office, leaving Alan fuming at the desk. I too was fuming as I began, 'Now look, young man, is it because of the way I am dressed? Yes or no?'

'Well madam, it's hardly the attire we expect in this restaurant.'

'Who's restaurant, is it?'

'I'm not at liberty to say.'

'Well I am! You get hold of Mr Higgins now and tell him Edith Trenchard is here and is being refused a table. Just see how quickly he comes. If you don't, I'll phone the police and won't you be in for a surprise! Now do it.'

He picked up the phone and dialled the number. Mrs Higgins answered. 'I have some trouble in the restaurant. There is a woman called Edith Trenchard asking to speak to your husband.'

'Who?'

'Edith Trenchard.'

'Put her on.'

The Maitre D' handed over the receiver.

'Hello Edith, what's up?'

'Please tell Charlie that my friend and I have been

refused a table because I am dressed like a whore.'

Charlie took over. 'Sorry Edith, I'll be there in ten. Put him on.'

I could hear an argument ensuing as I walked out of the office and back to where Alan was waiting.

'Come on,' he said, 'let's get out of here.'

'No, this one's on me. You watch.'

The Maître D' came out, full of apologies and took us to a table. Several pairs of eyes followed us.

'What can I get you?' he asked.

'Don't worry. Charlie knows what I like and sure enough, within a few minutes, he arrived with a lovely bottle of Mercier, chilled to perfection and full of apologies. I stood up and he came over and kissed me on both cheeks. He turned to shake Alan's hand. 'This is Alan, my lover,' I announced.

'Edith, you *are* a shocker!' Charlie said. At that, we all burst out laughing.

'Alan, are you prepared to leave things to Charlie? I know he will choose something wonderful.'

'Yes, that's fine but I will pay for it.'

'All right, but the champagne's on me,' Charlie added.

'Lovely, thanks,' Alan replied. 'Now come on, how did you manage this?' he asked as Charlie came over to pour the champagne.

'Charles, please join us.'

'Just a glass then.' He poured himself a soupçon, raised his glass and said, 'What shall we toast?'

'Edith,' Alan replied.

'Wonderful idea. To Edith. I'll leave you two lovebirds alone. I am sure you will enjoy your meal.'

'Come on now, how did you manage this?'

'He's a client. I know a lot of important people.'

'I wish you didn't.'

'Now Alan, don't spoil it.'

'But you know already that–'

I interrupted him, as I could see it in his eyes. 'What?' I asked.

'That I love you.'

I reached over the table, squeezed his hand and smiled.

We enjoyed the rest of the evening although he seemed a little quieter than he was on our first date, but he cheered up when we arrived back at the shop. Must have been because he was on his own territory and not out of his depth.

'Come on, I'll make you a cup of coffee. And next time, I'll take you out and we'll have fish and chips.'

'That reminds me. I've got to go to Southend on Friday to look at some furniture. Would you like to come?'

'I would love to, but I can't tell you until tomorrow as I'll have to speak to the cat sitter.'

'You got a cat?'

'Yes.'

'Can you phone her?'

'Of course, I can.'

'Use the one in the office.'

I went into the office, picked up the phone and dialled our number, which even in those days was ex-directory. I could sense that he was listening.

'Could I speak to Mary, please? That was the code as Maud came to the phone.

'Mary, can you look after the cat on Friday please?'

'Is that all night?' Maud asked.

'Wait a minute.'

I went to the foot of the stairs and shouted, 'Will that be until Saturday afternoon?'

'Yeah, if you like,' he replied.

'Yes Mary, until at least midday Saturday. Oh that will be wonderful. Thanks Mary, you're an angel.'

I put the phone down and quickly looked out of the

window, taking in all that was necessary to do the job.

'I'm yours all day and night,' I said, returning to his side.

I made the coffee and we sat in the lounge. 'Did you really mean what you said, that you love me?' I asked. 'But you don't even know anything about me. The problem is Alan, I think I am falling in love with you.'

'Come on, it's getting too serious! Let's go down to the shop and sit on that lovely chaise longue.'

I loved it. He was such an expert, gentle and caring as well as exciting. Then up to the bedroom for another serious talk as he wanted to tell me he didn't tell all his other girlfriends that he loved them. I brought him back to reality when I said, 'I never tell my clients I love them either.'

'You are special, Edith.'

'Pull yourself together ... what do you want me to wear on Friday?'

'Something sexy.'

'I can't be sexy all the time – maybe just at night. I could wear something nice to meet your clients.'

'Okay.'

'Now you book the hotel but I'll pay. If you say no, I won't come.'

'Okay.'

'What time shall I be here?'

'I could pick you up.'

'No, No, No. I don't want you to see my ...' I paused ... 'My place of business.'

'The Temple station at ten o'clock.'

'I'll be there. Don't be late. I won't wait.'

He was so gentle as he undressed me, teasing the clothes from my body and pulling me close to his chest. He held me powerless in his arms as he took me, all night. Where he got his energy from, I will never know, but I remember beginning to feel bad about setting him up, especially when I didn't want to leave him.

I made him breakfast, full English with toast and tea and sat down with him in total silence, behaving as though it was the last time we would see each other before making the same journey home.

I remember I even met the same copper.

'I see you've been to the same party then?' I said before he had the chance to reply.

I thought he was quite observant when he said, 'I see you've changed though.'

'You noticed, you naughty boy!'

Bif soon arrived and took me home. 'Did we get what was needed?' he asked.

'What do you mean?'

'Oh, come on Mother, you know very well.'

'Yes, I did. It's a very easy entrance at the back, but you'll have to have a look today as he is only away Friday and Saturday. Sheila goes home early on a Friday and normally the shop shuts around five o'clock. I think it will be earlier with Alan away from the place.'

'It's Alan now is it, Mother?'

'Yes it is, and I like him, but business is business.'

I walked in to be greeted by Maud. Thank God we were alone.

'What have you been doing? You're walking like a stuffed camel. On second thoughts, don't tell me. Now Edie, for God's sake be careful – he's a bloody villain and a major fence.'

'Maudie ... something's happened to me. I can't help myself. Do me a favour and leave the Victorian chaise longue that's in the far corner, together with a few other pieces to make it look like there was no room. By the way, the keys for the van are in the desk in the office.'

'Just be bloody careful and remember what I said,' Maud replied.

D-Day arrived and I was soon on my way to the station, worrying myself silly at what Maudie had said. It was spot on ten o'clock when I arrived, wearing my black velvet suit, white polo-necked sweater and black boots. II was carrying my suitcase with all my other gear in it – just what every business woman needed.

Ten minutes went by and no Alan. I couldn't believe he was late. In fact, I thought I saw him drive past. It was now half past ten and I was beginning to get upset and wanted to leave, but just couldn't. 'I'll give him another five minutes,' I said quietly to myself, only to be asked:

'Has he stood you up, love?'

'I think so,' I replied.

'More fool him.'

'It was a her,' I said mischievously which caused him to disappear quickly.

I had now given him forty-five minutes, something I wouldn't have dreamed possible, when the horn pipped, and he was there. He leaned over and opened the door. I opened the back, threw my case in and jumped into the front.

'I thought you weren't coming,' I said, almost in tears.

'I wanted to know how you felt about me. If someone's late, I won't wait.'

'Oh, you cruel bugger. You know I love you.'

'That's all I wanted to hear.'

We drove along the Mile End Road and out towards Southend. He looked like the cat that got the cream – as smug as you like.

'Well, do you like what you see?'

'Yes, you look beautiful, Edith. You're too good for me.'

'What? And you kept me waiting for forty-five minutes! You wait till I'll get my own back.'

We arrived at the hotel in Southend. It was nothing out of the ordinary but it was clean and convenient. I hadn't wanted it to be too expensive for obvious reasons. We were just in time for lunch, but with enough time to see the solicitor beforehand to confirm the arrangements for the afternoon. The secretary confirmed that we should meet at 45 Benmore Road.

We had a lovely walk along the promenade with this lovesick woman holding onto him like a besotted schoolgirl. He walked so proudly with me on his arm; he seemed to want to show everyone.

—You know, Mr White, our group of friends and acquaintances knew what I was worth financially and would have liked a taste of the money. Here I had a man who wanted me for what he thought I was, just an ordinary woman, doing a bit of business. It was like Maudie's Peter.

'Only he wasn't a villain,' Maud interrupted.

It was refreshing and lovely and I responded to it.

Lunch over, we went to the house – a very large double-fronted mansion which had been lived in by a woman on her own for over fifty years and it had been in her family longer than that.

'Do you want to wait in the car?' Alan asked as we pulled into the drive.

'No, I'd like to be with you.'

'Come on then, let's go.'

Mr Springbourne, the solicitor was waiting for us. 'Good afternoon. Springbourne … David Springbourne,' he said, holding his hand out.

'Alan Wright, and this is my …' He paused momentarily. 'Assistant. Edith Trenchard,' I answered for him, holding my hand out to shake his. He took it and smiled.

The preliminaries over and we began our survey, entering the drawing room first of all, only to be confronted by three beautiful chaises longue, which made us to burst out laughing. I explained to the solicitor that we had just turned down six others. Alan squeezed my arm when he thought no one was looking.

I loved doing this as I adored our antiques at home, and by the time we had finished, I had it all marked up and away.

'I'll let you have our offer next week and tell you when we can remove it.'

'I bet she's worth her weight in gold,' Springbourne whispered to Alan. 'She knows her job!'

'Yeah, she does, and keep your mitts off!' They both laughed together.

It was the autumn and becoming a little colder every day. I hadn't thought to bring a coat with me, so Alan decided that he would buy me one and no matter how much I objected, he was insistent. We called into several shops before he saw the one he wanted me to have.

I couldn't believe it. It was a continuation of the posh whore theme. An off-white leopard-spotted fur coat that cost £80. It was a little expensive in those days.

'Oh Alan, you mustn't! It's beautiful.' I could have been sick, but hadn't the heart to tell him. It really didn't go with the black velvet, but I must confess it went well with the whore's outfit which is what he wanted me to wear in the evening.

We returned to the hotel where he had booked us in as Mr and Mrs Wright, giving his correct address, surprisingly. I decided to change early as he was taking me to the Pavilion Theatre for a variety show and then for the promised fish and chips. He was a strange fellow for he loved me as the common-looking woman, a bit of rough, but the moment I put the whore's outfit on, he wanted to take it off. I think he had me four times before I was able to leave the room dressed in my outfit and new fur coat.

'You look lovely, darling,' he said as he put my arm through his, walked me down the stairs and into the street. He decided it would be nice if we popped into the Last Post for a quick drink before the theatre.

'Chavin?' he asked.

'Half a bitter, please.'

'Right love, wait there.' He sat me down on the bench seat all on my own, encouraging all and sundry to stare or chat me up.

'On yer own darlin,'?' was the first.

'Well, yes at the moment, but me date's over there buying us a drink,' I answered in a cockney accent.

I did look a dog but he loved it, and I loved him. Theatre followed the drink and my long awaited walk on the pier with a bag of chips ended a lovely day. We began to walk back to the hotel when I realised that Maudie and the boys were in the middle of their burglary and I began to get worried. What if something went wrong? Would the boys get locked up? That was something I didn't want to happen.

'What's the matter?' he asked. 'You seem upset.'

'I am. I'm going to work in the south of France for the winter. I won't be back until March, and I don't want to leave you.'

'Edith, will you marry me?'

'I can't. You don't know anything about me.'

'I don't care. I just want you.'

'I can't. Come on, let's go back to the pub. We can just get a quick one in if we hurry.'

We sat in the snug, just staring into space like an old married couple who had run out of things to say to each other.

We finally got back to our hotel and lay in bed thinking for a while when he asked again if I would marry him.

'We've only known each other for a few days.'

'Well, come and live with me. I can afford it. You needn't work. I make enough for the two of us.'

It was really tempting. 'Can I stay with you over the weekend?'

'Yes, please.'

I fell asleep through sheer exhaustion, but poor Alan had to wake me up and have his wicked way – twice. By now I was getting used to his desires.

We were up bright and early, and when I asked him what he wanted me to wear, he replied with a huge grin on his face:

'The coat!' He was like a little schoolboy who had given the teacher an apple.

We set off for London with me snuggled up to him in his coat the whole way, only to be greeted by David in a dreadful state when we arrived at the shop.

'We've been robbed!' he yelled. 'Everyfink's gone. They've taken the van as well and no one saw a thing. They thought we were working late.'

Clever old Maudie, I thought.

'What do ya mean, "Everyfink's gone"?'

'Just that! It's gone – the safe – the lot! There are just a few pieces left.'

'Call the police,' I said.

'No, don't do that. I'll get it back. I'll find out who's done this. Don't you worry. Someone will talk.'

'Alan? Call the police!'

'I can't.'

'Why not?'

'It's business.'

I made him a cup of coffee and we sat down to talk about it.

'It will finish us. They've taken all the cash as well.'

'It won't. You'll get the Southend lot. That will keep you going.'

I eventually convinced him that he still had a chance. Not only that, he still had the chaise longue, which at least brought a smile to his face.

The phone rang. It was the police, reporting that Alan's

van had been discovered at Blessington Hall loaded with their furniture, which had been stolen a couple of weeks before.

'Look, darlin', I don't want you mixed up in this. I think it better you go.'

'I don't want to. I want to stay with you.'

'Look, it really would be better for both of us if you went. I couldn't bear to see you caught up in this mess.'

After about an hour of pleading, and a phone call from the police to say they were coming over, I left. I remember asking if I could keep the coat. We only managed a few kisses before the taxi arrived.

'Please don't forget I love you,' he said as I got into the taxi.

That was it. What started as a prank turned into a romance that I didn't want to end. I left mouthing the words, ' I love you too'. I went through a similar ruse to avoid being identified and arrived home to a very joyful Maud who had succeeded in not only returning the stolen property, but also taking £2,300 from Alan's safe which she gave to Dr Barnardo's in Alan's name.

I wrote to him saying I was on my way to France and would write again with my new address when I got there. Alan was remanded in custody for receiving stolen goods and asked for a number of offences to be taken into consideration. He got four years and had to serve a minimum of three. It was all very sad because I enjoyed myself for a short time.

As I said, Maud was full of it when I returned, explaining how they came near to disaster. 'You tell it, Maudie.'

Maud continues ...

It didn't need much planning as they never dreamed they would be robbed, so we decided to take a Mini Cooper as our getaway car because we could easily lose any followers, particularly down the back alleys in London's East End and, by now Bif was an expert driver in this car.

We arrived at the rear to find the van had been parked up as expected, very conveniently so, having reversed up to the back door. We immediately started work. Within two minutes, we were all inside .The only real security in place was the back door, but that was easily overcome by going through the rotten window frame just at the side. The main door could then be easily opened from the inside.

I was cross with myself for overlooking one of the main points: a lorry delivering potatoes to the chip shop five doors away – ten hundred weight sacks of Maris Piper potatoes. I'll never forget them. The lorry was blocking our escape.

We either had to carry them for him or move the car and then the van. We discovered the Mini had got a puncture. It was getting like Piccadilly Circus. Edith never said it was busy.

'I didn't know, did I?' Edith interrupted.
Bif volunteered to carry the spuds. Half a ton of them, the forty yards to the chip shop. The driver couldn't help as he had a bad back. Half an hour later, Bif had finished and then had to repair the puncture, whilst I helped Stanley to carry some of the goods to the van.

'Is Big Al there?' a voice suddenly said, as Bif was struggling with the wheel. He nearly jumped out of his skin.

'Oh! Bloody hell. You scared me. Who are you?' he shouted.

The two of us stopped work and quickly hid behind the furniture, daring not to breathe in case whoever it was came in.

'Fillibut Willey.'
'Who?'
'Oh, just tell him Willey wants him.'

'I'll get him.'

Bif returned to the shop where I told Bif to tell him Big Al was on the phone and that he would see him later.

'Big Al thought it would be you,' Bif told Willey on returning outside.

'He always does, the little bastard,' said Willey.

'He's on the phone,' Bif continued, 'and we've got to get this lot out, otherwise the bloke won't have them. Can he see you later?'

'Okay, but tell 'im it's urgent.'

Bif came back into the shop. Big smiles and we all breathed again. I felt like saying he was as big a liar as his mother ... in a nice way.

He went back to changing the wheel and eventually, covered in grease, came back to help us.

It took us another two hours to finish loading the van. During that time, you have never seen so many people passing by, oblivious to the fact that we were robbing the place. They must have been locals who thought we were working late.

One of them commented: 'He's keeping you late tonight. 'Ope he's paying you well.'

Stanley was sensible enough to say nothing as we all knew businessmen wouldn't pay that well unless it was dodgy.

I left the rest of the loading to the boys and went to the safe – my speciality. It was a cranky old thing with a mind of its own. What with the noise in the alley and the traffic outside, it was difficult to listen to the sound of the tumblers and open the safe. It took me about forty minutes instead of twenty, the last ten of which was causing Stanley some anxiety.

Every two minutes or so, he would say, 'Come on, mother. Leave it. We've got what we came for.'

Finally, the safe was open and we retrieved all the

documents and £2,300 in cash. Bif and I went off in the Mini and Stanley was to follow. We set off down the alley and waited and waited. No Stanley. Bif backed up the road to find out what was wrong. Stanley finally arrived in a state of panic, and swearing like a trooper. He wasn't used to driving a van so Bif told Stanley to go with me and he took over.

The Bedford had a diesel engine with a heater fitted and this had to be pressed until the green light went off and then the engine would start. Bif's tractor had a similar starting mechanism.

We arrived at Blessington Hall around eleven o'clock that night and left the van in the middle of the drive, hoping it would be found the following morning. It was a wonderful feeling to have some good come out of a burglary like this. I think it helped Edie as I believe she was in love with this Alan and would perhaps have done something silly.

'I suppose I was beginning to like him very much,' Edith added, 'but I realised I could not go on with Alan, not because he was in prison, but because he had a picture of me in his mind that didn't exist. I was not a whore ...'

'A bit of a floozy perhaps,' Maud interjected.

***

Edith finishes the story ...

It was a game, but I did love Alan for what he gave me. He wanted me for who I was ... not for what I was worth. After a few weeks in Nice, a couple of dates with Laurent du Pont and several fabulous parties, I realised that there was life after death. I did miss his lovemaking though.

However, I felt guilty about what I had done and duty bound to help Alan and David indirectly. They won the contract to buy the antiques at Southend, which gave the shop a new lease of life with plenty of stock, which I had to bank roll. David agreed to pay 10% of all sales to Charlie from the restaurant, and he looked after the money for me, acting as the telephone-go-between.

Poor Old busty Sheila lost her job and I assisted in appointing a new secretary, who was a very good bookkeeper, and manager, paying her a secret bonus each half year to encourage her to stay. By golly, she sharpened David up too, as I had explained about David's slovenliness. No longer did he have the dirty suits, scruffy shoes and unkempt hair – he began to take a pride in himself.

I had to help David run the business, which was mainly done over the phone through Charlie and I would call him back. I also called David several times to ensure he was okay. In fact, I think David thought of me as his mother because I would shout at him if I had been told he had his breakfast or dinner on show. I told him that he was in charge and that it was his duty to run the shop as he was the businessman now. I could sense his chest was expanding when I made him feel important. It didn't happen straight away but he did prove himself and the calls for help became fewer. He paid me back all the monies lent, through Charlie. After three years, Alan was released from prison and went to see Charlie to ask if I would contact him, but I couldn't. That had been a different life.

Charlie told me that Alan was a broken man, very grey and had lost his gruff macho image, but he was so grateful I had helped him and would never forget me. He also said he would never sell the chaise longue in the corner of the shop. It would be kept there until I wished to fetch it. He told Charlie to say that I would know what he meant.

I never did see him again, but I did call at the shop a few times and it was still there. However, I would add that in the end, they had a very successful and legitimate business.

Chapter 13
Time and Tide

Maud was as keen as ever to have a break and enjoy the sun. We immediately reinstated our tickets and took the Blue Train to Nice which was not as pleasant as it had previously been. It had lost all its glamour and this was the last time we travelled this way. From then on, it was by aeroplane, which at the time was more expensive and unexciting, but of course, that didn't matter as it was a lot quicker.

There really was nothing like the Blue Train in its heyday – so much atmosphere. The cabins were luxurious with plenty of room and the chefs in the dining car were second to none. It was a magical feeling looking out of the window whilst you sipped your claret. You passed the little stations lit by a solitary gas light over the station name. Eventually, you arrived in Paris into the dimly lit Gare du Nord to take on a few more passengers, before continuing onto Lyon and the south. You returned to your cabin and fell asleep to the soporific melody made by the wheels over the lines, only to be broken momentarily by the little rumble as it passed over the points, ensuring we were going in the right direction. Then sleep would follow until the steward tapped on the door to announce:

'Madame, we will be in Nice in one hour.'

Father would never allow us to eat in our cabin, and that continues today, so it was the dining car once again. Where they got those fresh, delicious baguettes and croissants from, I will never know. I can smell them now.

However, I am digressing. On this occasion, we took the train, Bif following in the car. It took him three days to join us. Mind you, he did go and meet Yvette somewhere along the way.

The fun started the moment we arrived in the south. The invites for afternoon tea or parties on a Saturday night, which seemed to be every Saturday night, came flooding in. There was even the occasional party midweek.

Bif was rapidly becoming a very eligible, good-looking bachelor. Of course, his potential wealth meant he was duly invited. But he wasn't interested; always having a soft spot for Yvette, the girl he used to play with in the streets of Ventimiglia when he was a boy. That light never dimmed. In fact, it blossomed on this trip and we knew it would end in marriage.

Yvette was, and still is, a lovely girl and never wanted anything more than a contented marriage. She never wanted the wealth that came with us and always seemed totally satisfied with her lot.

I always had a strange feeling when I saw Bif with his wartime mother, as I called her. I was never jealous, even though he was very affectionate towards her. I actually thought it was lovely. Maud would often advise me to be careful in case he decided to want to stay. I was philosophical though and accepted that if he wanted that at his age, it had to be. He always came home though and even when he married Yvette, they came to live at the Hall.

***

I believe the most exciting burglary we ever did was shortly after we arrived in France. As I said the invitations came rolling in and we had accepted most of those we had received, but although pleasant, one was very much like the other, and things were becoming a little boring.

One particular invitation fascinated us, which we

accepted; in fact all the family were invited. It was a wild extravagant party, hosted by Michael Freisman to celebrate his son, Donald's selection to the Nice First Team at polo. It was also Donald's birthday. He was a good-looking boy and loved the ladies. 'Anything from sixteen to sixty,' he was known to say. He would often take his lovers, of which there were many, to a little hotel at the back of the town near the railway station, which allowed that sort of thing. He would always spend the night with them, have his wicked way a few times and then dump them.

He was not a nice person, always bragging about what he had got, never what his parents had done for him. He had never really worked and his father simply gave him an allowance. He tended to knock around with eighteen-to twenty-year-old lads where he could be the king dick and they would take advantage of his generosity, which he threw around in abundance. He was simply a lazy self-opinionated bastard.

The family were nouveau riche and really lived up to the fact. It was now their chance to mix with the permanent rich and the so-called minor aristocracy – as I am sure you are aware polo is a rich man's sport. Their house or villa, as Michael loved to call it, was situated in the old town, overlooking the sea. It had a beautiful terrace which ran the entire perimeter of the villa on the ground floor, with an identical terrace on the first floor, where there were ten beautiful bedrooms. It was also blest with wonderful views of Nice and the surrounding countryside, and only five minutes' walk from the sea. The gardens were magnificent, almost a carbon copy of the Mediterranean gardens at Rayol Canadel between Le Lavendu and St Tropez. Absolutely spectacular. I think it belonged to one of the early film moguls from the turn of the twentieth century.

We arrived at the party, which was to be held both indoors and out as it was a lovely warm evening. The host and hostess, an elegant couple received guests at the main entrance. That said, Michael Freisman should have at least found out the guests' names, instead of introducing himself and then asking each one who they were. I can't tolerate this sort of ignorant snobbery and it gave me a lovely opportunity to tease.

'Good evening,' he said. 'I'm Michael Freisman and this is my wife Mary, and you are?'

'Oh, I'm Edith Trenchard and this is my housekeeper, Maud, Yvette our cook and this is Bif our head gardener,' I said, causing Yvette to titter somewhat. 'Now you two!' I said, turning to the youngsters and surreptitiously winking at them, 'I want you to behave this evening. We are guests in this gentleman's house.'

I hope you don't mind, Michael,' I said, taking his arm. 'There were six invitations and I didn't want to waste them. Hopefully, Alice and Stanley will be along shortly. They do the cleaning; they don't get many treats.'

You have never seen two people so completely taken aback. Mary was wide eyed and open-mouthed and our host was speechless. I grabbed him by his arm and waltzed him into the villa, to be greeted by the butler for want of a better expression.

'Thank you, Malcolm, you better go and attend to your other guests,' I said, quickly being corrected by Philipe the butler.

'It's Michael, not Malcolm.'

'Oh dear. No matter. He didn't know my name either.'

'Edith, you're terrible. You shouldn't behave like that,' Maud said.

'Why not? We could have some fun!'

Then of course, his forgetful father had to introduce Donald Duck, his wonderful son.

'Donald, this is Edith Trenchard ... her housekeeper,' he said, gesturing to Maud, 'the head gardener and the cook.

She thought she would use the invitations up as the others couldn't come,' he added, still in a state of mild shock.

Naturally, Donald had to leave because he did not consider us important enough to stay and chat, so we were simply brushed off and encouraged to mingle with the ever growing crowd.

Of course, we knew many people and many knew us or of us, so we were soon comfortably in the thick of things. This scenario fascinated Mary, our hostess and she couldn't take her eyes off us. It seemed she couldn't understand why so many people would bother to greet the chief cook and bottle washer, and kiss them on both cheeks, as is the French way of greeting. I remember noticing her standing in the doorway of their lounge when she was drawn into a conversation with one of the groups passing through. You could tell she was intrigued, especially when I heard her ask:

'Who are those people over there?'

'Those next to Edie and Maud Trenchard?' the one asked.

'No. Those with the woman in the red dress.'

'That *is* Edith Trenchard! And you don't know her? the guest replied, somewhat surprised. 'Good Lord! That's her sister Maud. They're one of the richest families in Britain. They live at Number 17 Watling Street. It's a big joke within certain circles.'

'Why's that?' Mary asked.

'All I know is that they live in a palace of a place, on a forty thousand-acre estate, not far from London.'

'Who's that young man with them?'

'That's Bif, Edith's son, and Yvette his bride to be. They were childhood sweethearts. Edith has two children and Maud has a son called Stanley. He's a city whiz kid and rumour has it, he doubled their fortune in just a few years, which was big enough even before that.'

I could see her scurry off to chat to her husband, both

returning to have a look at the guest list.

I saw them staring in our direction and gave them a little wave, only to be saved by the bell as Donald Duck and some of his teenagers arrived to liven up the place. The disc jockey also began with a few of Elvis Presley ballads, to put us in the mood. It worked, that was until Michael Freisman decided to make one of his many announcements. The band stopped with a roll of the drums and there was silence.

—Mr White, I told you earlier about Maud's kleptomania problem and the difficulties she had as a child. Unfortunately, this has carried on into her later life. I know she won't mind me telling you but when she is not occupied or becomes bored, there is a danger she will amuse herself by removing things that don't belong to her. It doesn't take long for boredom to set in and this occasion just happened to be one of them.

Michael began:

'Ladies and gentleman. This little get-together is purely and simply for a few friends to have a good time and celebrate our son's twenty-fifth birthday. As you will all be aware he has been selected to play for the Nice Polo Team. To commemorate this, we have bought him this lovely watch and would like him to come and accept it.'

Of course, we all clapped and cheered and congratulated him. I suppose it was quite an achievement. He then announced that the buffet would be served in the lounge and on the terrace, and for us to help ourselves. The champagne and other drinks, on the other hand, were constantly served by a team of waiters, brought in for the night. It was well organised.

By now, Maudie was bored stiff and went on the rampage, only to return with her handbag, which was now bulging.

—I tell you, Mr White, she was good at it!

'Edie! Help! I've got too many,' she said.

'What, darling?'

She opened her bag to reveal an array of wallets and ladies' purses.

'Where can we put them?'

'Oh God! Where does Lady Bountiful keep hers? Pop them in her bag. It will give her something to think about.' Lady Bountiful was, of course, our hostess. Maud quickly closed her bag with a struggle because we could see Michael approaching us. I think it was more out of duty than anything, but this time showing more interest in our well-being than previously.

He looked straight at me first of all. 'You're Edith?' he asked, 'and you must be Maud?' he remarked, smiling at her.

'Yes,' we replied in unison.

'Well, Edith,' he began. 'May I call you Edith?'

'I think you already did.' He smiled nervously, perhaps to hide his embarrassment.

'You are a tease,' he continued. I just smiled and he signalled for his son to come and meet me.

'You have some lovely paintings and I am envious of one or two of them,' Maud suddenly announced, which made Michael grow in stature.

'I'll show you them if you like?'

'Yes, I would love to see them,' Maud replied, showing genuine interest.

'Hello Donald,' I said as he approached.

'Oh! You know my name?' he said, sticking his chest out.

'Of course I do. I think everyone does. Your father has just told us all it's your birthday,' I replied, causing his chest to shrink back in. Michael then formally introduced us to Donald.

'Edith, I'll leave you in Donald's capable hands. Come on, Maud, I'll show you the works of art.'

Clutching her bulging bag, Maud went off with Michael, leaving me with wonder son.

We chatted for a while before he asked me to dance.
'I love Presley, don't you?' he said, leading me onto the dance floor to rock and roll.

He was such a smoothie; really fancied himself especially now that he was wearing his new watch. He was so proud of it, telling everyone in turn that it was a Rolex and cost over £15,000; glorifying in the price rather than the quality. So typical of the nouveau riche but he was a young lad and ... tempting.

The dance finished and I was left like a little wallflower waiting for someone or other to invite me for the next one, when Maudie came back, looking very excited. She told me she had been to Michael's study to look at the paintings and discovered a little safe behind one of them – a safe very similar to one she opened in the Bahamas.

I was intrigued by Edith's latest revelation about the Bahamas but Maud suddenly castigated her for having mentioned it. This further aroused my curiosity and I had to ask Maud what it was all about, but she was as secretive as ever. All she would tell me was that she had been sent to the Bahamas to open and steal the contents of a safe because an important person over there was believed to be involved with the Nazis. All the papers were given to Mr Churchill and the War Cabinet. Edith realised her mistake and apologised for mentioning it.

Where's the booty?' I asked, noticing that her bag was empty.

'Oh! I saw a handbag in the study and popped them in whilst he was showing me some delicate art work. I hope it was his wife's,' she said, chuckling like a naughty schoolgirl.

Donald came back and invited me onto the floor again, this time for a quickstep which was actually all he could do – just step quickly, but at least I was getting to know him and he was holding me tightly, which was my cue.

'Mmm, you're strong,' I whispered, looking into his eyes and smiling. 'I love to be held tightly like this.'

He visibly grew taller and I could almost hear him thinking what he was going to do to me. And all the time I was thinking that he was already mine and I would play with him a little. We had been dancing for a few minutes when he asked me to have a drink with him, which I did, giving me a chance to enjoy the amazing buffet.

It consisted of almost every type of shellfish available from the Med, almost all the different meats, the freshest of vegetables, and salads and fruits from all over the world. It was impressive to say the least. Donald managed to eat a little but after couple more glasses of champagne, he was becoming playful, easy meat now, so to speak, especially when we tried to drink the last one linked through each other's arms. As for the sausages on sticks – now there was a double innuendo.

Maud came over again with her little bag bulging and whispered, 'Can you keep him occupied? I'm going to take a look at that safe. Don't let him go into the study.'

Well that was manna from heaven for me. 'Have you been at it again?' She nodded. 'Where are you going to put them? Silly question. In the safe?'

Maud nodded again.

On Maud's orders, I got down to my task of looking after Donald, only to realise that everyone was becoming aware of his demeanour. One caring guest reminded me he was a terror with the ladies. I nearly shouted, 'Mind your own business.' Instead, I asked Donald if he wanted to show me what a terror he was.

He nearly fell over himself to say yes. 'Where?' he asked excitedly. 'Your car?'

'Don't be silly. Your bedroom, of course.'

'Oh, I can't … my father …'

'Oh I'm sorry. I thought you were twenty-five,' I added, putting the knife in.

'I am! Hang on a minute. I'll see what I–'

'Don't be silly. The moment will be lost. It's now. The moment is now.' I turned round to the buffet table. 'I think I would prefer one of those pork pies,' I said, not realising the impact of such a remark.

I walked over to the table and helped myself to one or two delights, including the pork pie, leaving his ego to deflate before me. I rejoined the others and was having a chat with Maud, when Donald approached and requested another dance. In fact, he pestered for some time before I broke loose and went to the toilet. Imagine the shock when he was outside waiting for me.

'Come on. I want to show you something,' he said, taking hold of my hand and leading me to his bedroom.

'I wonder what that can be?' I asked cheekily.

He opened the door and pulled me inside despite some false resistance on my part. He closed the door, quickly turned the key and began to strip off, leaving me to stand and watch. He certainly had a lovely physique.

'Edith! Which do you prefer now? This or the pork pie?' he asked as he was now sans underpants.

'Well, I did like the chipolatas.'

He stood there like a Greek god, totally naked, and obviously very fit. He didn't bother to take my dress off; he simply went straight to the knickers. A crash onto the bed and he was away. I must admit I did enjoy the Bratwurst for breakfast and it was lovely to have a young body enveloping my soul. I know he really appreciated what I had to offer. The session was ruined by none other than Maudie, who having successfully done her duty, had seen Donald follow me to the toilet and hadn't returned. She thought I might be in difficulty.

She listened carefully to the noises emanating from the

rooms and I was disgusted to think that she thought we were having it away against a door.

We heard her call out: 'Edie, are you all right?' No reply forthcoming, she then knocked on a door, causing some man to pop his head out and tell her to piss off. She never did see who the female was. At the third attempt, I came out of the room, looking reasonably respectable and inviting Donald to do the same.

He was now very embarrassed, especially when I said, 'Maudie, you know Donald, don't you?' She nodded.

'Now Donald, don't be shy. You were very good. Come on.' I took a bemused Donald by the hand to the top of the stairs and left him to join Maudie who was on her way to the bathroom.

'What on earth have you done with him?' she asked me. 'He looks as though he's been hypnotised.'

'Given him a lesson.'

'In what?' she asked rhetorically, as we walked down the stairs, with me having not a care in the world.

'Well ... did you see inside?'

'Of course I did. It was like old times.'

'I see you managed to deposit the booty.'

'Yes, it's safe now.' She burst out laughing at her little pun.

'Anything interesting?'

'There were just business papers and a little money, which I left, but what about this?' she said, opening her little bag to reveal a most beautiful diamond bracelet. It really was quite exquisite and she loved wearing it when we got home. I was extremely jealous.

The party went well and we all enjoyed ourselves. That was until we saw a few people appearing perplexed and looking under tables, having mislaid some of their possessions.

'I'm sure I was sitting somewhere round here,' one lady said to her husband, who was also looking for his wallet.

It was time for Maud to stop giggling as she was getting me going and that would look obvious. I decided it was time to leave, mentioning to Michael that if he found a little red clutch bag, it was mine. I was now one of the unfortunates who had lost something.

Bif and Yvette had left early, preferring their own company so it was a taxi for Maud and I. Poor Donald's appetite was whetted, and he was once again pestering me, not wanting me to go. Quite flattering actually, but now he wanted to take me out. I must admit I fancied the idea and agreed to meet him sometime the following week.

We chatted to our host and hostess for a few minutes, thanking them for a wonderful party, which it was. We said our goodbyes and took our leave, wondering how on earth they were going to explain away all the stolen goods and what Michael would do about the bracelet.

The following Wednesday Donald picked me up in his little TR4 sports car and drove into Nice where we had a few drinks before driving to this bijou three-star hotel near the railway station. I remember we arrived just after nine o'clock and walked in, where he was obviously known and where he had his key to the room already in his hand – room number 126.

The concierge greeted him as we passed the desk on the way to the lift, but the way he looked at me was not pleasant. It was as though I was another of his client's easy meats, which to him I suppose I was. It really upset me, but at least this was a new experience. The lift was one of those old- fashioned contraptions where you slid a concertina iron gate across, then another on the lift itself, and the reverse when you stepped in. The moment you pressed the button to go up, the whole world could see up your skirt as the lift ascended.

—I wish I had been wearing knickers, Mr White.

'Edith!' Maud shouted. 'Don't be so disgusting.'

—Just kidding, Mr White. I was really. Well, at least I was wearing them on the way down. Anyway, Maud, Mr White is surely not one of those men who think a woman's place is in the home, are you, Mr White?

I didn't answer.

We stood side by side staring into space as the lift trundled up to the second floor.

'Donald darling, are you nervous?'

'Good Lord, no,' he replied, continuing to stare into space.

'Well, we are a chatty little soul, aren't we?'

He was saved from further embarrassment as the lift shuddered to a stop at the second floor. The gates clanged as he slid them open to reveal a long corridor, which was only lit by the light that escaped from the lift. As the lift descended, the pitch black darkness was broken by Donald's experienced hand pressing a well-positioned time delay switch on the wall, giving you about thirty seconds to enter your room. We had arrived at room 126.

He opened the door, allowing me to enter first. It was adequately furnished – bathroom en-suite, settee and a pair of very large comfortable chairs set around a gas fire and of course, the double bed, surrounded by a dressing table, and even a writing desk and chair.

'What are you expecting?' I asked, causing him to be embarrassed once more.

'I thought er … you …er …'

'You what?'

'You wanted er … um …'

'I do, but you could be a bit more subtle.'

'Sorry.'

'Come here and I'll let you sample the delights of experience.'

I gently and subtlety teased the clothes from his body until he was naked. Well, not wholly naked – he still had his bloody watch on.

'Now run the bath,' I said as I slipped off my clothes down to my slip and followed the naked young man into the bathroom.

He was a romantic lover, you know. I told him to get into the bath and I followed. Then he began:

'It's waterproof, you know.'

'What is?' I asked, somewhat bemused.

'My watch, of course.'

'Oh,' I replied, sighing. 'Fantastic.'

This was the so-called stag with his own bordello, and here he was in the middle of a session, talking about his watch. It didn't do much for my ego I have to say, so I decided to get my own back.

'Well, this is a sorry little thing,' I teased, feeling around in the water. 'Whoops, it's gone! Now where is the little boy? You're … a virgin!' I exclaimed. 'Oh dear, our big tough boy is a virgin. Wait till I tell them at the club.' That pulled him up by his boot straps.

'I'm not!' he protested.

'Oh, yes you are! Come here, my little virgin. Let's see what you've got.' I splashed around in the water, pretending to search for his manhood. 'No, can't find it.' This put him off even more as he protested vehemently, so it was now time to relax him or I would miss out. After a little more wriggling in the bath and a gentle massaging here and there, things started to improve.

From his behaviour, he had obviously been used to a quick bonk and an 'off you go' type of arrangement. Certainly not one that enjoyed the pleasure of the chase and the capture, Although we now had the pill, most women were still very nervous of having sex in case the contraception didn't work. I wasn't the least bit worried. Anyway, by the time we had finished in the bath, he was exhausted, the water had gone cold and he was still wearing his watch.

'Has it stopped?' I asked.

'What?'

'Your watch.'

You would not believe the panic on his face until he checked all was well.

'No, it's fine.'

We dried off and he began to get dressed. 'What on *earth* are you doing?' I asked.

'We'll have to go.'

'What! Does Daddy want his little boy in by eleven? I thought you were a big boy. Now get your bum in that bed. I haven't finished with you yet. And another thing – if you think I'm going home before breakfast tomorrow morning, you've got another think coming. And ... if you are able to walk to the lift after I have finished with you, I will have failed in my duty.

His mouth dropped.

'Get in, or I'll tell every member of the Nice Polo Club what you are like in bed! Now get in!'

Believe it or not, he took his watch off and put it on the bedside table!

He was hard work but by the morning, he needed to take the lift down to breakfast. We hardly spoke to each other as we ate fresh croissants, pains au chocolat and a cup of the very best French coffee in one of those very large bowls, which were popular in those days.

It was obvious that the norm for Donald was to leave before breakfast especially as the proprietor, who was also acting as a waiter, came over to the table and explained in French to Donald that this time he would have to pay for breakfast.

He answered in a bravado sort of way: 'Pas de problème.' Being the arrogant sort, I guessed he wouldn't for one minute think I could speak French, so I laid on the flattery.

'You speak French then?'

'Of course.'

'What was all that about?' I asked.

'Oh, it's nothing. Just a little arrangement I have with the owner. He's a friend of mine.'

I tried not to laugh as he struggled to his feet and hobbled out of the dining room. Every now and then I would enquire of his well-being if only to maintain my advantage and keep up the pressure. We returned to the room to collect our things, but before doing so, I opened the windows and shutters and walked out onto the balcony to take a welcome breath of fresh air. It was a typical French building, but this was a little different as there was one continuous balcony to the front and individual ones to the rear. It was a delight to see a few trees and flower beds. His room was at the back, freshly painted, not dim and unkempt as they often are.

'It's quite nice out here,' I remarked. 'Come and look.' He was reluctant, as I discovered my little one-night stand had never been outside on the balcony because he suffered from vertigo. I took hold of his hand and led him outside. I could feel him tense up.

'Come on, I'm sorry,' I said as I led him back inside. 'You poor old thing. Come here and let me hold you.' He was like a little boy doing as he was told and it wasn't long before he was on the bed again, putting the finishing touches to the last few remarkable hours.

'Edith, you are unbelievable and fantastic. Can I see you again?' he asked as we walked out of the room to the lift.

'We'll see. Let's take the stairs.'

'I couldn't.'

'What? A young buck like you? Amateur!' I almost skipped down the stairs, beating the lift and waited for him to open the gates. He struggled with the doors and hobbled out towards the front desk.

'What's the matter?' I asked, laughing.

'I think I have just pulled a muscle.'

'Liar.'

I stood at the desk whilst Donald requested the bill and had a chat, in not very good French, with the proprietor.

'Did you have a good night, Monsieur Donald?'

Well, he need not have gone into detail but he was boasting a little. However, it was flattering to be called a sensational lover and very sexy, but it was off putting when he began comparing me to others in his little book, or should that be, in his little brain. They joked with each other about sex and women for a few minutes before he paid the bill, but not before the proprietor asked if he would see him tomorrow. That was when I decided to teach him a little lesson.

'Monsieur. Are you the proprietor of this establishment?' I asked in perfect French, speaking very quickly to prevent Donald, who was now standing at the door, getting the gist of what I was saying. My outburst surprised and shocked the proprietor. 'Donald came highly recommended,' I continued. 'Several women have found him a little exciting, but the price I paid for his services and for the night's entertainment were extortionate. What is worse, he is not very good. In fact, he is an amateur and as such, it should be free. Is he learning the job?' The proprietor looked nonplussed and stood open-mouthed as I continued in full flight.

'If you are going to continue to run your establishment like this, you will need better young men and they need to be trained properly. Merci.'

I returned to Donald who was standing motionless in the entrance hall.

'Close it, Donald.'

'What?'

'Your mouth. It's wide open.'

He came to with a bang. 'I didn't know you could speak French?'

'You didn't ask.'

'Well, have you anymore surprises up your sleeve for me?'

Yes, you male whore. Wait till our maître d'hôtel demands a percentage from your immoral earnings, I thought as he asked what I had been saying to the proprietor. I grabbed hold of his arm, snuggled into it, then turned to the proprietor and winked.

The proprietor suddenly twigged and laughed loudly, waving to me as I waltzed him out of the door to the TR4 which was still outside. Within a few minutes, he was pulling up in our drive and leaving me to take a well-earned bath and rest.

He must have asked a dozen times for another date, but I found it more interesting to keep him on a very long leash.

'Give me a ring in a few days and we'll see,' was my final comment as he smouldered in anticipation.

Chapter 14
Donald's Demise

We all received invitations to Donald's inaugural polo match. He must have rung me a dozen times, insisting I attended. We accepted the invitation but I kept him guessing, keeping him at arm's length, to create the desire. It certainly worked because he was like a cat on heat.

We had given Bif the pleasure of choosing which cars to bring across to France. Of course, he chose his two favourites – the Duisenberg and the Bentley Le Mans. For him this was his first executive decision to have both of them shipped out. It was a bit over the top, but as he said the climate in Nice was superb and it would do them good to be used for a while.

It was a glorious day as we rolled up in style in the Bentley, which certainly created a great deal of interest amongst our group. Maudie and I were dressed in befitting costumes, myself as one of the Charleston Flapper girls; probably a bit late for the Charleston period but it looked good. Maudie wore a very posh lady's outfit. It wasn't fancy dress but we loved dressing up and having a good time.

'She always did love making an exhibition of herself, Mr White,' Maud interrupted.

Michael Freisman had certainly pushed the boat out for his son's first match. He laid on a marquee and once again, an endless supply of champagne and a delicious buffet. You had to hand it to him; he was certainly trying to ingratiate himself with the so-called establishment. We were welcomed by the host himself, who told us to park the car by his marquee and then personally escorted us inside. A far cry from the previous occasion.

We all drank champagne together and ate freshly picked strawberries with cream whilst waiting for Donald to make the grand entrance in his polo garb and looking the part – minus his horse, of course. He came directly over to me, which was quite flattering, took both my hands in his and simply said:

'Thank you for coming, Edie.'

'How could I miss coming to see this big, strong, strapping man?'

'Could I see you after the match?' he asked, almost pleading.

'Of course, you can. Get the match over first and I want to see you win.' It was though a weight had been taken off his shoulders and he began to relax.

He seemed to ignore the rest of our party which caused Maudie to whisper, 'I think he's got it bad, Edie.'

I enjoyed the match and he played well, but I suppose the half-time break spoiled everything. He had once again come over to see me just for a quick chat, before joining one or two other players. Maudie had her back to them a step or two away when one of them asked Donald, 'What are you doing with her? Don't you think she is a bit old for you?' As I said, he was an arrogant boy. Anything that did not affect him, he simply ignored, and this applied to Maudie here. You remember he had even been introduced to her outside the bedroom and been in our company. Yet he didn't even recognise her; either that or he didn't care what he said.

'Mr White,' Maud suddenly said, interrupting my story, 'I have always defended my family. We were always brought up to respect people, not to take advantage, but also not to be taken advantage of. I know Edie is a bit loose at times. I sometimes teased her, calling her 'the tart with the heart', but I know she would not knowingly do anything to upset or hurt anyone. When I heard Donald responding to his friend's question, I was furious and I was determined to teach him a lesson.

'He turned round, looked at Edie and said quietly: "I've never had a woman like her. She goes like a train and she loves it. I'll introduce you when I've finished with her. She'll teach even you a few tricks!"'

Maudie hated having to tell me what had been said but, I've always been a realist and never expected or wanted anything other than a good time. I wasn't overly bothered but the more I thought about it, the more I realised how dastardly he was and how hurtful were his words.

It's interesting that no matter what gender you are, there are some people who take things on the nose and don't respond to insults. They forget there are many lovely ways to get your own back, and Maudie was determined to plot my revenge.

I was hurt and hadn't the courage to tackle him directly, I suppose. To ease my situation, I began flirting, not outrageously, and turned my attention to Michael, Donald's father who turned out to be just as eager as his son.

'Michael, you have put on a splendid buffet for us and the champagne is out of this world,' I said as I walked into the marquee towards him.

'Do you think so?'

'Oh yes, it's wonderful.'

'Grand timing as I was just about to open this bottle, which a friend has just given me. Would you like to try it?'

'Oh yes, that would be lovely.'

Got him in one. Donald, you have lost your chance, I thought, as I followed Michael into the back where the refrigerators were. We were alone among the bottle crates and the rubbish.

—A very suitable place for a liaison, don't you think, Mr White?

A loud popping noise filled the air, followed by a whoosh as the ice cold champagne came oozing out of the bottle into a large fluted glass. The bubbles toppled over the rim as Michael poured the first glass for me. He held his glass carefully as he poured his own, but was unable to stop the sensuous liquid from caressing his hand.

'Don't waste it,' I whispered as I took his hand and subtly kissed his cool skin, licking it teasingly with my tongue.

'Here's to us,' Michael said as we clinked our glasses.

'To us,' I added, our lips only separated by two champagne glasses.

It was too much for him to resist and as our glasses parted, our lips were joined. How on earth we managed to find somewhere to put the glasses, I shall never know, especially as our lips were locked together in a kiss which was gentle yet firm; the sort you dream of, or see in films. It was only broken when we were on the floor and I got my just reward. It was a stupid place when you think about it – the storeroom floor of a marquee, especially when so many people had the opportunity to come in. Even when one of the waiters walked in to collect another bottle from the refrigerator, Michael was too far gone and didn't stop. He did pause for a few seconds when we heard his wife asking if anyone had seen Michael. 'Sorry about that,' he said, and continued.

We finished our champagne, aware that the bubbles were still rising, only to realise that someone had removed our half empty bottle. They must have noticed the two half empty glasses which were near it, not least two pairs of feet protruding from behind the fridge. We tidied ourselves up and thanked the Lord that everyone's attention was focused on the game of polo – that being the most important attraction of the moment.

He wasn't a bad lover, and like his son before him, he asked if I would see him again, to which I agreed. There was *one* problem however – this one was married.

Donald no longer interested me, especially as I now had his father, so I was decidedly cool with him even though the match was won by Nice and he had played well. But his fire was still burning. Even though he was being fêted by some of his team mates, he would make those quick casual glances in my direction.

We decided to take our leave, Maudie agreeing to drive. We both looked the part, wearing the big goggles which were a must in the open-topped Bentley Le Mans. Our departure – the reversing and roar of the engine as it started up, attracted more admirers than we did. Maudie couldn't resist playing to the gallery and drove along in front of the marquees, stopping to thank our host. I received a crafty squeeze of my arm from Michael as she roared off. I also caught a glimpse of Donald looking somewhat po-faced as we left. Strange that.

'I saw that, Edie,' Maud shouted over the noise of the engine.

'What?' I asked.

'Him squeezing your arm.'

'Who?'

'You know. What have you been up to now?'

'Getting my own back.'

'What? With his father?'

'Why not, after what you told me?'

'There was no doubt, Mr White,' said Maud, 'that my sister Edie was somewhat loose, but she was right. There was no way we were going to allow a jumped up little squirt like Donald make such comments about her. After all, she taught him a few worldly ways.'

Yes, they may have been wealthy but he was a bit

backward in that respect, unlike his father.

It seems Donald was very upset that I had left early, particularly without saying goodbye, so much so he began to telephone me every hour. Fortunately, the housekeeper answered the phone, but eventually I took the call.

'Why did you go without seeing me?' he asked in a plaintive voice.

'I thought you said I was too old for you and that when you had finished with me, you would pass me on to one of your friends.'

'No, I didn't. I wouldn't say anything like that.'

'But you did! Maud was standing next to you and heard it all.'

'If I did, I didn't mean it. Edie, I love you. Don't do this to me ...please.'

'No! You don't love me, but I forgive you, so forget it.' I could feel the pain in his voice disappear as he sighed with relief.

'Would you like to come out for a meal?' he asked, his confidence rapidly returning.

I agreed to go for a meal as long as it was at Le Coq d'Or and it was my treat.

'As I mentioned, I was determined to teach this lad a real lesson,' Maud said. 'He had invited Edie out for a meal, and I have got to give it her – she looked not only sexy, but quite sensational. I had a plan and knew it would succeed ...'

—Do you know Mr White, I now realised I could be very cool and calculating when my back was against the wall. Edith interrupted, 'I could smile at him, make Donald feel so important, as if he was the most perfect man in the world and yet, I could have the dagger at his throat and boy, did I now want the dagger to sink in.'

I hired a driver as Bif was out with Yvette and was chauffeured up to Michael's house in style. Their housekeeper opened the door, and without hesitation, invited me in.

'Madame Trenchard?'

'Oui.'

'Deux minutes, s'il vous plaît.'

She went off to find Donald just as his father came out to see who was at the door.

'Edith! How nice to see you. What brings you here?' he asked loudly ensuring Mary could hear, his eyes nearly popping out of their sockets in surprise. A sly little squeeze and a kiss followed.

'I left early from the match because some naughty little man seduced me,' I said, whispering in his ear.

'I felt dreadful leaving early and so have asked your son if he would accept an invitation to dinner as an apology. I'm taking him to the Coq d'Or. It was an excuse to see you,' I whispered again.

'Take your coat off a moment and come and have a drink with us.' He spoke loudly as though he wanted Mary to know he was being the good host.

He turned to go back into the room, at which point, I really laid it on. I simply waited. He turned to see why I hadn't followed him, but I stood there with my arm out ready to link his. He twigged and came back, his arm out and crooked. I put mine through and we made our way towards the lounge.

'Sorry Edith,' he whispered.

'I just wanted to hold you. Now give me a kiss and don't be silly. It's just the way we have been brought up,' I said softly, laying it on a bit thick. 'Oh! I do love powerful men.'

I could see his chest protrude noticeably.

We came into the lounge where Mary was seated on a plush sofa.

'Mary? You know Edith, don't you?'

'Of course I do,' she replied sweetly, not knowing which

way to look. 'How nice to see you. Come and sit down.'

'What would you like to drink?' Michael asked.

'A nice dry champagne, if you have one.'

'Yes, I'm sure we have,' he replied, ordering his butler to bring one.

I could see Mary absolutely itching to know what I was doing, going out with her son. In fact, she couldn't wait and just blurted out.

'How do you know my son, Donald?'

'From your lovely party! He took me out for dinner and it was purely on condition that I paid for the next one ... if he wanted to go again, of course ... that I'm here. My sister and I also left early after the match and I felt somewhat rude,' I said with a touch of irony in my voice.

'But you're er ...'

'Much too old for him?' I suggested.

'Mary!' Michael exclaimed, obviously embarrassed.

'I actually have friends from all walks of life ... from prime ministers to peasants ... and from all age groups. Perhaps he wants me just for sex,' I whispered, much to Michael's amusement.

Mary simply sat dumbstruck, not knowing what to say.

'Serves you right, Mary.'

'No ... seriously, we are just going out for a meal. So don't worry, I'll bring him back a virgin.'

'What's this about a virgin?' Donald asked, entering the room at that moment, wearing an obviously new, cream linen suit. 'Wow,' he said, drinking me in as he came over to give me a peck on the cheek.

'Thank you,' I replied in a coquettish manner .

'Now, what's this "virgin" business?'

'Oh, it's nothing. Your mother was just asking if I was too old for you ... which of course I am ... but I explained that we were just good friends. Donald simply glared at her. 'By the way, did you find my little red clutch bag? I think

I left it here by mistake.' That was the devil in me. I was dying to know the outcome of the missing purses and wallets.

'We did find one or two things. I'll go and look,' Michael replied. He returned in seconds. 'No sorry. Nothing like that.'

'No matter. If it turns up, you know where I am.'

We had another drink, followed by some difficult small talk. It was obvious that Mary could not get over the fact that Donald was taking me out. It was time to go.

'Don't worry, I'll take care of him,' I said cheekily to Mary, trying to get her to smile. That made matters worse. The look that followed would have killed an entire battalion. I thought I should leave quickly before I did anymore damage.

'Would you like to borrow the car, Donald?' his father asked, noticeably changing the subject.

'Oh, no it's my treat,' I said. 'Barry is outside. He's my chaperone and chauffeur. Come on,' I ordered, and with that, took hold of Donald's arm and waltzed him out of the room to the waiting car. Round one to me I thought as the car glided down the drive. That lad was a randy devil. We hadn't gone a hundred yards before he began kissing me and misbehaving, but not before he pulled the blind down with his free hand so that the chauffeur was not a witness.

'Come on,' Donald urged. 'He can't see.' A further struggle ensued until he put his hand up my dress and found to his surprise I had my bathing costume on.

'What's this?' he asked.

I turned on the sexy voice and began stroking his arm and running my fingers through his hair. 'I'm going to give you a treat … something you have never had before.'

'What? What's that?' he asked like the spoiled child he was.

'Just be patient. It will be worth waiting for.'

'Come on. Please tell me. Don't keep me in suspense.'

'Wait and see. Just be patient.'

He was now really anxious, so I undid his trousers and like some excited little boy, he ejaculated everywhere, missing me, thank goodness.

'You're not going to be much good to me, are you? I think you ought to come back when you grow up.'

'Just you wait,' he bragged, but I could sense it had really annoyed him.

'We'll see.'

Just at that moment, Barry announced our arrival. Donald started to panic as his cream linen suit was in a mess.

'Don't worry.'

'Barry, could you get a damp cloth for the young gentleman. He has had a nose bleed,' I said through the intercom.

It seemed ages before Barry returned with one of the restaurant's towels and a damp cloth. It took Donald another ten minutes before he was ready to make the grand entrance. He was a spoiled little brat and now I was determined to take him down a peg or two before the finale.

'Do I look okay?'

'Of course you do! You might have worn the brown shoes instead of the sandals, but you're such a good-looking young man, no one will notice.'

Barry opened the car door, allowing Donald to get out first. Like his father, he immediately began to walk over to the main entrance of Le Coq d'Or – one of the most fashionable in Nice at the time. It took my chauffeur to remind him of his manners. He sidled back to the car, helped me out and we both walked to the entrance. Once again, the thought of a chauffeur scolding him went completely against the grain, and I could tell he was very angry.

The Maître D' opened the restaurant door. 'Madame Trenchard! How lovely to see you ... and you, sir.' He had such a beautiful French accent. He then showed us to our table, commenting on how I looked, which made me feel even better and as he continued to speak to me in French, another wonderful opportunity occurred.

'What did he say?' Donald asked.

'Oh, I'm sorry. I thought you spoke French.'

It couldn't have been better. He was angry at me making fun of him, angry because the chauffeur had reprimanded him, angry at my comment about his French, and embarrassed as he walked through the restaurant, trailing like a puppy on a lead, the marks on his lovely cream suit quite evident. I never really wanted to do this but the boy was so arrogant and his behaviour so bad, he really did need to be taken down a peg or two.

Once seated, the waiter asked what we would like to drink. To calm the troubled waters, I suggested Donald choose. This helped him restore a little self-respect, but I knew he would choose the most expensive wine. He made a great play of it, asking for the Bollinger 1960 in a raised voice, so that everyone in the restaurant could hear.

'Don't worry about your suit. It's only the front of your trousers that show the marks. Everyone will think you tried to screw me,' I said, whispering, but loud enough for those at the adjacent table to overhear.

'Keep your voice down!' he muttered in embarrassment. His discomfort had returned and the moment the drinks arrived, he downed the first before I was even halfway through mine. I poured him another, much to the wine waiter's disgust.

'Je suis désolé, Monsieur.'

'What's he say?'

'He was sorry he didn't get to you quick enough to pour your drink.'

'Oh, that's all right,' he replied, waving the man away like some nonentity. More embarrassment.

We spent a few minutes studying the menu which was all in French, so I began to translate it slowly for him. More humiliation ... another self-poured glass of Bollinger and a further, 'Je suis désolé,' from the wine waiter.

'You choose for us,' I said, placing the menu down.

He gulped down more champagne but not without the waiter's helping hand this time. We sat there in silence whilst he stared blindly at the menu. Suddenly, he raised the menu in the air and flicked his fingers.

'Garçon!' he shouted. The entire restaurant must have heard it.

'Madame Trenchard! Please would you ask him to keep his voice down. He is disturbing the other customers,' the Maître D' snapped.

'He is a spoiled little brat and I am trying to teach him some manners. You can see that at the moment I'm not succeeding,' I replied in French.

'What did you say?' Donald asked, slurring his words a little.

'I simply told him you would be ordering for us.'

The couple at the adjacent table were smiling. It was obvious they had been listening to the conversation and found it as enjoyable as I did.

'I would like steak frites,' he said, asking me to translate.

'Donald ... they don't do chips here.'

'God, it's a bloody restaurant, isn't it? I want steak and chips,' he replied in a raised voice.

'Then darling, you can have steak and chips. I'll go and sort things out. I left the table in search of the Maître D', who wasn't very far away.

'Bernard, you can see I am having some difficulties. Is there any way you could cook this young man a few chips? I know it is difficult and not on the menu but I really don't want to leave at the moment. If you have a problem with this, please ring Bertroni and tell him Edith is here and requires some chips for a young boy.'

'Madame Edith, that won't be necessary. Of course you can have chips,' he said in an agitated tone.

I went back to the table to find that Donald had finished the first bottle of Bollinger 1960 and ordered another. 'Well, you have been busy, Donald. I am pleased to tell you the chef is doing steak and chips especially for you.'

He was past the embarrassing stage and virtually three sheets to the wind. He was only just about able to string a sentence together and I was sure another drink would have finished him, but he was trying. We hurried our main course, after which, I decided it was time to leave.

Bernard telephoned the chauffeur and we started to make our way to the entrance, but not before Donald grabbed the unfinished bottle of champagne, took a swig and tucked it under his arm.

'Bonne chance,' a guest at a nearby table proclaimed.

'Don't worry. I'm well paid for this. I'm just the au pair. I've now got to fix him up with a woman for the night,' I announced to the nearest tables. The look of horror on their faces said it all.

I was glad Barry arrived to help me get Donald out of the restaurant and into the car. The moment he was inside the car, he collapsed in a heap.

'Take us to the beach opposite the Negresco, please Barry. I need to be there in ten to fifteen minutes and I would like all the blankets from the boot laid out on the beach.'

'We'll be there.'

Donald was still almost out of it when we arrived, but amazingly, he could remember the promise I gave him.

'You promeeshed me shumfin exshitin.'

'And I'm going to give it you, in just two minutes,' I replied purposefully.

The two minutes became ten as we finished the Bollinger and staggered down the steps to the beach where, as arranged, Maudie was waiting.

'Am I glad to see you! He is a pain in the ...'

We took him down to the beach, stripped him of his clothes and laid him on the rug whilst I pretended to make love to him. That began to sober him up a little. I then stripped off to my bathing costume and continued seducing him. His Marks and Spencer Y-fronts indicated that my attempts were working ... Now was the time.

'Come on, you. I promised you something special.' He was all mine! We grabbed him by the arms and tried to get him to stand – easier said than done because the beach was very stony. We dragged him towards the sea.

Dipping him in the sea did little to revive his senses; he was very drunk and only just on this earth. I managed to relieve him of his Y-fronts, getting soaked in the action, and signalled to Maud to carry out the next stage of the plan. She ran up the steps, grabbed all our clothes and blankets and disappeared.

We were now stranded. I only had my lovely bathing costume on, with a skirt attached and he, the poor thing, was stark naked. But the best was yet to come.

Maud had arranged for two well-seasoned prostitutes to take him back to their room where he would spend the night. It cost us £300 each with a promise of more if they kept him there until ten o'clock in the morning, after which, they would send home in one of their outfits.

In the meantime, I found Maud had mysteriously missed my pair of pumps which I had kicked off at the water's edge. I quickly put them on and ran off after her.

This was their cue. Out of nowhere, two sexily dressed sixty-year-old ladies suddenly appeared and took pity on this nudist-loving young man who was sitting down on the pebbles and crying his heart out. Maud was supervising events and was just out of sight.

The ladies had been well-briefed by Maud who then joined them on the beach, clutching her camera. Donald was completely unaware of the events that ensued whilst the camera was clicking. Maud, an expert in psychological warfare, finally managed to convince him that he was falling in love with these two prostitutes who wanted to take care of him.

Like a lamb to slaughter, and totally unaware he was naked, he was trundled along the streets to their hotel room in the centre of Nice.

In the meantime, still very wet, I ran as fast as I could to his father's house. I had hardly finished knocking when the door was opened.

'Madame Trenchard, que faites-vous? the butler enquired, taken aback by my attire.

Once again, Michael arrived to see what the kerfuffle was all about.

'Edith! What on *earth* is the matter?'

'I cannot believe how stupid I have been. I shouldn't have asked him,' I replied, pretending to be grossly upset.

'What? Asked him what?'

'To return the dinner date.'

At that point, Mary appeared at the front door and dismissed the butler.

'Come on in,' Michael said plaintively. 'You're wet through. Mary, pop upstairs and get Edith a dressing gown, would you? She's soaking. In fact, Edith, go with her and dry off.'

Mary took me upstairs to the bathroom, gave me a few towels and left me to clean up. She returned after a few minutes to check if I was okay. She lent me one of her least glamorous gowns and escorted me back to their lounge.

'Thank you both for your kindness. Could you order me a taxi and I'll get out of your way.'

'Nonsense Edith! I'll take you home, but first have a drink,' Michael said.

'A cup of tea please. That will do nicely.'

He ordered the tea and then asked what on earth had happened. I laid it on a bit thick. 'We left here and I could tell he was annoyed. Things became worse at Le Coq d'Or. He ordered a bottle of Bollinger and almost drank the lot, becoming very drunk very quickly, especially, after the second–

'Glass?' Mary interrupted.

'Bottle,' I replied.

'We were politely asked to behave ourselves. Barry took us to the beach as I thought it would be a lovely idea, and it would sober him up. Instead, he got worse. We ran into the sea only to see someone stealing our clothes.

He couldn't do anything. He was far too drunk and in the nude so it was left to me to run after the thief. I had him in sight for a while and then he totally disappeared between some houses.'

I could see Mary squirming.

'I came back quickly to help him, only to find him flirting with two of his girlfriends. I won't tell you what he said to me but it was very rude and upsetting … and he told me to … well, you know. I know I am older than he is, but I had no intention of a romantic liaison with Donald, and in any event, I could tell he knew them very well … and they were a lot older than me. I left him to come to you for help, as it was the nearest place.'

By now, it seemed I had succeeded in my bluff. The tears helped.

'We are so sorry, Edith. I don't know what comes over him.' Michael seemed genuinely concerned.

'Michael, may I phone for a taxi?'

'No Edith, I said I'll take you home. I'll go and get the car and we will have a look for him.'

I chatted to Mary for a few minutes and then dropped the dear lady another little bombshell.

'Mary, I think those women were prostitutes. He seems to want women like that. It didn't do my ego much good either. I think you should get Michael to have a word with him.'

Her chin dropped a few inches and I was rescued by the butler informing me that Mr Michael was waiting.

'Good night, Mary. I will return the robe tomorrow, and thank you so much for your kindness.'

I got into the red Ferrari Berlinetta and could feel the power the moment Michael touched the accelerator.

'Oh, I would love to drive this. No … I would love *you* to drive this … fast.'

'Would you?'

'Yes, I find speed exhilarating.'

'Let's go,' he said, grinning like a Cheshire cat.

'What about Donald?'

'He deserves all he gets. I am sick of baling him out of trouble.'

Wonderful, I thought to myself as he put his foot down, making his way to the N7 out of Nice where he let rip. The car reached 100 kph as I began to squeeze his leg tightly. At 120 kph, I was rubbing him in excitement. At 160 kph, I was over him like a rash. He braked, swerved off the road and pulled into the next quiet lane. I climbed out of the car, ran round and managed to straddle him in the driver's seat. Oh my, he was as anxious as his son. Certainly, one of the most difficult things I have ever done … and in a Ferrari.

'Come back to our place and let's do it properly.' That was just too much for him. He couldn't refuse. The foot was almost down to the floor and fifteen minutes later, we were pulling into our drive.

'Some place you've got here.'

'It was our father's. He was very well off,' I replied, trying to play it down a bit. 'Come on in. I'll let you help me get dressed as I need to give you this robe back.'

I took him by the hand, opened the door, which was seldom locked in those days, and took him straight to my room.

He led the way in. I kicked the door closed behind us, opened the robe to show my attributes and within seconds, he took advantage, or so he thought. I had him on the bed and for the next forty-five minutes, he made up for what his son sadly lacked.

We walked down the stairs in total silence a while later. 'Sorry for Donald's behaviour,' he said as he opened the door.

'That's not a problem. It was a lovely excuse to see you. Thanks for the lift home. Oh, I forgot … here's your robe,' I added taking it off, exposing my naked body.

'Can I see you again?' he asked.

'I would love to.'

Poor old Donald. He certainly got his comeuppance. He was featured in the local *Nice Matin*, walking in the centre of Nice, accompanied by his two girlfriends and dressed in a tart's clothes, minus the wig and make-up. The incident was put down to his youthful exuberance and the fact that he had played well at polo on his debut for the Nice First Team.

Chapter 15

On Tenterhooks

Maud had by no means finished with Donald yet. She had her gander up and nothing stops her when someone has offended any member of our family or staff. In any event, she wanted his watch.

'I certainly did,' Maud said, taking over the conversation. 'I prefer people to be honest, say things straight to my face, rather than gossip and exaggerate to someone or another. Perhaps he wasn't,' she added.

'Wasn't what?' Edith asked.

'Exaggerating.'

'Maud! Don't be so mucky. What *will* Mr White think of me?'

'Oh, don't worry about me. I'm just enjoying the experience,' I replied.

We all laughed, including Mr Higginbotham, who I believed was as amazed at the revelations as I was.

Maud has her say ...

The opportunity soon arose for Donald to enact his co-called revenge. Donald kept phoning Edie, and each time, she rejected his requests to see her. He wanted to make her jealous and like some spoilt teenager, he would find out where Edie was and would just happen to turn up with one of his bimbos by his side.

I worked out a plan of action. We knew he would be taking at least one of his lady friends to his hotel room, which from what Edie had told me, allowed comparatively easy access. It was also the only time we thought he would take his watch off, which is what we were after. I also intended to steal their clothes, regardless of who the lady might be. After which, I would tip off the *Nice Matin* about a male prostitute ring operating from the hotel, and in which Donald was involved.

We planned everything in detail – our equipment, the clothes we would be wearing, which of course would be black and included balaclavas. We would be ready at a moment's notice.

We knew it wouldn't be long before Donald was up to his old tricks, the creature of habit that he was. He always took the young ladies to expensive restaurants, throwing his money around, giving the impression he was rich. Then a quick dalliance in the hotel bedroom, and home.

All Edie had to do was find out when he would be there and make sure he stayed all night. I would then enter Room 126 from the balcony and hopefully steal the watch and leave. All we had to do was to wait.

A few days later, Donald rang and I answered the phone.

'Is Edith there?' he asked.

'No, I'm sorry. Is that Donald?'

'Yes it is. Where is she?'

'She's out for the afternoon, and again this evening. Can I take a message for you?'

'Where's she going?' he asked, sounding annoyed.

'I think it's the Coq d'Or,' I said, hoping that this would be our opportunity.

By now, Edie was standing next to me and we both realised that this could be it. She made the reservations for the restaurant and now had to find someone to go with her at short notice.

I telephoned several people and asked if they would help us out. It was short notice and the only person I could find was a very dear ally who would only come if he could bring his friend with him. They were Henri and Philipe. We knew them both very well and you could not imagine a more camp couple. Philipe was the more feminine and was always insanely jealous of anyone showing any interest in Henri. They had lived together for more than thirty years and were very much 'husband' and 'wife'.

We wanted Henri to put on a bit of an act and be very attentive to Edie. Under normal circumstances, this would be easy, but Philipe, who often preferred to be called Phillipa, depending what mood he was in, decided to be awkward from the start even though we explained it was only a ruse.

I remember when they arrived at the house for pre-drinks, you would have thought it was a convention for the near feminine community. We had to endure the exaggerated pucker-lip kisses on both cheeks from Philipe. He behaved like a little girl on her first day out with her school friends without an adult present.

He squealed in a girly voice: 'Oooh, darlings, isn't this just so exciting!' Henri was noticeably quiet.

'Would you like a glass of champagne?' I asked.

'Oooh! Yes please. I just love the bubbles. They go right up my nose.'

Henri was not a bad-looking man – a retired actor. No, that's not fair. He was an actor that had been retired through lack of demand. I went to town on him, suggesting he looked on this experience as his greatest part. It worked; he took it very seriously, especially when we told him how important it was to us.

Bif rolled up in our latest Rolls-Royce Phantom V and took the three of them to the Coq d'Or. They were going there in style.

Edith looked the part; she really could turn heads when she made the effort and that night she certainly did. I was always a bit jealous of her looks. I never liked telling her because she was big-headed enough.

'Only kidding, Edie dear! You tell Mr White what happened next.'

Edith continues ...

I knew the moment we got into the car we were set for trouble. I opened the door to get in. Henri was behind me and was about to sit next to me when Philipe shouted:

'No. I want to sit next to Henri, not you.'

He really was behaving like a very precocious child. Henri then went round to the other door to sit the other side of me when Philipe began screaming and crying like a baby, stipulating that only *he* could sit next to Henri. I now had Henri leaning over me in order to comfort Philipe, followed by both of them leaning over me and kissing and cuddling each other.

'I'm sowwy,' Philipe said quietly and then added almost shouting, 'but I still want to sit there!' He pointed to the other side of me, indicating that he wanted to sit between Henri and me. I then had to suffer the indignity of Philipe clambering over me to get to the other side. Not only that, I swear he tried to tear my dress in the process. He then sat in the seat as smug as one could be, wearing a smile like a bloody wax model. All this going on and we hadn't moved an inch from the drive.

Despite further attempts to explain that Henri was only acting, Philipe cuddled up to him, gripping his arm throughout the entire journey.

'Bif? This is not going to work,' I said as we pulled up at the restaurant.

Henri jumped out of the car, raced round to open my door and made the grand gesture of holding my hand to help me out. He then continued to hold my hand until we reached the restaurant door. Bernard, the Maître D' was there to greet us.

I looked round. No Philipe. 'Where is he?' I asked impatiently. 'Bloody hell! He's still in the car.' We all went back and there he was sitting in the middle of the back seat in tears and pouting.

'What's the matter?' I asked.

'I want him to do that for me.'

'What, for God's sake?'

'Help me out and hold my hand.'

By now I had lost it, as they say in today's parlance. I just snapped. 'Get out of the bloody car or I'll send you back home.'

Henri intervened quickly, holding the stupid sod's hand to help him out of the car and then to the restaurant door, where Bernard, poor chap, was still waiting patiently.

'Madame Trenchard! How lovely to see you. Your table is ready for you and I hope you won't mind but that young boy you were dining with the other evening is also dining here tonight.'

'Don't worry, Bernard. Aidez-moi, s'il vous plaît. I have another idiotic person with me tonight and I might need your assistance. I know it may sound stupid but please call him "Madame" too,' I said, continuing in French. Bernard was quite taken aback. He didn't know what to say. I simply put my hands together in prayer and said: 'Please.'

After a signal from me, Bernard came to the table, addressed Philipe as 'Madame' and then held the chair for him to sit down first. Once again, he had that smug look all over his silly face. Bernard then came round to my side and did the same for me.

'Master Bif is not joining you, Madame Trenchard?'

'No, he's had enough already,' I replied, making sure Philipe heard.

'My usual, please Bernard ... and quickly. I am in need of a drink. Are you going to join me in a bottle of Mercier?' I said to the others.

'Oooh! The bubbles again. Yes please.'

Bernard took the hint. Thankfully, within a minute or two, he was back, serving Madame Philipe first, which at least shut him up for a few minutes and gave me chance to think of a new strategy; the present one was certainly not working. Every time Henri touched me we risked a scene.

'Look Philipe, let me tell you something. I do not want to take Henri away from you. I love someone else. Now don't all turn round, but there is a young man with a brunette, sitting at the table to your left. I was his girlfriend and he has finished with me. You and Henri have offered to help me get him back. I was hoping that you would make him jealous, so that he would want me again.'

'Edie, why didn't you say? I thought it was a trick so you could have Henri all to yourself. I'll behave, but I do like the waiter calling me "Madame".'

I had had enough and went to the ladies room. It was really just to have a break from the stress, but who should I see waiting for me as I came out – none other than Donald.

'Hello Edith,' he said. 'Why are you avoiding me?'

'I'm too old for you.'

—Note the psychology, Mr White. If you want to put someone down, you say, "You're too young for me," but if you want to keep the way open, you say, "I'm too old for you." You are then in control.

'You're not,' Donald said, a little despairingly, just like a rejected lover.

'You've treated me very badly, talking about me to others and saying what you would do when you have had enough of me.'

'I haven't! I haven't,' he replied, trying to keep his voice down.

'Well, you were overheard and I bet that little bimbo won't stay until breakfast like I did,' I said, trying to sound a little jealous and turning away to return to our table. I immediately called Bernard over and asked him to phone home and tell Maud to get ready as we may have some business to do later on.

Philipe had finally begun to behave himself. That was until Donald came over to the table to see who my guests were.

'Hello Edith,' he said, pretending he hadn't spoken to me earlier.

'Oooh! We are a lovely looking young man, aren't we!' Philipe exclaimed. 'Edith, aren't you going to introduce me then? I love nice young men.'

'This is Donald. He's a very dear friend of mine. Donald ... this is Henri, a family friend and this is Philipe.'

'I'd like to be your friend too, Philipe piped up, causing Henri to wince a little. He hadn't finished. 'I could give you a much better time than she could.'

'Philipe! That's enough. You've had too much to drink. Bif will take you home.'

'I'm sorry, Edith. I won't do it again.'

'Do what? You don't know what you have been doing. You're drunk. Henri? Take him to the car and please come back.'

Philipe was back in his spoilt brat mode, apparently more so when Henri left him in the car, but at least he was out of the way.

Henri returned a few minutes later and demonstrated to the world how sorry he was to have left me alone, ensuring, of course that Donald could hear. He played his role superbly and sat down, pulling the chair closer as if we were lovers. He was a superb actor, at least at that moment, and we could tell Donald was becoming more annoyed the more he could see Henri's attentiveness. It made him overly attentive to his partner; sometimes this was obviously over the top, even surprising her. It was quite comical.

I felt at this stage that our plans would come to fruition. All we had to do was wait to see whether or not he would take her to the hotel.

They finished well before we did. At least, Donald acknowledged me as he left, putting on an act of bravado, but failing miserably. He even made sure he put his coat on whilst facing me, which I chose to ignore, smiling to myself that I had this hold over him. Strangely, I was beginning to feel sorry for him and wished that I could call off our plan, but I knew Maud would be mad at me.

By the time we finished our meal, I was absolutely convinced the bait was taken and asked the Maître D' to phone home and tell Maud to get ready. He was intrigued by the cloak of secrecy I was adopting. I quickly returned to our car, stripped off in the back, knowing I was safe with Henri, put on my dark clothes and waited for Maud to arrive. Fifteen minutes later, she rolled up on the scooter and we were away to put the finishing touches to our scheme.

It took about an hour and a half before Maud was ready for action at Donald's 'special' little hotel. His room was only two floors up and she knew it wasn't going to be difficult to reach his balcony. However, at the last minute she chose to go to the adjoining balcony and watch. Open curtains and lights off were a sure sign the room was empty. We 'masked up' as they say and Maud began.

She threw a line with such deftness that it caught with hardly a sound, and within seconds, she was on her way up. Once there, it was a short jump to balcony 126. The French never expect to get burgled from outside, especially from two floors up, and with a simple flick of her penknife, the shutters were open. She gingerly opened them and looked in.

—Honestly, Mr White, Maud was quite impressive!

'Thank you, Edie. I did something right then!' Maud added.

Our problems began when a visitor on the other side of

the courtyard happened to see me and shouted at me. I could see he had gone back into his room and was probably going to raise the alarm.

'Maudie, you tell Mr White what happened next.'
Maud continues the story ...

Donald and his lady friend were not in the room. I was just about to give up when I noticed there was a chink of light coming from under the bathroom door. Again, with a flick of the knife through the window lock and a gentle jolt upwards, hey presto I was in. I looked back and saw the man was back at the window shouting instructions to someone. I simply shouted 'Four' to Edie who immediately left the area on the scooter. It was our pre-arranged signal for where to meet me should things go wrong.

They were having a real splash around in the bath and from what Edie had told me, he was now trying what he had previously enjoyed. I quickly searched round for his beloved watch, which was nowhere to be found. I could only deduce that it was, once again, still on his wrist.

'It worked underwater you know, Mr White,' Edith explained.

I have never really liked any form of violent action because you never know what can happen. So I quickly threw all their clothes out of the window and then decided to use my wartime training. I had no alternative; speed was essential now. I quickly put the desk chair under the door handle, then quietly went over to the bathroom door and listened. They were certainly enjoying themselves. It seemed a shame to intrude, but I tapped on the door. There was a massive splashing and then ... dead silence. I heard him say, 'Ssssh!' quietly. He got out of the bath and I could hear a squelching noise as he came over to the door. I was waiting.

—I don't know whether you know this, Mr White, but when men are naked in difficult situations, they do not stand up straight.

He cautiously opened the door and peeped out. That was where he made his mistake. It was easy – a swift blow to the back of the neck, and he was out like a light. The trouble was the bimbo let out a piercing scream. I hurried into the bathroom where she was still sitting up in the bath, put one hand across her mouth, my finger to my lips and whispered, 'Ssssh.' I then ran my hand across my throat as a warning to her to be quiet, and just to make sure she thought I was a man, I fondled her somewhat full bosom. She was petrified and simply shivered in silence.

Poor Donald was lying there, sparked out, and sure enough, his watch was on his wrist. Naturally, I duly relieved him of his prize possession.

I could hear voices outside the room and realised it had to be the concierge with reinforcements.

'Are you all right in there?' he called out in French, at the same time trying to use his pass key, but the chair prevented to door opening.

Two men charged at the door but still it didn't open.

'Ouvrez la porte! C'est la police!' one of them called out.

That was it. I had all I wanted and I was on my way. I collected the rope and the grappling iron and threw it up to the roof. It rattled down and caught on the guttering. I could hear the noise in the room as the two men were beginning to break down the blocked door. I started to climb as quickly as I could, passing the third floor. I then heard the door break in and the commotion as two men ran to the window.

A gendarme called out first, ordering me to stop and come down. I didn't answer and carried on, but he grabbed hold of the line and began to yank it. In the darkness I could just hear and see that the joint in the guttering was beginning to crack and pull away from the wall. Every time the gendarme pulled at the rope, and every foot I climbed, seemed to cause the guttering to come further away. He pulled again and I had to stop climbing as I could now see a gap in the wall where the guttering had been. More gendarmes arrived, bringing with them a battery of spotlights which they immediately trained on me and the surrounding area.

Before I could decide whether or not to give myself up, the gendarme yanked the rope again, only this time the guttering swung out. I could not get back, so I made a great effort to climb the last yard to grab hold of the corbel that held the guttering in position. I managed to grasp hold of it just as the gendarme pulled again, causing the piece of guttering to slide down in front of me. The grappling hook was still attached to the metal as it had twisted round, but my arm was now entangled. I tried desperately to shake it off, but the guttering was beginning to fall. I was now holding on by one hand and could do nothing as the metal fell until it jolted to a halt, almost dragging me down with it. I hung on like grim death as if my life depended on it, which of course, I suppose it did. Finally, the guttering spun off the rope and detached itself from me. It crashed to the floor, narrowly missing balcony 126 and the gendarme.

I hung there, praying my fingers would hold out. I spun round, hoping to catch the corbel with my other hand, but missed, to the astonishment of the small crowd that had now gathered below. I tried again and missed, causing the same shocked reaction from below. The third time I succeeded and caught hold of the corbel. Now at least I stood a chance as I had the strength in my two arms to pull me up. However, I still had the grappling line attached to my arm, which was making things difficult for me as it kept getting caught on the brickwork of the building; it was also swaying from side to side as I moved.

Within seconds, I felt my strength being sapped from me as I held onto the eight-inch corbel. Like a gymnast, I managed to lift myself up and was now almost horizontal with the roof. I then began to slide my left leg onto the roof, but accidentally kicked a tile which dislodged and fell to the ground, to more gasps from the ever-growing crowd. My leg was now firmly on the roof but I still couldn't move as both my hands were needed to support me. I saw one opportunity to throw the grappling rope to the apex and hope it would hold; the trick was I had to release my right hand from the corbel which was under my left one and both were supporting me. Luckily, the rope was still twisted around my arm.

Hanging by your fingertips is not something I would recommend. How I did what I did, I will never know. The pain was excruciating but somehow, I managed to extricate my right hand and unwrap the rope from my arm whilst keeping hold of the end. It was now free but my troubles were far from over. I could now hear the sound of a fire engine on its way.

I was still balancing on one hand when I wrapped a goodly length round my arm and began to swing the rope back and forth in the hope of reaching the apex when I was ready.

I counted to three and hurled the grappling rope with all my remaining strength. It missed, I lost my balance and began to fall. I managed to grab hold of the corbel and was now hanging by the fingertips of my left hand. The crowd was deadly silent and even the gendarmes were motionless, looking up at me. The grappling iron slid down the roof, drifting to the right. But then I could hold on no longer and my fingers began to slip. The crowd gasped, some even screamed as my grip failed, and I fell from the roof. I thought my number was up when suddenly, I stopped falling. It was like a dream; I was pulled up but not before banging against the wall several times. I thought my arm had been pulled out of its socket, such was the jolt.

The grappling iron had slid down the roof and stuck in the remaining guttering.

I couldn't believe it. I looked up and down in total shock, unable to move. Survival instinct kicked in and I knew I had to get onto the roof quickly. Once again there was a deathly silence as I managed to climb and reach the guttering. This was tricky. I had to try and roll onto the roof. I slipped again and fell back into the previous position, but thankfully the rope held and caught me in mid-air.

After a further attempt, I was on the roof and sliding along until I could feel that the remaining guttering was safe enough to take my weight. It was a wonderful feeling to look down and feel secure. The crowd and even the gendarmes were equally relieved; they were shouting and clapping.

I was grateful for their concern but I had but one thought – to get away. I still had the grappling iron which I slung over my shoulder and set off up along the roof to one of the chimneys, where I could work out my options. I climbed up and put my arm round the chimney. I could have kissed it as I knew from then on I would be safe, although not necessarily from the gendarmes. At least, everything I did from then on would be within my control. Within a couple of minutes, I got my breath back and was able to think rationally. I set off over the roof tops, taking a pre-determined route towards my rendezvous with Edie.

I thought it would be straightforward until I noticed the gendarmes below were running along various roads in the direction I was travelling. A few brave souls were also appearing on nearby roofs through skylights in an attempt to stall me. Eventually, I could see I had lost all but one of my followers who was in hot pursuit. He was slower than me, thank goodness until I came to the end of the building. There was a narrow alley, way below and a slightly taller building opposite. There was no way I could risk jumping to it, so it was decision time again. It was either give up to the fast approaching man or try to use the grappling rope. In the end there was no choice. I quickly wrapped the rope round my arm and hand and began to swing the rope until I had enough motion to enable the weight of the iron to take the rope to the other side, about fifteen feet away.

I let go. Perfect. The rope landed on the other building which had a flat roof and a walled terrace. Once again, on each floor there were those lovely balconies. I tugged on the rope and knew it would hold. A quick look behind me to see that my pursuer was now only some twenty feet away. One more tug, and firmly gripping the rope, I jumped off the edge of the building, legs straight out in front. I bumped into the opposite building. In fact, I was only inches from the balcony, which within seconds, I was standing firmly on. I was deciding what to do next when who do I see but my lovely sister who had been quietly following the situation and was now waiting at the end of the alley some forty yards away.

I flicked the rope and brought the irons down and within a minute, I was running towards her. My pursuer just stood looking down at me as I got onto the back of the scooter. We were away. Edie zigzagged all over the place, down side roads and alleys until finally ... we were pulling into our drive.

I can't remember anything else after that. The moment I sat on the settee, I fell asleep, totally exhausted.

'Not before she took out this beautiful watch and waved it at me,' Edith interrupted, proudly presenting the watch. You see, Mr White, this became another of our trophies.'

'Was it worth it?' I asked.

'It could have got us caught because we made a simple mistake,' Edith added.

It was my mistake. The following day, *Nice Matin* reported the robbery and the chase in great detail and stated that the robber was believed to be a woman.

'How could that be?' I asked. 'I thought you were all wearing black balaclavas?'

—Indeed, we were, Mr White. The gendarme who had nearly caught up with me was observant. He watched me get on the scooter and saw me adjust my bra strap as it has slipped down in the excitement. It was just a simple move, but he noticed, Clever fellow, don't you think?

'Very observant,' I added.

'I'll give you this, Mr White,' Edith said. 'Mr Higginbotham will supply all the details. You could sell the story to Nice Matin. It could be worth a few bob! Still interested?'

'Silly question,' I replied.

'In that case, same time next week? I think we should call it a day now. You get a little tired as you get older.'

'Yes, that's fine. See you next week,' I replied.

***

I was becoming very fond and protective of my two old ladies, not only for their candour but also for their endearing qualities. They stood up, wished us good afternoon and disappeared, leaving me in the tender care of Mr Higginbotham.

A few minutes later, he showed me to my car and within seconds, I was away. By now, I wondering what on earth was coming next. I thought I had enjoyed an interesting and full life ... but from my perspective, these two took the biscuit!

Chapter 16
Russian Roulette

I returned to my office at the *Mail* with more little gems for the newspaper. Another two robberies were now solved, but the jewels had been found.

Almost immediately, my editor, George Stevenson called me into his office.

'Clive, good morning. This is Sir John Fitzpatrick,' he said, addressing our visitor. 'Sir John, this is Clive White, one of our most talented reporters. Let's sit down.'

The three of us sat round the table and, after the usual niceties, George dropped a bombshell.

'Clive, I'm sorry to have to tell you that we have been served with a D-Notice regarding the two Trenchard sisters and at the moment, I am at a loss to know what this is about.'

It is rare for me to keep things from George, but in this case I had no alternative. I told them briefly about the alleged robbery at the bank and my visit to the police station when they were in custody and how I had offered to help the police and the sisters in ensuring their identification and safety.

Sir John interrupted: 'Mr White, there is really no further discussion needed. You are to drop any investigation into this robbery with immediate effect and the paper will not publish anything that refers to them. They are to be left alone. Do I make myself clear?'

'Perfectly,' I replied.

He looked at George who nodded his agreement.

'But why? I asked. 'I'm not investigating the robbery.'

'Yours is not to reason why, Mr White, but I will tell you it is a matter of national security, and you have been to their house on several occasions.'

'This is ridiculous, As I said earlier, I went to help them as I thought they were vulnerable at the police station and as a result, they invited me to afternoon tea. I met their sons and daughter and saw parts of their house and Bif's cars.'

'You're forgetting one thing, Mr White.'

'What's that? 'I asked.

'Mr Higginbotham.'

'For God's sake. I phoned him about them and he was invited too. Are your men watching the place? Are they spies and very dangerous at ninety-one years old?'

'No, Mr White. It's what they know and what they have seen that is important to this nation. As I said, you are not to investigate further.'

'I have been invited to tea yet again next week and I *am* going.'

'Be careful, Mr White. Do not overstep the mark of common sense. You know what will happen if you do.'

'I won't, don't worry. But I will continue to see them if I am invited.'

'Should you wish to write anything ... anything at all ... you must contact me first ... and only me. Is that understood?' Fitzpatrick added, addressing both George and me.

With that he stood up, picked up his smart navy blue trilby and made for the door, turning only to warn us again of the consequences. 'Good morning, Stevenson ... White.' With that, he left.

'Arrogant bastard,' George said almost within earshot of him. 'Now what the hell is this all about, Clive?'

'Nothing yet. I'm trying to put a story together but it's

obviously been spiked before I start.'

'You wouldn't be keeping anything from me, would you?'

'George? How long have you known me?'

'Clive, just keep me informed ... I'm intrigued.'

Not long after that meeting I had a call from Chief Inspector Baldwin who invited me along to have a chat. Strangely, the moment I arrived, he invited me out for coffee as he wanted to talk to me off the record. It was rare this sort of thing happened but there it was, and not even in Baldwin's area. He drove in total silence past Number 17 when suddenly he asked what was so special about the two women. I told him what I had seen, how beautiful everything was, how wealthy the ladies were and what a strange existence they had. Strange, in the sense that one of their children Bif, was the chauffeur and Alice, their daughter was the cook, for example.

Suddenly, Baldwin said, 'Clive, everything is off the record. No one must know we have met to discuss the case. I have been told to stop the investigation into the two old dears with immediate effect by none other than the Chief Constable. Not even his deputy is aware and all the records of the case are to be quietly destroyed. I need to discuss with the Chief Constable what I am to say to my two constables and then the matter is closed. What was astonishing was that when I went to the custody record book, all reference to the ladies had been professionally filleted. That in itself would have caused a stir had it been noticed, but as yet ...'

He took me to a little café in Rickmansworth. It was obvious he was on edge, constantly looking in his mirrors before finally pulling up in a side street.

'What's going on?' he asked. 'I think they were connected with some dirty business some time ago, particularly the one called Edith, and involving some seedy politician or other. Any ideas?'

'Off the record?' I asked.

'Off the record.'

'I think you're wrong. It's Maud, the quiet one who I think worked for MI5 or M16 on very special work. The fact that Edie was a little indiscreet about Maud's actions in the Bahamas during the war began to point conclusively to a very secret career. But we are both in the same boat ... the paper's been spiked as well.'

We chatted about this and that, with a few more references to the two old dears, each trying to glean a little more information from the other. I didn't want to spoil my chances at this early stage, but as we parted he asked to be kept informed. Naturally, I agreed, as far as the job allowed. From my point of view, it would have been the biggest scoop of the year.

I couldn't wait for the day to arrive when I returned to Number 17; all this intrigue had made it far more interesting. I was bang on time on the due date, feeling that if I had been late, they would have possibly gone out or mysteriously had another appointment. Bif was in the drive with his Bentley Le Mans, which I had to look at that before I was invited in by Mr Higginbotham, of course.

'Ah Mr White, how lovely to see you again. Come and sit down,' Edith said chirpily, at the same time directing Mr Higginbotham to sit down in what was becoming his usual place.

Edith continues ...

Where were we last week? Yes ... I remember we were still in France; in fact still in Nice, when Maud had another bout of kleptomania. It always seemed to happen when her mind was not occupied. She had done her damnedest in Lafayette's with several rather nice watches – Breitling and Longine, plus a new coat and gloves, which I went and paid for.

Lafayette was very busy and we were now making our way towards the entrance when someone tried to steal Maudie's bag. She felt her bag open and instinctively spun round, grabbing the wrist of a young teenager. He tried to pull away, but within a split second, she had his arm twisted behind his back.

'Francais?' she asked firmly. He didn't answer. She twisted his arm a little more and he yelped with pain. 'Francais?' she asked again.

'Oui. Algérien.'

'Young man,' she began in French, 'if I see you doing this again, it will not only be your arm I will break, it will be your neck. Do you understand?'

'Oui, Madame.' Another tweak of his arm and she let him go.

He ran off, yelling a few obscenities, turning round as he did so to give the V sign, but it became obvious that he was back at work within a few minutes. Maud decided to take matters further and began by watching the young man from a discreet distance.

It was a classic duo game. He would steal a bag or pick someone's pocket, run along and quickly put the goods in the basket of a young woman walking towards him. She would immediately cover the goods over with her shopping and walk away. The young woman then met with an older man, linked his arm and they both walked to a quiet place where she handed him the items. He then handed them to another man waiting in a nearby car park. In the meantime, the woman would return to the scene, changing her head scarf, and casually indicate to the young man that she was back on the job. So the process began again. This was a very professional operation and we could see at least three teams at work. Maudie insisted on finding out more.

We discovered that some were working the railway station, others the markets and, of course, the group on the street near Lafayette. They always changed their clothes after a couple of hours and always had something slightly different to wear, such as a reversible coat, a hat, scarf, sometimes even using a pushchair. What was interesting was that they were always under the control of the man. He was the only common denominator and the only one who was allowed to go the car, thus ensuring the pickpockets could not identify those further up the chain.

We spent the next few days watching the operation and were astonished to find they were making at least twenty hits per day and that was from the three groups we were watching. We also discovered that they changed the car, the driver and the rendezvous point several times a week. We now had to track the cars because we did not believe the boss of the operation would be involved in the menial task of collecting the money. Therefore, we had to have our Vespa on hand. They were clever. Even the driver of the car did not take the goods to the boss; instead we believed he put everything into a metal-edged case and took it to the left luggage boxes at Nice's main station. We followed him and watched. He hung about outside for about half an hour and then gave the key to a taxi driver returning from a fare. The taxi driver immediately left to deliver the key to wherever. We had lost him. The only thing we could do was to wait until the case was collected.

Maud secured the scooter not far from the main entrance to the station and we both waited. It was six hours before the case was retrieved by a tall, well-built, but rough-looking North African man wearing jeans and a light coloured T-shirt. Of course, the shades and the big white hat obviously indicated he didn't want to be recognised! We took photographs of him; in fact, we took photos of the entire operation. He sauntered into the left luggage section, looking all around him – a dead giveaway for someone up to no good.

Maudie immediately disappeared to collect the scooter whilst I kept watch. Thankfully, he took his time which enabled Maud to be ready to go. I casually followed the man out to a gleaming new Mercedes parked outside. He opened the nearside rear door to reveal a thin dark-haired, hatchet-faced man, Mediterranean in skin colour, who took the case and closed the car door. The car slowly drove away, leaving the African standing there. The African waited a second or two before a Volvo Estate pulled up with three other men inside and began to follow the Mercedes at a discreet distance. Maudie was concerned at the degree of security we faced, but nonetheless she was determined to do something.

We followed the Volvo, keeping just out of sight. That was until we sensed they had clocked us. They pulled onto a grass verge and waited, but Maud was not at all concerned as she rode past.

'You take a quick glance as we pass,' she shouted. That's just what I did and sure enough, they pulled off the verge and followed us. Maudie just continued on for several minutes, turning off on a couple of occasions until she stopped, got off the scooter and walked up the drive of a nearby house. 'Stay there. Any trouble, sound the horn. I'll be back in a minute.'

She disappeared for a few minutes and left me worrying about the Volvo behind. It had stopped some distance away and was obviously waiting to see what we were doing. Maudie returned, got back on the scooter and rode up the drive to the back of the house. She had been riding along casually, looking for a house that appeared empty and as luck would have it, this one was. We put the bike behind the garage and hid ourselves behind some shrubbery with a reasonable view of the entrance. Sure enough, the Volvo slowly drove past, first one way then the other. We waited some twenty minutes before leaving the house, waving and shouting goodbye, and then returned from whence we came at a slow pace. There was, however, no sight of the Volvo on the main road until we espied it parked up on a side road, with two of the men standing nearby. They had given the game away. I now had a mental note of their location and we returned home to work out our next move.

We believed the hatchet-faced man was the boss and that the Mercedes was his car, so we decided to watch him every day and night to gauge his routine.

'It was terribly exciting, Mr White!' Maud interrupted.

With the help of Bif, the three of us noted all the man's movements and luckily, he was a creature of habit. Every Monday night he had a game of boules. On a Tuesday, he visited a few pimps who were running his prostitute ring every Wednesday, and that was the day which interested us most. He spent two hours gambling in the Palais de la Méditerranée, a casino on the Promenade des Anglais, and from ten o'clock, he let his hair down in the bar at the Atlantic Hotel, where he was king for the night.

It was Maud's suggestion and I don't think I will ever forget it. She thought it would be a good idea if I took a room for the week at the Atlantic. On the Wednesday evening, I was to play a little roulette and use my talents to prevent him going back to his house, whilst she went and looked round Hatchet Face's house to see what the security was really like. It reminded me very much of the Vauxhall Bridge Road job, but there was no way this man was an Alan Wright.

I hate gambling; it goes completely against the grain, but Maudie reminded me of the poor sods who lose their money, their passports and their holiday. She suggested that I may even get a little bit of the other. Put that way, it didn't sound so bad.

I booked in, wearing a blonde wig and made sure I was labelled as a big spender. After a shopping trip, I entered the foyer, loaded with designer label bags of a few tempting clothes which I was to wear on the Wednesday evening.

I took a taxi to the casino and sure enough, I arrived at almost the same time as Hatchet Face who was accompanied by a few of his henchmen. I suppose his entourage made him feel big and powerful, especially as they were fawning over him all the time. We acknowledged each other courteously before going our separate ways.

Up close, he was an evil-looking man and I don't think any woman would have fancied him, even with all his money. I realised I didn't want to go through with it; he just made me feel uncomfortable. However, I went into the lounge for a drink before playing, and sat by myself, just watching the world go by, when he entered. Once again our eyes met; he nodded in acknowledgement. I could see even through the crowd he was staring at me. I gave the occasional smile but always turned away. I called the waiter to order another drink, but he was intercepted by one of Hatchet Face's bodyguards, another large North African, who also fancied himself and was also wearing the shades.

'Monsieur Jacques Valantin is buying you this one,' he announced in French. In fact, I didn't hear English spoken all night.

I signalled to the waiter to carry on with my order and said, 'Please tell the gentleman that it is very kind of him, but I don't know him and I do not accept drinks from strangers. If he would like to offer me a drink, it would be usual for him to approach me personally.'

He returned to his boss to relay the message. It did not go down well and you could tell he was absolutely furious. They all turned to look at me but that was my cue to leave. I walked out to the tables and began with roulette on the table with minimum stakes of 500 francs. (£50) It was just simple bets on red or black but my stakes were £1,000 a time which was a lot of money in those days and after a win, I doubled up. I was about £2,000 up when Hatchet Face joined the table and sat next to me, but not before he had quietly but firmly removed the gentleman who was sitting next to me.

'Hello! Thank you for the offer of the drink,' I said, making polite conversation which seemed to relax him.

'Faites vos jeux, s'il vous plaît,' the croupier called.

'Two thousand on black,' I called back to him.

Hatchet Face didn't bet; he simply watched me. The croupier spun the wheel. That familiar sound – the ball rolls round and round and then begins bouncing over the numbers as it slows down. All faces were intent on seeing the very last bounce before it nestled in a number. This is when fortunes are either made or lost – the despairing looks as another loses his shirt, countered only by the smiling faces of those lucky winners. The wheel stopped. Vingt-six noir. I had won, doubled my stake and placed the £4,000 on red. The wheel spun again, followed by a deathly silence as all eyes watched intently. Click, click, click and the ball bounces into a slot.

'Quatorze rouge,' the croupier announced. It looked good to have all the chips being pushed towards me, especially as it was impressing Hatchet Face or Monsieur Valantin as I shall now call him.

'You're bringing me luck, Monsieur Valantin.'

'Good,' he replied. 'Now perhaps you would allow me to buy you that drink? Now that I am no longer a stranger,' he announced, his voice like his face – evil and hatchet-like. I knew that my refusal had niggled him. He was obviously not French; his accent appeared Eastern European, possibly even Albanian; whatever it was, it had a sleazy tone.

Not many people in my life have sent shivers down my spine but this one did. What added to my repulsion was his habit of dribbling every time he opened his mouth. His saliva would somehow land on you, every time he spoke. I convinced myself that the need to make friends with him was just for the cause.

He called the waiter over and ordered a little pink champagne for the 'lady' and he would have his usual, which turned out to be a dry martini in a champagne coup. The waiter arrived and handed me my pink champagne in a manner suggesting I was Valantin's little concubine.

'Santé,' I said, gently clinking his glass.

'Santé,' he replied, a missile of saliva just missing my arm.

I turned my attention to the table and began to play again, which seemed to annoy him, It was as though I had to stop everything because he had bought me a drink. This was something I was not used to and carried on.

'Faites vos jeux, s'il vous plaît,' the croupier announced again. I put £2,000 worth of chips into my handbag and placed the rest on the table. I carried on for a few spins until my drink ran out and he offered me another.

'No, let me buy you one. You have brought me good luck.'

'No,' came the reply. 'You are with me; I will buy you the drinks.'

At this point, I really began to feel nervous. His voice was sinister and threatening and I was now wondering how I could extricate myself. I decided to play another table.

'I am going to play Blackjack over there,' I said, pointing to another table. I put another £2,000 worth of chips in my handbag and collected the rest. Just as I stood up to leave, he took hold of my wrist and held it firmly until I sat down again.

'I want you to sit next to me and I buy you more drinks,' he said quietly but menacingly. Even fellow players were beginning to notice the tension in the air.

'I don't want another drink, thank you,' I said the moment the glass was empty, but Valantin insisted on another little pink champagne.

'After this, I must go back to my hotel. I am getting very tired and I've had too much to drink already.'

'Where are you staying?' he asked.

'The Atlantic.' Why that slipped out I will never know.

'Oh good. I will take you there. I am meeting friends there at ten o'clock.'

'No, it's okay, thank you. I'll get a taxi.'

'Nonsense. I'll take you,' his voice and demeanour becoming more obnoxious. He signalled to Doctor Death, the one who always wore the large white hat and shades and still did, to fetch the car. He then firmly took hold of my wrist as I stood up. I looked at him sternly and didn't move until he let go, which further annoyed him. I walked to the cloakroom accompanied by the other African who at least waited outside the door, whilst I collected my coat and looked for an escape route. Unfortunately, the security at the Palais de la Méditerranée was as it should be – secure, with all the downstairs windows barred up in non-exotic areas.

He was there waiting for me. At least he offered to help me with my coat and escorted me to the entrance where he opened the rear door of the waiting Mercedes, our well-mannered host already inside.

'I don't like to be kept waiting. I told you I am meeting friends and I will be late. Get in,' he exclaimed. Some people have a way with words and women, but he was not one of them.

I had no option but to get into the car as muscleman behind was hustling me in. He then slammed the door with some force, earning a rebuke from the boss. Of course, the child lock was on so there was no escape. By now I was terrified, trying desperately not to show it.

He turned to me, put his hand on my knee and for the first time, offered me a compliment.

'You are a beautiful woman.'

I could see by the driver's face he knew what was coming and sure enough, Valantin leaned over and began to kiss me, pulling my face close to his dribbling mouth, whilst his spare hand went up my dress. I tried to stop him, pushing him away. Instantly, I realised that my only way out was to give in. I leaned over him and began to kiss and caress him. This annoyed him so much that he became violent and pushed me away, almost banging my head against the door He wanted to control and was not having any woman taking it away from him.

'Come here,' he shouted, undoing his trousers. I could see in the mirror that the driver was grinning. I'm sure he wanted me to give him a blow job, but I refused which made him even more aggressive. He grabbed hold of my hair and pulled me towards him. Instant shock when my hair came away in his hand. Realising it was a wig, he started to laugh uncontrollably. He couldn't stop thank God; it saved me from further torment.

I was somewhat dishevelled by the time we reached the Atlantic even though we had only been in the car for ten minutes, but worse was to come.

'What's your room number?' he demanded.

I didn't want to say but I had no alternative; there was no way I could get out of the car and there was no one around to see my plight.

'Deux cent trente-deux.' (232)

Valantin nodded to the driver to go and get my key whilst the other man came round to help me out of the car, obviously to prevent my escape. He took a vice-like grip of my arm, walked me straight to the lift and up to my room, but not before I had demonstrated my reluctance. Valantin followed a couple of minutes later, and because he was well-known at the hotel, was able to make a plausible excuse at reception.

Valantin walked straight into my room, went to my

wardrobe and rummaged through my clothes before choosing a dress for me.

'I want you to meet my friends and I want you to look good. You have twenty minutes and you will not be late. Wear this,' he ordered, throwing the dress at me.

I was desperate to phone Maudie, but I was not given any opportunity. In fact, I was becoming more terrified by the moment.

—Mr White, it may be hard to understand the lack of resistance women might have in this situation, but they are so frightened, it is impossible to think straight. There was no time to sort out a strategy. I felt like a caged animal. Here was psychologically disturbed man who controlled two giant African men who would kill or rape for their boss, and you are alone with one of them, frightened to scream for help because of the consequences.

I was left in the tender care of Dr Death. Obviously, the boss was afraid of me being left alone. I really couldn't fathom out what he was after, and I am sorry to say, too scared to ask or do anything about it. All the African was interested in was seeing me naked and perhaps take advantage.

'Turn your bloody back,' I shouted, accidently making it known that I spoke English. I had managed to make myself look half decent when the phone rang. It was Valantin. My guardian confirmed that I was ready and would bring me down in the lift, which he duly did, all the time holding me by the wrist.

The lift doors opened and who should be standing there waiting but Hatchet Face, his hand outstretched to take mine.

'Good,' he muttered, whereupon I was hustled into the bar. 'A pink champagne for the woman and my usual,' he ordered. The African sidled up to him and said a few words in his ear.

'You didn't tell me you could speak English,' Hatchet Face exclaimed.

'You didn't ask.' That earned me a kick in the shins.

'What else have you not told me?'

'That I speak German and Italian and some Spanish?'

'Right,' came the reply.

I was then pushed into a corner with one of the stooges to ensure I behaved myself, whilst he made lewd comments about me to one of his friends. The Maître D' came over to me, asking if I was all right, but before I could answer, he was intercepted and politely told that should he wish to speak to Madame then he must ask Monsieur Valantin. I made several attempts to go to the ladies room alone but was immediately accompanied by one of my chaperones.

I walked over to the bar and explained I was tired and going to bed, but with a quick nod of the head, Doctor Death took me back to my corner.

Eventually, many of the men began to take their leave until I was left alone with Valantin and his two goons.

'I'll take you to your room,' Valantin said.

'Don't worry, I can find my way.'

'*I* will take you,' he replied, almost snarling the words.

I knew I was in trouble but I didn't know how much trouble.

'Come on,' he ordered, flicking his thumb in a commanding gesture.

The three of them escorted me to the lift and then to my room. Valantin had the key and was about to open the door when suddenly, he grabbed the back of my head and banged it hard against the door. I was knocked senseless and didn't know where I was. Then he did the same again. This time, the door opened and I was almost thrown in, falling onto the floor.

'Get up. Get up,' he snarled, but I was too dazed and injured to do anything. He called the goons who lifted me and held me up. He slapped me across the face and shouted, 'When I tell you to get up, you get up.' He then slapped me on the other side of my face. My head had dropped and I was unable to take anything in. I was still being held up when he grabbed hold of my dress and ripped it off me, followed by the rest of my clothes, before being thrown onto the bed. The goons left me in his tender care and it was tender; he thrashed me, thumped me and even kicked me before he had finished.

He sat me up on the bed and leaned over to give me a kiss on the lips; all I could see was saliva coming at me. It was instinct that made me push him away which earned another tremendous thump across the mouth this time, knocking me sideways. Again he sat me up, trying to be tender. 'Now give me a kiss and mean it.' This time I gave him a kiss, putting my arms around him.

'Say goodbye, chérie,' he said as if nothing had happened. I didn't answer. He yelled, 'Say goodbye, chérie!'

'Goodbye, chérie,' I replied through swollen lips.

'Goodbye. We must do this again. You would like that, wouldn't you?'

'Yes, chérie.'

'That's a good girl.' With that, he took a wad of notes out of his pocket and threw 5,000 francs (£500) onto the bed.

It took all my strength to get to the phone on the other side of the bed and dial Maudie. I could hardly talk, I was that bruised.

'Darling! What's happened?' were the first friendly words I had heard for a while. I managed to explain in part, and within fifteen minutes, she was with me.

As a reporter of everyday events, I am party to unsavoury incidences, cruelty and even traumatic experiences that take place. This is all part of my job and over the years, my skin has thickened to it.

That said, Edith's recent account of the dangers she had subjected herself to, came as a shock to me. Despite certain aspects of her behaviour, she was a kind, endearing and compassionate soul, who in her own way, only wanted to right some of the wrongs instigated by a heartless and supercilious section of society.

It was obvious that Edith's recent ordeal also severely impacted on Maud. She is about to continue the story …

Chapter 17
Just Desserts

When I opened the door to Edie's hotel room, I could not believe what that bastard had done to my sister. I was so distraught that the tears welled up in my eyes.

My initial reaction was to phone the police, but Edie would have none of it. She said no one would believe her plight and in a way, I suppose she was right. She had disguised herself, gone gambling, been drinking at the bar with a group of men and then invited this man to her room. It would have been his word against hers in that he paid her for so-called rough sex to which she was totally agreeable. She wouldn't have a leg to stand on in court. That was her argument and I suppose she was right.

—Mr White, being a reporter, you will know that women seldom get a fair hearing. It's always them that seduce the men, never the men who force their intentions.

I ran a bath to get rid of the smell of that beast and bathe Edie's wounds. I organised clean sheets and put her to bed, staying all night to ensure her safety; she was not fit enough to go home. The hotel staff were aware something terrible had happened, but I assured them all would be well. She obviously didn't sleep very well; she had a nightmare and woke up screaming several times in the night.

I took her home the following day. The Maître D' himself approached me in the foyer and said he had tried to warn Edie. He knew what a vile creature Valantin was, but he had been prevented from getting anywhere near her. He used the word 'Mafioso' as if that would justify everything.

She rested for a week before we could even speak of the horrors of that day. I felt terrible because I felt responsible for much of her ordeal. It was another two weeks before she could go anywhere without wearing sun glasses and begin to look her usual self. She did have one lovely surprise which helped raise her spirits. Donald was still interested in her, and every woman likes to know they have someone interested in her. I told him that Edie had been mugged in Nice Centre and had been knocked about and wasn't well enough at the moment to receive visitors, but it didn't stop him phoning. Apparently, he even told his father of her ordeal.

I was extremely angry and certainly not prepared to let matters rest, with or without Edie's help. I need not have worried; my constant talk about getting our own back sped her recovery, and for the next few days we thought of nothing else. However, we knew our best ammunition would be to study this man's psyche, and his obsessive behaviour to control anyone or anything. We also realised that when he wasn't in a controlling mode, he could become out of control, if you see what I mean.

What was most important to me was I knew that if we could avenge the situation, the ghosts in Edie's mind would be laid to rest.

Whilst Edie had been in the casino on that Wednesday of the awful incident, I had taken a look at the grounds of Valantin's house and found it to be totally unguarded except for, what must have been two household staff – the cook and the cleaner. Valantin obviously thought his house was safe and it was only himself who was at risk, hence the need for his two bodyguards.

Therefore, if we were to do anything it would have to be on a Wednesday. We checked for a couple of weeks and sure enough, the ritual was the same: a little gambling and then the rendezvous with his friends at the Atlantic.

We came up with a simple plan: Bif, who would be armed, would take care of the driver at the Atlantic, whilst I would sort out the other African. We would be fully kitted out in dark clothes, including our balaclavas, of course, and for the first time since the war, I would be armed with a .38 Smith & Wesson with a silencer, for which I still have a permit, I might add!

The special treat in store for each of these despicable men was to be a little injection that would knock them out and thus keep them under control, whilst we did our worst. I really didn't care what happened to that dreadful man, or me for that matter. After a little more planning, we were now ready.

We decided to rob the house on that Wednesday as soon as we saw them leave. Sure enough at eight o'clock prompt, they departed.

We had considered all the options of how to get Valantin up to the bedroom at the hotel, but Edie knew she would be able to do that.

'Maudie, you forgot I returned to the hotel and booked in for three days, Edith said. 'Some of the staff actually remembered me and were pleased to see me feeling and looking much better, including the Maître D'. I took him into my confidence and told him I was going to get my own back.'

'"Be careful, young lady," he said to me in this glorious French accent. 'It must have been the young lady bit that flattered me, but he continued with the warning. "He's dangerous."

'"So am I," I retorted.

'You see … Maud was right. She did put the fight back in me. Just so that you know I wasn't prepared to expose myself unnecessarily – if you know what I mean – I didn't stay there on my own. It was just to make sure we had the same room and also enable us to prepare. We put my clothes in the wardrobe to make things appear real.'

Maud continues the story…

We parked carefully out of sight near Valantin's house but in view of the road that the thugs would drive along on their way to their evening's entertainment. We waited until the Mercedes passed us and was well out of sight, checking that there were three of them in the car.

We drove up to the house and on went our balaclavas. I opened the large wooden gates and Bif gently drove the car up the drive. We had changed the registration plate, of course. Bif parked in front of the house, Edie got out and knocked on the door. It was so simple.

The cook opened the door; the cleaning lady peered cautiously over his shoulder. They were obviously not expecting visitors. Neither were they expecting a revolver to be pointing straight at them. I did not enjoy frightening the pair in such a way but we had no choice. We were told everything we needed to know.

The safe only took a few minutes to open and it was full of identity cards, passports, medical cards … you name it. There were hundreds of documents, all stolen identities. What was noticeable by its absence was the obvious – the cash.

I put the gun to the man's head and asked him where the other safe was, but he was too scared to tell me. I made him kneel down and asked him again. No reply.

'I am very sorry,' I said slowly in French.

That was too much for the woman. 'No don't! Please don't. I will take you.'

I took the gun away from his head and followed the pair of them to the wine cellar, leaving Edith upstairs to find whatever she could. One of the wine racks was on very cleverly concealed rollers which moved easily with care, once a catch had been released. There it was … another easy safe. In fact, it was similar to one of the models I had trained on during the war. I remember we had a maximum of twenty minutes to sort this one and it usually took me about ten, but I was out of practice.

Fifteen minutes later, I could not believe my eyes! The safe was stacked with cash – dollars, sterling, French and Swiss francs and when we counted it back at home, there was the equivalent of over £350,000!

The French couple just stood there opened-mouthed and fearful of what was to come. They were obviously an item as he put his arms around her to console her. I gave them each 100,000 francs (£10,000) and told them to collect their belongings and leave immediately. I hastened to tell them I was contacting the police and that the monsieur and his African friends would not be coming back. They shot off, packed their belongings and left. I felt awful that I had terrified them, so before they left, I asked where the man's favourite café was and when he frequented it.

I know I'm sentimental but I wanted to do more for them. A few weeks later, I saw them sitting outside the Podium Café and approached them with a parcel.

'Marcel Laine?' I asked.

'Oui.'

'That man over there has asked me to bring this parcel to you.'

'Où?' (Where?) he asked.

'Il est là. (He is there.) He told me to tell you there will not be another.'

I was dressed as a little old lady, slightly stooped. 'Good bye. I hope all will be well with you,' I said, giving them a wink. From a distance, I could not help but notice their utter amazement ... and joy at the parcel's contents – a further £10,000.

They kept looking to see "that man over there" but after a while, gave up. Perhaps they'd worked out the significance of the wink.

Anyway, back to the story. It took some while to carry not just the money but the gold, silver, diamonds and other objets d'art that Edie had discovered. The robbing bastard had amassed a fortune out of unsuspecting tourists as well as the locals. There was considerable information to suggest that Valantin was head of a people smuggling organisation; there were records of all his contacts all those concerned with the pickpocketing racket; forgers' names and those officials on his pay roll including two senior police officers.

I relocked the safe, leaving all the passports except two for evidence, and we quickly returned home to change out of our clothes.

***

Edith continues ...

Bif took the Mini Cooper and drove us quickly to the Atlantic, dropping me off a short walk away and Maudie at the front entrance, just in case. He then parked the car in the front parking area. Together, we hurried through the swivel door, up the stairs and along to Room 232. Maudie was carrying a suitcase of tricks, its contents unknown to me, although I could hazard a guess.

It was now half past nine and we were ready. I was to go down to the lounge whilst Maudie remained upstairs to do her part, which she had kept to herself. I was tingling with anticipation and at ten o'clock on the dot, Valantin walked through the swivel doors, followed by Doctor Death who was wearing the same outfit as he had worn weeks before; I thought he must stink. Valantin walked straight into the lounge to be greeted by his usual friends, all full of themselves. Doctor Death remained some distance away and to my horror, he was joined by the other African. Had Bif failed in his part, I wondered? But as they seemed to be unconcerned, I thought perhaps the opportunity hadn't arisen.

Some of the 'lads' noticed I was sitting in the corner and signalled to Valantin. He turned towards me, looking very surprised and walked over.

'Bonsoir Madame. Pourquoi?' (Good evening, Madam. Why?)

'It was the biggest thrill of my life and the money wasn't good enough.' He burst out laughing. 'And you owe me double, and I want it,' I added over his laughter. 'This time, it's 10,000 francs in advance, and I'll show you a trick or two!'

I left him standing and walked over to the bar to order another drink, knowing that several of his friends would offer. I knew it would annoy him and I was right. 'I'll get it for my woman,' he said loudly, ensuring everyone heard, causing them to tease him somewhat and making him even angrier.

'Go over there,' he snarled, directing me with his arm to my corner. I dutifully went.

Once again he came over to see me, only this time he tried to kiss me and I turned away. He was embarrassed, grabbed hold of my face and kissed me full on the lips. When he pulled away, he left his trade mark saliva on my face, which I wiped off with a flourish. Another point to me, I thought. He could see his friends looking and he was becoming very annoyed.

'Give me my 10,000 francs or I am leaving.'

'You're going nowhere.'

I quickly drank my pink champagne, marched defiantly to the bar and asked if anyone was going to buy me a drink. That did it. He nearly lost it there and then. He grabbed my arm and held it so tightly I could have screamed and then, almost throwing me, forced me back in my corner, ordering the waiter to bring over my drink.

'Would you ask the monsieur to bring my 10,000 francs?' I asked the waiter in English. All of them spoke English, as all the best hotels employed English speaking staff.

His face was a picture when the waiter asked him for the money in front of his friends. He was so embarrassed, not least, seething. I was winning. It was quite funny. I stood up again, appearing to leave which caused him to call out to one of his Africans: 'NDoko! Look after her. Don't let her out of your sight and where's Beeno?'

'He was having trouble with the car, boss. Shall I go and see?'

'No. Watch her. I'm not putting up with this shit from a woman,' he said quietly, although making sure I heard.

I held out my hand, expecting the money and, to my amazement, he told NDoko to give it to me. He put his hand in his pocket and pulled out 1,000 francs and gave me that.

'Dix mille!' (10,000) I ordered, still holding my hand out. He looked at Valantin who nodded his approval.

I had the bastard; he was already fuming and I hadn't finished with him yet. One of the Africans had not returned so now I knew Bif had despatched one of them. I finished my drink and banged on the table, waving my glass in the air as if to demand another.

Valantin brought over a bottle himself, and leaning over snarled, 'What room are you in tonight?'

'Have you forgotten darling?' I replied cheekily, pulling him off balance and pushing his head into my boobs, which caused a few, including NDoko, to laugh. He tried to extricate himself but slipped further down, getting his nose caught in my dress between my bosom. I held his head by the ears and waggled it between my breasts before he was able to extricate himself. NDoko was still smiling but the look Valantin gave him made him shudder.

'I'll have you tonight,' he said, waving his finger at me. 'Now wait there and shut up.'

'But I want to go to the toilet.'

'NDoko. Take her.'

He followed me to the toilet and stood outside the door. I deliberately kept him waiting, so much so, I heard Valantin come and ask him what the hell was happening.

'She's in there, boss. There's no way out.'

'Go in and knock.'

'But boss!'

'Go in and knock. Now!'

He walked in. There was only my door locked so he knocked. 'Um, er ... Madame? Monsieur Valantin wants you. Now.'

'Tell him to go away. I'm reading my magazine.' I heard him go out and the door close behind him, but I could still hear everything that was said. He was even being told by hotel staff to calm down as he was disturbing the other guests.

This was all too much for Valantin, especially after he had been told that I was reading a magazine and wouldn't come out.

He opened the door and shouted, 'I will count to five and if you are not out, I'll smash the door in. One, two, three ...'

I opened the door gingerly and peeped out. 'Is my little chicken cross with me?'

He was shaking with anger almost uncontrollably. Once again, he grabbed hold of my arm and dragged me to my corner. I could now see Bif and the Maître D' coming to my rescue, but I managed to signal to Bif that all was okay, and he in turn, stopped the Maître D'. The latter still felt he would come and speak to me.

'Are you all right?' he asked in English.

'Don't worry, I'm all right, nothing serious will happen.'

'Be careful he is–'

'What's he saying?' Valantin interrupted.

'He just asked if I was all right.'

'And what did you say?'

'I told him everything is okay and that my husband is a bit jealous.'

With that, he walked back to his friends who in turn stared at me. I then committed the cardinal sin. NDoko had been ordered to walk me back to my corner and as he did so, I put my arm through his and held him close to me, my head leaning against his arm. I could sense NDoko felt uncomfortable, but the more he tried to shake me off, the tighter I held him.

Valantin stormed over and grabbed hold of my face with one hand. He wanted to know why I had insulted him.

'Well, NDoko is a big handsome boy, isn't he?' He let go of me and turning to NDoko said:

'Go and check the room.' NDoko stood there, shrugging his shoulders.

'What number did you say it was?' Valantin asked.

'I didn't.'

'Well, what is it?' he asked, spitting the words out. His saliva was bad enough when he was calm, but this lot was enough to sink the Bismarck.

I gave Valantin the key, who in turn gave it to NDoko. He started to leave when I got up to follow him.

'Where are you going?' Valantin asked.

'With NDoko, to my room.'

'No, you're not. Sit down.'

'No! I want to go with NDoko.'

The lounge became silent. You could hear a pin drop, and even Valantin could sense everyone was listening, so he decided to accompany NDoko and me to the lift.

So far so good. Our plan was working and I sensed he was beaten before he had started. He was so full of anger he could not think or rationalise, and he hadn't even noticed the other African hadn't returned. NDoko called the lift but was joined by Bif, so I decided to take the stairs to the lower floor, linking Valentin's arm to ensure he would do the same. He didn't even ask where we were going.

I walked him out into the open air and stood there, simply looking at him. I needed to keep him away from anything or anyone until I felt Bif was safe. He didn't say a word so, after a few minutes, I led him back into the hotel, up the stairs to the second floor, along the corridor towards Room 232, only to be faced with Maudie coming the other way. We did not acknowledge each other and I moved over to allow her to pass.

—Mr White, she was amazing!

It happened so quickly, I didn't know what was going on. Maudie kicked him so hard in the crutch he bent forward, unable to breathe, and then with another mighty kick which landed under his chin, he was unconscious. Bif was waiting anxiously by the door to my room, propping up NDoko against the wall and ready to explain to anyone passing that his friend was non compos mentis due to excessive alcohol intake. We dragged the bodies into the room and by the time Valantin came round, he was stark naked; hands and feet were handcuffed to the bed and as a precautionary measure, his mouth was taped with an industrial version of the product.

We sent Bif down to the car to look after the other African.

'Hello chérie, do you love me? Come on … tell me you love me. I can't hear you, chérie. Come on, tell me … now!' I yelled. 'Oh pardon, chérie, you can't. Your greasy little mouth is all taped up.' I yanked the tape off his face, which obviously caused severe pain, but he was such a hard bastard, he simply swore and spat at me, finishing with the words:

'I will *kill* you!'

'You haven't the guts to do it yourself, so who would do it for you? NDoko? He's on the floor here. Your other stooge is tied up in the boot of your car, and … whilst we speak, your safe at your villa has been opened and is being inspected by the police. We mustn't forget the safe in your cellar. I wonder what happened to all that cash? The dollars? The Swiss francs? And the pounds?'

'I'll tell you what happened to all that money, I took it for services rendered. Expensive services, don't you think?' I continued.

By now, Valantin was trying to sit up, at the same time, staring at me in total disbelief at what he was hearing. 'I bet you've never paid £350,000 for such short-lived moments of self-gratification, have you?'

At this moment, NDoko was showing signs of life. Bif had administered a quick-acting drug, which lasted about 30 minutes but NDoko now opened his eyes slowly and suddenly realised his predicament – handcuffed, feet tied, and naked. At least he could sit up to see what was happening.

Maudie introduced herself and told him that his boss was about to be castrated. 'And possibly you too,' she said dismissively.

With a sharp intake of breath, NDoko capitulated: 'He's the boss. I just work for him.'

'Liar!' I shouted 'You do everything he wants you to. You've even killed people for him.'

'But he made me. I had no choice,' he pleaded, his voice rising a few octaves. As far as we were concerned, we were finished with him. He was ready to be locked up, but we had different plans for Monsieur Valantin.

'Here is your money, Monsieur Valantin,' I said, producing a tightly rolled wodge of cash. 'Now come on, open your mouth.' He spat at me again, mouthing obscenities. I grabbed his nose tightly. He was struggling violently and it was necessary for another little calming jab.

I left Maud to sort him out whilst I propped up NDoko to watch.

'What's that, dear?' I asked Maud, who was holding what looked like a roll of wire.

'It's only cheese wire.'

'What on earth are you going to do with that?' I asked.

'Just what farmers do to dogs that worry sheep. They castrate them!'

'You can't do that!'

'I'm not. He will do it himself if he moves.'

I left her to it and when she had finished, Valantin couldn't move without the wire cutting into his genitals. If he did, he would regret it. I felt that was a bit unfair seeing that the monster did not have sexual relations with me; he simply got his erotic pleasure from beating up his victims. I was at least thankful for that.

When he woke up again, he found it was only his hands that were handcuffed together. He tried to sit up only to experience extreme discomfort as the wire tightened round his nether regions. I then explained what would happen if he made a false move.

'Now open your mouth,' I asked again, giving him a gentle push to remind him of his predicament and the pain of movement. 'Now ... open wide.'

He did as he was told and I gave him his money back, taping his mouth again for good measure. We made sure NDoko was incapable of doing anything else and bade them farewell.

A job well done, we thought. We telephoned the American and British Embassies, then the Gendarmerie and told them what we had done, supplying all the passport details as well as the photographs of the operation. This was to ensure that any attempts of corruption by the French would be impossible; thus the investigation could proceed smoothly.

I believe the three villains got their just desserts. They admitted numerous murders and were later executed.

Chapter 18
Like Father, Like Son

We had a few weeks' rest after my ordeal. Not wishing to cause me any further upset, even Maud behaved herself and refrained from her kleptomaniac activities ... well, almost. She managed to secure a beautiful cashmere sweater but couldn't remember where from, so I let her keep it.

We informed our friends that we would be returning to England for the spring and summer and that they would be welcome to visit if they happened to be passing Number 17. Few people ever came our way as it was off the beaten track, but we still had visitors.

A week or so before we left, I remember I was on my own at the villa; it was a very warm day at the beginning of March so I decided to sit outside by the pool and enjoy the sunshine when I received a visit from Michael Freisman.

'Hello Edie, I understand you are leaving for England soon?' he said as he walked over to me. 'Why didn't you tell me?'

'We've only just decided in the last day or so,' I replied.

I moved across to the settee and invited him to join me. He sat down and immediately put his hand on my knee.

'What about us?' he asked. It suddenly dawned on me that he might be getting serious. I put my hand on his and squeezed it a little to let him know I was fond of him.

We had been chatting for a few minutes when I thought I would find out what happened about the missing wallets and purses.

'Michael, did you ever find my little red purse after your party?'

'Edith, you are not going to believe this,' he began, looking very ashamed. 'I know I can tell you, but we had the most bizarre burglary you could imagine and it must have been one of the guests.'

'Why? What on earth happened?' I asked, trying to sound genuinely concerned.

'When everyone had gone I went into the study and there on the table was Mary's handbag, and it was bulging open. I couldn't believe my eyes. The handbag was full of the guests' wallets and purses plus other things ... jewellery, trinkets and the like.' I managed a puzzled expression. 'The wallets were full of money and cheque books. There were gold compacts, gold and silver cigarette lighters and cases and several watches. I just could not believe it.

'I stormed in to confront Mary, and without thinking, asked her what on earth she had been doing, stealing all these things.

'"I don't know what on earth you're on about," she replied, almost in tears. I took her to the study and showed her the handbag. She nearly passed out. She seemed to know nothing about it and then she remonstrated with me.

'"Why would I want to steal when I don't need anything? And anyway, I have my own money," she added.

'The fact that I had even doubted her in the first instance caused an almighty row. Once she had calmed down she asked what we were going to do about the problem.

'I hadn't a clue. I wanted to phone the police and bring them into things, but it may have caused embarrassment to some of the guests. I then looked in the safe.'

'Ooh! Have you got a safe?' I asked.

'Much good that was. The thief pinched the only real thing I had of any value. It was a beautiful diamond bracelet which I bought for my mother and when she died,

I always intended to give to someone special. Edith, if I get it back, I shall give it to you.'

At that remark, I gulped. A sudden sense of shame came over me and the most I could do was feign a weak smile.

'The thief took the bracelet and filled the safe with the wallets and purses and then relocked it. I could not understand why he did that and how he could have taken all those things without being noticed by anyone. Not one of the guests saw anything and yet he collected all the items together and then left them behind. Doesn't make sense, especially as there was a lot of money in the wallets.'

'Perhaps he got disturbed?'

'Yes, that's a distinct possibility and it gives me an idea. I will write to all the guests telling them there was thief at work; he must have been disturbed and dropped them all in his effort to escape. That will save the embarrassment and they will think it was one of the hired staff.'

It's interesting that Michael thought the thief was masculine; I've never looked at Maud in that way. I've always thought she was very feminine even when she was in the Navy with all those handsome blokes, but I suppose it's always assumed that only men perform robberies.

'Let's not talk about it anymore,' Michael said. With that, he put his arm around me, leaned over and kissed me. It was very pleasant and I responded accordingly. What girl wouldn't? Anyway, one thing led to another and the kissing became more intent; that was until we heard a car pull up in the drive at the front of the house.

'I'll just pop in and see who it is, and get rid of them.'

'Great,' Michael said, looking a little deflated at the interruption.

I ran barefoot into the house to see who it was. To my horror it was Donald.

'Deux minutes!' I shouted through the door and charged back to the garden to Michael.

'Michael, it's Donald at the front door.'

'What the hell is he doing here?'

'How the hell do I know!' I snapped back. 'He's just arrived as you did.'

'Edith, he can't see me here, I've got to hide.'

'What about your car? I've seen it at the front.'

'Oh God! Make some excuse.'

'Michael! Go! I've got to let him in.'

'Where? Go where?'

'Quick, go to my bedroom and wait there till I come and get you. Don't come out.'

I quickly spruced myself up and walked to the door full of smiles.

'Donald! What a surprise, how lovely to see you.'

He didn't greet me but simply shouted: 'What's my father doing here? Where is he?'

'What do you mean "Where is he?" He's not.'

'What's his car doing here and why did you take so long to come to the door?'

'I was naked and I didn't know who it was. If I thought it was you, I would have opened the door … naked …' I whispered sexily in his ear.

'Edie, I know he's here and I want to see him.'

'Donald, he's not.'

'Then why's his car here?'

'Donald, your father asked us if he could leave his car here as he had just met a man he was doing business with. They told us they would be an hour or so and drove off.'

'Where's Maud then?'

'She had just gone out a minute or two before you arrived.'

'Edith, I don't believe you!' Donald immediately began searching the house, much to my pretence of annoyance. He looked in all the downstairs rooms and then started to go upstairs.

'Donald, you can't just go up there searching our rooms. That's not very nice.'

'Look, I know my father's here. I know he is and I'm going to find him.'

'Donald – no!' I shouted, more in an attempt to warn his father of his impending doom. This only made him more certain his father was in the house. He now stood outside Maudie's bedroom with me trying to stop him entering.

'Edith, I don't believe you. Where is he?' He pushed me away from Maudie's door and looked in. Of course, there was no one there. 'I know he's here,' he remonstrated. He walked further along the corridor.

'That's my room, Donald and he's not in there either.'

He walked in and looked under the bed. 'I am sorry Edith,' he said and walked slowly towards me. He put his arms round my neck, pulled me gently towards him and kissed me. I wasn't sure, but somehow I could sense that Michael was in the wardrobe, listening to all this. By now, I was a little out of my depth.

'I'm sorry I didn't believe you,' Donald whispered. 'But I have just heard you are leaving and I don't want you to.'

'Donald, you are welcome to visit us any time at Number 17. I would love to see you,' I replied, trying to act casual.

I'm sure he felt that I was being a little aloof as he suddenly remarked, 'Is everything all right? You seem … distant.'

In for a penny, in for a pound, I thought and put my arms around him. He tightened his grip and gently pushed me onto the bed. For the next half an hour, he made passionate love to me.

I must admit I thoroughly enjoyed myself. When I realised my predicament and started to laugh, I had to turn it into a scream of delight.

'Edith, you are fantastic, please stay. I don't want you to go … I think I am in love with you.'

'No, you're not. Now don't be silly,' I said, trying to reassure the man in the wardrobe. 'You want to get a young woman more your own age, someone you can fall in love with. I am too old for you.'

'Edith, you're not.'

I wondered what on earth Michael was thinking. I had to put a stop to it and told a white lie. 'Is that your father arriving back, or is it Maud?'

It was his cue to get dressed, all the while apologising for doubting me.

'Oh, don't worry,' I replied, kissing him passionately on the lips and escorting him downstairs to the door.

'Please come again,' I said with conviction. Thank goodness his father was still upstairs.

'Don't worry, I will. I love you,' he said again.

I raced upstairs to my room to find Michael was already out of the wardrobe, sitting on the bed and looking very cross.

'Why did you seduce my son and why did you make love to him?'

I was now cross. 'Michael, darling, you were in my wardrobe and your son thought you were having it away with me. If I hadn't had sex with him he would have found you. I had to make it convincing, didn't I? You are a married man in a very responsible position. Do you want people to think you are having an affair with me?'

'Well, yes Edith, I do. I want you.'

I couldn't believe what I was hearing. I wanted to put my head in my hands and start screaming. I now had a father and son wanting me. I was only thankful there wasn't a grandson.

'Michael, come here. Come and make love to me. On second thoughts, let's run a bath together and make love in the bath. I'm a bit sweaty.'

What an afternoon. The naughty man had me over the

bath. Then we had the bath; then we got into bed for a rest, or should I say, for the rest. Father and son were so generous with their affections. I felt we ought to return the items we had stolen from them.

We finally got dressed and returned to the garden. He lay across me on the settee with his head on my lap whilst I caressed him. I was in paradise for a while and could have stayed there forever until he spoiled things by saying:

'Edith, I think I am falling in love with you.'

What a mess I was now in. What made it worse, I was now very fond of them both. We lay there until Maudie returned to impart the most exciting news of the day.

'Hello Michael. What are you doing here, or need I ask? I've just seen Donald sitting in his car round the corner. Is he waiting for you?' she asked with a knowing grin on her face.

'No, he's not. Bloody nuisance.'

'Maudie? Would you help us to get out of this mess, please? Michael needs to be taken down the road and dropped off away from here and doesn't want to be seen by Donald.'

'Of course, he doesn't. You got yourselves in this mess. You get out of it.'

'Please,' I begged. 'I won't ask you again. Please.'

'Come on then,' she said, showing a little annoyance. 'You'll have to get into the back of the car.'

I put my arms round Michael's neck and kissed him goodbye, which annoyed Maudie even more.

'Come on, put him down and hurry up.'

He crept into the back of the Rolls and Maud drove off, but Donald wasn't that stupid. He followed the car. Thank God, Maudie saw him and drove to a friend's house.

Eventually, Donald got fed up or thought I was telling the truth and left the area, giving Michael the opportunity to pick his car up and, of course, to see me again.

'Big head,' Maud interrupted.

Before we took our leave of Nice for the summer, I went out a couple of times with them both; at different times, of course.

***

I remember it only took four hours door to door when it would have taken us two or three days using the other methods of travel. Bif shipped the cars back and we resumed our lives at Number 17.

It was lovely to see Stanley and Alice again. To our amazement, Stanley had made a small fortune for us in a few share deals and investments, but the biggest surprises were two weddings – Stanley's and Alice's. We had a very busy summer indeed. They were wonderful affairs with all our friends, many coming over from France. Even Michael and Mary made the effort to come, which must have been an effort for Mary; I believe she may have known about my liaisons with Michael!

Stanley was betrothed to Elodie, a lovely French girl. Alice never told James, her fiancé that she was well off until they had been engaged for a couple of months, James being a normal lad from a normal family. Both couples were married in the lovely little church in Fracklington village.

Unlike most newly-weds, they had the opportunity of moving into the Hall or buying a house of their own or even building one on the estate. Both chose the latter. Stanley kept his office at the Hall and became the Estate Manager; Alice now looked after the household as we had a full-time staff of twenty, which took some looking after. Maud, in conjunction with Stanley managed all security aspects of the estate, particularly because times were changing. There were more villains about and more sophisticated robberies taking place, which required ever increasing vigilance.

I had a couple of visits from Donald which upset him as he still held a torch for me, but he was embarrassed to tell me that he had put one of his bimbos in the club and was going to marry her out of decency. No basis for marriage as far as I was concerned. At least he was finally beginning to grow up. Michael was furious as you can imagine; he would have liked a grand affair, but it wasn't to be. However, both Maudie and I flew down to it and it was lovely.

Donald had now joined his father's business and began learning the trade. He has remained my friend as did Michael who became a regular visitor. Sadly, Michael died a few years back; he was another man I fell for, but had to settle for a loving friendship. I do miss him so.

—Mr White I think it's time I called it a day. I am becoming maudlin. Same time next week?

***

There was still time in the day for me to pop back to the office at the Mail. George was due to report to the Home Office and was keen to get an update from me on the latest events at Number 17.

I really didn't want to say too much for fear of compromising my situation. Neither did I want to make it difficult for the two old dears; I had grown rather fond of them, their candour and their joie de vivre.

***

'Right then. Let's have it, Clive – from the roots up with the bark off!' George exclaimed the moment I walked in.

'George, I can't explain. These two old women have an incredible story, particularly Maud, the quiet one as I think of her. I am convinced she was sent over to the Bahamas during the war to open the safe of a very senior person who was known to have Nazi sympathies. She was to either steal certain papers or photograph them, and I have the feeling I'll hear more in the next day or so.

'Working as a team they have been instrumental in exposing several illicit schemes carried out by many rogues. They've given their ill-gotten gains for want of a better expression, to various charities in the name of such villains. You remember the French gangster, Jacques Valantin? He was one of them. They also caught that far right Nazi, de Clancy before the war. You know the one we were mixed up with?'

'I remember it, Clive, but I wasn't around then and neither were you.'

George's secretary suddenly interrupted us. He was required urgently by the paper group's chairman. George suspected it was to do with this story and quietly told me to disappear for a few days and get the notes written up, which is exactly what I did. It is very difficult for a reporter to write up a story when he or she knows there could be so many other interesting things under the surface which would make the story not just ordinary, but sensational!

Chapter 19
A Sting in the Tale

I was relieved that both my boss and I were spared any further visits to the *Mail* from Fitzpatrick. Hopefully, I was keeping my cover and spent the next week researching all the rumours and insinuations the two sisters had made. That only created many more questions than answers. I looked forward to our next meeting like an excited child.

Naturally, I arrived at Number 17 prompt at 2 o'clock and was ushered straight into the conservatory where the ladies were already waiting for me.

'Mr White, I hope you don't mind but we thought we would have a change of venue and meet in here,' Maud said chirpily, glancing up from her knitting.

'Not at all, it's very pleasant. In fact, the whole house is very pleasant,' I replied.

'Thank you, Mr White, said Edith. 'That's very kind of you. Now I would remind you I still have all my faculties, despite my age, and I can remember exactly where we left off.
Edith continues the story ...

The estate ran like clockwork and there was very little for Maud to do, with the result she made several incursions to London to top up her habit, but as CCTV became more and more sophisticated, she was caught more and more. Fortunately, she was made a special case and even when one of the shops decided to take matters further, it was found that due to her illness, it would not be in the public interest to prosecute her. She was convinced they were deliberately putting last year's stock in her way and even had the audacity to ask if it was the current year's fashions!

Our doctor suggested that Maud try a hypnotist to help her overcome her problem. We had heard that a Mercedes Grant was very good; in fact Grant himself was boasting exceptional achievements – even the posters in his clinic guaranteed 100% success for stopping addictions. We have to remember though that her wartime training had given her extraordinary powers of resistance.

Maudie turned up at Grant's clinic for the first time and sat in this lovely waiting room, skimming through the magazines, showing all the latest household equipment on sale, which in reality, would have been her next target.

She did not realise she was being watched. In fact she had been waiting over half an hour when she decided enough was enough and called the receptionist to say that she was not going to be kept waiting any longer and was leaving. That was Grant's cue; he came in quickly, apologised profusely and explained it was part of his technique to cure problems. Naturally, she accepted the apology and went into his room to begin treatment.

Mercedes Grant was like Perry Como, the singer/entertainer. He adopted the 'Mr Casual' approach. In fact, he was trying to be so casual, I think she may well have fallen asleep and when he tried to put Maudie under his influence, he couldn't even get close. In the end she pretended to go under and when he had finished she told him he hadn't succeeded. He could not understand why, so she told him she had been trained to resist all forms of psychoanalysis, including hypnotism and did it automatically. As she left his establishment she turned to him and pointed at a poster on the wall.

'What?' he asked.

'You didn't get me, so it's not 100%!'

Within days of her visit she had been caught again. It was

always the same routine: they would telephone me, Mr Higginbotham or Stanley and explain the circumstances, leave her with the goods and we would send the money.

The only cure for Maud's problem as I have said before and will undoubtedly say again, was to keep her busy and what happened next was born out of tragedy, but it certainly kept her busy.

We were often invited to parties at Wilbur Thornber's house. I say 'house'; it was a wonderful place with many acres of land and woods around it. Wilbur was about my age and very fit. He was also a very wealthy American, and held dual British nationality.

His wife Aletha, was an attractive woman, but was well known for playing away from home with all and sundry – a bit like me I suppose, except I wasn't married to a lovely man. Anyway, that's where I came in; I always helped him in his hour of need. We had a lovely arrangement we would go out together with no strings attached. I would often attend functions with him and pretend I was his PA, which often didn't work as I was as well-known as he was.

The Thornber's parties were extravagant events and within a couple of hours, both the host and hostess were always missing. He was always with me and she was with anyone, which was just accepted. On this one occasion, the party was in full swing and we sneaked off in our usual fashion. Everyone knew where we were going. He was making love to me and I was in the missionary position when he suddenly, he tensed up and yelled out. I thought he was just enjoying himself and had reached a climax. Not the case. Everything stopped and I was stuck there. He didn't move for what seemed like a few minutes.

'Come on, Wilbur darling, I know I'm good but this is a bit–' I stopped, realising something dreadful was happening. He then rolled off me and hit the floor … dead.

I couldn't believe it! He was a very fit man, in the prime

of life and this had happened. I got dressed and went to look for Aletha, who was missing as usual, so I phoned the police. It was probably the worst thing to do from Aletha's point of view, but in the long run, the best for me. I actually felt something was wrong, but couldn't put my finger on it.

The police arrived along with an ambulance and the party came to an end. I was of course the last person to see him alive and I had to tell them what I was doing. The police were a smutty lot of sods and thought they would have a laugh at my expense, enjoying what they thought would be my discomfort, concentrating their initial questions on the sexual side.

I felt there was no point in concealing the fact so I told them I was having a party bonk.

—Not quite in those words, Mr White.

I told them I was having intercourse with the man; that he was a very good friend, and we had known each other for years. There wasn't much more I could say.

The police officers left me to concentrate on the rest of the guests who all quite rightly so told them he went to bed with me; thankfully some said it was nothing unusual.

About half an hour later, Aletha arrived back. She was immediately given the news that Wilbur had died and that I was in his bed at the time it happened.

Well, Sarah Bernhardt could not have put on a better performance! She told the police she had left the party to be on her own and had been walking round the grounds because she was upset in the knowledge that I was in her bed with her husband.

Maud had overheard Aletha telling a police officer that Wilbur was trying to get rid of me, that I had threatened him if he didn't leave his wife, and that I was after his money. Well!

That was a foolish and elementary mistake for Aletha to make because it made the police take a thorough look at the situation, just in case a crime had been committed. It also made them investigate my association with Wilbur and the allegations she made about me.

Everyone was questioned and eventually allowed to go home – except me. I was asked to go to the police station to help them with their enquiries, which of course I did, accompanied by Maud, who would never let me down. She had also phoned Higginbotham who arrived there just a few minutes after us.

I was taken into the interrogation room where I refused to say anything without my solicitor present, who duly arrived and insisted that the evidence at the moment, pointed to a heart attack and that we should wait until the autopsy before jumping to conclusions. However, Maudie had told Higginbotham what she had heard Aletha say and he jumped in with both feet.

'I understand you have been told my client was after his money. Are you aware who this lady is?'

'Edith Trenchard,' the copper replied.

'I would suggest you refer to *Who's Who*,' Higginbotham responded. 'Her fortune is more than that of our Queen. Why therefore would she want this man's money? They had been friends for years and I would suggest you look at his wife's behaviour. It is well known. Officer, you have no reason to detain my client as you have no evidence against her. Are you going to charge her? If not, we are leaving now.'

With that, he took my hand and marched me out of the station.

—Maud, you tell Mr White what happened next.

Maud takes up the thread …

The police doctor's initial diagnosis revealed Wilbur died of asphyxiation and in consequence Edith was taken in once again to be questioned. Thankfully, she had Mr Higginbotham with her again. He was wonderful.

'Just doing my job, Maud, just doing my job,' Higginbotham said.

' I just felt they knew I hadn't done anything wrong,' Edith added. Yet I felt as though I were a criminal. They sat me down and I was given a warning that everything was being recorded and may be used in evidence et cetera. At that point, Mr Higginbotham seemed to take over and he began the questioning:

'You say you *believe* Thornber died from asphyxiation. So you don't know?'

'No, not exactly,' the constable replied.

'So what do you believe ... exactly?' he asked. The constable was that flummoxed he did not answer.

'You don't know. Let me clear up a few points before you start. Were there any signs in that bedroom that indicated something had been used to suffocate the man? Where there any signs of a struggle? And while we are on this subject, don't you think a man built like Wilbur Thornber would resist the woman he is allegedly trying to get rid of and try and stop her killing him, bearing in mind the positional advantage he had?'

'We only have her word for that,' the other officer chipped in confidently.

'That's not correct, officer. My client stated that he was on top of her when he fell off and hit the floor. Had she been on top of him, she would have simply got off and dragged him off the bed, and there would have been markedly different injuries. Or haven't you examined the body yet?

'My client will not answer any further questions until after the autopsy has been completed. I would ask you to look at the possibility of the poison aconite being administered because this gives the appearance of asphyxiation. I would also request that my pathologist is given the opportunity to attend the autopsy or alternatively carry out a private one as soon as possible.'

You are an expert on poisons now, are you?' the constable asked sarcastically.

'Indeed, I am. I have often been called on by the Home Office to advise on such matters. I see you do not have anything to charge my client with. As this has now been a waste of time, I will send you my bill and my client and I will leave now.'

We just upped and left again.

The autopsy did reveal Wilbur was poisoned. The news hit the press like a dose of salts. They were everywhere for a story, particularly the *News of the World*. They can always smell a good one: 'Rich People's Romps' or something like that. However they were called off and it took me some time to realise why, but I'll tell you about that later. The story about Wilbur's death was reported, but the details were left out.

I knew Edie would be cleared of everything. Quite simply, she wouldn't do anything like that to anyone, let alone a friend and lover of many years. She is a bit of a floozy but that's Edith. There is not a bad bone in her body and I was furious that the Aletha woman could have made comments like that about her; I couldn't forgive it.

The cause of death was poisoning. Mr Higginbotham had requested details of the poison used, but as yet, and this was some days later, they hadn't discovered which one or what family of poison it was.

It was common sense to think that something was amiss by Aletha's attempt to throw the scent away from herself and onto Edie. I was convinced it needed investigating, especially after the police arrived at Number 17 and told us they did not believe Edie was involved, for several reasons. They then apologised for their treatment of her.

I started to make enquiries about Aletha amongst her family and close friends. Her relationships with her male friends were particularly interesting as were her everyday habits. Some amazing results came to light.

She was first and foremost a shopaholic and had run up incredible debts at Harrods and other major stores, including the designer jewellery outlets. To my surprise, I learned that Wilbur had warned her he would not cover her debts if she continued in this vein.

I decided to break into the matrimonial home to take a look at their financial records, specifically her credit cards. It was quite easy because in those days, the police were not as diligent as they are today in protecting scenes of investigation. I left a trail of clues as I went into the house, which was deserted, having had to run several hundred yards over the grass and soil because I couldn't park anywhere near the house for fear of being seen. Police patrols passed every now and then, the occasional one going to the front door and taking a cursory look around the place, for security purposes.

Careful to avoid any confrontation, I managed to gain entry through one of the downstairs windows with a simple pen knife and a little tape.

It was fortunate that the house was empty as it took me ages to find the safe, which was well hidden. It was of a type I had not seen before and it took well over an hour to break into it. I photographed the contents to look at them later on and hurried to Aletha's bedroom to look for anything that could shed light on her behaviour. I knew they had separate bedrooms as Edie, hussy that she is, had often told me. It's often a sign that the relationship has ended when this happens.

I searched all her handbags, cases, coat pockets, you name it. She was most certainly in debt, right up to her pretty neck, having hidden dozens of bills, credit cards and payment reminders from Wilbur's scrutiny. Again, I photographed all these and returned the contents to their rightful places. A casual look in one of her handbags revealed a very small photograph of a young man in his mid to late forties. Inside one of her lockets in her jewellery box I discovered another picture of this man. I hadn't a clue who he was, but I knew it wouldn't take long to find out.

I went over to Wilbur's room only to find he had another safe hidden behind a picture. Like all careful men, it was obvious he had removed this one from downstairs and replaced it with the new one. Quite rightly so as I had it open within minutes. I took more photographs but had to finish my search quickly as the dawn began to break and I realised I would be seen making my getaway. I returned through the window, closing it behind me, across the lawns, and down the road to some fields where I had discreetly parked the Mini.

The following day I began to develop the pictures and was astonished to find Wilbur had made a new will and poor Aletha was not mentioned. His entire estate went to his niece in the States. Good for him, I thought. But it was unsigned leaving the question of whether this was a copy. At least there was now a motive for his killing. Did Aletha know she was being cut out of the will?

I called Wilbur's solicitors, Honeyford and Spellman in the High Street; I knew them very well as they acted for our tenants and farmers when we had legal matters to sort out. We paid their bills promptly; Father always said it was the best thing to do. Miss Honeyford who was a glamorous fifty-year-old, had kept her maiden name for business purposes. Her father and grandfather before her had run the business and had a notable reputation for honesty and straightforwardness. They were also family friends and I confided in her the problem Edith had and the fact that I believed that Aletha and or her boyfriend were guilty of killing Wilbur. I confessed I had a copy of his intended will and asked her to confirm whether it had been signed. She was reluctant until I gave her my copy.

'Yes, we do have a copy on file and yes, it is signed,' Miss Honeyford replied. But it was when I asked if Aletha knew of the will that the can of worms opened.

'I shouldn't really tell you this but under the circumstances ... I will. Wilbur was emphatic he did not want her to know because I am sure he knew she was going to walk out. He also had a few problems which we were dealing with because Aletha had run up many thousands of pounds of debt. There a few court actions pending and now she will have to face this herself. It will surprise you to know he has left over ten million pounds and has half a million in cash.'

'Good God! That's a motive for murder if anything is,' I remarked.

The next port of call for both Edie and I was the home of Jason Williams, the alleged boyfriend. Within a couple of days, we not only found out all about him, but most importantly, his address in Marlow. He was also a notable villain – into both hard and soft drugs, and using his car dealership as a front. This time however, and from then on we began to take photographs of everything.

He was well worth a look at, especially after our first sortie when we witnessed Aletha and him in the house together. It was a disgraceful situation when you think Wilbur was still not buried. Of course, when the autopsy concluded that Wilbur *was* poisoned, the spotlight fell firmly on them.

We kept a close eye on both, to see what, where and when they did anything, but the circumstances although self-inflicted, were tragic.

I had decided to look more closely at Williams' house, and after our thorough investigations we found that Wednesday morning was the only time the house was left unattended.

Bif drove me to the house whilst Edie kept watch. The first thing that troubled me was the alarm was not set; it was not like him to forget, but at least it allowed me easy access. I immediately went for the safe and could not believe its contents. There was one £150,000 in cash and some of the jewellery that we had noted from the receipts in her handbag. I was looking at everything when I heard some movement above and quickly but quietly crept up upstairs.

I couldn't believe my eyes. Aletha was sitting at a dressing table in one of the bedrooms and appeared blind drunk. It was obvious too that she had been beaten up. She saw me, but thankfully I had a balaclava on; there was no way she could identify me or converse with me for that matter.

It was time for me to leave. I pulled a sheet off the bed and dashed downstairs, wrapping everything I'd retrieved in it to make a bundle. I could not take any further chances with her in the house as it was still daylight. This was not the moment to find the drugs, but I suspected they would be there somewhere.

Dr Barnardo's received a welcome addition to their funds with the compliments of Jason Williams, including his address. I reported anonymously that I had heard a woman's screams coming from Wilbur's house and that I believed that someone was in danger. I don't know what the outcome was, but I know the police went to the house and a woman was taken away in an ambulance. The trouble was I believe I had inadvertently given Williams an excuse, seeing that the house had been burgled that morning.

We kept tabs on him and one could see he was no longer interested in poor Aletha. He was now a regular at the Elephant and Castle and was meeting a very sexily dressed long-haired brunette. From their demeanour, it seemed they knew each other well. I decided to warm things up a little and walked in.

'Hello Mr Williams. It is Jason Williams?'

'Yes, that's me. Who wants to know?'

'I'm Polly Bottle from the charity, Dr Barnardo's. I was told I would see you here. We want to thank you so much for the £150,000 donation you gave to us recently. Such generosity is overwhelming and we were wondering if you would appear on television with us? His eyes nearly popped out of his head. He sat totally immobile and speechless, just staring at me whilst several people around him began congratulating him.

'No, I don't want to know things like that. 'Op it.'

'He's a very generous man, folks. He gave £150,000 to Dr Barnardo's,' I announced to everyone in the pub.

As I turned to go, I couldn't resist the sting in the tail: 'Mind you, we have reason to believe he acquired these funds from selling drugs and he's mixed up in the murder of the American businessman Wilbur Thornber. Good Night. See you Jason!'

'You fuckin' will!' he yelled, but by now I was outside and away. I saw him outside shaking his fist. I just waved to him through the car window.

We continued to check his movements and eventually followed him to an industrial complex in Harlesden where he had a warehouse unit, which made paper bags. It was, by all accounts, a thriving business; they certainly received a lot of orders, and certainly had many deliveries to and from the place. I believed that this was a front for his main business – drugs. It was a simple matter for me to look over the place. I broke in and found a small laboratory tucked away at the back. This one was for the police. I did not want to disturb anything and give him an excuse to get away with it this time. Even so, whilst I was building up a picture of the man, I still could not tie him into the murder.

Williams had become ultra-careful in all his dealings; he had even obtained a bodyguard who travelled with him everywhere and furthermore, he now had a house sitter who remained in the house at all times, which made things difficult, so we decided to put pressure on Aletha. This time, Edie went to see her on the pretext of finding out when the funeral was.

Edith continues ...

I walked up the small drive to the front of the house and rang the bell. A heavily-built man opened the door.

—Mr White, I don't know whether you remember Arthur Mullard, the film actor? He was a big gruff actor with an equally gruff cockney accent and looked the epitome of a villain. Well, this man was the spitting image of him.

'What d'ya want?' he demanded.

'Is Aletha in? I've come to see her ... to find out when her husband's funeral is.'

'I'll get 'er.'

'Gosh! What on earth has happened to you?' I asked as she came to the door.

'Edith? It is Edith?' she asked. 'What are you doing here?'

'I came to find out when the funeral is. But more importantly, what's happened to you?'

'We were robbed and I was beaten up,' she replied. 'I've only just come out of hospital.'

'Good Lord!'

'How did you know I was here?' she asked.

'The police told me.'

'I thought you were a ...'

'Suspect?' I interrupted.

'Well ... urm ... yes.'

'No, not at all. They knew it wasn't me from the start. You told them you thought I was trying to force him to leave you. I simply told them he was concerned that you were spending too much money, which he told me just before he died. That cleared me because I had no motive. I didn't want to fall out with you, Aletha or for things to become unpleasant between us. I'd better go. Perhaps you would let us know when the funeral is? We would all like to pay our respects to Wilbur. Good bye.'

I left her a very worried woman and when Maud decided to look at the house again, she went prepared for a fight. This time she was armed with a .38.

'Licensed to carry, I assure you, Mr White,' Maud chipped in.

When Maud arrived at the house, the door was again opened by Bully Boy.

'Yeah! Wadya want? he enquired in his polite, welcoming manner.

'Is Mr Williams in?' Maud asked.

'No one's in.'

'Good,' she said and immediately sprayed his face with C.S. gas. He fell to his knees, whereupon Maud touched a pressure point, and he was out for the count.

She opened Williams' safe, taking another huge chunk of money, a Rolex watch and all his papers, plus a notebook with some very useful contents. She emptied his cupboard drawers and wrote all over his walls, *Murderers! You will be caught! Aletha is the number one suspect and Jason is the number two. One of you is going down. Which one will it be?*

She relocked the safe and seeing that Bully Boy was coming round, decided it was time to go. She also put copies of the photographs we had taken all over the place but the pièce de résistance was the photographs she put in Aletha's handbag, depicting Williams' cosy liaison with the busty brunette.

Maud stayed around, waiting for Jason to come home. He was greeted by Bully Boy who was waiting at the gate, ready to tell him what had happened, and terrified of what might happen to him. The noise which emanated from the house for the next half an hour was enough to wake up the entire population of Marlow. It was when he must have been checking his safe that she thought the atomic bomb had been dropped.

Jason's notebook revealed a multitude of sins. The fact that we had another £85,000, which we were donating to Barnardo's in his name was beginning to put him into difficulties with his creditors. I continued the pressure by prompting the press, giving them a regular update of what was happening, which meant they were there almost all the time.

The family too kept watch on the place and it became increasingly obvious that Aletha was constantly being kept in a drunken state and was seldom seen out. We sent more photographs to Aletha. Finally, the balloon went up, especially after one showed Jason in a passionate embrace with his brunette. Aletha finally walked out in an inebriated state and managed to get back to the former marital home.

We had divided the two guilty parties and knew we could conquer, but we still did not have any proof of where they had acquired the aconite and who administered it to Wilbur. Aletha seemed not only too soft, but incapable of knowing what to do, and therefore we concentrated our efforts on Williams. It was obvious that Aletha was totally besotted with Williams, otherwise she would not have put up with the beatings he gave her or lied about the break-in. We concluded that Williams must have supplied the poison. As to who gave the fatal dose, that remained to be seen.

—Maudie, you tell Mr White what happened next.

Maud finishes the story ...

We knew Williams wasn't stupid. Careless perhaps when he was annoyed, but I could not imagine him leaving any sign of poison at his home. He would know that the police would do a thorough search if he became a suspect.

You can't buy this poison from anywhere; it's not like arsenic or other well-known poisons, where you can obtain it from legitimate sources. It had to be made and somewhere other than Marlow. His little drug laboratory in Harlesden was the obvious place, but again, he was unlikely to leave any clues lying around.

I decided to take another look at his warehouse unit, which again was simple as there was no security. I think he assumed no one knew about the place. He was probably right; it was also a long way from his home in Marlow.

I went back to the factory late one evening to find there were a few people still working there. I kept my distance, noting who went in and out. A lightly-built man came out and got into a new Peugeot 105 and I decided to follow him. He stopped outside a semi-detached house in Willesden and went in, using his own key. I stopped further up the road and waited to see what might happen. Within a few minutes, he came out again, wearing a change of clothes and got back into the car. Again, I followed him to a car park near Willesden Green underground station where he parked the car and hurried to catch the Tube. I did the same, accidently bumping into him at the ticket office after he had bought the ticket. I now had his wallet. We caught the train, and to my astonishment he went to the Elephant and Castle where he met the busty brunette.

Concerned that Williams might come in, I positioned myself out of sight but within earshot. The man's wallet revealed his identity – a Charlie Watts of 277 Harlesden Road, Willesden, which is where I saw him. He was single and lived with his parents.

Charlie soon realised he was without his wallet. Not easy to create an impression on a lady when in that predicament, but to my utter surprise, the brunette overcame the problem and actually bought the drinks.

It was obvious to me how desperate Williams had become to maintain control of the situation. He was using his girlfriend's talents to make up to Charlie. I thought I would stoke the fire a little by going to their table.

'Wow, you're slumming it, aren't you? What's Jason Williams going to say when I tell him?'

Charlie immediately got up and hurried out of the pub. I went straight after him. His pace quickened and by the time I was within a few feet of him, he'd started to run.

'Charlie Watts, how nice to see you!' I shouted to attract his attention. 'Can we have a chat?'

He turned round to face me and stopped in his tracks.

'What about?'

'Can we go somewhere quiet?'

'It'll do here.'

'Sure?'

'Yeah.'

'Well,' I said loudly. 'It's about your complicity in the murder of the American, Wilbur Thornber.' He grabbed hold of my arm and pulled me to one side.

'Please keep your voice down. I don't know what yer talkin' about.'

'Oh yes you do, Charlie. You made the poison.'

'What poison?' he asked a little cockily.

'Aconite ... and you know perfectly well.'

The colour drained from his face.

'Y ... y ...you can't prove it,' he stuttered.

Yes! We've got them, I thought to myself.

'Not with £10,000 in your bank and the drugs you make? We have all the evidence. Now can we go somewhere quiet?'

'Who are you?'

'MI5.'

We walked to his car and got in. By now, he was quivering like a jelly. I switched on my tape recorder before continuing:

'I am telling you this so that you know exactly where you stand. We have been after Jason Williams for a long time. We know, and you know he makes, buys and sells drugs. We also know that he, along with his girlfriend Aletha Thornber, murdered Wilbur Thornber. She has already confessed. We know you made the aconite. Therefore, you will get life as well as them. Why did you do it?'

'He made me.'

'Who did?'

'Jason Williams.'

'No, he didn't make you. He *paid* you £10,000.'

'I gave him the aconite and he threw the money at me.'

'You have two choices. You can tell Williams about our conversation and he will kill you, or you can keep quiet because we only want Williams. I would go to the doctor if I were you and get a fortnight off work. By then, it will all be over.

'I think I'll take the second option. He really did make me do it,' he insisted as I got out of the car.

We had what we wanted. I returned home to put the case together with Edie, after which, we visited the police station and arranged to see the Chief Superintendent with Mr Higginbotham.

Poor old Charlie couldn't believe his ears when he was arrested. He was protesting that as he had confessed his part in the affair and they had arrested Williams, he would be released. Of course, the police knew nothing of the arrangements with MI5.

Williams was more devastated than Aletha when he knew there was no money for her and he had wasted so much time and effort in trying to get it. Poor Aletha had been so infatuated with Williams that she was buying all the jewellery she could and giving it to him, in the hope that he would want her. When she came to court, she was a shadow of her former self and yet still seemed to hold a torch. Williams and Aletha got life and poor Charlie, ten years.

Interestingly enough, the poison was a delayed action variety and deadly. I believe if Aletha hadn't suggested Edie was involved in Wilbur's demise, she may have got away with it.

Chapter 20
On the Run

The next year brought sadness to the family. Bif's grandfather, the Earl of Boothtown passed away. Bif had grown very fond of both his grandparents and went to see them regularly. Maud was as upset as I was. Despite our loss, I was honoured to be told first of all and to be invited by the Countess to stay with her until after the funeral.

In fact, it was a lovely affair, if funerals can be considered lovely, especially as many of the very old politicians were there, together with some of the current and new, including the then leader of the Labour party, Harold Wilson whom I always felt was a good man.

We stayed with the Countess for a couple of weeks whilst Bif decided whether or not to take the title. He was like us, not one for hereditary titles. However, with my support, his grandmother persuaded him to accept because we knew it would have been his grandfather's wish. Bif inherited all their estate, which wasn't a great deal; in fact, the Hall itself was in desperate need of repair.

He put the matter in the hands of Stanley who organised and managed everything. We even supplied her with a groundsman, housekeeper, chauffeur, and one of our cars. She was better looked after than ever before which was important as she was now very elderly and frail.

It always caused a bit of humour in the family because we now had an earl and Yvette was now a countess. Bif took his seat in the House of Lords and it was a lovely moment for his grandmother to see him installed, but he never took part in the debates. The moment he took the title, he and Yvette were in great demand: opening fetes, charity events, school presentations and even just being on the guest list at functions. It was obvious why Yvette was asked, as she had the most glorious, may I say, sexy French accent and she was a stunner. Bif was a lucky man, but as I said earlier, all she ever wanted was to be with him.

Whatever anyone thought about the Labour Government under Wilson, the industrial section of the Stock Exchange had its best run since the war. Stanley could not go wrong, more than doubling our asset value, in spite of the huge tax bill it gave us; but our philosophy has always been that if you make money, you pay your taxes. He actually began advocating, using the money sensibly, and investing more in property, capital goods and works of art.

He thought it would be a wise move to buy our own plane, which we did. It gave us the advantage of going to France for the weekend or anywhere in Europe for that matter at a moment's notice, and it was on one of those trips we encountered a man called Gereber Leibhold. He was either an Austrian, German or a Swiss art dealer. We never did find out, but we knew he was working for the East German Government or someone very high up in its political structure.

We set off for a week's break at the villa in Nice. Francesco was due to pick us up, but at the last minute, due to unexpected heavy snow, we were diverted to Marignane, the airport at Marseilles. What was worse, Francesco could not drive to Marseilles because of the weather.

We decided to put up at lovely five-star hotel in Marseille and have a couple of days there; however, we did not expect the weather to be so cold and did not have the right attire. Maudie was in her element – shopping for clothes. We spent a lot of money in rue Paradis although she somehow managed to acquire several items free of charge. In fairness, I took them back and paid for the leather fur-trimmed coat. How she got that one out, I will never know.

We were near Vieux Port (Old Port) a short walk from the centre, but as it was a little too cold for me, we took taxis everywhere. It was on one of our little jaunts that I noticed an advertisement for an exhibition by the Russian artist, Boris Tubalov. We thought it would pass an hour or so which it did, I must say, and was most enjoyable. Maud and I have always liked to encourage talented, young artists; so many struggle to survive. We bought six of Tubalov's pieces. They were not expensive and they agreed to deliver them to our villa free of charge. You never know what the future holds as far as value goes. The important thing is to enjoy them for what they are and I knew they would look just right in the hallway of the villa and give a fresh feeling to the place.

I was talking to one of the exhibition organisers, a David Timberlake who asked us what paintings we had, and when I told him we had several of Monet, Picasso, a Renoir and several other well-known artists, you can imagine his astonishment.

'We don't keep them all at home. Some are on loan to various exhibitions in New York, London, Milan.'

I mentioned en passant that we were now in the market to purchase other works of art of the Impressionist era. 'It was just by chance that we are here. Our plane couldn't land at Nice, so we are spending two or three days in Marseille. I don't suppose you have any of those?' I said, laughing.

'I never get any of that period,' Timberlake replied. 'They are mostly sold at auction where they attract better prices, but I do hear of the occasional private sale. I often have some very good paintings in my own gallery. I will let you know. Here's my card.'

I gave him our contact details in France and left it at that. It seems he did some research on us by phoning round various exhibitions until he found one that we were supporting. They in turn phoned us and told us a Mr Timberlake had been making enquiries about us. He was a little confused and gave the impression that we may want to sell various works; we explained the situation and they were satisfied.

We arrived at Marignane to board our plane to Nice when Maudie saw Timberlake talking to some rather plump Germanic fellow. We both stood for a while staring in Timberlake's direction. Finally, he noticed us, raised his hand in acknowledgement, but immediately turned away sharply and ushered the man away out of our sight. I thought it strange, especially as he had previously made a bit of a fuss of us.

Maud's super second sense told her that both men continued to watch us at the airport, especially as we did not travel on schedules flights.

Francesco picked us up at Nice. The following morning the Tubalovs arrived, and yes, they do look lovely in the hall. We have had them twenty years now and they look as fresh as the day we bought them. He specialised in the 1920's beach scenes. The delicacy of his pastel shades are beautiful.

I suppose it was some three weeks later after we had returned to Number 17 when we received a very anxious call from Francesco saying that a Mr Timberlake had been trying to contact us urgently. He told him he would have something very special for us to see, and if interested to give him a ring. I did of course, and to our surprise, he had a private client wishing to sell a Gainsborough.

We had planned to go to the villa the following weekend so it worked well. Francesco took us in the Rolls to Marseille and to Timberlake's gallery, where we were entertained. After much hype, the moment came and he pulled a curtain back to reveal a beautiful Gainsborough painting of a genteel woman.

'How much?' I asked before I examined it.

'One point two million. However, the vendor would like the sale proceeds sent to an offshore account.'

That immediately sent out warning bells. From my experience, I would say it was possibly genuine and therefore worth sending for proper analysis and provenance.

I phoned Stanley for his advice and was told that the tax matters were for the seller and not for us to worry, if the sale particulars were right. He was delighted we had consulted him with regard to the capital.

'I will arrange for the money to be transferred to your account within twenty-four hours of all the conditions being met satisfactorily. We will fly the painting to London tomorrow and hopefully, everything will be cleared in one week. Would that be all right?' I asked.

'I will give you a reference for you to phone our bankers who will confirm funds and also the guarantee of security and insurance to cover the painting whilst it is not in your possession. Our solicitors, Don Crofts & Co. will also confirm all is genuine from our side.'

'I'm sure that will be okay. I like people who can make their minds up quickly,' he said excitedly. I don't suppose you would be interested in a Matisse. It's not your style though, is it?'

'Why not? We have two.'

'I thought you would find conventional works more appealing,' he remarked, which annoyed me beyond belief.

'Well, let's look at the Matisse,' I said, losing my patience. 'I never judge a book solely by its cover.'

'It is not here but I can have it here within the hour.'

'Fine, we'll be back then. Can we ship the painting now?'

'As soon as I have verified all your points.'

'In the meantime, pack it ready for collection. Send it to Marignane to be collected by Trenchards and organise the paperwork for customs.' I gently marked the back of the canvas and the frame to ensure there was no fiddling, and with that, we left to have another look around Marseille.

We returned an hour or so later when we were introduced to the man we saw with Timberlake at the airport some weeks earlier – Gereber Leibhold.

'How do you do?' I said, taking his hand. I hate men with a flabby handshake and this one was one of those, but as Father used to say, 'You don't have to sleep with them to do business with them.'

'She does!' Maud interrupted.

Leibhold was a gross individual. You know the sort – beer swigging, loud and pompous. I never really knew what his nationality was, but from the start, Maudie felt he couldn't be trusted.

—I've probably told you, Mr White that I've always had an interest in art, which I'm sure I inherited from my father, He spent hours showing me how to identify various aspects of a painting, how it's framed and how a piece can be forged. Whilst I am in no way an expert, I know how to get some help from those that do, particularly when I smell a rat.

He unveiled the Matisse and within a couple of minutes, I felt the picture was not right and said so, in spite of the attractive price. He tried to assure me it was genuine, but I would have none of it unless once again its provenance could be verified. He then unexpectedly showed us a photograph of a magnificent Holbein, which I liked. In fact, I had either seen a picture of it or the real thing before the war.

'Where's this one been?' I asked.

'It's been in a private collection in Switzerland for over

sixty years and the family have lost a great deal of money,' Leibhold replied. 'They would also want the money transferred to a private offshore account.'

'Wouldn't we all!' I said, chuckling, a remark Leibhold struggled to understand. 'Have you anymore on your books? Because I really do like what I see so far ... as long as they are all kosher.' That little word changed it all. Both Maudie and I saw him wince at the word "kosher".

'I want to take a look around the place,' Maud whispered immediately. 'It's not right. I can smell it.'

'We would like half an hour to have a chat. You've whet my appetite,' I said, feigning a smile.

'Yes, of course,' Timberlake replied, but I could detect a little reticence from Leibhold. We were away to the nearest café.

'Did you see his reaction when you said "kosher"?'

'Yes, yes I did,' I replied.

'There's something drastically wrong,' Maudie continued. 'No one suddenly brings these works of art out of a conjurer's hat. They have been stolen from a Jewish source, I'm sure of it. How come a man like Timberlake is mixed up in this? He doesn't have the wherewithal to do this sort of thing. It's too high profile. And what's that fat slob doing with these paintings?'

'I want to take a look at this place tonight. Any chance of you looking after Timberlake for a couple of hours or so?' Maud asked.

'Let's see.'

—You see Mr White, Maud sits there, all matter of fact, and has the nerve to criticise me for my loose behaviour. Then she had the nerve to ask me to use it!

'I didn't ask you to go to extremes. You could have just had a scintillating conversation.'

'Tell me, Maudie dear, what man would want a scintillating conversation when he thinks it's on offer?'

We returned to Timberlake's premises and had another look at the photograph of the Holbein; it was really tempting. I then asked Timberlake if I could discuss one or two things with him privately.

'My sister and I have considerable funds available to us and ... ' I said, stopping in mid-sentence and changing tack. 'Would you have dinner with me tonight? I would like to put our cards on the table. We are changing our investment strategy and are now in the market for a few more works of art.'

'I would love to,' he replied, 'but can I just confirm Liebhold hasn't booked anything for us this evening?'

He shot off and returned a few minutes later, full of the joys of spring.

'That will be lovely.'

'No doubt you will have done much research on me by the time we meet. So where and when and what would you like me to wear?'

'Come as you are,' he replied.

'I couldn't. I've been in these clothes all day. You know Marseille, so you choose the venue. I'll pick you up from wherever. And it's on me.'

'Do you like fish? There is a lovely fish restaurant towards Cassis not far from Marseille.'

'Love it. Why don't you book a table? What time?'

'Come casual, and pick me up from here, say seven?'

When we left, Maudie and I were in high spirits at the possibility of buying a 'kosher' Gainsborough for a fair price ... and the possibility of others, but Maud was convinced that they were from Nazi hoards.

Together with Francesco, we booked into a charming little hotel for the night. I left Maudie to her own devices whilst I went to buy a few clothes for the evening. Francesco drove me to Timberlake's place at seven and on to the restaurant. I was pleased I had made an impression, which meant there was a good chance of keeping him for most of the evening. Arriving in the Phantom IV at the restaurant certainly did the trick because the service was excellent.

We chatted for a good hour about our change of investment strategy and the move towards acquiring more works of art, making it clear that we would not keep them at Number 17 but loan them out to suitable galleries.

'What sort of figure are you going to invest?'

'David, that's naughty!' I said, squeezing his hand a little. 'You don't ask an investor in the art world how much he is going to pay. That immediately puts the price up.

'Sorry.'

'Oh, don't worry, but between you and me … not that Herr Leibhold, we have in excess of twenty million.' His eyes nearly popped out of his head.

'That's a lot of investment.'

'Of course it is, but I know you have been looking into us, so come on, what have you found out?'

He told me about our entry in *Who's Who*, the banker's references and the personal opinion of their banker who had spoken off the record to ours; at least we had a clean bill of health.

'Are you married?' I asked.

'Divorced. You?'

'No. I lost my husband during the war. I have two children though, but they have both recently married so I am on my own.' He immediately squeezed my hand.

Business was banned during the meal. It puts you off the champagne. After two fine bottles of Mercier and a lovely meal, it was time to go home.

'Would you like to come back to my hotel?'

'I was going to ask you back to my flat. It's not far from the office. Would you like to?'

'That would be lovely.'

I didn't want to call Francesco out so I ordered a taxi and we made our way to his flat. Once there, I wasn't sure it was his flat. He struggled to find the right key to open the door and seemed very confused about where anything was. At least the coffee was good.

He sat me down on the settee and then sat on a chair opposite. I thought, this is no dammed good. 'Something wrong?' I asked to his astonishment.

'Of course not.'

'In that case, come and sit next to me and tell me why you have brought me here. Because it's not your place, is it?'

No, it's a friend's,' he said, looking deflated. 'My flat's a bit poky and I wanted to impress.'

I questioned him on all aspects of his work and found out that he had only just met Leibhold. He was known as a big art dealer and he had contacted him to see if he had any old masters.

'That office is not mine, it's Leibhold's.'

'Don't worry. If the Gainsborough is genuine, you'll get your commission. I'll see you do.'

'Thank you.'

'Where does he live?'

'Above his office.'

My heart sank as we thought the office would be empty, especially as I was with David. 'Is he there tonight?' I asked, trying to sound casual.

'I doubt it. He'll be trying to get hold of others. He knows who you are.'

I just hoped he wouldn't be there when Maudie was, although I knew she could look after herself. The little relief I felt was put into the clinking of coffee cups and a toast to the deal, which ended in a kiss and several more until we were sprawled across the settee.

He couldn't get his trousers down quick enough, and

before I knew it, I was naked before he was. Thank God it was a warm night because even in France, it can become very cold especially if you are sprawled naked on the floor in the lounge as we now were. We decided enough was enough and spent the rest of the night in bed. Whose, I do not know until we heard someone opening the front door. David leapt out of bed, frantically searching for his clothes.

'David? I thought you would be gone by midnight,' a good old-fashioned English accent sounded from outside the bedroom.

'I'm sorry, George. Seem to have got a little involved,' David replied sheepishly.

'Well, never mind. Come on, introduce me,' the stranger said, walking straight into the bedroom, deliberately hoping to catch me unawares.

I was prepared. 'Hello,' I said, 'I've just heard you're George. I'm Edith. How lovely to meet you. Do you want us to go?'

'No, of course not.'

'Then I would suggest we have a drink, and I'll make it,' I said, taking charge. 'Tea, coffee or something a little stronger?'

We all settled for coffee. David told George all about me which was very indiscreet. I found out little about George.

'I think we should get some sleep,' George announced once we had finished our coffee. 'You two take the bed and I'll sleep on the settee.'

'George, don't be silly. It's a lovely big bed we could all get in it. Top and tail if you like. But I would prefer us being a little more conventional … Ménage à trois?'

Well, if you could have seen the faces on those two young men! Absolute picture. George stood open-mouthed although his eyes showed he had the appetite for it, whilst David simply grinned, revealing he too was interested. It was a wonderful experience for me and the boys and I kept them busy for most of the night, just as Maudie would have liked.

It was a delight to wake up and have breakfast with two lovely boys, both of whom wanted to see me again. I couldn't imagine why. I saw David quite often afterwards, especially once we'd paid for the Gainsborough, but it was an expensive series of sexual encounters.

'Maudie, you tell Mr White what happened next.'

'Edie, I'm astonished. You never told me that! Mr White, she is a trollop – an out and out trollop!'

Maud continues ...

When I got to my appointed destination, I twigged straight away that it was not Timberlake's apartment but the other man's. Quite amazing what he had in it. He was without doubt a dealer in stolen art, but had a few genuine ones to make him look like Mr Clean.

This to me was very important; we lost both our men to the Nazis and I was not going to allow them to benefit from their crimes. I took a miniature camera with me just in case and sure enough when I opened the safe, there were the names and addresses of people who had bought the paintings and which ones, together with a list of all the paintings he could get his hands on.

There weren't just details of paintings, but sculptures, carvings, rare books, silver and gold ornaments. It looked like the inventory of the National Art galleries. Naturally, I photographed these lists but there was no way I could ascertain where these treasures were stored.

I looked over the apartment, which was enormous and eventually found a strong room, cleverly concealed in the bathroom. You stepped into the airing cupboard where there was a panel below, under which was the mechanism for the safe. You then had to find the combination to open it. It was impressive stuff. I could say I was an expert, but this one was a challenge. I achieved it, but it took some doing, a couple of hours in fact, and certainly tried my patience.

'You told me it was similar to the one in the American Embassy in Grosvenor Square which you looked into during the Korean War in '48. You were asked to go back for a few weeks to help MI5 because our government wanted to know what the Yanks were doing,' Edith suddenly blurted out, much to Maud's disgust.

—Mr White this is still classified. Edie should not have told you that. They knew it had been broken into, but I made sure they thought it was the Russians ... just in case. From then on they really did improve their security.

Well, my luck was out, I had left the tell-tale chocks in the door just to make sure. Forearmed was forewarned and sure enough, Fatso entered the flat. He wasn't a spy or trained in that field, so he didn't notice anything unusual, not even when I closed the safe and started to make my getaway. I had taken a few pictures of the works of art in the safe, and as I was leaving, I couldn't believe my eyes. His walls were covered in either very good copies or the real thing.

I hid at first in the bedroom and when I heard him wandering round, I slipped into the cloakroom and then outside, picking up my chocks as I went.

An hour later, I was waiting for Edie to come back. I had so much to tell her, but as is her wont she was out all night, making some young buck tired.

The following morning she joined Francesco and I for breakfast, looking like the cat that had got the cream. Need I say more!

'Do you want me to get the car, Maud?' Francesco asked.

'Not just yet, Francesco,' I replied, delving into my bag. 'Here's 500 francs. I'd like you to buy a large bunch of flowers for your Jeanette. I don't think it fair that we kept you away all night.' In truth, I needed him to disappear for a while because I wanted to talk to Edie privately.

'Edie,' I said, 'I need to go back into that flat. I think we have stumbled on something very big and dangerous. I know Leibhold is dealing for the ex-Nazis. I have looked in his safe, I have photos of documents, names and addresses of those that have bought from him and the pictures he's sold, together with almost a catalogue of what they had on offer. Anyway, he came back; I managed to get away without any trouble, but as I was leaving I noticed he had dozens of paintings on the walls which are either copies or originals. It's a fantastic place to hide them, but I want to go back and have another look, just to make sure.'

'Please don't ask me to keep Leibhold occupied,' Edie said, when I had finished outlining what I had seen.

***

Edith takes up the tale ...

We outlined a plan of action: Maud was keen to go back to the flat that evening and I was to invite David to organise a meeting with Leibhold for the same evening. If the Holbein was genuine, I wanted him to think I would buy it. I was also to pretend I was very anxious to get hold of some other works and would like to see them quickly. I was to tell David that we would take them anywhere at any time. It worked perfectly. The meeting was set up and I let Leibhold choose the venue and time. He was to come to our hotel first, have a drink together about seven and book the table for eight to eight-thirty.

This would give Maud up to four hours to have a look at Gereber Leibhold's place and study some of the paintings on the walls, plus look at what other artefacts he had in there.

I dressed for the occasion – a bit loud – in anticipation of what I thought Leibhold would like. As I said earlier, a some-what fat beer-swigging, raucous, uncouth man. I was right.

'Tarty, I would say, Edie. A role you always perform well,' Maud added.

David and Gereber, which I was now invited to call him, arrived at seven o'clock on the dot, as all good Germans do.

We sat in the lounge where there were several other guests. This was a mistake. The first beer Gereber drank didn't touch the sides of the glass, and after the third, he became a little louder. However, I managed to get some sense out of him before he was too far gone. He told me the Holbein was in Switzerland and he would contact me the following day to arrange a quick viewing.

The restaurant was like the Oktoberfest Beer festival in Munich, it was that rowdy. God knows where it was as I had a hell of a time trying to stop his wandering hands, let alone concentrate on the route. The meal must have been good – he ate all of his and most of mine. David decided it was not for him.

I was getting cross until I saw Gereber's inflection of the eye and nodding of the head, prompting David to leave, but not before he slipped his phone number in my pocket. We sat on long benches for the meal where the waitresses continually topped up your 1-litre beer glass. Many of the women were dressed in traditional Germanic dress, where all of them, which now included me, sat astride their partners to help him or her drink the beer. It was also an excuse for another grope by either party. I suppose I entered into the spirit of the occasion because I do not remember going back to the flat with him. I knew I had been safe as I found him on the floor absolutely sparked out the following morning.

But there I was in his flat, where Maudie had trodden before and I didn't have to make a secret of it. It was useful for me to take a look at some of the exhibits as well, although Maudie had seen and noted everything.

He was like a time bomb at seven-thirty when he woke up, gruff as you like.

'Guten Tag Fraulein,' he said on seeing me standing over

him. 'Did you have a good time? he asked. He was wide awake with no apparent side effects, from the booze.

'Yes, fabulous,' I replied, not knowing whether I had done or not.

'So did I! We must do it again.'

'Yes, we must.'

'You were a naughty girl,' he added, laughing on his way to the bathroom.

'God! What have I done?' I asked. There was no reply so I followed him. 'Oops! Sorry!' I had walked in, not realising he was on the toilet.

'You don't remember? Then it will be my little secret.'

'You terrible man,' I replied, pretending to be anxious.

'Last night you said we could go to Switzerland to see the Holbein. I can be ready at a moment's notice. Can you ring me at my hotel? I must go and change.'

Francesco collected me and once again I joined Maud for a full English breakfast and a decent cup of tea. She had been busy; we now had a criminal file which could blow a hole in the organisation. She verified that some of the paintings were originals, but was even more excited when I told her we were going to see the Holbein in Geneva.

Leibhold telephoned us later that morning and arranged for us to take him to Geneva. I phoned the airport at Nice to reserve our take-off slot, leaving it to the pilot and staff to organise the flight preparation. It was just a simple journey to pick up Leibhold and get to Nice.

I arrived at Leibhold's apartment and rang the doorbell.

'Come in!' a loud voice replied.

My hand touched the door which opened and I walked in.

'Good morning Fraulein,' Leibhold said, approaching the door. He kissed me on both cheeks.

'Can we take some paintings with us? It will save me considerable time.'

'What are they? I asked, taken aback by the sudden request.

'Oh, they're just good copies of old masters. I don't think they would interest you.'

'Of course you can, but you will have to get customs approval for them, which will be difficult at this short notice.'

'That will be fine.'

We carried out four pictures, duly packed in strong wooden frames and put them in the boot of the Rolls. They only just went in. I thought the packaging was a bit over the top for copies, but refrained from commenting.

'You made no mention earlier of requesting that Mr Timberlake come with us?'

'There's no need. He does not get involved with the detail. Anyway, I want you to myself. I will take you to my private club.'

'I will have Maud, my sister with us. Although I make the executive decisions, she does like to be involved.'

That's all right. She can come with us. There are plenty of men.'

'Oh no, she's not like me! She'll prefer to stay in the hotel.'

'Hopefully then, Fraulein, it will be just you and me at the club.' I nodded my agreement, not really knowing what to say.

We arrived at Nice airport and dropped Leibhold with the pictures at customs. Within a few minutes he was back with the papers signed and sealed. This was ridiculous; it could not have been done so quickly, especially with French bureaucracy being what it is. Something odd was going on.

'That was quick,' I remarked.

'I am well known and trusted.'

I didn't believe him, but it suited me to agree. 'I am

pleased about that. At least I know I am dealing with an honest man.' We smiled at each other and within minutes, we were called to our plane. Three hours later, we were at Geneva and taxiing to the private landing area.

The moment we were off the plane and heading toward the exit, Maud and I were requested to attend the Customs Office.

Thinking it may be something to do with the paintings, I asked Leibhold if I could have the necessary papers.

Strangely enough, after giving me the papers, Leibhold went through customs without a hitch.

'Wait for us, Gereber. I don't think we will be long.'

We were taken into the Customs Office and escorted to a holding area to be questioned. To our horror, Spencer, our pilot was already being held in a room there.

'What's he doing here?' Maud asked.

'All in good time Ma'am,' the escort replied. 'In here, please,' he continued, opening the door and directing us in. 'Please sit down. We won't keep you very long.'

We sat down at a table where Maud insisted I sat opposite her. She told me later it was a technique she learned in the service where the interrogator would be at a disadvantage if he had to look from one side to the other when questioning. She always seemed very confident in these circumstances.

I was about to speak to Maud when she gently kicked me under the table, indicating for me to be quiet. We sat waiting for well over twenty minutes when two men and a woman came in. One man sat at the table and the other two stood behind us.

'I'll introduce myself,' the senior officer began.

'No need to. I know who you are. You were very junior when we last met,' Maud said.

'Yes, I wondered if you would remember me.'

'I don't forget,' she replied firmly.

'The two behind you are Officers Mary Whitely and Michael Potts.'

Maud didn't even turn round to acknowledge them. She simply asked:

'What's this all about?'

'I was about to ask you the same question.'

'Don't be silly,' Maud added. 'Why are we in here with our pilot next door and you having allowed our passenger to go?'

'I think you know. We believe you are involved with the theft of numerous paintings, which have been smuggled out of Germany during and after the war,' the senior officer said.

'Don't be so stupid. If you thought that you would not have let our passenger go, would you? Particularly as he is the one who got the appropriate papers for them to be exported from France. So come to the point, or we will leave, especially as you have no jurisdiction here. You know as well as I do this is a social call to warn us off.'

'My colleagues said you were sharp.'

'It would seem,' Maud continued, 'that we have stumbled into an investigation which we might compromise. Is that right? Of course it is. And what have you done?' she asked rhetorically. 'You have compromised your own investigation ... if it is yours, by not pulling in the man who is so obviously involved.'

'He's not been stopped? the officer asked, completely surprised.

'No, he appeared to be allowed through without any checks. If you are quick, you may be able to stop him leaving the airport and arrest him for drug smuggling or something. Bring those paintings you have removed from the plane and search them in front of us. He does have the appropriate papers for the pictures to be shipped. Do I have to tell you how to do your job?'

He shuffled in his chair, very embarrassed at the turn of events. Even more so when I wanted the names of his two line officers, which he quite rightly refused to give. A quick inflection of the head sent Officer Mary Whitely scuttling out and down the corridor to the Swiss police section. It seemed they found Gereber, cool as a cucumber, sitting in the Arrivals area waiting for us. They brought him back to the Customs Office and we were all ushered into another room where the paintings had already been placed.

'What have you been doing, Gereber? They think we are smuggling drugs,' I said, the moment I saw him.

'Quiet! No talking,' the customs officer shouted in French, German and English just to make sure we understood.

They made great play of unpacking the paintings. Of course, they found nothing. Leibhold was devastated when they started taking the frames apart.

'There is nothing in them. They are just copies of famous paintings and made to look authentic. They cost many thousands of dollars and you are wrecking them,' he said angrily. 'Who's going to pay for them? You? You?' he said, looking at each of them in turn. 'I have the papers. They were inspected in Nice and they were satisfied.'

The inspector then turned his attention to me. 'Why have you come to Switzerland?' he asked.

'To see a Holbein painting which we are hoping to buy from Mr Leibhold who is the agent. We have only seen photographs of it so far. Our lawyers have checked Mr Leibhold's credentials. They are in order and that's good enough for us. We will naturally need to have the painting examined and subject to a satisfactory outcome, we will buy it.'

'And what's your interest? he said, turning to Maud, who does not waste time in dealing with bureaucrats.

'You've seen my passport. You can see we are sisters and

she has answered all the questions for me.'

'I want to hear them from you.'

'Well, I'll be here all day,' Maud began, 'and I would like a drink and something to eat. I also want a solicitor to be present and I don't care what you do. The whole thing is ridiculous and you know it. We have never been in a situation like this before and it will not happen again.' From that moment on she just shut up.

The pilot had nothing to offer, but was told to wait whilst they searched the plane. As soon as that was done, we were all to be released, but not before Maud got a telling off for her attitude to a man who was only doing his job. We gave the details of where we were staying, which was the Hotel du Parc des Eaux-Vives and for how long. Finally, we were off. We had been delayed for over four hours and were completely fed up, but we now knew we had discovered there was an ongoing investigation.

We called at Chez Bouvier for something to eat and a decent cup of tea. Most importantly, we chatted about the experience and what to do. As far as I was concerned I just wanted out. I didn't even want to bother with the Holbein. Maud would have none of it. She wanted to screw them all to the wall.

'When can we see the Holbein?' I asked, Maud having told me to act excited.

'This afternoon at two o'clock. I will collect you at one forty-five from your hotel,' Leibhold said.

Sure enough, he arrived promptly. It was a short drive from the hotel, but when Maud saw the building, she knew this was the place. The many cameras gave it away as did the eight-foot perimeter wall.

Leibhold sounded the car's horn and the gate was opened. We drove thirty or forty metres to the front entrance of a building where we were met by two Gestapo-looking men who opened the car doors. We were ushered into the building and straight into a studio, cum library, where in front of us was a covered easel. I wanted to take the cover off, but was stopped in my tracks by our host who was obviously in charge.

'Wait. Bitte warten,' he said in a strong Germanic accent. He was tall and thin and wore bottle thick spectacles. Despite his age, which must have been eighty plus, he had jet black hair. 'I am Walter Specke,' he said, holding out his hand to shake ours. 'And you are the Trenchard sisters?'

'Come on,' I said. 'Don't keep us in suspense any longer.'

With that, he pulled the covers off. It was a very regal picture of Henry V111, which I was sure I had seen before, but Specke pointed out a few minor details which differed from the one in the National Gallery. I spent well over an hour studying the painting before I asked about the price and its provenance. Like the Gainsborough, this one looked the real thing.

'Can I bring my own expert to have a look at it, or send it to London?' I asked. 'I can give you all the necessary assurances.'

'I know you can, Miss Trenchard,' he replied purposefully. 'I also know you are in the market for other works of art.'

'News travels fast.'

'Not really, Miss Trenchard, especially as Herr Leibhold only informed me the other day.'

'Well, what other delights have you got to show us?' I asked.

'We do have other works, but not before I have taken you to the Beer Fest tomorrow night,' Leibhold announced.

'Do you like Beer Fests, Miss Trenchard?' Specke asked.

'It would appear so, but I can't remember too much about them,' I remarked, causing Specke to smile, an expression which nearly cracked his face.

'You're very quiet,' Specke said, addressing Maud.

'I haven't got anything to say as yet, but I might ask my sister if I can join her tomorrow night.'

Wishing to return to the business in hand, I asked again if we could have the Holbein examined, to which Specke replied: 'See how you feel after tomorrow night.'

We all left the house and returned to our hotel, keen to get rid of our chaperone and have a private chat.

'It's a knock-off. Or it's Jewish,' Maud said without hesitation. 'I want to have a look round the outside of the place now. Just in case I need to go in. We hired a car and quickly returned.

I parked up as far from the entrance as was physically possible, leaving Maudie to do her stuff. There was no doubt she was an expert in her field. Armed with her grappling iron, she disappeared to search the grounds. Half an hour later she returned with all the information she needed. She was very impressive in these situations.

The following afternoon we received a phone call from Leibhold who told me he was picking us up at eight o'clock. He insisted that Maud came along, and that he would not take no for an answer. We both had something to eat first, knowing what they were normally like, and as usual we were picked up precisely on time.

He drove us well out into the country to a large pub where we were introduced to Maud's escort who was none other than one of the two men who opened the car doors for us. Maud could sense there was trouble in the air and whispered to me to be careful.

At nine o'clock, the band started playing and the beer started flowing. I suppose there were about 200 people there, with perhaps a few more men than women, but the strange thing was the evening seemed to have a military reunion flavour about it. Maud didn't like the feel of the place, nor her chaperone or the other man from the house who had suddenly appeared.

Again the usual long rows of tables where we were supposed to sit alternate male and female, so I was next to Leibhold, with Maud's chaperone on my right; then next to Maud was the other man.

'Mr White, I knew we had got trouble and I had to speak to Edie quickly,' Maud said.

It soon became obvious the evening was an intended orgy and without so much as a by-your-leave, everyone started having sex with anyone who they fancied. I had heard about these sort of parties but never experienced anything like it.

Maudie signalled another visit to the loo. I took the hint, placated poor old Gereber by helping him with a litre of beer.

On the way, Maudie made it clear we were in trouble, and I should try to remain as sober as possible as we may need to escape. Not only that, I was not to be surprised if we were followed.

Sure enough, two men were waiting surreptitiously nearby when we came out of the cloakroom. We made our way back to the bench to resume our so-called fun.

Despite all the research they had done on us, they failed to find out what a wonderful pickpocket Maudie was – the best MI5 had trained. She quickly managed to extract her young man's car keys and his .38, so at least, we were even.

It was now approaching midnight and I have never in my life seen such debauchery from such a large number of people, many of whom involved in some sort of intercourse, and all the time the beer was flowing down all of us. Not only that, Leibhold was out like a light under the table.

I could tell Maudie was becoming more anxious and I knew we had to get away.

'Wait there,' I said as I extracted myself from what had now become an ensemble, and once again went to the loo.

Only this time I was accompanied by one of the men, who was only just compos mentis.

I was sure these two were under orders not to let us out of their sight. This became obvious when Maudie made an excuse and followed me, only to find she too was being accompanied.

'Come on Fraulein, what are you up to?' the man asked me in a sinister tone.

'Don't be silly,' I continued. 'I am only going to the toilet, nothing else. I'm here to enjoy myself and help you enjoy yourself. So you wait there.'

As I went into the toilet, I could see Maudie approaching with her escort. I opened the door and called mine in. We were on our own and I felt it was my job to put him at his ease. The trouble was the other one was curious to know what was happening and came to look. So he too joined in and soon I had them naked from the waist down, kicking their trousers under the cubical partition.

This was Maudie's cue. She quickly retrieved their trousers and placed them in a large waste bin, but not before pocketing a further set of car keys. We now had to get out of the place as we were in far too deep to think we could do much more.

I left the men at their most intense moment; they were now of course too far gone to notice they were in the ladies loos, and a few women were getting very annoyed that two homosexual perverts were using their toilets.

'Come on, let's get our stuff and go. We can use one of the cars,' Maud whispered.

'Two perverts in the ladies!' I shouted in German, as we quickly headed for the exit, grabbing our stuff as we went.

Much commotion could be heard in loud German style. You can imagine what they would think of the two English women who had ruined their evening when the 'perverts' had to explain the situation.

After various attempts, we found a match for a set of the car keys and managed to get out onto the road. Things were now desperate and I drove for all I was worth away from the place. It was pitch black and all we had were the headlights to tell us which way to go, as I hadn't got a clue where we were heading.

I drove along the road for what seemed like miles and noticed the tarmac was disappearing and becoming a dirt track. We were now approaching a parking area, which went no further, except to a wooden chalet that was long closed. It had obviously been a tourist spot.

'We're being followed by what looks like a convoy,' Maud said, on seeing numerous sets of headlights some distance behind us. 'They will expect us to go on, but we won't. We'll leave the car here and double back, return on foot, taking cover behind the hedges. Hopefully, they won't see us. We'll make for the nearest town where there is a police station. Quickly, come on.'

By the lights in the distance, she knew we were only 10 or so miles away from a village at least. That was easier said than done; Maud was the only one with sensible shoes. I was wearing three-inch stilettos.

We ran down the track until the headlights became dangerously close and hid behind the foliage until the last of seven vehicles passed.

At least our eyes were becoming accustomed to the dark and we could make progress, but we had a new problem as the wind was getting stronger and the cloud layer was drifting, exposing the moon. We were now very vulnerable as our silhouettes could be seen for a distance, so we had to take the lower ground. Then of course, I broke a heel and Maud had to snap the other off, but it did make things easier.

'Pick it up,' Maud said. 'We shouldn't leave any tracks. Take them with you,' Maud ordered. We continued for well over half an hour when Maud saw the lights from one of the vehicles coming back in our direction. 'They're looking for us. Get over there quickly,' she whispered.

We concealed ourselves well into the ground behind a mass of scrub. They would have had to be very clever to see us, but I could see the passenger leaning out of the vehicle, brandishing a shot gun. It slowly drove past, but we remained in our position until we could hardly see its rear lights.

We had once again reached the tarmac-surfaced road and were making our way quickly towards a public house when Maudie realised there was insufficient cover for us. I was feeling extremely cold, mainly because I was not dressed for jungle warfare, so we thought it would be better to make for the nearest house away from the road. We set off across country again towards the lights of the town when we spotted a house. It was now three o'clock in the morning and I was all in, so it was there or nothing.

Maud took the initiative and made her way to the front door. In the darkness, we could just about see it was a big house. She banged on the door, having rehearsed what she was going to say.

The door opened. 'Welcome Frauleins. I somehow knew I would be seeing you two again,' the sinister voice of Walter Specke said. He stepped back to invite us in. 'Come in, you must be very cold, wandering all over the countryside.'

'Thank you,' we both said in unison, too shocked to say anything else.

We followed him into a room, where even at this time in the morning a huge log fire was burning. Within two minutes, we could see the reason why. He had a night watchman who immediately asked if we would like a warm drink. Of course I said yes whilst Maudie remained reluctant, but in any event he brought in two hot coffees.

It's not drugged, young lady,' Specke said casually. 'The doors are locked. You cannot get out, so there is no need to drug you, is there? You wouldn't get past Felix either. You caught my two young men napping, as you English say. The way you disarmed them and took their trousers away was ingenious.'

'They had to spoil things and show us they had guns. We were terrified,' Maud said, putting on her little girl lost routine. 'You know our situation and how easy it would be to be robbed.'

'I don't think anyone who can take a gun away from an experienced soldier is frightened, do you? Now, which one of you has the gun?'

'I've only got the heels from shoes and I can't put them anywhere, can I?' I replied.

'I had the gun. It had slipped out of his pocket, when I was tickling his balls,' Maud replied unabashedly, 'and then it fell onto the floor. I kicked it under the table and left it there. I didn't want to have it. I don't like guns.'

I looked at Maudie and mouthed, "tickling his balls". I couldn't believe she would even think those words, let alone speak them.

'I will give you until dawn to produce it, otherwise I will leave you in the capable hands of Felix, and he won't be put off by having his balls tickled – he hasn't any. One of our men will go back to the restaurant and have a look, just to give you the benefit of the doubt. Now, warm yourselves up and let's hope we find it. Felix, they won't leave the room, will they?'

'No master.'

'Now Frauleins, we want to know why customs stopped you and not Herr Leibhold?'

I just blurted it out. 'Because they thought there were drugs hidden in the parcels. They asked us if I had packed them and I told them that it was Mr Leibhold who had done so, and that he had gone through to Arrivals.'

'She also told them that he would have to wait for us as we were taking him and the paintings to a dealer,' Maud added. 'Apparently, he was sitting, waiting for us to come out. I think they just damaged the painting out of sheer cussedness because they had made a mistake. Not the actions of a guilty man, don't you think? And then you spoiled everything by sending two gunmen to chaperone us.'

Specke seemed to accept our explanation about the paintings but was concerned about the gun.

'Perhaps I was a bit pre-emptive, but it's too late now, so when the boys get back we will have to think of something, won't we?'

He turned to leave the room, but not before he whispered something to Felix. We were left to think about our situation with Felix breathing down our necks.

'We've got to get out before they come back,' Maud whispered, which earned her the first clout from Felix.

'Why? Have you got the gun?' I asked. Maud nodded.

'No talking you two,' he shouted in German.

That incensed Maud. 'Don't touch me, you bastard,' she snapped.

That earned her another clout but he didn't anticipate Maud's reaction. She flew at him with everything.

'Get him!' she shouted at me as he started laying into her. I did as I was told, still holding the two stiletto heels. I dropped one of them as I jumped onto his back, and grasped him round the neck. I pulled hard and he began to lose balance. Unfortunately, as we fell backwards, my remaining stiletto entered his nasal passage with such force he screamed out. Made worse when Maudie took advantage of the situation and pushed my hand holding the stiletto, ramming it further up his nose. We fell backwards and he landed on top of me. He pulled the stiletto out, banging the back of his head on mine and nearly knocking me senseless. Once again, Maud came to my rescue with a hefty kick to his temple. That laid him senseless, but to be sure, she finished him off with a fire iron.

We began to search the house for a way out. Room after room we tried, but all windows and doors were locked and we had no means of opening them; the glass was unbreakable. We then came to one locked door which had a large, old-fashioned keyhole, which suggested that the sort of key would not be one you would carry around with you. Maud deduced it had to be nearby. It was that simple. The key was on top of the door casing. Once again, there was no way we could get out but this room proved to be a real 'masterpiece'.

We had no time to do a thorough search. It was full of the most priceless works of art you could ever wish to see. We came out of the room, locking it as we went, and continued looking for an exit. We then found another room, the master's office, where the opportunity to escape presented itself, but here again Maudie wanted more. Behind the desk there was a small safe, which she opened in a minute or two and there, just as we thought, were records of payments to a neo-Nazi organisation in Germany with branches in Austria.

We heard a car pulling up outside. It was time to get out fast but not before Maudie relocked the safe. It was too late; we heard several men entering the house. Specke called out for Felix. Of course, there was no reply which immediately put them on their guard. Specke began shouting instructions to his associates.

'Stay close. Edie,' Maud whispered. 'Get behind the door.' She took the .38 from behind her back and we waited, knowing one of the men would eventually come in.

We watched as the door handle turned slowly, followed by the door being opened. A man looked round only to feel hard steel pressing into the back of his head.

'One false move and you will be dead,' Maud whispered in the man's ear, at the same time removing his gun. As quick as a flash, she hit him across the back of his head and he was despatched. She grabbed hold of the man's limp body as he fell and signalled to me to help put him behind the door. We could hear some movement and whispering at a distance as she handed me his gun. Maud led the way to the front entrance, which was open. I immediately hurried to get out and was almost at the opening when Maud whispered loudly:

'Stop! It's a trap.'

I almost fell over in my angst to get out, only saving myself by grabbing hold of the door casing.

'Come back to me here! Wait! Keep your eyes open and cover our backsides,' Maud ordered like some bloody sergeant major.

She went to the door and looked out in all directions, trying to see where the other two were. It was then that Specke made a big mistake. He shouted:

'You won't get away, Frauleins!' She now knew where the voice came from and roughly where he was.

The garden was not well-maintained. It was an old shrubbery and the leaves were almost out in full. We knew that if we could get outside we had a chance of escape and, the advantage of both being armed.

'I'm going to fire over there,' Maud said, pointing in one direction, 'and the moment I do that, I want you to run over to those thick shrubs and when you're hidden, start firing over my head. I will then run over to you. Okay?'

'Okay,' I replied.

'Go!' she shouted and opened up into the area. Two men fired at me but I'm sure Maudie got one of them because only one person was firing when she ran across to the bushes.

'Stay here. I'll take the car. Don't move until I call you.'

Maud moved away and after she was out of sight I couldn't see or hear a sound. It was as though she had disappeared. It seemed like a while before the shooting started again. I heard someone yelp as if they'd been hit and a few seconds later, Maud called out:

'Edie, come on, let's get out of here.'

It seems Specke was one of three who had been caught in the firing line. We took his car keys from his pocket as he lay there and made a dash for it.

The car roared out of the drive onto the road and we were away heading towards Geneva just in time for dinner.

Before that, we called at Geneva Airport and requested to speak to the Head of Security and to make a call to the police in England. But it was easier saying MI5 or British Intelligence, so Maud used her code to get through to the department head, a chap called Porky Rice. He was a plump individual when he started in the service but became a very good operative and now a department head. Maud quickly outlined our story and dilemma and within minutes, we were surrounded by police and security staff assigned to protect us.

Maud gave them all the details we had discovered, including the names and addresses of all the purchasers, saving the juicy bits for Porky's department. At least the Gainsborough was one of three pictures with a genuine provenance and we were lucky enough to buy it.

All the other paintings and works of art were being held by the Swiss Government until the Jewish owners or their descendants claimed them; otherwise they would eventually be sold off and the money held in a special account.

***

Seldom in my life have I seen Maud so determined, not just determined to finish a project, but determined to stop the

Nazis benefitting from anything. They had taken Peter from her; he was everything to her and the only love of her life. It made her feel so much better to know that all those involved in the dirty business were arrested, charged, found guilty and served long sentences. There were dozens involved. Some were found guilty of murder and got life.

Then of course there were all those greedy people who bought the works of art knowing their ghastly history. They hadn't bothered to check the provenance or didn't want to check because they simply wanted the self-gratification of ownership. They got their comeuppance once the authorities retrieved the pieces and returned them to the Swiss government for safe-keeping. And then we had those who were not only greedy but stupid; those who bought the forgeries for the real thing and paid a top price. It was amazing how many of them declared they had to be genuine due to the price paid. What's more, their anger was directed at us for exposing the dreadful affair as their dream was ruined and their 'assets' confiscated.

Naturally, buying a forgery is not a crime; only the forger was guilty, but he or she was rarely caught. You would need to be a brilliant artist as well as a genius to be able to copy something as detailed as some of these old masters and be able to fool the experts. What did upset many of these buyers was the fact the money was going to help the criminal section of the Nazis and a very far right wing the neo Nazi Party; some of those people were descendants of the families that had suffered.

Whilst Maud felt she had done her duty once more, she felt a great loss. Peter was always on her mind and for many months she retreated into her shell and did very little. Several years passed before she began to get back to normal.

Maud was recognised for her work in this case, but was diplomatically warned to keep out of matters that didn't concern her; we could have jeopardised a long, ongoing investigation. She politely told them to piss off. No, that's not true – those were her actual words.

Of course, Mr Higginbotham knew what we were doing. In a way he was as guilty as we were, but he did his best to stop our silly games, warning us that our luck would soon run out. He even committed the cardinal sin of telling us we were getting *too* old and this would cause us to make mistakes. We were in our sixties to seventies and whilst Maud hadn't lost her touch in cracking safes, pickpocketing and even shoplifting, our problem was more of a physical nature such as breaking into establishments, climbing up ropes, or even getting through windows. Maud was always fitter than me; her military training had made her that way, When she came out of the Navy, she always kept up with the fitness, the running, the jumping and the skipping, often at some ungodly hour in the morning, As for me, it was my regime that kept me slim, not the exercise. We could still make ourselves look tidy as they say and not look our age, but I suppose that's where the money comes in.

'Mr White, Edie has always been a lucky bitch,' Maud was prompted to say. 'Look at her. She has always looked twenty years younger than she is and always able to pull them in. Even now she doesn't look her age, does she?'

I must admit I had to agree.

***

At this juncture, we decided to stop and live the rest of our lives in boredom – a more favourable choice than being in Holloway with other female thieves.

We were still being invited to functions, but now it was out of duty and not out of desire. In spite of our 'joie de vivre', we could tell we were being looked on as those two silly old biddies in the corner.

I was really lost, as I still would have liked to have

continued my shenanigans with the younger opposite sex, but how many young men really like an old lady where the skin underneath the facade has begun to wrinkle; the boobs are shrivelling, and the bum starts to sag. Even if they wore a mask, they would still know that those soft undulations had long disappeared.

—But it didn't end there, Mr White. I soon learned that if a woman looks reasonable, a little sexy perhaps and kept the bulk of her clothes on, there would still be the chance of a little bit of pleasure. The clothes would often get creased but what did that matter. I could always get them pressed. What I did notice though, the clientele just got older.

'Edie, you're bloody disgusting!' Maud declared, almost shouting.

'I'm only trying to explain to Mr White how our lives changed.'

'Well don't include me in that. Do you know, Mr White,' Maud continued, 'Father never brought us up to brag about what we had got and that's what she's doing. She's always managed to get a bit on the side.'

'He always said there were many people less fortunate than ourselves and it was our duty to help them. That's why we always gave the cash we stole to various charities,' Edith added in self-defence.

'Edie, shut up. You know that's not true. We gave it as a punishment for those creeps that stole it in the first place.'

'I was only joking.'

'Yes, we were getting older in the flesh, but not in spirit. It doesn't matter who they are, or what status in life, the young do not really respect age, and this is another of the many reasons you are here today, Mr White,' Maud said, changing the subject.

Chapter 21
A Lesson in the Learning

Maud and I decided on another sojourn to the villa. We were sitting in the airport lounge waiting for the crew to organise our departure; Maud was knitting as usual, with not a care in the world and I was just daydreaming when some youngsters appeared on the scene. It soon became obvious that they thought they would start taking the piss out of two old women on their own, which I suppose we were to them; that would include anyone over thirty-five. I suppose it was Maud's knitting that helped to give that appearance.

'Where are you going to?' the first one asked in a loud voice, assuming we were deaf.

Have you noticed the older you get the louder some people talk to you, particularly in hospital?

'Nice,' I replied, to which he turned to his friends and mimicked me in a posh voice.

'Ooh! Nice. We are too, so you will have some company.'

'Oh, that will be lovely,' I replied which again brought hoots of derision over my accent. They then turned their attention to Maud who always had the ability to ignore everything when she was knitting. For the next half an hour they derided us and just made a nuisance of themselves.

'On a cradle-snatching mission, are we?'

The mere fact we ignored them only added fuel to their fire. They persisted for about fifteen minutes and were beginning to annoy some of the other passengers. I was thankful when Flight 252 to Nice was called and they began to move to their departure gate but not before one of them yelled:

'The flight's been called.'

Another lad followed suit: 'The Nice flight's been called. Come on.' He went to the gate and I heard him tell the assistant what he had said, to which she replied:

'Oh yes, they are the Trenchards, so don't you go upsetting them.'

He just ignored the advice and when the flight was called for the second time, they came en masse to inform us, and assumed our hearing had further declined.

The leader, as I will call him, leaned over Maud and repeated in a slow loud deliberate voice, 'You ... will ... miss ... your ... plane.'

'Thank you,' she replied, remaining where she was.

'Where have you put your luggage?' he asked.

'We don't have any, but thank you.'

Egged on by his mates, the youngster persisted with his jesting, but by now Maud had reached the end of her tether.

'They will call us when our plane is ready, young man.' She paused. 'Ah, look, it's ready. They're bringing it out now. No doubt we will see you in Nice and perhaps there you won't be so rude,' she continued. He yelled in pain as she grabbed him by the ear and pulled him over to the window. 'Look!' she shouted angrily, pointing to the Cessna taxying to the loading area. 'Our plane is just coming out of the hangar. It will be at least another fifteen minutes. So why don't you go with your friends and we'll meet you at Nice.'

Then with a last tweak of his ear, she said, 'Bye, Bye,' much to the amusement of the fellow passengers.

But the best was yet to come. When the lad arrived at the departure point, he couldn't find his passport. He searched his rucksack, his pockets and then came running over to us to see if he had dropped it nearby.

'What are you looking for, young man?' Maud asked.

'I've lost my passport.'

'Oh dear,' I said, as Maud had gone back to her knitting.

He raced back to the departure point where his friends were becoming worried about the situation. He remonstrated with the staff, but was clearly told he would not be able to travel. He then became a little unruly and security had to be called.

There was no time left for him to argue as the passengers filed through the departure gate. He said his sad farewells and promised to see his mates in Nice the following day.

A very dejected little soul walked round the seating area, retracing his steps. No one felt sorry for him due to his recent behaviour and rudeness.

Once again he came over to where we were seated. This time he was very subdued and embarrassed as passengers stared at him. Many, you could hear, were commenting that it served him right.

He sat down, put his head in his hands and remained there for several minutes.

Aware that it was too late for the lad to board his plane, Maud miraculously found his passport under a nearby seat. She had, of course, picked his pocket when she had grabbed him by the ear.

'Look! I've found it!' she said loudly in her silly girl lost voice. Some passengers nearby could see the funny side of things and probably realised the truth of the situation.

Maud handed him his passport and he, very sheepishly, apologised for his rudeness. That was worth everything to us.

'Don't worry, young man,' Maud said, 'bring your hand luggage and come with us. What's your name?'

'Robin, Robin Brunel.'

'Well, Robin Brunel, have you learned anything today?'

'Yes, Ma'am.'

'And what's that?' Maud asked.

'Not to be so rude and stupid. It was just the excitement of the trip.'

'Come on, we don't want to be late,' she said, smiling.

Like a little lost lamb, Robin followed us. The young assistant who had been at the gate earlier reminded him just how lucky he was and suggested he remained on his best behaviour.

He was totally confused until I told him we were taking him to Nice and that we would be there before his friends arrived. He would of course, have to wait for his luggage to arrive from the other plane, but at least, it taught him a lesson.

He has kept in touch with us and now works in the City. Stanley knows him very well and they often do business together. A changed lad now. Stanley was very clever with the financial markets and passed on much of his expertise to Robin. In fact, he gave the lad several of our accounts which set him up for life.

Chapter 22
Villains of the Square Mile

It was Robin Brunel who gave us the enthusiasm to do our last job. He had stumbled across a plan to manipulate the prices in a number of shares and in government bonds on the stock market. There were several major partners in stockbroking firms involved and what was worse, there were senior officials in three major banks also involved and an insider in the Treasury Dept. He told Stanley it was a huge conspiracy which needed to be exposed.

They were going to offload huge numbers of shares on the FTSE 100 list which would send shivers down the exchanges and hopefully create a mini crash. They would of course, sell at the top and buy them back at the bottom and thus make millions. It was totally unscrupulous, and in our opinion, they should not get away with it.

We decided to do something about it; the problem was we had no proof except Robin's word. He was a young man and no one would believe him. The newspapers wouldn't have touched it with a barge pole and it would be put down to the rantings of two rich old dears who had nothing better to do with their time. The only thing we could do was for us to secure the evidence ourselves.

Our starting point was the offices of Arbuthnot, Gideford & Bedford, Stockbrokers of London, They were an old-fashioned establishment, situated at London Wall, where Robin was already a junior partner. Through Robin they managed several of our large portfolios, which gave us an easy entry. Robin told us he had seen the plan on Graham Gideford's desk a couple of weeks previously and that they were probably in his safe, obscured by a large velvet curtain at the back of his office, near the window.

'I'll explain this to Mr White, Edie,' Maud suggested. 'I was very much concerned with the timing and planning of things.'

Maud takes up the story ...

We had to find out first when events were likely to take place as it affected the way we would operate and how quickly we would have to put our plan into action. Stanley contacted Robin to see if he could arrange a visit for me and Edith to see how some of our funds were performing.

In other words, it was an excuse to visit their offices and scrounge a boozy lunch, which was normal in those days. Not for us I would hasten to add. We were seldom seen in the City. Stanley was a different kettle of fish. Incidentally, I did ask Robin to get the name of the safe before our visit, just in case I couldn't. The safes in these old offices were often as old as the buildings themselves and were usually opened with a large safe key. It would therefore be far easier to make an impression of the key and save time.

We had to take Robin into our confidence and outline what we were going to do. He was extremely concerned and tried to persuade Stanley to stop us getting involved.

'How can they get into the office? How on earth could the sisters open the safe?' Robin asked, and when Stanley told him he began to panic.

Stanley told me that he sat Robin down and explained that his mother was very capable of doing a small task like that. That seemed to make him panic even more.

Anyway, Robin organised a lunch time visit with the senior partner, Graham Gideford who was to be the host and tour guide. However, he made a big mistake by excluding Robin from the proceedings. Robin of course, was a junior, but as far as we were concerned he was the one with our accounts.

'Where's Robin, Mr Gideford? I asked.

'Call me Graham.'

'That's nice. Where's Robin?' I asked again.

'He's busy and we thought you would want to meet the senior partners,' he replied as Robert Bedford joined the group. 'This is Robert ... Robert Bedford, my partner.' Stanley made the introductions.

'Oh good. Maybe he will be able to tell us why Robin is not here. He is the one that manages our accounts and I would have thought you would have organised that better. What is our account worth to you?'

They both stuttered and coughed, not knowing the answer.

'Gentleman, what is our portfolio currently worth?' Same response as before; they hadn't got a clue.

'I will tell you that the portfolio is currently worth twenty-one million and you earn in commissions in excess of £100,000. The next time we come, I will expect you to have some clue of who and what you are dealing with and have the courtesy to have our account manager ready to discuss matters with us and enjoy the lunch, which our commissions will pay for. Furthermore, Robin is the only reason we are with this firm and you would be well advised to remember that. Good day, gentlemen.'

'I am sorry. I will get Robin,' Gideford announced, getting to his feet. 'Of course Robin will join us for lunch. It was my intention in any event.'

'Liar,' Edith whispered, kicking my leg.

—Mr White, we were investigating a possible conspiracy to defraud millions. I would not normally have behaved like this, but I had no respect for them and wanted to belittle them. They were thieves in the making and were intending to ruin the savings of hundreds of investors.

Suffice to say, we needed to make sure our own investments remained secure.

They summoned Robin, and of course, made a great fuss of him in front of us. To ensure there were no further embarrassing moments, we immediately went to lunch, along with Robin and some of their management team to Robert Carrier's restaurant.

'What can we get you to drink, ladies?' Gideford asked.

'Well, I would love an ice-cold dry champagne,' Edith said, and I concurred.

'Stanley, what are you having? I suppose you're the driver, Gideford added with a snigger.

'No, he's waiting with the car. I'll just have a bitter please.'

'Would you please arrange for our driver to have something to eat?' Edith asked.

'I don't think they will do that, Mrs Trenchard.'

'They will. Just tell them it's for me, Edith Trenchard. It's our building.' That knocked the pompous smile off his face.

'I have to say Edith, you look lovely,' Robin suddenly said.

'Why, thank you Robin,' she replied.

Robert Bedford decided to agree and made a similar comment. I could see Edie growing in stature by the minute.

We all got a bit tipsy during lunch; Edie was the centre of attention and I could sense it was going to lead somewhere; just where remained to be seen.

To be honest, Edith did look lovely. No one would put her above forty-five. She always had a lovely girlish attitude, especially when she had been drinking champagne. It was very appealing to the male sex, more so when she used it to flirt, which was on every occasion, It soon became obvious that Robert had the hots for her.

Robert was sitting next to Edie and it didn't take much imagination to work out what was going on under the table. The expressions on both their faces said it all, not least the fidgeting.

I was a little annoyed with Edie. I did not want her to forget why we were here. I leaned forward and whispered, 'Edie, I'm going to the loo. Coming?'

'Yes, indeed.'

She had to give Robert one of her tantalising smiles as we got up. Reciprocated, of course.

'Edie! Use it, don't ruin it. I want to know what's in his office. Nothing else! You can see him after. That's if he is not in gaol.'

That brought her back to reality, but the moment we were back at the table she was off again.

After lunch, we returned for a guided tour of the office. Robert showed Edith his office and I swear I saw them kiss. We had a final cup of tea in Gideford's office, where I came into my own. They were so minded to make sure we had a good time, they forgot the rudiments of office security. During our lunch I had 'borrowed' Robert's keys and made an impression of the only key belonging to a safe. I knew I had the right one when I saw it in the office.

Now it was only a matter of when I was to open the safe and what the next step was. There were several different firms operating within the building, which was on four floors: solicitors, accountants, quantity surveyors, as well as Arbuthnot's, the latter occupying the entire third floor. It was not unusual in those days for firms to organise their own security and from my investigations, there was no reception service at the entrance, no daytime security and only minimum lock-up security at night. The keyholders, usually one of the employees were given the responsibility to be the first there and to open up in the morning.

I decided to take a look after hours; it was so simple. Only the cleaners were there and I noticed that they collected the contents of the waste paper bins separately from the other rubbish and placed it in marked bags. These were then collected by a special unmarked van and taken to Kennington Oval. This was very interesting as all our private business would be in the hands of the criminal fraternity – or opportunists.

I told the police anonymously what was happening as I did not want any opportunist sniffing out what we had discovered.

—You may remember this, Mr White. The *Mail* ran the story and the villains were given community service. At least it sharpened up the security surrounding waste paper.

My plan of action was to enter the building just before the cleaners finished, slip into the toilet and wait for them to leave. I would search the filing cabinets and the safe in the partner's offices. Despite her pre-occupation with Robert, Edie had managed to give me a detailed description of where everything was. Just how she did so is beyond me.

Bif drove me to the offices in the Mini. We always liked to use this car as it was so fast and very manoeuvrable . It could get in and out of spaces you could not imagine and down alleyways you would not think possible. Anyway, we arrived at the offices about ten to seven. I walked into the building, up the stairs and into their offices, slipping unseen into the toilets.

I listened carefully; there was just the noise of the hoovers that were operating in the adjacent room and the chatter of the women working. Then suddenly, I heard one of the women coming in my direction. As she neared the door, I darted into the last cubicle and stood on the toilet hoping she would pass. But No! The toilet room door opened and she came in.

'Please don't come in here,' I kept repeating to myself.

Suddenly, another woman shouted, 'Madge! Give us a hand.'

She called back, 'Two minutes, Dot.' She opened the toilet room door again and stood there for a second or two. I'm sure she could have heard my heart beating as my breathing had stopped and that was the only sound. She then opened the first cubicle door and sat down on the loo to have a quick fag.

After a couple of minutes, I presumed it was Dot who opened the toilet room door and shouted impatiently, 'Come on, Madge.'

I could hear her shuffling about and blowing into the air as though she was trying to disperse the smoke and a hurried, 'Coming, coming,' seeming anxious to not get into trouble. She flushed the loo and left. I nearly collapsed, I had held my breath that long. I waited several more minutes when I heard them saying goodnight to each other and the sound of their voices fading. Once silence reigned, I ventured out and went straight to Gideford's office where the safe was. The key fitted perfectly.

I took all the papers out of the safe and began to look through them. What I didn't hear was someone entering the building. Neither did I hear a woman's footsteps until they were close. As she ran past the office I was in, I fell to the floor keeping perfectly still, simply looking up at the safe where I had left the door open. It is not a mistake I would normally make. I could do nothing but hope. I didn't dare move. Seconds later, the woman ran past and descended the stairs to the ground floor. I heard what sounded like a door slamming and once more, I could breathe again.

I photographed all the papers, including each page in Gideford's diary. In fact, I included the previous year's pages as well, thinking it might be pertinent. I relocked the safe and did the same with the filing cabinets before turning my attention to 'luvver boy's' office. I didn't find anything of consequence there, but photographed his diary just in case. It took well over an hour to complete the search.

Finally, as arranged, I caught up with Bif at the Albert Memorial and we were home within the hour. The results of the night's work were soon put on the screen for us to study and I must say, my new camera was amazing; it produced very sharp and clear pictures.

There was definitely something afoot and Gideford was in the thick of it. The minutes of all the meetings were noted and the duties for all participants were defined. The problem was that the names of those present and involved were in code.

The first meeting outlined in detail what they were going to do. However, once again, they used code for the company shares involved. It was therefore necessary to find out who the other participants were and we needed one or two other clues before we could break the code.

The following day, we invited Robin for a meal, which Alice prepared for us. Afterwards, we sat in the drawing room to discuss the problem. When we put the pictures on the screen, Robin's eyes opened wide as did his mouth.

'I told you my mother would get into the safe, didn't I?' Bif announced proudly.

'She's amazing!'

'Yes, she certainly is,' Edith said. 'Now we need to find out how Robin can help us decipher some of this information.'

Edith continues ...

'Robin, can you remember who came to the office on the 16th of last month? And what about the meeting with J.P.W. on 12th December last?' I asked.

Fortunately, Robin's memory was good. Anything he wasn't sure about, he made a note of and would get back to us if he discovered anything.

We continued the picture show and the questioning for well over another hour, when Robin suddenly said:

'I remember that meeting last December. It wasn't a

meeting, not at the office. I remember Gideford made some joke about having an early Christmas dinner. He didn't come back that day.'

'Right! Now I want you to list all his contacts that you can remember whose initials are J.P.W., P.T.A., L.T or S or anything similar. It will be a start. See if you can remember him mention where he went. He may have made the arrangements, so check with his secretary's diary. You can use some excuse for her to look. Say the boss recommended the place and you would like to go there as we are treating you to a thank you dinner for all your hard work. Get the idea?'

'Yes of course,' Robin replied, getting excited about the prospect.

'Nobody uses code in the Minutes of a meeting unless they have something to hide,' Maud interjected.

Before Robin left that evening, he insisted on showing Bif his pride and joy – a beautiful second-hand MGB GT in teal blue.

The following day, Robin managed to get the name of the restaurant where the Christmas lunch was held. It was at The Belfry in Berkeley Square, a restaurant, which I often used and as Robert had invited me to dinner, I thought it would be nice to go there on our first date.

I rather liked Robert and the thought of a lovely dinner would just set things off. That said, I was ten years older than him and perhaps a little too old, but I made the effort and arranged to pick him up at the office at six-thirty.

We would have a few drinks first and then on to The Belfry. After the lovely 'touchy-feely' lunch we had previously, I thought I should pull the blind down in the back of the car, winking at Cedric our English chauffeur as I did so. I thought Robert might become amorous. No such luck. The drinks at the Savoy turned out to be tea and a chat and then at eight o'clock, we continued to The Belfry for dinner,

'Good evening, Edith,' the Maître D' said as we entered.

'Good evening, Charles. This is my companion, Robert Bedford.'

'Good evening, sir.' he replied.

'Robert, I want to surprise you. Would you let me have a word with Charles privately?'

'Sure. I'll go to the table. Don't you be too long.'

Alone with Charles, I immediately asked all the necessary questions and sure enough it was booked, but in the name of Gideford's secretary. I then asked if he happened to remember who any of the guests were.

'Let me think ... Yes, there was Sir Harold Wilmot and Gideon Peters. Like you they are regulars here, but I don't know any of the others.'

'How many were there?'

'I seem to remember five. Why the interest?'

' Oh, just Maud wanting to know where someone was, but it doesn't sound like he would have been with them. That's most helpful. Thank you, Charles. You choose the menu for us and we'll start with a bottle of the Mercier.'

I walked over to the table where Robert and the waiter competed to see who could be the most attentive. 'I *love* an attentive man,' I said as we sat down just in time for the champagne to arrive.

'Tell me about yourself and how you fit into the firm?' I asked, getting the conversation started.

'Well, what is there to say? I am fifty-six years of age, single, been married, no children, lonely. I am a senior partner in the firm but my forté is commodities. I suppose I could be considered one of the top advisors on commodities; the stocks and bonds side of the business I leave to Graham. I have little if anything to do with it.'

I felt I wanted to hug him. A man who was honest enough to tell me he was lonely was someone special.

The first course arrived which was the prelude to a

superb meal and for the first time, I thought he was falling for me. I could see it in his eyes by the way he looked at me. He was different to any of the men I had known. Still with the same needs, I am pleased to say, but I could feel he had a genuine desire to be with me.

'Mr White, she fell for all of them and often got hurt,' Maud interrupted.

'You've had your turn. I'm telling this story,' Edith replied like a petulant schoolgirl.

I didn't want this, especially as we were investigating the possible criminal actions of his firm, even if it was by his partner. They were partners and each was responsible for the other's actions. I wanted to warn him.

We had a little contretemps on leaving because I insisted on paying for it, but when he asked if I would like to go to his place for a coffee, how could I resist? On arrival at Robert's beautiful three-bedroomed flat in Chelsea, I sent Cedric home, assuring him I would get a taxi back.

It wasn't the prim and proper place I would have normally expected for a man in his position, but it was situated in a very desirable mews. The furnishings were tasteful and practical, but very much a bachelor pad. There were clothes everywhere; it was generally untidy but clean. He quickly removed a pile of clothes from the settee and invited me to sit down.

'Come and sit down next to me. We can have the coffee in a few minutes,' I said, tapping the cushion.

He immediately sat next to me and turned to look at me. I knew from that moment he was in love with me. It was so flattering; I just loved it, but I couldn't allow it. I was too old for him. I held his hands in mine and said:

'Robert, please don't do this to me. You don't know me and I am far too old for you.'

As Maud said, I didn't want to get hurt. Every one of my men has taken advantage and I've let them.

We talked for ages whilst he admitted how much he loved me. Despite my repeating that I was too old for him, he tried to convince me that the age difference didn't matter.

'We've only just met. How could you possibly know someone in that time?'

'I know what I see before me and that is enough for me,' he replied.

The talking became kissing, the kissing became lovemaking and the love-making became one of the most wonderful evenings of my life. He was so tender; every move was one of warmth and gentleness. I could not remember how I got into bed and I have never woken up with any man's arms around me. It was as though he did not want to let me go. It was wonderful.

We were awake for only a few minutes, just lying there in total silence, when he said, 'I must go to work. Please say you will see me again.'

'Of course I will. How can I resist you now?'

He took me in his arms. 'Tonight? Please?'

We agreed and enjoyed another equally wonderful evening together. I got home the following day armed with information that excited Maud beyond belief. It was possible that everyone in some way was linked to a chap called Wilmot, who was chairman of one of the major banks. Peters, a very senior official at the Treasury was also part of the scheme of things. The next job was to confirm the involvement of both parties, take a look at their offices, or in Peters' case, his home.

—I have said Maud was a very clever cookie and could read the criminal mind. Well, it takes one to know one, Mr White and she was clever!

Maud assumed that Peters would not leave any papers around in the office; he was a senior civil servant and open to public scrutiny. It was unlikely he would carry them round with him unnecessarily, as again it could create difficulties. Therefore, they had to be at his home and we needed to take a look.

This was easily achieved, as Peters lived in a very large and pleasant semi-detached house in suburbia. The study contained some beautiful first edition books on the shelves. Maud could not understand why there was insufficient security; the double-glazed windows were all locked and bolted, but the only lock on the front door was a simple Yale and on the back door was an out-of-date three lever lock. The back door took less than two minutes to open and she was in. Even the dog didn't make a sound – in fact, I remember Maud saying the poor thing was terrified of her.

She had to make this job appear to be a normal burglary, if any burglary is normal, which was not difficult. Peters had little imagination and had simply put the papers in the drawer of his desk, leaving the key in the lock. He made it so simple that she found everything in minutes. Once again, she photographed the papers and then dropped them on the floor with the other contents of the desk to make it look as if the drawers had been rifled.

Upstairs, Maud was astonished to find Peters and his wife slept in separate rooms. She found his wife almost dead to the world; she was in such a deep sleep as a result of the telltale sleeping pills next to the bed. She also slept with a great deal of cream on her face which I suppose would put any man off. Maud looked through the drawers and found a few pieces of jewellery which she took before going to his room. Peters had very little, so she simply took some money and credit cards.

When Maud returned home she realised this little job had given us many clues and ideas, and now felt that Peters was undoubtedly a weak link. No one on earth would be involved in a conspiracy like this unless there was a mistress on the scene. That together with the fact he didn't sleep with his wife suggested there must be a mistress somewhere and, presumably he would need money.

We were, for the moment, to concentrate on Peters. Maud felt that by watching his every move 24/7, we would see who he met and could put names to the code (initials). We would also see when, where and at what times they met and from now on, we would always be able to get the minutes of any meeting from Graham Gideford's safe. It would be no problem finding out what transpired at those meetings. She also felt it would be a quicker, cheaper and a less risky way of solving the problem.

We took turns and watched for many days, but it was the same routine; Maud thought we should try another tack and turned our attention to Sir Harold Wilmot. We found this much easier as he lived in a large flat just off King's Road, Chelsea and had his office in Threadneedle Street; he was also driven everywhere in his Rolls-Royce Silver Cloud. Being somewhat larger than life, it was easy to keep an eye on him.

Being a senior Treasury official, news of the burglary at Peters' home made the press but did little to thwart their activities. They continued with their meetings and Sir Harold certainly did not think there was anything untoward. In fact, he seemed blessed with a new energy, scurrying from one meeting to the next. It became doubly difficult to differentiate between what was criminal and what was his normal daily activity. We needed to find out the names of who Sir Harold met to see if they matched any of the codes and also what position in the conspiracy he held. At that point, we had the distinct impression he was the leading man.

It was also necessary to look at his files and those of his secretary, which meant breaking into their offices; not as simple as it may seem because these were blessed with decent security.

Maud carried out her usual surveillance routine – the

twenty-four hour security, receptionists' hours and the cleaning arrangements at night. She concluded that the weakest link, and there always is a weak link, would be around eight o'clock in the evening when the cleaning staff had finished and the three security men had done their first patrol. She also noticed that the security men fraternised with the cleaning staff a great deal and Maud considered that this sort of role would suit me. After the inspection at around eight-thirty, all the cleaning staff and the three security men left, leaving only one man on duty. That was when we were to 'attack' the place.

I was to dress as provocatively as possible, walk in at around eight-fifteen, approach the reception desk and inform the security guard that I had a job interview with Mr Philips of ACE Cleaning Services at eight-thirty. As I was a little early, I was to ask if I could wait. As Maud would say, it was my job to chat him up. I was to find out how the doors opened and what his routine was. Mr Philips wouldn't turn up so we would have to repeat it on the second day when I would ensure the doors were left open for Maud to enter.

I arrived at eight-fifteen on the dot and walked up to the desk, dressed up to the nines.

'We're closed, love,' the night guard said.

'I've got an interview wiv Mr Philips of ACE Cleaners. For a job 'ere,' I said, using my south London accent. 'He said he'd be 'ere 'bout eight firty. Can I wait fer 'im?'

'Corse you can. Corse you can,' he replied, repeating himself. 'You can sit over there if you like.'

'I'd sooner chat to you 'ere, if that's okay?'

'Corse it is love. Corse it is.'

'What's yer name?' I asked.

'John.'

I began to ask him a whole series of questions; how long he had worked there, how old he was, whether he was married – all that sort of thing. By now the evening staff were leaving and the girls began calling out: 'Night, John.' Other remarks followed: 'You be careful with her.' And another: 'Mind what yer doin' John, she'll eat yer alive!'

Well that did it. I leaned over and said, 'Do you mind what yer doing, John?' He just could not resist glancing at my cleavage as I leant over.

'Well?' I asked.

'Well what?'

'Do you mind what yer doin'?'

'Not very often.'

'Ooh, come 'ere. I love a man like you. No wonder all those girls fancy you. What time do you finish?'

'Not till after two o'clock,' he said with a sigh.

'That's too bloody late and it doesn't look like the boss is coming, do it? I suppose I'd better go?'

'You can stay a bit if you like,' he replied.

'Can we go somewhere a bit private then? Everyone can see us 'ere.'

'Yeah, I use the canteen to make me a cuppa tea. You can come wiv me if you like?'

'I'd love a cuppa tea.'

'Come on, then No one ever comes in at this time. It won't matter.'

He took me over to the lift and we made our way to the canteen. We chatted for half an hour or so when I said, 'I don't want to, but I fink I'd better go. I'll get you into trouble.'

'No you won't, don't worry.'

'No, come on. I'll probably 'ave to come back tomorrow so I'll see you then.' We walked back to the lift where he attempted to kiss me and missed.

'Come 'ere,' I said and kissed him.

Well, I've never had so many ups and downs in my life before, but I'll tell you it's a bit different in a lift, especially when it's moving! It was quite an experience and most unexpected!

'What have you done to me? You are naughty, yer know. I'm not normally like this. I'm a good gel, I am. I don't care if the boss don't come. I'm comin' to see you anyway. I want a bit more of that! Big boy.'

Having halted the lift halfway down, we eventually arrived on the ground floor. 'Tidy yerself up, John, I said. 'Yer look as though you've had sex. See yer tomorrow.'

I walked to the door when he shouted after me, 'What's yer name? I don't know yer name.'

'Doris,' I replied. 'Doris Endicott.'

'See you tomorrow, Doris Endicott.' I waved and left.

I could not get a taxi for love nor money; it must have been the garb I was wearing, or the stocking I forgot to pull up, but it was a little disconcerting receiving offers I didn't want to refuse. But there you are. Eventually, I arrived back at Number 17 and gave Maudie the details of my activities, leaving out the juicy bits. I suggested that I could keep John out of harm's way for at least three-quarters of an hour and that I could open the automatic door.

The following day, Bif took us in the Rolls to Bank Station. It was about seven-thirty; the City is still alive at that time so we decided to have a coffee before we started work.

Maud made sure I knew what part I was going to play and what I was to do if things went wrong. At eight-fifteen on the dot, I arrived at Wilmot's offices. It seemed sad as John was so pleased to see me and I knew it would be the last time.

'Ello John. Missed me?' I asked, smiling, I'm sure I looked the part with my new tarty, black, tight leather trousers, skin-tight red sweater, and four-inch stilettos to match. I slinked across to the desk and gave him a peck on the cheek.

'You look luvurly, Doris.'

'Pardon?'

'I said, you look luvurly.'

'Don't be daft,' I replied, having nearly dropped a clanger by forgetting I called myself Doris.

Once again, we chatted until the girls left and once again the comments came, only this time there were twice as many. I was a little concerned when one of the security team was late away and asked what I was doing there. I was amazed to hear John say I was bringing his snap because he had forgotten it. The team left and we were once again on our own.

'Shall we have a cuppa tea then?' John asked.

'Ooh luvurly. Come on then,' I said, throwing my handbag behind the counter and following him to the lift. As the lift doors opened, I suddenly ran back to the desk to collect my handbag, at the same time switching the electronic doors back on. He held the lift doors open for me and I ran in. The moment he pressed the button for the fifth floor, I kissed him. He was like an anxious bull. My trousers were too tight for him to get them undone. It seemed like ages before I could stop wriggling my way out of them. When I did, it was all over in no time at all.

We had only been in the lift for five minutes. Maud needed at least twenty-five minutes, so I had to keep him occupied for that length of time and I could hear her words in my ears if there was an emergency: 'You know what to do to keep him occupied.' We all know what some men are like after they have climaxed. Well, he was one of those.

'Come on then, let's 'ave these off,' I whispered in his ear as I began pulling his trousers down again. I had to work really hard to renew his interest. In fact, it required every trick in the book and a great deal of perseverance before I was able to say: 'Wow! We 'ave lift off. You clever boy. And aren't we a big boy now?' It's always good to let your target know he's a real man; it does wonders for his self-esteem.

I had to laugh as he was almost bow-legged by the time he put his trousers back on. Then he had to help me into my gear.

'How do I look?' I asked before we exited the lift.

'Fantastic, Doris.'

'Right John, let's have a cuppa tea.' I offered my arm which he took and he led me into the canteen, where he began to pour his heart out.

'Doris, you're special.'

'Now don't start getting sentimental wiv me. You don't know me. I'm not what you fink.'

'I like what I see and that's enough,' he replied.

'John, I fink you are nice, very nice, but I am a working gal and I 'ave lots of clients. They would not allow me to leave because I owe them a lot of money. They are dangerous men and I wouldn't want you mixed up wiv them. I know you wouldn't understand all the different men I entertain. Let's just remain friends. Come on, one more time!'

My rejection of him made him temporarily despondent. That was until he got in the lift and I tickled his fancy once again. We had been over an hour and I was sure Maud would have completed her part of the plan. The lift opened and immediately closed again as John wanted to kiss me for the last time. They opened once more and he led me back to the desk and pressed the switch to allow the main doors to open. I walked towards the exit but nothing happened. He pressed the switch again. This time they opened. I turned to see him staring as I left. A quick wave and I was away.

To my absolute joy, I saw Maud waiting at the bottom of Threadneedle Street. 'How did you get on, dear sister?' I asked, mainly out of annoyance. She appeared so refreshed whilst I stank of sex and sweat and simply wanted to get home to a cleansing bath.

'Don't worry, I phoned Bif in the car. He'll be here in a

few minutes,' she announced, seeing my discomfort. 'You will be pleased to know we have got Gideford hook, line and sinker. Everything! He has recorded everything on paper, typed up by his secretary and she too stands to make a fortune. She's well on board too.'

The paperwork photographed in the secretary's office showed there were other people involved and gave their names. It also verified the names of those coded by their initials. It was a complete record of everything that had taken place and signed by Sir Harold Wilton. Not only that, it included some notes he had added to various pages.

It was a clever sequence of events in that not everyone involved knew who the other members were, but they all knew what actions they were going to take. Not only was Sir Harold the boss, but he also acted as the go-between for the parties to ensure that the secrecy remained.

One thing was certain. These few individuals concerned controlled a great deal of the country's investment portfolio and were in a position to cause havoc if they acted together.

How they could have kept secret this exclusive club and their goings-on, I will never know, but Maud was able to open Gideford's safe a number of times, which enabled us to keep abreast of their modus operandi and when they intended to carry out the attack. It was to be the day Parliament returned after the summer break.

They were to sell heavily for the first four hours of trading and keep selling at a moderate level for the remainder of the day. A similar pattern would take place on the second, third and fourth day. On the fifth day, they would pounce, buying the stock back very cheaply.

I couldn't help thinking of those poor sods that could well lose their life's savings, whilst these greedy criminals would possibly make millions. We had three months to decide the best course of action.

I went out with Robert many times over the weeks and

became quite close to him. I began to stay a couple of days a week at his house and he stayed a couple of days at Number 17. Things were becoming serious, and knowing that we could ruin the man I was becoming very close to, became a matter of deep concern. I had to resolve it, and quickly. Maud and I had many discussions on how I should approach the subject and it was agreed I would take the bull by the horns. The only aspect that I didn't like was that I had to imply we had heard about the matter from a Treasury source which we hoped would save Robin being involved.

I will never forget the evening I told Robert that his partner was mixed up in a very big criminal conspiracy, one which may cause him to be sent to prison and lose much of his money. I was so worried how to tell him, so worried that I might lose another man I had grown fond of, and so worried I might ruin him. I moped around all evening in silent, tense mode which began to exasperate Robert as he knew there was something wrong. After a while, he could no longer put up with the tension and finally snapped.

'Come and sit down, Edith. It can't be as bad as all that. I want to know what the matter is. Is there something you're not telling me? Do you want to call an end to our relationship?'

'No! No,' I said exasperatingly. 'I don't want to do that. I love you.'

'What is it then? Please tell me.'

We sat on the settee facing each other. He took hold of my hands in his. 'Come on now … spit it out.'

I made him promise not to divulge to anyone what I was about to say. I then gave him all the details, omitting our part in the investigation. I could see the colour slowly drain from his face, coupled with a look of bewilderment.

'Robert, you mustn't tell Graham. I know he is your partner, but he is involved in this right up to his neck.'

I stayed with him for two wonderful days. I had never had anyone that I could take care of before. I felt part of him and that it was our joint struggle to overcome such adversity. We spent hours going over his partnership contract, which I immediately gave to Mr Higginbotham and others for advice. To our astonishment, they all told us there was a clause in the agreement, making it null and void if one of the partners was involved in any criminal activity. However, this clause in itself would become null and void if the other partner was aware of such activity and did not prevent it.

Robert was unaware until the investigation was underway and Higginbotham felt his partnership share would be unaffected, which was a relief to us all; at least after a few days Robert calmed down. However I was surprised when he told me he had always believed that Graham had been involved in a few dodgy deals.

All that was left was to decide what to do. Hand the information to the police or MI5? Or pass it to all the newspapers?

We took the matter to the police – in fact, to the Metropolitan Chief Commissioner himself. The problem was it was not in the public interest because no crime had been committed, and it would be an easy defence as they would simply say it was a doomsday scenario which they were looking at, in order to prevent such a thing ever happening.

We therefore decided to involve a few real friends in our plan to scupper the criminals, which comprised of two major investments banks, our own bank, several wealthy friends and a major pension fund.

I would say that Maud was so angry that they were cheating the little man that we as a family decided to put our entire fortune on the line to protect them, which was in excess of one hundred million pounds. With the other monies available to us, there would be several billions and we felt we could counter their moves. We had to teach them a lesson.

On the first second and third days, we knew it would look like a disaster zone and they would be very exposed, having sold much of their stock at the top, forcing the prices down. They hoped the rest of the market would follow suit and they would buy back on the cheap on the fifth day.

We decided to buy back heavily in the last half an hour of trading on the third day. At the same time, we passed the information to all the media both here and in the USA, the police, members of Parliament and the Bank of England. In fact, to everybody that we thought ought to know about it. Everything was set. We were all on tenterhooks for the whole of the month of August.

Robert and I went to the villa mid-August for a long holiday to get out of the way whilst Maud held the fort. She made sure that she checked the contents of Gideford's safe on regular occasions to ensure all was well, which it was.

The day arrived. The market opened at eight o'clock and within half an hour, there was panic in the air. The early morning news broke the story which added to the problem. All major stocks were being hit and by the end of the day, second liners had taken a thrashing. All sorts of stories were circulating as to the reasons for the crash but none were anywhere near the truth.

On day three, stocks were still falling and over 25% had been wiped off the value of the market. There had been billions of shares sold short, which as you are aware Mr White, is selling stock you haven't got in the hope of buying it back on the cheap – a very dangerous practice.

At two-thirty that day, we went in with all guns blazing. By close of play at three o'clock, the market had regained half of its losses. By four o'clock the police were at the offices of all the protagonists and the story was on the BBC

News. The late edition of the *Standard* also carried the story, showing a picture of Wilmot on its front page. Of course, the following morning the story broke in the dailies with great force. I think the worst thing that happened was that the criminals and their firms were suspended from dealing with immediate effect and could not buy back the stocks.

Every one of them faced the full force of the law, and following an investigation, all went to prison. Graham Gideford was suspended and dismissed from the Stock Exchange, having been found insider dealing on a number of occasions as well. He received three years in prison and was declared bankrupt. Robert bought some of Gideford's share in the business, which straightaway went to pay the receiver and we bought the rest, which we gave to Robin. Out of interest, Stanley was Robin's best man at his wedding and Maud felt she had avenged the poor.

—Mr White, if I told you we doubled our investment for our troubles and so did all those who had helped us, you may think we were as guilty as the criminals themselves, but as I said, no one would do anything until a crime had been committed. We did give several millions to our favourite charities. At least that eased our consciences.

***

I suppose we were all very pleased with what we had achieved, particularly Stanley; he had netted the family business over fifty million pounds and even Robin had netted himself one million. Most importantly, I had met the third love of my life in Robert Bedford. I loved him dearly, but for the first time I felt I was too old for what he wanted, which was marriage. I was worried he would not want me in a few years' time and would feel trapped if we were married. Lack of confidence, I suppose. I was wrong in this decision as we stayed together until he passed away in his late seventies. I lived with him at his flat three days a week; he stayed at Number 17 two days a week and every time we went to the villa he was with me full time. In truth, it was a good compromise.

Chapter 23
Enforced Retirement

Both Edith and I were relieved this whole stock market fiasco ended. About six months after the financial crisis, things settled down and we were almost back to normal. On one particular afternoon, Stanley was outside at the front of the house, bidding farewell to George Simon, one of our investment bankers. I was watching and listening from an upstairs window when I saw a car drive up and two men alighted.

'Hello George. What are you doing here? Or need I ask?' one of the men said, going over to greet George Simon.

'You two obviously know each other, but I don't know you,' Stanley remarked.

'Sorry … John Fitzpatrick and this is Edward Sutherland, one of my associates. I have known George for years, so forgive me. I was hoping to see Maud Trenchard.'

George duly said his goodbyes and departed.

'Where are you from?' Stanley asked Fitzpatrick.

'That doesn't matter. We just want to see her.'

'Sorry, it matters to me. Good morning,' Stanley snapped and began to walk away.

'Just a moment,' Fitzpatrick called out. 'I only want to see her and I am sure she will see me when you tell her I'm here. Anyway, who are you?'

Stanley stopped in his tracks. 'You obviously do not know my mother so please make an appointment and remember, she is a very busy person. Good morning.' He continued walking away.

'I'm from the security services,' Fitzpatrick said hurriedly.

—I felt so proud of Stanley, Mr White. He had become so protective of me and Edie, for that matter.

I couldn't let them suffer any longer and shouted down, 'Good morning John. And what brings you here? I think I know! Show them in, please Stanley.'

Edie appeared just as I met them at the foot of the staircase. Surprisingly, John gave me a hug, and with the introductions over, we went into the drawing room for a private conversation.

As there were no secrets between us, I expressed my wish for Edie to remain in the room. That said, John got straight to the point.

'Maud, I really don't know how to say this because you have done so much good for the service, but you cannot go round breaking into safes in people's offices. It's illegal. And that goes for both of you. We know you broke into the office of Sir Harold Wilton and stole certain information.'

'I did not steal anything. I merely photographed information.'

'That's stealing,' he said firmly.

'Prove it.'

'And you, Edith could be locked up for kidnapping the security guard and keeping him in the lift.

'I didn't kidnap him. I went and had a cup of tea with him after I had taken his snap in for him. Unfortunately, the lift broke down.'

Everyone smiled.

'Look,' I said, 'had they not pleaded guilty and found out where the information came from and that it was obtained illegally, they would have got away with it.'

'Maud, we knew you were up to something when you were seen entering the stockbroker's office after hours, so we decided to find out for ourselves and–'

'This wouldn't have been necessary if the Chief Constable had taken the matter seriously,' I said, interrupting him.

'And MI5, for that matter,' Edie added.

'It was a very tricky situation. There were so many high-profile figures involved and you know how difficult that can be.'

'This is my point!' I snapped angrily. 'If any of these had been a stoker or a dustbin man fiddling his tax, he would have faced the full force of the law. Things wouldn't have been softly, softly. My Peter lost his life fighting for the ordinary man and I was not going to see his ideals wasted on that band of crooks.'

Fortunately, the tea and scones arrived and I was forced to come off my soapbox.

John changed his tack immediately after the tea and concentrated on the break-ins and the way we had carried them out. He knew about the early ones in France and even the one with the gangster, Valantin.

'Maud, remember,' he went on to say, 'you have worked for us, you have trained several of our agents and staff and you have even helped the police so we know your style. You are too professional to be an ordinary villain. You do a job which is so good that it has to be one of us and you are one of the best. I know we can't prove anything but with a concentrated effort, we could make things difficult.

'The two of you will have to stop this. The world is changing and it is becoming a far more dangerous place. Look what happened to Edith in France.'

'All right, you have made your point,' Edith said.

'Furthermore,' John continued, 'we have stopped the police investigating your kleptomania and your other activities, so what I am asking you to do is to retire, like ordinary folk do. We have to keep our eyes on you, Maud. You are aware you hold too many of the nation's secrets in your head, so we will be around for some time. But please try to stay out of trouble.'

We chatted for about an hour, small talk mainly and I noticed Edith had made a hit with John. He kept looking at her and would look away when Edie met his eye. I knew it would lead to trouble and when it was time for them to leave, John asked if he could use the loo and Edie foolishly offered to show him the way. I knew it had begun. She escorted him along the hallway and opened the cloakroom door for him.

Edith takes up the story ...

'I thought you looked extremely sexy in the Royal Bank of Scotland the other day ... on both occasions.' I smiled as he closed the cloakroom door.

'Thank you. It's the whore in me, you know,' I said when he came out.

'I wish I could sample some of that!'

'Of course you can, When are you free?'

'Well, I'm free on Thursdays,' John blurted out.

'It's a date. I'll see you in Lyons Corner House at Parliament Square. Seven o'clock and don't be late because I won't wait.' Memories of Alan came flooding back.

We rejoined the others and showed them the way out. Maud looked at me in disgust.

'What are you up to?' she asked when they had left.

'What do you mean?'

'You know very well what I mean. I can tell by the look on your face you're up to something. You're disgusting, Edie.'

'You didn't say that when I kept the bloke in the RBS busy, did you?'

'That was business.'

'Sometimes Maudie, I need to have a little bit of pleasure. I can't think of King and country all the time. Anyway, he is one of the heads of the Secret Service, so I am doing my duty.'

TWO OLD DEARS

Maud shook her head. 'And what would Robert think? That certainly brought me back to earth with a bang.

Thursday came round too quickly, but whatever I might be, I wasn't going to lose the opportunity to try out the Secret Service. John arrived at seven o'clock prompt, shook my hand and we sat down.

'I have to keep things formal, particularly here in front of Parliament. I'm known by all in the Cabinet. Would you like to have dinner with me?' he asked.

'That would be lovely, thank you.' I quickly finished my cup of tea and walked out to his chauffeur-driven car. At his office, he picked up his Jaguar and off we went. I don't know where we had dinner, which was lovely, but I do remember the little house in Bourne End.

He offered me a coffee which I then made and sat me down on the settee, where he began to show me the photographs they had taken of us. Then it came to the tarty ones of me: 'Why does every male on this planet like the whore look in every woman other than their wives?' I asked.

'I don't know,' he replied, 'but looking like that, I desperately wanted you. It did something to me.'

'Make it next Thursday and I'll do it especially for you.'

The rest of the evening was taken up by straight sex on the bed and a very boring evening all round. But the following Thursday I did go for the whorish look and he was a different animal. It was strange; he met me again in Lyons Corner House and I was looking like a tart. Never mind the House of Commons, it was straight to Bourne End. This time it was a fantastic performance by a very grateful man.

'One for the road?' he asked as we lay together in silence for a while.

'Of course, and this time, put everything into it!'

He drove me back home in his car, which had a bench

seat at the front so I made the most of it and cuddled up to him. I could feel him relaxing. It's surprising how many men feel good when the woman they are with feels vulnerable and needs to be close.

We arrived back at two o'clock in the morning. It was a reluctant goodbye on his part because I'm sure he wanted to stay the night, but even I had had enough. Maud heard the car arrive and came down to see me dressed as I was, making little effort to show her disdain.

It was me however who decided to end it; I was too fond of Robert and I didn't want to lose him.

One serious note came out of our liaison: John told me they were having to keep their eye on Maud. She had broken into the offices of the Third Reich in Paris during the war and stolen some highly classified papers, which would effectively expose a senior British official who was involved with the Nazis. It seems a far right organisation was aware of this and were trying to find out more about it. This information would not only embarrass Britain but France as well. John also believed that those involved were extremely dangerous and we needed to take care.

It was not the sort of thing I wanted to hear after a night of sheer delight; another reason why I thought our relationship should end.

I wanted to break the news gently to Maud about the far right organisation, but she had already guessed that something was up. On several occasions when we were out, she had noticed we were being watched. She wasn't a bit worried; in fact she was more worried about me.

It was one of the main reasons I began to think of retirement. This, together with the constant words of Mr Higginbotham urging us to do so, kept us out of mischief for several years. However, it was fortuitous that we had Secret Service protection, although it did not concern us. They had spotted a gang of villains watching Fracklington

Racecourse. We actually leased the course for a modest fee to the racecourse company. When it wasn't being used we grazed it. MI5 informed the police of their suspicions and sure enough, two well-known figures were seen around and were believed to be planning a raid.

The police wouldn't inform us of the plans, but we did hear them discussing which route the criminals were likely to take and when. It was feasible to assume that Saturday would be the day they would choose because of the volume of people arriving in the village and on the course on Saturday race days. On a fine day, there was always a great deal of money passing hands.

The police had reason to believe that a raid would take place on the Saturday just before the last race. We were just going to watch, but Bif had other ideas. Early on the Saturday morning, he took our JCB out and dug a ditch across the intended escape route, putting up a barrier which blocked the way to warn people of the ditch.

About four o'clock in the afternoon the only thing we heard was an enormous double bang as a Range Rover hit the ditch and another hit the back of the first. The villains hot-footed it but were soon caught. It was quite a farce as we later heard they could not believe how they could have missed an enormous hole in the road, having double-checked everything was in order on the Friday night. It happens to be near a little copse of beech trees which is now called 'Robbers Folly'.

We were nearing the end of 'dare devil' existences. Sadly, we weren't even involved in the episode at the racecourse. I suppose we were now becoming old and unwanted, except I had Robert and was never again unfaithful. Our love got stronger as the years progressed and I finally lost him when he was seventy-nine I dearly wished I had married him when I was younger and had his children. That said, we were very happy and never had a missed word.

I found it so difficult being without Robert and missed the things we did together. Maud could not get used to being unable to shoplift without getting caught or being unable, because of her age, to pick pockets. In fact, we were becoming two useless, boring old farts.

Stanley continued to lucratively run the business side of things. Bif and Alice and their partners were very successful too; they were considering opening the house to the public in conjunction with the National Trust. It was not that we needed the money; it was simply because we were in a 1920's time warp and surrounded by all the old masters, which the public had never seen. It would be a delight to allow others to enjoy what we had.

Maud and I were now the only ones to be living in the house and we only used two rooms, plus two bedrooms. The parties were long since over and most of our friends were like us – old, and past it. Many, of course, had died.

Chapter 24
The Final Showdown

Age is a great killer of enthusiasm; yet Maud and I still got excitement out of doing things we shouldn't. We still didn't like being told what to do, where to go, so the rebellious streak in us made us want to do one last job. It was to be the National West Bank in the Kensington High Street, London.

We spent weeks watching the place, noting every move outside and inside the bank until we were satisfied that we had the full picture, particularly the positioning of CCTV cameras and alarm systems. No one would suspect two old dears who were always dropped off outside the bank two or three times a week to do their shopping and occasionally popping into the bank to cash a cheque. The preparation was very exciting; it gave us something to do and certainly made us feel we were alive again.

Just when we thought we had organised everything in minute detail, the problems of age came to the fore. We had forgotten our escape plan! How would we get away? We didn't want to involve Bif because he was my son. Should he be caught, he would undoubtedly go to prison. In fact, we couldn't and wouldn't want to involve any of our children. We didn't care for ourselves; we were just in it for the excitement and looked no further as to the consequences.

We had to prepare a getaway plan – prevent people

running out of the bank after us – stop them phoning the police, which of course was easy twenty years ago. Living outside the 21st century, we failed to realise that almost everyone has mobile phones. The other thing we didn't realise was that all banks were fitted with bullet-proof screens and doors that would lock at the press of a switch, and we could be trapped inside.

However, fortunately Maud watched a film on television which showed a bank robber putting a chair in the way of the door to stop it closing; at least we covered that problem. She also watched endless films that showed you could wear a plastic face mask. That was something we could use, except Maud thought it would be a good idea to disguise ourselves as two old ladies.

'No one would believe we were two old ladies really. Would they?' Maud asked, trying to convince herself. She was the expert. I hadn't a clue. Of course, we had to consider the fact we were older and didn't walk so quickly. We were thinner and less agile; we did not speak with the same fluency of a younger person. We may even be a little confused at times and as in my case, we may need to go to the loo. You can imagine a bank robber asking to be excused for a moment and then return with guns blazing.

All these points Maud thought would be covered by our disguises. 'People will think we are acting the part,' she would repeatedly say.

Maud decided we could overcome the need to say anything by carrying written instructions on cardboard in number order so we wouldn't get confused. The first one would say: 'This is a stick up. Empty your drawer into this sack'.

She then realised that if the sack were full, the cashier would not be able to push it under the counter. We needed to think hard about that one.

The second sign would warn that we would shoot if

anyone tried to stop us. Making such a statement worried us. There was no way we wanted to kill anyone or carry real guns although Maud was still licensed to do so, but hardly ever did. We asked Bif if he would make something for us and we would use blanks. He converted an old shotgun by sawing off the barrels and blocking them. It would just fire blanks and make the appropriate noise.

The third sign would warn that the place would blow up if anyone tried to follow us or phone the police. To do this, we bought a bundle of white candles, dipped them in light brown paint to give the appearance of dynamite, wrapped them in a bundle with an alarm clock set to go off five minutes after setting. It would have a radio aerial sticking out to make it look as though we had control.

So far, we thought we had covered every angle until I went in to the bank to cash a cheque and found that none of the chairs would budge. They were fixed to the floor as part of the modern décor.

I immediately lost my confidence and tried to persuade Maud that our plan was not such a good idea, but she wanted desperately to do this one last job. She had always been there for me ... what could I do?

Bif thought all along that we were just playing silly biddies and were not really serious. He became terribly upset when he realised we were deadly serious. No matter how hard he tried, he couldn't dissuade us and began to worry even more. He had the mad idea that if he helped us, he could stop us getting into trouble. Keep an eye on us so to speak.

We chose to use a car from Bif's collection; it was the 1966 Austin Mini Cooper, which only had 8000 miles on it from new. Originally green and white, he had sprayed it red especially for the job, using a paint that would wash off. We simply had to pray for a fine day. The final touch were the false number plates.

—Mr White, you'll recall that the car was very small, very powerful and could outrun anything in the London traffic, going into places where few other cars could.

'Robbing somewhere a few years ago was easy. I could break in at any time, open the safe and get away,' Maud suddenly announced. 'Nowadays, the fun's gone out of it. There are cameras and security all over the place, and time-locked safes that cannot be opened in the conventional way ... It's just not fair,' she added, laughing.

Bif insisted on driving us, and so it was agreed that if he were caught, we would naïvely say he knew absolutely nothing about it – forgetting he had painted his car a temporary colour and was driving it with false plates. He knew the danger we faced but just wanted to be there for us. We checked our getaway strategy and double-checked everything we planned to do. Now we were set.

Thankfully, it was a fine start to the day and we arrived at the scene a few minutes early. We waited until just before four-thirty when the bank was due to close, and then went in disguised as two old ladies. Maud approached the counter and handed the cashier note number one, demanding that she empty the till into the bag. The cashier just laughed. That was until Maud produced her sawn-off shotgun, whereupon the cashier screamed at the top of her voice. This immediately caused Maud some confusion. The trigger was very light and the shock of the scream jolted Maud's hand. The gun went off with a hell of a bang and the recoil blew Maud right across the room, throwing her against the opposite wall. I had no alternative to pull out my pistol and take control.

'I will shoot this young lady if you don't pass the money under the counter,' I shouted.

—Now I ask you, Mr White, what criminal in their right mind would say: "I will shoot this young lady"?

'That said, you could see the staff were terrified

especially when Maud, having struggled to her feet, pulled out a parcel from her coat and gave another cashier a note which stated that the bomb she was holding would be triggered in thirty seconds if the money wasn't handed over and if any electronic devices were used to raise the alarm.

After such a performance, I was surprised the cashier actually put the money in the sack. Add to which, no one had noticed that the shotgun was only loaded with blanks and there was no damage done when it went off.

'The bomb is now primed so please be careful,' Maud shouted.

—Mr White, again what villain would say "please"? All our plans had gone for a burton and both of us had said something. We had even forgotten to put something in the way to stop the door closing!

I just prayed that they wouldn't lock the door on us and as luck would have it, they didn't. We were able to walk out, but not before I set the alarm to go off a few minutes after we had left. I looked around, checking all was okay. Thankfully, it was quiet. Maud turned right and I went left and tried to get into a parked car until she shouted:

'Come on. This way.' I was so relieved she didn't say my name. We scurried along, past the bank again and stopped in the first doorway we came to, where we took off our fake faces and put them in a bin nearby. We then took our coats off and placed them in the holdall containing the money and walked as quickly as we could to the end of the pavement, turned right again, expecting to see the car.

We walked along to the next road just a few yards away. Still no car. We never gave a thought to the police cars that had arrived at the bank as we walked back towards it, turning left this time. No green and white mini. Panic began to set in when we heard Bif's voice nearby. 'Come on Mum, I'm here.' The car was a few paces away. We had forgotten it had been sprayed red!

Bif got back into the driving seat as we hastened towards the car. I got into the front, slamming the door. Bif suddenly realised Maud was still outside on the pavement. I had also forgotten it was a two-door car, so I had to open the door and struggled to get out again. I pulled the passenger seat forward for Maud to climb into the back. It seemed to take an age. Old bones don't perform as well as younger ones and by now, even Bif who was usually very calm, began to get flustered. Finally, I managed to get back into the front and we drove away slowly.

We had done it! We had robbed the bank of £8,000 and got away with it. The weather had been kind to us, the car hadn't changed colour and we were on our way home. But it didn't end there; we were held up by a burst water main and we had to pass through some pretty deep water and be sprayed by other cars. You can guess what happened. The car very quickly became a green and white one. This was where Bif came into his own. He turned off the main road and raced down the side streets and alleys until we were out of the built-up area and heading for Number 17 over the fields, through the woods and into the garage.

Bif was now concerned for our well-being. He removed the rest of the temporary paint work, changed the registration plates, burnt all our clothes and started praying.

Maud nearly had a heart attack when we were featured on the Six O'clock Today programme that evening. There were images of Maud being blown over by the recoil of the shotgun. More emphasis was placed on the fact that we were armed and dangerous and believed to be women than the robbery and the value of the money stolen.

Aside from seeing herself on television, Maud was not a bit worried; she was more annoyed than anything. She said it made her look foolish. The raid was described as amateurish; it was because Maud had her favourite necklace on that day, which is what the young cashier saw.

Ah, that is why you were able to anticipate the Chief Inspector's question regarding the necklace,' I said, turning to Higginbotham. *'Sharp.'* Higginbotham smiled. *Not bad, I thought as Edith continued:*

—Mr White, we feel we should give you the money to give back to the bank and give the young cashier £1,000 for the shock we gave her. But I would emphasise that her scream nearly finished Maudie. She was all of a dither after the gun went off.

Things died down and I thought we had heard the last of it. That was until we were unlucky enough to walk through Marks and Spencer's and Maud accidently bumped into a young woman. Maud apologised to her, but the woman stopped and stared at her.

'I may be getting on,' Maud said, interrupting, 'but I knew I had seen her before and I knew exactly where. She tried to engage me in conversation and I was sure it was to check my voice. I smiled and walked away. I knew she would report the matter and told Edie that the bank clerk had recognised me and to watch out. There was no point in leaving as we had arranged for Bif to pick us up at four o'clock I think, so we carried on shopping.

'The next thing we knew was that this young woman was running towards us, accompanied by a large policeman. She called out: "There they are – the two old women who robbed the bank." The policeman stopped in front of us and told us he was going to take us in for questioning because he believed we had been involved in the robbery at the National West Bank. He radioed for a police car, and before we knew what was happening, we were in a room at the police station. We may have seemed confused at that point but in truth, we were.

'I remember some of the folks in Marks saying: "It's ridiculous, arresting two old women like that." Some complained about the way we were bustled out of the store. Initially, I was well aware of what was going on but then began to play the very confused old dear. Age does play some funny tricks and finally, I was totally confused, so I went into knitting mode.

'Edith took over and conducted all matters at the police station and was wonderful, don't you think? Then you came along with Mr Higginbotham and we knew all would be well. So we are very grateful to you and always will be.'

'You can now see why Mr Higginbotham wants us to retire, can't you, Mr White?' Edith said. 'Maud seems to think nothing will come of the incident.'

'Why do you think that? I asked Maud.

'Well, for the first time for a very long time, I noticed MI5 about the place, not in numbers, but there nonetheless. They don't want to lose me this way. I'll tell you something, Mr White. The worry and trouble we went through has certainly put us back into retirement and we will never do anything again ... bored or otherwise.'

.

Epilogue

As a reporter, this sequence of events has been the most interesting of anything I have ever been party to; in fact I cannot remember any other comparable story and I know it would be the scoop of the century if I were allowed to divulge it. But I am sworn to secrecy and will respect that. Edith's words come home very firmly: 'When we are dead and gone, you can reveal the whole story as long as the children and grandchildren are excluded.' I wouldn't want to break my vow for anything.

Shortly after my last meeting with the ladies, I was summoned to the Editor's office to be faced with an elderly Edward Sutherland from MI5. Strangely enough, I remember the name and the circumstance. He questioned me about my meetings at Number 17 and made me sign the Official Secrets Act. That spoiled it for me, but little did he realise that the sisters had told me all their intrigues or most of them, I thought.

I remember asking Maud what she actually did during the war which was so secret. The sisters both turned round to Higginbotham who nodded his approval.

'She worked for Naval Intelligence and for the SOE,' Edith answered.

'Yes I realise that, but what did she do?'

'It is still classified, Mr White,' Maud replied, answering for herself just this once.

'Come on! I've signed all the papers. I'm bound hand and foot. Give me a clue.'

Higginbotham once again nodded his approval, which Maud acknowledged.

'Well, Mr White I was a burglar and specialised in safe cracking. I was dropped into many countries to steal or photograph secret documents from safes in France, Germany, Holland, the Bahamas and even the American Embassy in London.

'I trained many others to do similar work and I can recognise the style of many of the modern cracksmen, which has helped the police. Fortunately, they have never believed a woman could do such a thing. The point is Mr White, I robbed a safe in the Bahamas, which if the contents were known even in this day and age, would rock the establishment, and I would prefer to see England as it is than any other way. Edith and I have always had a wonderful relationship in spite of her constant dallying. I was a bit jealous of her good looks which she always used to the full. But I wouldn't have changed things for all the tea in China.'

'So was this little woman lost, all an act?'

'Oh no Mr White, that's real. It's all been too much for me.'

She looked into my eyes as she said that and smiled the compelling smile of a vulnerable, little girl.